Praise for Come the Morning

"Philadelphia's art world at the turn of the century receives close inspection and serves as the historical backdrop for *Come the Morning*, a novel about a struggling gallery owner.

"Evocative, reflective, and historically revealing, *Come the Morning* does a fine job of dovetailing a sense of self with a sense of place and purpose, also revealing the plights of women, artists, entrepreneurs, and the circles that both support and defeat them.

"Readers seeking a moving story of artistic circles and life change will find that *Come the Morning* operates smoothly and is compelling on many different levels, making it a top recommendation."

--***Midwest Book Review***

"A deeply satisfying novel of scope and depth. A beautiful book. *Come the Morning* brings to mind Crane's *Maggie*, Sinclair's *The Jungle*, or the more genteel worlds of Henry James and Edith Wharton. I loved it."

--**Tim Bazzett, author of the memoir, *Booklover***

"An unforgiving world of poverty, boom-bust, the growing women's movement, European migration [and Ezekiel Harrington's] single-minded quest for wealth and revenge. A superbly engrossing sequel to Burt's earlier, *The Seasons of Doubt*."

-- **Jerry Berberet, PhD, American Historian**

"*Come the Morning*, the sequel to novelist Jeannie Burt's *Seasons of Doubt*, will immediately captivate readers as they continue to explore the life of Ezekiel Harrington, a good friend of Robert Henry Cozad, later to become Robert Henri, one of America's greatest artists and art instructors. While *the Seasons of Doubt* explores the community life of Cozad, Nebraska, *Come the Morning* returns to the life of Harrington although now he is now living in Philadelphia and then Paris, along with his continuing friendship with Henri who is now an aspiring artist."

--**The Robert Henri Museum**

"*Come the Morning*: hardship and grit, a life journey twisted by reality. Catch your breath before you start to read."

--**Manuel Cobarrubias, Visual Artist**

Also by Jeannie Burt

The Seasons of Doubt

When Patty Went Away

Lymphedema: A Breast Cancer Patient's Guide to Prevention and Healing

What You Need to Know to Show Your Dog

COME THE MORNING is based on historical record. The story refers to real events, true locales, and actual historical as well as fictional figures. The dialog and characterizations of actual individuals reflect the author's interpretation. The novel as a whole is a work of fiction.

Jeannie Burt

Publisher's Cataloging-in-Publication Data

Names: Burt, Jeannie, author.
Title: Come the morning / Jeannie Burt.
Description: Portland, OR : Muskrat Press, 2019.
Identifiers: LCCN 2019930010 | ISBN 978-0-9895446-6-5 (paperback) | ISBN 978-0-9895446-7-2 (ebook)
Subjects: LCSH: Artists--Fiction. | Prostitutes--Fiction. | Wealth--Fiction. | Man-woman relationships--Fiction. | Historical fiction. | BISAC: FICTION / Historical / General. | FICTION / Literary. | GSAFD: Historical fiction.
Classification: LCC PS3602.U76955 C66 2019 (print) | LCC PS3602.U76955 (ebook) | DDC 813/.6--dc23.

MUSKRAT PRESS • PORTLAND

Come the Morning

A NOVEL

JEANNIE BURT

For Roger

"It is easier, I think, to paint a good picture than it is to paint a bad one. The difficulty is to have the will for it."

"Shame makes a small man give up a lot of time smearing over and covering up his rough edges."

"Cherish your own emotions and never undervalue them."

--Robert Henri –*The Art Spirit*

1883

Chapter 1

Ezekiel Harrington stood under an enormous, round-faced clock, the size of a house. Half an hour ago, the Philadelphia Broad Street Station had swallowed his train as if it were a tidbit. Cries of a thousand babies and "all-aboards," screeches of trains, children's whines, and swats from their parents bounced from walls made of marble. He resisted the impulse to plug his hears and close his eyes.

He had just spent four days of his life on trains from Nebraska to come to where he had been told to come by his aunt and uncle, people he had never met. They had written that they would be here when he arrived and meet him under the clock. But the train arrived early. He was here and they were not.

Everything moved; nothing but the hard walls seemed to stay put. He squinted, and his lashes culled some of the frenzy but not all. He had spotted a hundred and fifty couples who could have been his aunt and uncle, dressed well and proud. All passed him by. But for an old photograph his aunt had sent his ma ten years ago, he had nothing that would tell him how to know them; they just as well might not recognize him. By choice, he was not dressed his best; he had chosen his oldest jacket, one too tight, sprung at the elbows, fraying at the neck, and patched from his mother's mending. His mother had made him a better suit that fit, but he would not deign to use it for this.

He had been ordered, like a child, to Philadelphia for the reading of his mother's will. He was fifteen years old, a man, and could just as well have stayed home in Nebraska and done this by mail or telegraph. But, for some ridiculous reason, the reading had to be done in Philadelphia, and he had to be at it.

Sam Schooley had seen him off at the train in Cozad. Ezekiel had never before been out of Nebraska. As he was boarding, he had turned to Sam and said, "See you in a few days," and he thought he saw a pooling in Sam's eyes.

He planned to stay the night, hear the reading of the will, then spend another four full days on the miserable trains back to where he and his ma had lived. The house was his now.

A high, wet, woman's voice rose above all else, "Ezekiel?"

He startled. She took him into her humid arms and began to sob. Behind her, what must have been his uncle, said, "Now, Dear."

She pulled away and dabbed her eyes. Totten reached out to take Ezekiel's hand. Ezekiel held back, then took it. His uncle's hand was firm and warm.

In the ten years since the photograph was taken, Totten and his aunt Prune had grown fat and his uncle, bald. Their clothes were overwrought: Totten's fine suit was draped with a gold fob thick enough to tether a bull, his aunt's breadth was covered in a flounce of shrieking taffeta. She descended on him again like a vulture, took him into her arms, and buried him in her ruffles and bosom.

They led him out the front where their carriage waited shimmering in the heat—a dark, waxen red, the color of blood. Their driver was letting himself down a step after strapping a small trunk on the top.

His aunt and uncle seemed to want to please him, were taking pains to drive him, at a slow pace, through a city he had no care for. He sat wanting to get on with the business and responded in simple yes's and no's to their entreaties. When his aunt warbled, "How *are* you, nephew?" He answered,

"Fine," and no more.

His aunt's voice, filled with high and wet enthusiasm, pointed out parks, three universities, a variety of social clubs, a couple of rivers, and stores she seemed to hope would dazzle him. His uncle said he wanted Ezekiel to get the lay of things before they left to go to their home in Chestnut Hill, some way out of the city. He asked questions that Ezekiel knew did not prompt much of an answer, such as, "What do you think of that, Nephew?" and isn't this or that grand?

The crush of the whirling, dodging city suffocated him. But for a few puny parks there was no space in any of Philadelphia. Nowhere was there sky to take him away and give him pause. The endless stores, the built canyons, the movement, the clanging clatter of trolleys gave no place for his eyes to rest or his lungs to take in air.

They drove along streets girded by buildings as high as mountains, which echoed until he wanted to shake loose of it. The tour went on and on, past Independence Hall, Penn Square, and two gentlemen's clubs. Finally, Totten said, "My office, Joseph," and the coach pulled in front of a building with a grill of white columns three stories high: Philadelphia National Bank & Trust, his uncle's bank. His aunt squeaked out, "Isn't this just something, Ezekiel?" as if he would think it was somehow God's gift. He hated it—hated that its grand face expressed what he and his ma could never have had.

A thunder storm came up as they were making it out of town. The storm settled him a bit. Thunder was something he could hold on to.

An endless hour passed before they made it to the town where the Humes lived. The driver geed the coach up a drive bordered by thick lawns. Their house was set high on a hill, the size of a hotel large enough to darken a good part of the sky. Dormers sawed at the fading day. The house leered over the street as if meant to impress. A columned portico constructed of over-fussed stone swallowed the coach as if it were something to eat. No building in all of Cozad, Nebraska, was as large as this, and there were only the Humes to live in it.

Inside, the floors ticked and muttered, the carpets swallowed his feet. A clutter of doilies covered tables. Antimacassars were pinned over the backs of chairs, and sofas fitted in thick, red upholstery. An arrangement of gladiolas sat three feet high on the center table beside a bible.

Fifteen minutes after they stepped into the house, Ezekiel was fed a meal that took two hours to eat. When he was so tired he could barely hold up his head, his aunt and the housekeeper led him up a broad, sweeping stairway where he would sleep. His quarters for the night consisted of a room with a bed and another with shelves filled with books, a leather chair and a desk. And there, in the corner, was his old trunk. How did it get here? Ezekiel belched and held his stomach against burn. The trunk belonged in his room at home.

He lifted the lid and knew what would be in it: his old school books, some of his ma's linens all tumbled about. But there was also the tin she had always kept by her bed. She had once kept letters from her sister in it, but they were lost to a fire. It held four dollars and fifty cents, now, a prune pit, and a loop of her hair he had tied with a ribbon. Why was it here? He was just going to have to wrestle the thing onto the train the next morning.

His ma had made a nightshirt for him not long before she died. He had not yet worn it. He took it from his valise. The scent of her sachet of dried roses still lingered on it.

He turned down a bed made of down, certain he would not be able to sleep. He folded his hands over his chest, and he waited for his mother, as he had waited every night since a child. He allowed the memory of her face to float over him, heard her whisper her nighttime blessing, "'Til marnin', Darlin'. God bless." He mumbled, "'Night, Ma." And a cloud of sleep took him.

Chapter 2

Morning lit a sliver in the drapes where the velvet did not meet. He rose, pulled back the window coverings, and began packing his bags, ready for the train back to Nebraska, back home to the garden behind the house that would have become overgrown while he was away, back to people he knew, back to the home he knew, back to dirt streets not yet cobbled, back to the hauling business he had begun after quitting school early a few months ago. He would be there in days, listening to the wind and the calling of the cranes at the river.

The sounds were strange here, the sounds of an unfamiliar bird outside, the tick of heavy and tight-fitted doors opening and closing downstairs, the murmur of his aunt and uncle's voices. It was odd hearing the voice of a man in the house. Ezekiel had not woken to a man's voice since his pa abandoned his ma and him a decade ago.

This room overlooked a garden so thick with flowers he could make out little but fuss and color. Back in Nebraska, his ma's gardens had mostly been given to whatever they could eat. She would have liked a garden with color if she had had time for it.

He went to the water closet and sat on the pot. Liquid rushed out of him, the filth and stench of anticipation and feelings held in.

He would leave this house the moment his uncle divulged what was in his ma's estate. His inheritance would not be a lot; he had seen his ma's accounts and had added to them from the pay he earned from his odd jobs. He anticipated bringing in more with his hauling as soon as he had developed his market.

He and his ma had discussed finances openly over the years. She had worked and saved and, with her dressmaking, had managed to buy them a house. She had sent small sums, amounts she did not share with him, to Totten in Philadelphia for safekeeping in his bank. It was that money, however little it was, that Ezekiel had come here to get his hands on. The rest, the money in the account at the Cozad bank, he would need while he established his business. He could still almost smell the scent of the Platte River and Mr. Simpson's livery where he still worked now and then. Three more days, four at most, he would be there. He closed his eyes, brought the image of home to him; it slowed his heart somewhat.

He heard the door crack open to the bedroom and his aunt's "yoo-hoo." Couldn't she wait until he was off the pot? She said, "Nephew, we have breakfast all ready for you downstairs."

The breakfast table sat in a room off the kitchen surrounded by small, paned windows beveled like diamonds. The table was filled with biscuits, sausages shining with fat, three kinds of jellies, a bowl filled with strawberries, another with thick cream. His aunt, flounced into a chair, said to a large woman in an apron, "Phoebe, you can bring him his eggs now." He squirmed; he was not used to being the center of things. His mother never had time to fiddle over him, and he had grown independent and used to fending alone.

"Did you sleep well, my dear?" she said.

He nodded. He had slept as if he were dead. He had not dreamed, had not gotten up even once in the night.

His aunt's eyes shone. She dabbed at them, muttered something about a piece of dust in them. She finished the napkin-patting and reached for one of the biscuits and butter. "I shouldn't," she said. "Your uncle and I already ate." She buttered half the biscuit, put it in her mouth, tucked it into her cheek. "It is so good to have you with us. We haven't had a boy to live with us since our Oliver and Cornelius left to school." Ezekiel knew from letters that one of her sons was at Harvard to become a doctor, the other studying to become a minister. "I am so grateful you will be with us."

Ezekiel did not know what to make of her, or this. He would not be here long enough to care. His uncle had told him he wanted to see Ezekiel in his home office at nine o'clock that morning. When that was done, he would be gone.

His aunt sat with him, chattering on while Phoebe set in front of him a breakfast fit for a dozen. All Ezekiel needed was a corncake, like what he had eaten every day of his life.

It was all so strange sitting in this cavernous place. His aunt and uncle might as well be from another continent. His aunt's flowery letters to his mother had never conveyed all this nor had the old photograph. Totten and Prune were young in the photograph, posing with their two boys who had been eleven and twelve, then. In it, his aunt had arranged herself in a dress of thick material with a flutter of ruffles at her throat and was surrounded by her fine-tailored husband and boys. They were all strangers to him, alien; they would never be more than that. He had eaten what the cook put in front of him. The rich meal made him feel sick.

Five minutes before nine o'clock, his uncle called him to his office, which overlooked the garden. There lingered in the house the oily scent of fried eggs and meat and gagging-sweet jams that made Ezekiel want to run outside and air himself.

The room smelled of leather and the oil of lemon wax. He motioned for Ezekiel to sit in a high wing chair across from his desk. Prune took the chair next to Ezekiel. As his aunt arranged the fluffs of her skirts, Totten gave Ezekiel a small nod and a smile that stretched his mustache. "How did you sleep, son?"

"Fine."

His uncle waited for Ezekiel to say more. "I thought you'd sleep well up there. You're in Ollie's old room, and he always slept like a pup in it."

The office spoke impressive comfort: the thick China rug, the desk with turnings, dark, inlaid woods and the groaning chair when Totten shifted in it. His dark banker's suit fit him as if he had been sewn into it. He pulled spectacles from the pocket of his vest. He checked his watch, a gesture that shouted he could mete out only so much time before he had to be somewhere important.

His aunt sat beside Ezekiel in a ridiculous dress of pinkish fabric that blended with her damp, pinkish coloring. Though her given name was Prudence, his mother had never called her sister anything but Prune. She sat there, as full as a fresh picked fruit.

Totten rested his hand on a file. "First," he said, "let me express again how sorry we both are for the reason you are here. We miss Mary and are grateful we could be here for you at this time." Totten removed his eyeglasses in a pageant of respect for his sister-in-law. Prune began to blubber. Was his uncle trying to make Ezekiel cry? He had not cried. He refused to now. "Her passing is a loss for all of us." Totten did appear to be touched, which surprised Ezekiel.

"Son, your mother left me in charge of closing out her estate. She leaves everything to you, of course. I know she has informed you of this." Ezekiel had never thought anything different. Totten sat back. "Your mother was a remarkable woman." Ezekiel swallowed three times at the ache. "She started from nothing. One might even say she started with less than nothing."

Ezekiel suspected what his uncle meant: that his pa was difficult, even before he disappeared. He also felt the word "orphan" lying on the desk as tangible as the file Totten fingered. He let the word and the implication lie there. He obviously believed Ezekiel's *less-than-nothing* pa was dead. He was not. "Your mother raised a fine boy. She made sure you were taken care of, best she could. Though I might warn you, as well as she managed, her estate is only a few hundred dollars."

He leaned forward. His fob clicked as he pressed himself onto the edge of the desk. "Son," he said, "we are your family now." Totten took up a gold pen. He watched his own fingers twirl it round and round in a thoughtful way that might have been tender. Totten cleared his throat, looked up directly at Ezekiel. "Son," he said again. Ezekiel wanted to scream out *I am not your son*! "I would like to be the father you never had. Your aunt and I want to make you a home."

"I already have a home," he said. His aunt laid her hand on his arm. "I *have* a father," he said. His aunt and uncle knew nothing. They only had a sense of him in the bad times, the times when his pa was not himself. They did not know of the times of tenderness and laughter. "I am *not an orphan*."

"That's right," Totten said. "You have your aunt and me now."

This was going somewhere Ezekiel could not abide. He had to dispel it right now. "I have people."

"Where?"

"At home." He *did* have people. He had Mr. Simpson. He had Sam Schooley. There would have been a time when he would have had his one friend: Bobby. "Where I live." His voice dropped, and his anger and sarcasm filled the room.

"This is your home now," Totten said.

Prune patted Ezekiel's arm. "Dear, you are ours now."

"My home is in Nebraska; I have friends there." On a warm day like today, Bobby might have looked for Ezekiel wherever he was working: shoveling offal in the livery or doing some job in the hotel, and he might ask, "When you done?" Ezekiel would tell him, and Bobby would say to meet down by the river after work, and he'd bring two poles. And if the crappy were good, they would fish, and if the fish were not biting, they would lie on the bank in the shade of the grasses, just at the edge of the water in the damp cool. They might talk about this or that and toss clods and proclaim a winner. And when they stood, their backs and rear ends would be damp. With their clothes sticking to them, they would pluck at their shirts, and air would puff under and cool them for a moment. But that was three years ago, before Bobby also disappeared and Ezekiel lost him.

"I have a home," Ezekiel said, "and it isn't here." His relatives seemed to believe his pa was dead. He would not tell them the truth. "My home is in Nebraska," Ezekiel repeated.

Aunt Prune wiped her eyes. "Darling, there's no one there for you any longer."

"Yes, there is." Why did he have to defend it?

"Who?" Totten said, the tenderness having bled from him.

"Sam Schooley." He blurted it and, in the blurting, knew it was true.

"No one *family*," Totten said.

Ezekiel gathered his breath, about to shout.

Totten thrust himself back in his rich chair and folded his hands over his stomach. He took off his eyeglasses and thumbed both of his eyes. Ezekiel moved his arm and let the hand of his aunt's drop from where it had lain on his wrist. Her hand left a puddle of warmth.

For a moment, neither Totten nor Ezekiel spoke. Ezekiel did not move. Prune daubed a tissue at her nose. Totten slipped on his eyeglasses and blinked. "It will be as I say."

"I am telling the truth. Sam Schooley *is* family." It was not far from the truth. Before she took sick the last time, Ezekiel's mother had asked, "What would you think if Sam came to live with us?" And Ezekiel knew they had spoken of marriage.

Totten took up the file with papers. It was marked *Accounts Mary Harrington*. "Your mother's estate was not large."

"There is the house," Ezekiel said. "We have the house." Talking as if his mother were still here reassured him.

Totten cleared his throat and shot Ezekiel a look that made him want to squirm. Ezekiel sat straight, not letting his spine touch the chair. His uncle, in his banker's voice, began to read the will. It started by saying that his ma wanted Totten to carry out things, as she'd indicated in letters over the years, and that she left discretion in the hands of Ezekiel's aunt and uncle. Totten began to tell him what it meant: that the cash his mother had on deposit at the bank had been put into a trust, administered by Totten, which would pay for Ezekiel's education. He would live with his aunt and uncle until he was finished with college. The "residue" of the money, if there were any, would be available to him after he had graduated. If he did not complete his college education, the residue…," *did he have to repeat such a word? It seemed obscene,* "…whatever is in your mother's estate will be paid you on your twenty-fifth birthday."

Twenty-fifth birthday? "The house," Ezekiel said. "I am going home."

"Didn't you understand?" Totten said.

"Understand what?" Ezekiel could hear his own voice rise; things were flying away from him.

"The house in Nebraska has been sold."

"It can't be."

Totten slid a telegram across the desk. At its top, written in large black letters, were the words: HARINGTON HOUSE IN COZAD SOLD. "Whatever remains of her estate, after you have completed your education, will be yours."

"From *college*?" Ezekiel said.

"From secondary school *and* college," his uncle said.

Ezekiel slapped the desk. It made a wet splat. "This is thievery! I'm going home."

"Oh, dear," his aunt cried. "This *is* your home now."

"You will live with us." Totten's voice was unperturbed and inflexible. Though he managed a smile, it was crooked.

"I don't want to," Ezekiel said. His voice broke high, like a younger boy's.

Totten leaned forward. "You don't have a choice."

"I'm not staying here." Ezekiel stood with such violence, the chair tipped. "My home is in Cozad, Nebraska. And I'm going back." He *did* have people, most of all Sam, who had sat by his mother's bed as she lay dying, caring Sam who had driven Ezekiel to the train, gentle Sam who had waved him off. "See you, son," he had said. "Have a safe trip."

"Going back to Nebraska would take funds," his uncle said.

"I have the money Ma left me."

"Your mother's money will go toward your future, and I will be the one to discern what that future will be. Now, *sit!*"

Ezekiel continued to stand as his uncle detailed and repeated each element of what was required before he got his inheritance: It would be given to him only after he graduated from a college of *Totten's* choosing. If he did not finish college, he would not get it until his twenty-fifth birthday.

Ezekiel shouted, "This is robbery! You are stealing my money!" He flung himself forward, leaned over the desk, put his face as close as he could to his uncle's.

"Sit," Totten said again.

"I am leaving this minute."

"You better have something in your pocket, if you do that."

"I do," he said. He did not say all he had was eighteen dollars and twenty-seven cents.

Totten was not backing down. "You will do what I tell you. You will finish your secondary education, *then* you will finish college."

"I have already finished it."

"There is no college in Cozad." His uncle's voice was low, warning. He was used to his word being taken whole and complete without question. "You will do what I say—or not see a penny."

"Secondary," Ezekiel said.

"You are fifteen years old." Another warning.

"But I did." Why must he defend this? He *was* finished. He had passed every class taught in Cozad. He had even been paid to teach reading and writing to some of the immigrant children who needed to learn English.

"Your mother said you do not lie."

"I am not," he said, "lying."

"We'll see," Totten said.

He did not sleep another night in that house. After his uncle went to work and his aunt left the house briefly for some errands that day, he threw his valise in the trunk, took the handle and skidded it down the long drive, and he loaded himself and his trunk into a train back to downtown Philadelphia. He had money in his pocket but not enough for a train ticket home. He asked the conductor where he might be able to find a room with a bed for a while. And, as they made their way into the city, the conductor told him he had a sister who ran a rooming house and gave Ezekiel a head full of directions.

Chapter 3

By nightfall he had moved himself into a room, paid a month's rent, bought himself a half loaf of bread for a supper, and had depleted nearly half the money he had in the world.

The room reeked of stewed cabbage and was small with only a narrow gap to sidle between the bed-cot and a desk. For clothes, three pegs had been hammered on a wall. The trunk left a mere toe-stub's couple inches between it and the desk chair. The door banged on a table in the corner and risked breaking the washbowl and pitcher on it. Under the table sat the bucket for his slops. The floor, ill-fitting boards and gaps, was not covered; a rug did not come with the room.

If he slept that first night in his rooming house room, he could not remember it. He threw the sheet off himself and listened to the city sounds that made it up the narrow space between his window and the next rooming house three feet away, abysmal sounds; ships' moans, endless streams of train whistles he wished were taking him home. He listened for the familiar: a night free of the screeches of trolleys and drunken shouts, a night marked only by wind and the rippling questions of goose calls, and cranes' cranky chatter, the scolds of coots, the crack of an angry duck, the winter snap of ice-break on the river, his ma turning in her bed.

The next morning, he found work for a day with an old man, washing windows at Reading & Reading Stationers. At dusk, he pestered the old man for another day's work and was given the job of unloading boxes. And when he was through with that, he asked for a steady job, but the old man told him he was too young for real work.

He walked the streets, entered three dozen businesses asking for work and found none. A week later, he made his way up the steps and through the toothy pillars of Philadelphia National Bank & Trust where he asked to see Totten Hume. In his pocket he carried a hand-written note:

> *If I am to comply with your demands, I will need to know to which college you are sending me. Otherwise, how am I to go along with your extortion?*
>
> *Ezekiel Harrington*

The clerk was a fellow not much older than Ezekiel, a tight sort with oiled hair and a collar officiously stiff and high. He huffed as Ezekiel handed over the note and asked who was inquiring.

Ezekiel swallowed bile. "His nephew," he said. "Ezekiel Harrington."

The clerk pulled a metal tube from the back of his counter and spoke into it. When he was done, he laid the tube back into its bracket and went to work counting money. A few minutes later, another bank official came in, took Ezekiel's note. In a few minutes the official came back, handed Ezekiel an envelope engraved with Philadelphia National Bank & Trust addressed to Ezekiel Harrington. The note was handwritten. It said:

> *Ezekiel,*
>
> *I have made arrangements through Mr. Wharton for you to begin class at his school of business. You and I both know that, because you are still a boy, this is nothing more than a trial. If you fail, you will be sent to a suitable secondary school of your aunt's and my choosing.*
>
> *Totten Hume*

Chapter 4

He watched his money dwindle. He had barely enough to last another month. He busied himself, bought a map of the city, and, on his own, found the university, a twenty-minute walk from his room. He began classes. After mornings, enduring the preaching professors and hot classrooms, he made his way through the city to the stationery store to beg work. The old man doled out coins whenever there was a box to open or a window to wash. The money he paid was a help but never enough. And, at the end of the day, Ezekiel ate his only meal of whatever the landlady put on the table. On a good day there was cabbage and gristle, on a bad day scorches and burns. When he was done, he went to his room and shut the door and every day found solace in his schoolbooks.

The landlady lived in the floor below, her room directly under his. The morning after he first came, she warned him he had better not wear shoes or boots upstairs again, or she would evict him and his noise. He had worn nothing but socks since.

He had heard no more from his aunt or his uncle, though, as the weather cooled, the end of the semester came upon him with its doling out of grades. The thought of it threw a cramp in his neck. He had attended every class, completed every assignment, written extra on every paper. Now and then, a professor would mark a grade, but some did not, and those worried him; a paper with no grade left him untethered. He craved certainty. He did not mingle with other students; he skirted their groups and clusters. He had no idea of them, no idea how these gatherings ever came together. And, as time went by, he was grateful he did not have to deal with it.

By the time the leaves turned, he could not sleep worrying he might not be able doing well enough to pass. Then what? It kept him at his desk with the lamp long into the night, heat blasting up through the gaps in the floor because the landlady kept her door open to the woodstove. Her room was so hot it baked Ezekiel, and he had to study under an open window. Later, when she finally closed her door for the night and closed off the heat, his own room grew frigid.

Not long after cold set in, a cat appeared at the window one evening. It was a dull cat with a coat the color of a rat's. It was missing one ear and had a scar running down its temple through a clouded eye. It was a squirrely cat that scrammed when Ezekiel made a move to pet it.

He began to bring gristle and bits from dinner and to set on the sill. The cat came again and again, swiped the gristle off the plate then disappeared. Each night Ezekiel put some scrap in the dish, and each night the cat came and took it until, finally, on a night of bitter snow, the cat took its scrap and it growled at Ezekiel, but stayed in the heat of the cracked window. It became habit; the cat would take up the scrap, look Ezekiel directly in the eye, and growl before it downed the food. And, when it was done, when the food was gone, it would sit on the sill soaking in the warmth but ready to leap if Ezekiel made any wrong move.

One night, Ezekiel reached a slow hand toward the cat and, though it tensed and looked out to escape, it held. And when Ezekiel gave one stroke to the head of it, it looked at him with an expression that seemed surprised the stroke had been pleasant. The cat began to stay while Ezekiel studied and to allow a stroke but never let itself come beyond the safety of the open window. The cat would always be gone by morning.

The tang of nerves filled the hall as students pushed and tugged to see the bulletin board. Ezekiel stood back as one after another of them pushed in, saw his grades, and gave a yip or a yell and banged another happily on the back or looked away and left without saying anything at all. Ezekiel stood planted away from the crowd until they had all gone. When he was finally alone, he closed his eyes a moment and tried to swallow. He took a breath and held it as he went to the board.

He put his finger on the listings, ran it down the alphabet of names to stop at the Hs. And there it was: Harrington, Ezekiel, followed by As after every class, along with the words: *Advanced to Semester Two.*

Chapter 5

For three years now, the city had trapped him, tied him like a dog at a stake. He had done what was required of him, had capitulated and proved himself with superior grades, better than the mere passing his warden Totten had mandated. He had broken all ties with his aunt and uncle, had not seen them, nor had any communication since the day he left their house. Release from this prison would come in one more year.

After begging a regular job for three months, the old man at the stationery store finally took Ezekiel on to work afternoons after school; the job paid for Ezekiel's room and keep with a bit more to pay for a morning meal at the rooming house. He knew the store now, even found some comfort in the crust of the old man, the routines, the heavy work cleaning and fussing with stock. But the idea never shook loose that in a year he would dust his hands of all of it. In a year he would be gone.

It was evening. Mrs. Hanson's stewed chicken and noodles had been cleared from the table an hour ago. Ezekiel was at his desk with his papers and books. The cat had finished his scraps of chicken fat and was making a comforting *thip, thip* with its tongue as he licked himself. He reached a finger toward the cat. In the three years the cat had never come farther into the room but had finally allowed a pet and a scratch. Its throat rumbled as Ezekiel dug his nail under its jaw. And, for a moment, he envied the cat, free to go, free to come. As ugly as the thing was, it had carved a life of its own making. And, for that moment the soft fur, the satisfied rumble made Ezekiel want to sleep, made him want to shake the endless hard tension that bound his neck. He yawned. The cat stretched up and looked down Ezekiel's throat. Its eyes went black at some evil cat-thought. Ezekiel took back his hand.

He tipped his head to one shoulder, tipped it to the other. It seemed to loosen the pain some. He picked up the text, *The Past and Present of Political Economy,* rifled a page. It was nonsense, a sort of discourse on socialism and private enterprise. Socialism was new to him; he had never considered socialism, had never heard of such a lofty, stupid concept until these useless classes. Books such as this with their endless ideas, and the finger-to-the-ceiling pronouncements from his professors, only solidified what he'd felt all along: one had to watch out, not for the good of society, but for oneself. For so long, Ezekiel had brooked nothing that might get in his way, neither friendship, community, nor association, let alone *society*, for God's sake.

He saw other students banding together to discuss classes and make plans to study together or go out somewhere after school let out, but he had never been one of them; he had made no friends at the school. When he first began his classes, he would position himself in the halls or sit somewhere in the back of the classroom, and he would take in how they behaved, how they laughed or mimicked some professor, or raged at a grade on some exam, or arranged where to meet to study together. He would wonder how coming together ever happened. How did they open a conversation? How did they come to learn one another's names? How did they link and group and find the common among them? He thought he could learn if he watched long enough, if he analyzed and learned, like he did any subject in school. But he did not learn; he never got to the point of approaching another boy or even saying hello.

The house was quiet, holding the late summer heat like an oven. The two other roomers, brothers, were in their rooms reading, or whatever they did after a day's work. He heard footfalls coming up the steps—not the clomps and thuds of the brothers' boots but the taps of the landlady's sensible lace-ups. The cat disappeared out the window.

Ezekiel waited for the steps to pass by his door; no one ever stopped at it. He took a pencil to make a note on his tablet.

He heard his landlady stop and heard her huff. "Mr. Harrington? I have a letter."

He clapped closed the text. His school notes fluttered to the floor. "A letter?" he said to no one. He had quit checking the mail basket long ago. In all the time he had lived in this boardinghouse, there had never been anything in it for him; no one wrote him; he had told no one but the university his address. Regularly, letters came from his aunt to the university, invitations to birthdays, Thanksgiving and Christmas dinners, a personal note now and then exclaiming about their sons and now their new grandbaby or some club event she seemed enraptured about. The letters were written in his aunt's smug flourishes. He'd read them and savored the anger each time; anger kept pain at bay. As time had gone on, as much as he had tried to hold onto it, the memory of his mother had faded. Sometimes he closed his eyes and willed himself to conjure her face, and she did not come. Those times a vacuum sucked at him.

He heard the rustle of the landlady's dress as if she were about to knock again. He put down his pencil, buttoned his shirt, opened the door. She handed the letter over. "You should check the basket yourself. This has been in it near a week." Without another word, she turned and went back down the steps.

The envelope was from the university. Inside it was another envelope addressed to him. It contained a letter, his name written in pencil with a heavy hand. The return address said Samuel Schooley, Cozad, Nebraska.

Of the entire world, besides his ma, Sam and Bobby Cozad were the people Ezekiel missed most. He had pushed them out of his head like a dog might look away from some piece of meat forbidden him. But sometimes Ezekiel could not hold remembering at bay; it flew at him in the unexpected hours until he could once again close himself and lock his thoughts from the hurt. Bobby had been his only friend; he had not had another friend since. As abrupt as Bobby's rush from his life had been, Sam had always hung on, slow and quiet as a late summer stream. Kind Sam had been there when his mother died. Sam and his Irish tenor's voice had been there through her last day.

He held the letter, felt the warmth of it, soft, almost, as a pillow. For a moment, he let the comfort of Sam sweep him up. Sam meant home. Sam's considered voice meant peace. Sam had stuck with Ezekiel and his mother, had gone for Dr. Chase during the worst of his mother's fevers. He had sat with her and talked with her those last days. Sam Schooley was as much home to Ezekiel as the Platte River, as Nebraska's tornadoes, as the skies filled with geese and cranes, the river muck singing with frogs, the fire in a stove, the spikes of winter hanging from eaves. The minute he was set free, Ezekiel would rush back to Nebraska and reliable, trusted Sam Schooley would be there.

He plucked open the flap, taking care not to rip it. The letter was written in pencil, humble and cautious:

Dear Ezekiel,

It has been over three years since I saw you off. I hope this letter finds you well.

I write to tell you there was a fellow come to town last week who says he is your pa Edmund Harrington. He was asking about your ma. It was David Claypool told him she had passed away. He then asked about where you went. I am the only one who knows you went to Philadelphia, tho he seemed all ready to know you had relatives there.

I hear from your uncle Totten now and then. He says you are not in touch with him, nor your aunt. He wrote that you are in the college. So I have sent this letter to the college in hopes you get it.

Ezekiel's hands began to shake. Bile went into his throat: *Sam was in touch with* Totten? He raised up the letter again:

> *I know this fellow cannot be your pa, as your ma was a widow. He is a drifter and the sort you want to keep from. He has left town now. Traber Gatewood found out he was wanted for robbing a bank in Plum Creek.*
>
> *It is not news I am glad to pass on but I think you need to know.*
>
> *Write soon.*
>
> *Your Friend, Sam Schooley*

Ezekiel crumpled the letter. What a fool he had been. Why had he not seen it? Sam's duplicity had sat right in his face; the house was sold even before Ezekiel got to Philadelphia. Sam knew Ezekiel was not coming back. Why else insist on the nonsense of Ezekiel's lugging the damn trunk with him? He had been blind, had seen none of it. His eyes felt filled with grit. Traitor. Sam had done Totten's bidding when he packaged Ezekiel up, put him on the train, and shipped him off to Philadelphia like so many goods. Sam had certainly been the one to help Totten finalize the sale of the house.

When he went to bed that night, Ezekiel squeezed closed his eyes until they cramped. He willed his mother to come. He whispered, "Ma." Though his voice was now a man's, it held a boy's plea. "Ma," he said again like a baby, but she did not come.

Chapter 6

The Reading & Reading Stationery Store sold cards, stationery of various rag, tarnished silver pens, and calendars. The business had fallen off greatly in the three years since Ezekiel had worked there. No longer did sales from the floor hold the business together. It was the engraving done in the back of the store that kept the bills paid. The Reading brothers had worked together nearly thirty years, until one of them died. The dead brother had been the one to do the engraving and carry the business end of the place. Nestor, the survivor, had a good hand with customers but was too shaky and feeble to engrave and too scatter-headed to manage the books. So, he hired a thin man to do the engraving, a dripping fellow whose lips shone, and the corners of his mouth perpetually leaked.

Ezekiel had worked there long enough to remember when Nestor Reading could stand without holding his back and could still make a reasonable attempt at writing his signature. The decline had been gentle but there nonetheless. At first Ezekiel had only done the physical work the old man could not manage; he stocked shelves, if there was stock, swept the store and the outside walks, washed displays, painted the walls, dusted shelves, rearranged display cases, even hand-painted signs for the old man.

Then one day, when Ezekiel had been there nearly a year, he came in early after his classes. From his stool, Mr. Reading looked up, saw it was only Ezekiel. "Won't pay you extra to start early."

Ezekiel asked if he could sit in the back and do some schoolwork before starting and added that he had an exam the next day.

"Exam in what?" the old man asked.

"Accounting."

"You know accounting?"

"Some."

"What kind of marks you get in it?"

"Good enough."

"What kind?"

"A," he said.

"How do you know? You haven't taken the test yet."

"Don't need to," Ezekiel said.

"How you know?"

"It's all I ever get." It was a lie. He had nearly failed civics until he did extra studies. It took him until the next year to bring up that grade.

"Can you do my books?"

Chapter 7

Winter set upon the city; the wind stripped the maples, killed back the flowers at Washington Square and left behind a bare, dim light. It was late November. In just seven months he would be gone and not see another winter in Philadelphia.

The weather kept people closed in behind doors. If they went out, they barged around like apparitions in heavy coats and mufflers and wrapped their children in wools thick enough they could barely move. When they walked, they bent into the wind, or sidled crossways, or crabbed backward squinting at dust and frozen tears.

Christmas. Holidays. The season of stretching, endless days.

Stores, of course, stayed open. Their display windows ran with sweat. Though the store was open, Reading & Reading's door rarely opened, its bell rarely rang. Ezekiel had been doing the store's books over a year by then. The old man said he did not have time to do books anymore. But time was an excuse; the truth was that the old man could no longer do them.

Reading & Reading was not doing well; even the holidays were not bolstering income. Ezekiel had started to prepare for the year-end inventory. Over the desk in the closet that served as Mr. Reading's office were shelves up to the ceiling that held decades of the store's old books. In some quiet moments alone, Ezekiel studied them. They revealed that the store had once been successful enough to handily support two families and to buy the building and stuff it with a great deal of stock. The inventory now was only a fragment of what it once was.

The Reading brothers had bought the building thirty years ago. It included the store and warehouse in back and the two stories upstairs, which were parsed into twenty-one rooms to let. The stationery part of the business had brought in customers from the harbor traffic three blocks away and from the banks and trusts in the financial area where the store sat.

Trouble came when Wanamakers started selling stationery, invitations, trinkets, pens, calendars, cards, waxes, custom seals, and everything else the Reading brothers had made their living on. And Wanamakers did it better and grander. In the last ten years, the department stores like Wanamakers, Lits, and Strawbridge and Clothiers had sucked business away from the Readings' neighborhood near the Delaware River toward the more fashionable Schuylkill, where the trains belched people and their money into the stylish new middle of town. All Ezekiel needed was for the frail, puff-eyed old man to hold on the few more months until he could finish with school.

At the boardinghouse, Mrs. Hanson closed down the kitchen the week between Christmas and New Year, in order to spend time with a sister in Delaware. Ezekiel holed up in his room, wandering out only to feed himself. There were no classes that week. There was no work, either; the store was shut. And so he read newspapers that he plucked from the diners, and he began studying next semester's texts. He hated Christmas—Christmas broke habit. The week between Christmas and the first of the year fractured things. He saw no one but the grocer down the street; he heard from no one but his aunt, who sent her inevitable invitation through the school's mail, asking him to spend Christmas with them. His aunt and uncle still did not know where he worked nor did they know where he lived. Yet still Prune wrote, never giving up. For three years her engraved envelopes had gone unanswered. Since storming out of their house, he had had no contact with either of them, though each year his school bills were paid.

After the interminable wait, classes finally began again. The peace of routine took over, and he was beginning to feel like himself as he made his way through sleet to the store.

It was cold, the walks slick with ice, wind screaming over the noise of the city. Brittle leaves threw themselves into a corner of the store's stoop. The old man would, he knew, bark out orders to sweep them up as soon as Ezekiel walked in, and he took some comfort in knowing it.

He went in, turned to close the door, expecting the old man to grunt orders. But no grunt came. Mr. Reading sat drooling and silent on his stool, leaning to one side. He said nothing, did not look up even when the bell dinged. Skin rippled slack from his face, an arm dangled at his side. It was as if the week had left him without muscle or bone. A customer stood at the counter in front of him, clearing her throat.

Ezekiel edged around her, nudged Mr. Reading's shoulder. The old man snorted awake, wiped drool on his wrist. The woman asked for a pen and pencil set. Mr. Reading grunted for Ezekiel to get the set from the case. Ezekiel laid it out, waited for Mr. Reading to rise to help the woman. But he did not rise, instead tried to conduct business from his stool, mumbling wet encouragements as to the splendor of the pen set. The customer left without buying.

The old man handed Ezekiel the key, told him to close when it was time and said he was going home early. It would be the first day the old man had ever missed an hour of work.

Chapter 8

One of his professors, Lewis, a lofty sort who, by way of his editorship of *The American Law Register and Review,* professed how one must be open to eventuality, how one must deal with uncertainty with flexibility and adjustment, and to allow oneself fluidity in his plans. "And," he said, "one must never commit to feeling one has things under one's total control, for it spells ignorance in the lay of things as they ought to be seen." *Drivel,* Ezekiel thought. *How, then, does one make plans?* He had always forced himself to *Certainty*, a word he thought of with a capital C. But he had begun to feel Certainty begin to slip, the fear kept him awake at night as if Certainty would abandon him, just as everything in his life had abandoned him, and that his life, no matter how perfect he had made it these last three years, would not continue to be so. Six months. That was all he needed. Six months to matriculate and get what his mother had left him.

———

No matter how thick a coat, how lined or furred it might be, the wind drove through it. The wind iced one's breath; it lifted skirts and sent anything not tethered down skittering. Ezekiel bent into it, carried his books strapped on his back to shelter himself as best he could it. A wet-dog scent rose from his muffler. His hands froze and went useless and numb. The heat of his studies ate at him every hour, and he could almost smell the end of it soon. A paper due in a week had kept him up long into the nights: Civics again, the inevitable study of how people work together. He did not know how to work with others, much less how this contrived to make a society, a government. He still did not understand the whys of any of the classes that touched on how people behaved. He did not understand the need or to carry on about the rights and duties of citizens. In his experience, the world was a solitary place, a place where one was inevitably and totally alone. In order to pass civics, the best he could do was to memorize then ape what he read and try to make his writing appear as though he had not copied it.

It had begun to snow ten minutes before he got to the store, the streets and walks already covered in white. He trotted toward the store and the warmth in it. He was to begin taking the store's first-of-the-year inventory that day. He looked forward to the mindless rhythm of inventory, the hope it might get him away from thinking of civics.

He got to the store, stood outside it, under the awning, brushing flakes from his coat. Two women were standing at the front counter when he went in. He could hear the jangle of the press in back where Kopke, the engraver, was working on an order. The women turned as Ezekiel entered. Mr. Reading's stool was empty. He went around the counter to find the old man.

One of the women pulled a sour face. "We *wondered* if anyone would wait on us."

Ezekiel unwrapped his muffler, set his books on the counter. "I'll find Mr. Reading," he said. He poked his head into the back room.

Kopke stood at the press, turning the crank. He was wearing an old, stained apron, his hands messed with ink. "Where's Mr. Reading?" Ezekiel said.

Kopke turned. "Sick, I guess. He let me in this morn then left and didn't come back."

"There are customers out front," Ezekiel said.

"I told them you would be right here."

The women stood by the case at the far end where Mr. Reading kept the items for sale. One woman counted her coins, put them on the counter. Ezekiel had seen her in the store many times before. She was a decade older than Ezekiel's aunt and was wrapped in a cotton coat with a crude, odd-colored shawl thrown over her shoulders. He thought she made a living by fighting down the prices of things then selling them again somewhere on the street. The old man had always humored her and seemed to like her and her pluck.

She huffed as if she had been waiting for hours. "I want to see that box there," she said, "the one with the scratch on the side." She pointed at a wooden stationery box. It had a compartment with a bottle for ink and furrows for pens. Ezekiel had never waited on a customer before. He did not like the prospect of it now. The old man had always made it look easy. How hard could it be? But his tongue welded itself to the top of his mouth. He could not utter a sound.

He took the box from the shelf, set it on the counter. "Ain't worth a dollar," the woman said, "with that scratch in it."

What would Mr. Reading say? What would he do? He had watched the old man work dozens of customers, yet Ezekiel had no idea how to go about it. He could not speak. He could not look at the women. She huffed again, through her nose. "Well?"

When he did not answer, she smacked the box back on the counter and threw an end of her ugly shawl over her shoulder. As she was going out, she turned back and said, "You sure ain't Mr. Reading, I can tell you that."

Kopke closed the store and locked it the first evening of Mr. Reading's absence, and for a week the place remained closed, though each day after class, Ezekiel traipsed to the store in hopes the old man was there.

Then one day Mr. Reading was back. He was thinner, his skin hanging on him, his chin turned into a wattle, red as a turkey's that quivered when he spoke. He held the walls as he moved. He grabbed at counters and shelves with spotted spider's fingers and braced his elbows on the cases without thought to the glass. Kopke did not return when the doors opened again. He wrote a letter that he needed solid work.

There was just Ezekiel, now, and the old man. Neither of them engraved and it was engraving that paid the bills. The old man grew frantic to find someone to replace Kopke. It was only then that Ezekiel's world began to throb and the fears to loop through his head. He had no one to confide in, no one to ask for advice, no one to listen and nod and pull his lips into a sympathetic mouth. He had no one to help dispel the nightmares. He once had someone he could call friend. But that was in Nebraska nearly a decade ago.

Now, neatness, organization, habit, and learning were Ezekiel's companions. He clung to them, excelling at school, straightening his room, studying, all in an immutable schedule while clinging to his job at the store. To live, to finish out what he planned, he had to have a job. He should have seen this coming weeks ago; he should have been looking for work, though finding another job would be scarce in winter. What would he do? He tried to convince himself nothing had changed, that the old man would find an engraver, and that his tired bones would hold out until Ezekiel was done needing him.

The store and his room at Mrs. Hanson's had been the only part of his life that seemed concrete. He began to see that the old man's hold on life was growing as porous as a sieve. For so long, he had clung to the idea he would be at the store; he had no mechanism to think beyond it, now. He had always positioned his life; positioning had always been his strength. But now the smug and smarmy memory of the predicament his uncle had thrown at him rendered him immobile. He shuffled through town thinking he should find some other work but saw only closed businesses and signs posting they were not hiring. He went to class but heard nothing. He tried to force himself to study, but his attendance at school became haphazard. He began leaving assignments unfinished, rested on the strength of his past grades, and hoped it would be enough.

Even his room at Mrs. Hanson's was slipping out of his hands. Books heaped themselves everywhere, papers scattered about on the desk and cascaded onto the floor. Neglected compositions and half-done essays lay on the windowsill, wet and stained from drips down the pane, and the cat sat on them, shooting Ezekiel accusing glances. He tried to convince himself nothing had really changed yet everything had. He could not sleep. He tossed in his bed until dawn. He tried keeping the light on. He tried reading. He tried pacing, but still sleep would not come.

The old man was slipping, and the store with him. Every column of the store's books was captured in the parentheses of loss now. If the old man could only hold on for another six months, Ezekiel would be finished with school; he would get his inheritance and thumb his nose at his aunt and uncle and be gone back to Cozad, Nebraska.

Snow ticked at the window. The landlady had gone to bed three hours ago. The cat had gone too as soon as the room cooled and Ezekiel had made a move to close the window. A draft froze his toes. He could not study. It was near midnight. Sleep was impossible. He got up from his desk, put on his coat. He tugged on a wool cap and slunk out. Ice prickled his face as sharp as an arm gone asleep. Ants crawled in his gut. A cur rounded a corner and snarled. Few people were out. Two women in too little clothes shivered against a tenement wall. Here and there, a saloon's windows sweated. Here and there a quick angry laugh filled the street.

The ice and the necessity of keeping himself upright on the iced walks kept him from thinking of Mr. Reading or the university or anything else. He slipped past the estate houses along Rittenhouse Square to Broad Street, past the lights of the Lafayette Hotel, where the night-shift hackers huddled atop their cabs waiting for fares, and slid onto Arch Street, heading nowhere.

He ducked deep into his collar, pulled the muffler over his mouth. And he walked until his feet were lost to the cold.

Chapter 9

Mr. Reading ran five-inch ads in the newspapers seeking an engraver. As if to test hope, the old man took a large stationery order for a wedding that would take many hours for an engraver to finish and print. It had to be done in a month. He took another order as well, an announcement of birth, and promised to have it done in ten days. For a week and a half, no one answered the advertisement. Mr. Reading grew frantic. Finally, with less than two days until the birth announcement was to be done, a fellow with flaring red hair came in saying he was an engraver. Mr. Reading pulled himself from his stool, laid his hand on the young man's shoulders and escorted him into his office. Ten minutes later, the fellow was put to work. His name was Jasper Hainsworth.

Men, dressed in suits and carrying briefcases, began coming into the store. They did not look at the merchandise, did not stop at the counters to niggle and buy, but went directly back to Mr. Reading's office. He began spending a good part of his days closed up in his office with one of them in particular, a fellow dressed in a dark, well-tailored suit. Ezekiel got a glance at some papers left out on Mr. Reading's desk, papers assessing the store's value for sale.

If the store sold, Ezekiel would be tossed out like dirt from a dustpan. This change, this disturbance, had taken him by the scruff and shaken him like a cat shakes a mouse. He should be looking for other work, should be making a scramble for another job, but hung there helpless to habit and familiarity.

The engraver Hainsworth had gone home half an hour ago. Mr. Reading had already put on his coat, was sitting in his chair, catching his breath before leaving, the briefcase with the sales papers balanced on his lap. It seemed as if everything about the old man were dry, his skin like dust, his scalp flaking, his fingers slivered with hangnails. Only his breath seemed to have juice to it and issued a wet rattle as he breathed. "Mr. Reading?" Ezekiel asked.

"You can go," Mr. Reading said. "There's nothing more to be done."

"I have something." Ezekiel faltered. He had thought about what he wanted to say so much it seemed like it had already happened. "I have something to propose."

"Propose?" It was as if Ezekiel had said a word the old man could not comprehend. Mr. Reading rubbed his eye.

"I would like to increase my hours," he said, "here at the store."

"Can't afford it," the old man said.

"I wouldn't plan on being paid more," Ezekiel said.

The old man fingered a plug of matter from his eye. It lay there, now, on his cheek. He looked straight at Ezekiel. His eyes were layered with thick veins. "No pay?" the old man said. "You mean more work hours and no more pay?"

"Yes," Ezekiel said. He had spent all of the previous night working on this in his room. The store meant security, the refuge of habit. Habit grounded things. But habit was predicated on keeping things just as they were, to keeping the job, to holding onto his room. He could cut back on classes, could beg sickness or some other excuse from the professors for his lack of attendance. He could even complete some of his work outside class. He could manage to get through school, keep his job just as he planned. Six months was all he needed. He had been saving a few cents each week. To sweeten his offer, for the short time he had left, he could cut back on that. "I am even willing," he cleared his throat, "to *reduce* what you pay me."

The old man's eyes crinkled, drew closed. "Reduce what I pay you?"

"Yes."

He took off his eyeglasses. "How much?"

"A third."

"I will pay you a third what I have been paying you and you work more?" The old man was getting frustrated, growing suspicious. "What you want for it?"

"Equity," Ezekiel said.

"Equity," the old man repeated, like it made no sense.

"To become your partner," Ezekiel said, "in the store."

"Me take a partner? A *boy*?"

"I can do anything needs doing," Ezekiel said.

"How much equity?"

"Ten percent."

"Hah, aren't you the one!"

Ezekiel had expected this. "In eight years, ten percent ownership." He would never last eight years, and he knew it. Mr. Reading was grinning now. "Two percent now, one percent for the next eight years."

"Aren't you full of surprises?"

"I got to make plans."

"'Plans,' he says. Hardly old enough to shave, and he's got to make plans."

"By first thing next week."

The old man's expression said this would be the end of it. To Ezekiel's surprise he said, "I got to think some on it."

Chapter 10

He had never believed in providence. He had never believed in order manifest outside his own making. His ma had often called him headstrong, then added, "A bit of stubborn may be good, but keep an eye out for too much of it." He had only ever believed in himself, in his own counsel, his own ability. The universe was laid out in constellations: Ursa, Pegasus, Hercules, Cygnus, and a dozen others, all talked about in some lofty room at the university, then forgotten. But this he remembered: He was born under the sign of Taurus. He was the bull, whom the Greeks called Zeus, a god who took on the form of a white bull to seduce the princess Europa. Ezekiel was not like Zeus in this way. He did not know what to do about females, had never felt at ease, never known where to look much less what to say to them, and in the unknowing, he had convinced himself he had no need for them. But, as with the white bull, power lay in him and in his will.

The bull cracked that February, its horns riven by vagaries that threatened everything. He had seen old men admitting to providence, to something about their lives that had been beyond their control. He swore he never would allow himself to be effete and powerless as one of them.

Even as Mr. Reading talked to men with their briefcases and papers, he agreed to Ezekiel's request, and Ezekiel worked harder than ever. For a few days, Mr. Reading and the store seemed to return to the pace, to resume the habit and custom likely much like the brothers when they worked together. But, as the days grew longer and damper, the old man's vigor dribbled away again, and he took to sitting in the back and letting Ezekiel take over the duties in the front of the store.

Ezekiel's palms still wept at the prospect of serving a customer, but at least he had learned to open his mouth and to speak when one came in. At night, aloud and alone in his room, he rehearsed, "Good afternoon, ladies," and he tried to put the lift into it like the old man. He rehearsed, "Let me show you…" and, "That's a good choice." "Lovely piece." "Elegant." But he sounded stilted as if he were pointing at the page of a book and reading. Without the old man out front, sales, once again, began to plummet.

Then one day, the old man did not come in at all.

They had taken in a shipment of vellum. Ezekiel had come in before opening to unpack and sort it. The back of the store had become his sanctuary. Every morning he came in and did more work arranging and organizing. Sometimes he had the odd impulse to whistle but did not. That morning, he had already spent hours working the back, making the storeroom orderly, clean, and dusted. He had sorted, labeled, and arranged stock on shelves and stacked boxes on pallets so they could find whatever they wanted and there would be room for the vellum. He had even managed to uncover a table suitable for a workbench and had cleared a dance floor's space in which to sort, unpack, and clean. In the front of the store, he had repaired a damaged display case and had washed the three high eastern windows that might never have been cleaned. Even with the low winter sun, they let in a dazzle of good morning light.

It was getting late, nearly time to open. Mr. Reading should normally already have been in. Ezekiel took off his work apron, put on his vest, wetted his hair, and combed it back. The store was lit, now, by a cold, hopeful winter's sun. He heard the front bell ding, expected it was the old man. He came out, but it was just Hainsworth taking off his jacket. "Good morning," Hainsworth said. He looked at the empty stool, and he stood there a moment, his brows high. "Mr. Reading not here yet?"

"He'll be a little late," Ezekiel said. He tried to make this sound certain, as if he knew why Mr. Reading was not there.

Chapter 11

It was always winter, when the days were frigid and brief, solid and bitter, that things seemed to turn for him in a way he could hold onto. They, he and Hainsworth, had made it, however clumsily, through the day without Mr. Reading. He locked up that night by himself but could not sleep, could not study, could do nothing but hope the old man was in the store the next morning.

He rose just as Mrs. Hanson was lighting the fire in the stove. To save a few pennies, he had given up breakfast, but his gut moaned when he saw the bread on the counter. A storm was coming in, the sky whitening in the east, the wind whipping at the intersections. He made it through the streets nearly empty but for a trolley or two, the nags throwing their heads and blowing puffs of breath. A few early schoolteachers bucked the wind going toward their schools, storekeepers pulled back the chains from their windows.

Ezekiel knew before he made it up the first step that Mr. Reading was not in. Not a light was on inside the store. He let himself in, turned on the lights, the dark maw of the windows sucked in a mere bleak winter light. Hainsworth came in not long after, chewing on a particularly dry piece of his lip. "What should we do?" he said. He was looking to Ezekiel for answers.

"Get to work 'til he's back," Ezekiel said.

Hainsworth put on his apron, arranged his hammers and burins, and went back to work, happily it seemed, on an order that had come in for an April wedding from one of the Biddle family. It was a large order that called for good paper stock on heavy linen. The Biddles had no plates for the order; Hainsworth would have to make them. The family insignia was elaborate enough to challenge even a jeweler. Hainsworth was working a third day on the plates, stopping only to go out front to help a customer when the doorbell rang.

That day, Ezekiel closed himself up in Mr. Reading's office. He pulled unpaid bills from the slot, sorted then into piles. He drew up lists, rifled through the past years' books. He made assessments, scrawled figures, made summaries. The old man was sick, as Ezekiel needed no doctor to confirm. What did this mean? What did it mean to his plans? What did it mean to the store? He found himself caring about the store more than he wanted. He scribbled notes to himself:

What happens if Nestor lives and comes back and is no more use than he was?

Nestor dies?

College?

wait seven years until I'm twenty-five for Ma's money?????!!!!!!

Competition (going broke)

Close up? Toss away key? Totten wins.

He underlined "Totten wins" and circled it three times.

Chapter 12

He had learned from the death of his mother that the time before and after death might be quiet but was never a still thing; it inched along like a worm, damp, naked, a muscular ripple mostly unnoticed, but vulnerable, subject to any heel or bird's beak.

After a week's absence, the old man died on the fifth of February. It snowed that day, a squinting white silence. The streets turned muffled, the crystals like dust, hillocks of snow on shoes, people slitting their eyes against the glare, noses and cheeks a furious red. By noon, the day of the funeral, the streets were slick, the walks treacherous. Ezekiel had begged time from his professors—again—and had gotten permission to take his exams later.

Hainsworth stuck with the work, though neither of them had been paid since Mr. Reading's last day at work. Ezekiel did not know why Hainsworth was still around, but guessed he was either dumb as a puppy or loyal as one. He knew Hainsworth still lived on the farm with his family so had somewhere to sleep, even if he did not get paid.

The afternoon of the funeral, Ezekiel printed a sign by hand saying the store was closed and would open again the following morning. After the burial, Hainsworth and Ezekiel returned to the store and continued to work as if nothing had changed.

Ezekiel began putting money from sales into the desk drawer, rather than the bank. His tiny equity was worth a few dollars if the store sold, but the time it would take to get through the estate and be sold made equity worthless to him now. He only needed the shop to provide for him for another few months, and to do that he needed cash; any money that came it was stashed directly in is drawer. Hainsworth finished the Biddle order.

Ezekiel cashed the check, gave Hainsworth a few dollars, and put the rest in the desk.

Four days after the funeral, two men came in, one an official type fresh-shaved, dressed in a gray coat and derby, and carrying a briefcase. The other was a rougher sort. The official set the briefcase on the counter, took off his gloves. He pulled an envelope from it and said, "I want to know to whom I should deliver this." It was engraved with the return of Rawle Law Offices.

"What is it?" Ezekiel said.

"Notice to vacate. The business is closing."

Chapter 13

Dolt. Fool. Imbecile. Like a gallop, there was a rhythm to it Dolt. Fool. Imbecile. He had thought these words many times about many people, when he judged them inferior, stupid, less. It was not someone else now, it was *him*. He had planned so carefully. He thought he had covered every patch, every hole. He had worked longer days for less, only to be jettisoned after all; he would not make it to graduation in June. Without a job he could not pay his rent, would soon not even be able to buy a biscuit. Fool. Fool.

The attorney and his associate had stood watch as Ezekiel and Hainsworth were escorted out of the store, "Before anything might disappear."

It was a miserable day of sleet, rain, wind, and as colorless as a tin can. He strode past storefronts that spoke of hard times, their displays thin, their windows filled with signs saying they were not hiring. But still they were open. They had held on as the finances of the country dived, just as the Readings had held on in the bad times. How?

He turned toward the rooming house he had been stupid enough to think he could keep until finishing school. His right shoe had a hole in it, his toes prickled and had lost feeling to the cold. He had scrimped, had saved, but to what end? He did not have enough to feed or house himself until June, let alone have his shoe repaired.

He had missed exams in every one of his classes, had not laid down a word on any of three essays, now past due. He had paid his rent through the month, but there were only two weeks left on that. When the month was done, then what?

His feet sloshed as he made it up the stairs to the room he would soon lose. He could hear Mrs. Hanson in the kitchen banging pots for supper. When she heard him stamp his feet on the mat, she came around the entry to see. She was wiping her hands on the skirt of her apron. "Oh," she said, "it's just you." She gave a pat to her apron and turned to go back to her pots. Over her shoulder she said, "There's something come for you in the mail. There in the basket."

One letter was addressed to him from the University of Pennsylvania.

Dear Mr. Harrington,

With regard to your status at the University of Pennsylvania and due to your nonattendance at classes, and to your lack of completion of your studies, you are no longer considered a student of this university.

A letter to this effect has been sent to Mr. Totten Hume.

Edmund J. James, Director

Chapter 14

A bed, unless it is used, is a useless thing, nothing but a wadded and cold temptress serving no function, no purpose. Down the hall, the snores of the two brother-renters vibrated through the door, their breaths synchronizing for a breath or two, then falling out until they came together again. There had been a time their loud rattling had been company during those long nights when Ezekiel sat at his desk or lay on his bed and read. The noise was intolerable now.

The notion that Totten was in his big house laughing at him sat like acid in Ezekiel's gut. He was beginning to understand hate. He had stuck to his plan and, until this moment, had made it work. When he was young, his mother had told him, "You won't be a dreamer." She had given a small toss to her head, and added, "Your pa was a dreamer." And she'd turned away, but not before Ezekiel saw the shimmer of wet in her eyes.

By evening, the rain had quit, but then the skies cleared and the night air froze. Ezekiel shrugged out of his nightshirt, threw it on the rumple of his bed. He could see his breath in the room. The cat had come, eaten its scraps, and gone. It was often staying longer now, venturing in to lie on his pillow on particularly cold nights. It closed its good eye and lifted its chin when he scratched its jaw and at the scar that crossed its milky eye. The scar was dry, and at times, Ezekiel put hair oil on it and the cat let him. Lately, if it was particularly happy with its dinner, it would suck Ezekiel's finger and make a rumble in its throat as it massaged Ezekiel's palm. He wished the cat were here now.

He shivered and his fingers were awkward. His private parts shrank in as he pulled on his pants. His shirt smelled of the tang of his tension the last few days. His shoes were still wet, his socks damp.

He unrolled a sock over his foot, yanked it up his calf. He had no garters. Garters were among the luxuries that would have come later if things had gone as he planned. As he manipulated the sock, the image of the old men of his youth sat on him, the old Nebraskan men, sitting on the porch of the immigrant house, canes between their knees, the breeze shifting their thin beards, pants hiked up, socks rippled around their ankles. They had no garters. He had always seen the old men as useless.

He pulled the sock higher and tighter, willing it to stay up. But he knew it would not. It would slip. It would ripple and fall like the old men's, sliding down into furrows just like life, attesting to his failures and stupidities, one ripple for staying too long at the Readings', another for the stupidity of offering—offering, mind you—to cut his pay and work longer hours in exchange for a gnat's share in the failing business. And the last, the most painful, his ejection from the university. Totten would be smiling, in the end. Totten would win. Everything was falling down around his damned ankles.

———

The trolleys had stopped an hour ago. The dark streets were layered with ice, the walks treacherous. No one was out but him, a lone man six or seven blocks in the distance up the street, his image lighting and darkening as he moved under the streetlamps. He braced an arm against buildings as he went, sometimes his feet slipped as he toed around the basement doors jutting into the walks. Everyone in the world but that man a few blocks ahead was inside, home, asleep, warm in their beds. The fellow ahead of him disappeared in a doorway, leaving Ezekiel the sole person in all of Philadelphia with nowhere to go.

He would never know why he went the way he did that night. It was not a direction he often took. He walked north, holding his head down, his feet sliding on the wooden walks of his tenement neighborhood, then coming to the new concrete as he left the rough canyons of the row houses.

He passed the enclosure at Penn Square, came to the station at Broad Street with its chuffs and screams of trains coming in. A few people rushed into the station, a few came out. At the Masons' Temple at Broad and Filbert, foot traffic had worn away a track and he had the vague sense of sure-footedness. The night air shifted and the cloud of his own breath blew back at him, he shoved his hands into his pockets, but they were too gone cold to warm. He was in a part of town he rarely went through.

He counted the blocks now, as if they were worthy of count; had walk-skated twenty-four. Light bled from a corner diner. He stopped. He steadied himself on the pole of a street light and began searching for a sign telling him where he was. In the diner, a man wearing a white apron was turning the sign in the window, closing up for the night. It was not a good diner, but cheap and tacky in a section of town where students from Drexel and the art school filled themselves on stale biscuits and cheap soups.

Five men sat at a table in a large bay window. They were young, near Ezekiel's age. The tones of their voices bled through the panes. They had finished their meals and were tipped back in their chairs, picking their teeth. On the floor, in a heap, lay a clutter of sketch pads, palettes, and rucksacks. One of the fellows was leaning slantwise to the window. He was talking, the others listening. He said something that made them all laugh. He stretched out one long, thin leg, and rested his foot on the brace of the next man's chair, chummy-like. He had thick hair, black as an Indian's. A too-long bang covered his forehead. He drew his fingers through it in a gesture familiar to Ezekiel from so long ago.

Bob Cozad, the only friend Ezekiel ever had.

Chapter 15

Providence. Until that moment Ezekiel had never cottoned to it, had been mortally bored by the concept in a required class with the high-minded title, *Intellectual and Moral Philosophy.* Professor Fullerton had discussed Providence endlessly, was he here, he would open a thick text and read aloud passages by Schopenhauer, or maybe Hegel or Schelling, and would have some arcane—and devotedly long—explanation as to how, in a city of more than a hundred thousand, Ezekiel could stumble on Bob Cozad.

The day he disappeared, Bobby had been fifteen years old, Ezekiel twelve. That was six years ago. Ezekiel had waited. He had never quit watching the trains, keeping an eye out for the Cozads' carriage, listening for news. None ever came. Here he was.

He was tall, thin, his hair still the same near black it always was, his cheeks so high they pushed at his eyes. He had the same sharp, pointed nose and the uneasy complexion. If three centuries had passed, Ezekiel would still have recognized him.

Ezekiel stood under the streetlamp as the waiter began turning down the lights. Bob and the men at the table started gathering their clutter. They stood, put on their coats and shrugged their packs onto their shoulders. The waiter came to unlock and said something cordial as he opened the door.

The men's voices, the rattle of their paraphernalia, and smells of cigars, rusted pots drying in racks, onions and pork grease, the toilet in the back alley, the droppings of rodents, the sawdust and wet rags pushed out the door. As they came out, Bob said to the next fellow behind him, "See you tomorrow."

The fellow answered, "Yuh, back to the grind."

Bob looked up the street as if planning how to manage the ice. The others began to scatter, watching their feet, slipping away in their particular directions. It was then Bob's eyes caught on Ezekiel clinging to the pole like a bum. And it was then, in a low voice, without even a hint that it was six years ago Ezekiel had heard his name called by this one, low voice: "Easy."

Chapter 16

How long did it take to reside in one place one moment, only to be lifted and dropped into another the next? A year? A day? A fillip?

Less. Less.

Nothing had prepared Ezekiel for this. If he faced one way, he was alone, pacing the streets in the ice of a Philadelphia night. If he faced the other, he was in an Arctic Nebraska winter six years ago before Bobby Cozad disappeared.

The night, back then, had been clear, with a moon so bright it lingered on the backs of one's eyes. Ezekiel had been in the house alone. His ma was still at work at the hotel. She still rented the house from Mrs. Gatewood, not yet able to buy it. Outside the window, heaven was endless, stars sitting on the panes.

He had been home from school for two or three hours, fed the goat, grained the hens, and was at his desk studying with no sound but the now-and-then hiss and flare of a moth taken by the flame of the lamp. His ma would not be home for an hour or two. She would be in the hotel kitchen cleaning up from the day's meals, bringing in enough meat from the icehouse to feed thirty or forty the next day. Leftovers from whatever she had cooked, she would bring home for Ezekiel. He would eat while she got herself ready for bed. She would sleep four, maybe five hours and be back serving breakfast at the hotel by daybreak.

Ezekiel had braced open his bedroom door with a shoe, catching heat from the coals in the stove downstairs. A knock came at the door downstairs. He startled. No one ever came to their house. Ezekiel put a marker in his book, *Nicholas Nickleby*.

Before he could get down the stairs, the door rattled again. He opened it. Three were standing in the doorway: Johnny Cozad, Traber Gatewood, and Bob. "River's froze over," Bobby said, "good and hard." They each carried ice skates, two pair were slung over Bobby's shoulder. He handed Ezekiel one of them. "Outgrew them," he said. He held out a foot. "Too little for my appendages. Should fit you."

Ezekiel got his coat. They traipsed in a line over the frozen ruts Cozad called streets, through blue-cold moonlight that died to black in the shadows.

Ezekiel had never ice skated before, Bobby helped Ezekiel into his skates. Johnny and Traber took off, scrabbling to the center of the river where the ice was smoother. Bobby gave a yank to the laces, double-tied the knots and said, "Let's go."

Ezekiel was slow, managing only a slip-step clowning progression, feet scrambling, blades slipping. When they were out in the middle, the moon glared white on their shoulders. Ezekiel could hear the others more than see them. He flailed in their direction but tipped too far forward, caught his hand on the ice, and went down. He could not figure out how to get himself back up. He trembled there, hand on one knee, inert.

Traber was making circles, gliding on one leg like a stork, holding out his arms in a competition of who could skate one-legged the farthest. Bobby was trying a one-footed figure eight. Johnny had turned around, was wobbling backward. He lifted one skate. His leg teetered, and the skate went out from under him. He yipped and went down. Ezekiel could hear the thump. Traber turned and flailed to get up. Bobby glided to his brother. "Hurt?" "Not much," Johnny said. He sat on the ice, brushed his hands on his pants. Bobby reached down, gave him a hand, and pulled him up. Ezekiel waited until Bobby came close, and he flailed himself around, making a drama of trying unsuccessfully to stay up. He yipped just like Johnny and went down. Bobby reached down. "Hurt?" he said.

"Not much," Ezekiel said and Bobby gave him a hand, just like he had his brother.

The memory made Ezekiel now want to lose his footing on the slick Philadelphia streets. The emotion was stupid, asinine; he was no longer a boy, but a man, or close enough to pass for one. But tonight in Philadelphia, he wanted Bob to reach down again and pull him up just as he had that night in Nebraska.

Here and there a saloon or a restaurant's windows were still lit. "I know a place," Bob said. "Not far." Ezekiel and Bob could have been anyone, friends going this way every night of the week.

The diner was a homely chop-house, its windows steamed over. The stale smell of rice in a pot and of spices leaked onto the sidewalk. A long plant with broad leaves languished in a corner by the window. They went in. The Chinaman folded his hands and nodded toward a near table. Bob called out, "Oolong," and held up two fingers. The Chinaman poured from an elaborate brass urn.

As they waited for their tea, Bob said, "It's been a long time." He said he was in his first year studying art at the Academy. Ezekiel could tell he was tired, and his fingers moved in a manner that suggested he was nervous. His chatter filled the silence with talk about how he was frustrated that a teacher named Eakins had been fired and was no longer teaching.

Why didn't you write?

The Chinaman brought the tea. It was speckled with bits of dark leaves. Bob took a perfunctory sip. The leaves settled.

"He let women in his classes with the men," he said. "Ridiculous *sin* that got him fired." He looked up and barked out a bitter laugh. Ezekiel laughed, too, and could hear the nervousness in the pitch of it.

Why didn't you write? Why didn't you tell me where you were?

Bob swirled his cup, sent the tealeaves roiling.

Ezekiel managed to mutter, "Well, that'll do it all right. Shouldn't ever mix a woman and a man." It was quick, meaningless, but at least it was something.

Bob chuckled. "Eakins was using *live* models. Studies of the nude."

"Men and women *nude*?" For a moment the idea overrode the shock of encountering Bob.

"Ah." Bob moved the leaves again. "Yes," he said.

"Oh," Ezekiel said. This *was* improper. Men and women in the same room with a woman *naked*? Imagine women painting a naked male!

For a few moments they sat, not saying a word. Ezekiel had not touched his cup. The thought of disturbing the tea made him nauseous.

Bob was quiet as if in a daydream, his eyes on his tea. "Nebraska was good times, Easy, Wasn't it?"

"Yes," Ezekiel said and he heard the longing in it. It had been a brief two years that Bob's family lived in Cozad, but those two years had shaped him, had given him Bob and laughter and possibility. And then in a sudden black abandonment Bob was gone. Vanished. Disappeared.

"So," Bob said. He looked straight at Ezekiel. "I wondered if I would eventually run into you."

Did Bob know I was in Philadelphia?

"Sam said I might."

Sam? Sam Schooley? *Had Sam always known where Bob was?* Knowing it would have changed everything. Ezekiel had known only what the rest of Cozad and Dawson County knew: Bob's pa shot Alfred Pearson. Pearson died. The people in town threatened to hang John R. Cozad, so he left in the middle of the night. Bobby, his brother Johnny and their mother left, and none of them ever came back. No one, not Sam, or Mr. Atkinson, or Traber Gatewood, or anybody admitted to knowing where they went. *Sam knew where they went.*

The family, all but Traber Gatewood, had scattered like dandelion fluff. Everything Bob's family had done to create a community fell apart: the mercantile closed up, the hotel shut its doors, nothing stayed the same.

Bob had once been light, quick with a sharp joke, a good laugh. He leaned over the table, now, turned his cup in his fingers. The leaves shuffled softly, but did not flail. Then, as if some explanation were in order, he said, "Pa was afraid he would be found out and sent back to Nebraska and hung." He paused, shook back his head like a dog shakes off water. He took a long breath. "We went to Denver first," he said. "But too many knew Pa had business in Denver. So, we came here."

"To Philadelphia?"

"To Atlantic City." He chuckled, an unhappy sound. "Pa opened a gambling resort." It would seem a good end. Everyone in Cozad said Mr. Cozad gambled to get all his money. A gambling house seemed to confirm it.

"Your ma?"

"Still makes Pa toe the mark." He gave a genuine chuckle, then he looked at Ezekiel straight on. "Sam wrote that your ma died."

Ezekiel felt himself begin to crack. He looked down, away. "Yes."

"I was real sorry to hear it," Bob said.

Ezekiel took a drink of the tea. It was bitter.

"I been doing all the talking," Bob said. "What you been doing, Easy?"

Ezekiel shrugged. "School, I guess." It sounded so mealy, so unimportant. He had his own secrets, his own silences; holding them tight had bolstered him. He would not say he had been robbed by his own uncle. He would not say he had been expelled from the school. "And business," he blurted. It flew from his mouth.

Bob drew up a hand in front of himself. "Business?" he said, like this was impressive. "What kind of business?"

"Stationery and printing mostly. Part owner of Reading & Reading." Ezekiel did not add he was now part owner of nothing.

Bob tipped his head. "Whoa."

Ezekiel wanted to hold onto this. He craved what it seemed to mean to Bob, the impression of something important.

The Chinaman came up, nodded to the pot of tea. Bob shook his head no. He yawned and rubbed his eyes. The Chinaman took up their cups and the pot. "Why don't you come up to the studio tomorrow night? Some of the guys are getting together to slop paint around." A thrill went up inside Ezekiel's gut. "Do you paint?" Ezekiel would have given anything to say yes. But he had never held a brush unless it was to whitewash a fence or a wall. "Not much good with a brush."

"Come along anyhow," Bob said. "After supper." He tore a page from a small pad he pulled from his pocket, penciled an address on the page. His handwriting was as large and grand as it was when they were boys, a generous script but without his boy's fancy flourishes. "Not far from here." He handed Ezekiel the note, grabbed up his gear. Then he stopped. He rattled a quiver of brushes into his lap, looked Ezekiel straight on. "There's something else, Easy." The old nickname felt like a warm hand on Ezekiel's back. "I want to ask you something."

"Sure," Ezekiel said.

"You got to promise to keep a secret."

"All right."

"For me."

"Sure."

"I haven't told any of the fellas about my dad, or anything about Cozad." His eyes jittered between Ezekiel's. "They don't know anything about me or my family."

"I see," Ezekiel said.

"I don't call myself Bob Cozad anymore." As if to make sure Ezekiel understood, he said, "No one knows anything about Nebraska, or Pa, or Ma, or anything about what happened. I can't tell them, Ease."

"Sure," Ezekiel said. "I won't tell."

"I don't call myself Cozad anymore since six years ago."

"What then?"

"My name's Robert Henri now." Ezekiel did not ask why that name; Bob's expression seemed to close down on further questions.

The attorney's office was on the fifth floor of a dry wood building, certain to be slated for tearing down and soon to be replaced with some new enterprise. The door opened directly into his office; he had no secretary, no clerk. The one window looked out on the tangle of fire escapes. Ezekiel had found the name in the directory at the Free Library.

The attorney was young, fresh from law studies, an unrefined sort, meaty-faced, thick-necked, better suited to a work crew hammering up cobbles in the street than in a law office. He wore a bad, too-small suit that struggled against three buttons. "I'm here to have a letter written," Ezekiel said.

"What sort of letter?" The attorney was endeavoring to grow hair on his lip. The hair was thin, fine, blond, losing a battle to give him some kind of refinement, or credibility, or whatever he intended.

"A letter that says I am a partner in a business."

"Are you a partner in a business?" The attorney's name was Sebastian Fennet. His desk was neat, spare. There was a file cabinet on the wall behind him with a lone label, "Clients S-Z," in the slot of the top drawer. Ezekiel liked that there seemed to be nothing hidden about Sebastian Fennet; that he was direct, understandable. Tact always made things difficult.

"A letter that says I am a partner who has the right to operate."

The night after he saw Bob, Ezekiel had slept as he had not slept since he could remember. It was as if seeing Bob had made something turn. He woke that morning clear-headed, knowing in a single thought what came next. He told Mr. Fennet what had happened at the Readings', and he told him what he wanted in the letter. The attorney said it would cost him two dollars. Ezekiel said for that much he would do it himself. They settled on a dollar and a half.

Ezekiel handed Fennet the letter from the attorney representing Mr. Reading's widow and he produced the document Mr. Reading had signed when Ezekiel made the deal for a share in the business. "Two percent?" the attorney said. "You own *two percent?*" A flicker of humor crossed Fennet's mouth. "I guess a partnership is a partnership however you cut it."

The lawyer's stationery was of the cheapest sort, light in weight, the engraving rough and of the lowest quality. As he wrote, Fennet's mouth moved, and he wasted two sheets before getting one to say what he wanted said. He handed Ezekiel the letter. The hand in which it was written was, at least, elegant.

February 25, 1887
Rawle Law Offices
211 S. 6th St.
Dear Messrs. Rawle,

Please review the agreement of partnership between Mr. Nestor N. Reading and Mr. Ezekiel Harrington which establishes Mr. Harrington as partner in Reading & Reading Stationery. Though the death of Mr. Reading is untimely, and my client is saddened by the loss, he intends to resume and continue conducting the business.

I am sure you will agree that, in order to perform in any capacity, Mr. Harrington must have immediate access to the premises. In this regard, unless Mr. Harrington is given access to his business by seven o'clock in the morning tomorrow, February 26, 1887, a letter of restraint and further court action will be immediately forthcoming. We would endeavor to keep this matter from the court.

Yours,

Sebastian D. Fennet, Attorney at Law

Chapter 17

The art studio was a convenient ten minutes from the Academy. Bob said he lived another three blocks down the street from it.

Ezekiel strode up the narrow stairs to the top floor. He could hear murmuring from a room at the end of a dim hall. The door was open and breathing out the smells of solvents. The floor was laid with old carpet, darkened in the middle and worn through to the wood in patches. Two lonely lamps made do for light.

He heard someone gargle out, "Damn."

Another voice—Bob's—said, "So, is it what you see?"

"Hell no," the other said.

There were five of them in the room, six counting Bob, who was wearing a ridiculous, collapsed topper hat as flat as a pie tin. It was an odd hat, seemed meant to proclaim him an artist but instead made his slanted face wild, severe, and ridiculous. He dressed in black as he had since boyhood, the same austere color his father had so long ago.

Ezekiel had never stepped a foot in a studio before but had formed an idea of what he would find in one: flowers on tables, windows with views onto rivers and meadows, bowls of fruit, perhaps, or a woman posing in fancy laces and pearls. This was nothing more than a large room, paint smears swiped everywhere a brush could reach, shoe prints crossing and recrossing dripped paints, and a forest of easels circling a woeful fellow sitting on a chair crammed into the corner.

No one had heard Ezekiel come in. The fellow posing in the chair saw him and began tapping his foot. He appeared to be an artist as well, his shirt open at the collar and bearing a yellow stain on the sleeve. Later Ezekiel learned models cost money and, to save, the fellows rotated the job. "Sit still, Skippy," Bob said.

"I'm trying," he said.

"Well damn, don't just *try, do* it," said one holding a stick of charcoal. He was short-cropped, short in the arms, stump-legged, his sleeves ruched up at his elbows, with hair tossed on his head like a rebellion. A couple of the others held onto palettes and were dabbing paint onto boards. Bob was in the middle of making his way around the room, assessing each drawing and canvas. In his left hand he held a charcoal of his own.

The one called Skippy noticed Ezekiel then. "Hey, get out. This is private."

Bob turned, then, waved Ezekiel in. The heavy-haired fellow turned, too. His face was handsome, but his brows were heavy, as if waging a battle with the hair on his head. "Don't need to come in if you aren't planning to work."

"Well, he isn't coming to work, Calder," Bob said. "He's coming to *look* at work." It gave Ezekiel a start, hearing it. It was, he supposed, true. But Bob's tone seemed to mean something else. They all looked up, then, even the model. It was as if Ezekiel's coming had taken on some significance.

Ezekiel sat on a chair pulled off to one side, an observer, as the rest painted and drew long after eleven o'clock.

Chapter 18

Night was only just giving way toward dawn, the skies across the Delaware beginning to lighten. He stood in the dark of the stoop. The eaves were dripping frigid picks from skies too heavy for snow. Ezekiel refused to shiver.

He had a key, he always had. He could have gone in. But, if the widow's lawyer ever came, Ezekiel did not want him to know it; he wanted to force the point of his rights and making the Rawle office hand over a key seemed a good way to make it. He tested the lock; by rights, the Rawle attorneys might have changed it, but they had not. He locked the bolt again and waited.

Ezekiel had no watch, but he knew it was some time past seven, the time his letter demanded they meet. As the minutes passed, he began to doubt Sebastian Fennet's plan, and to think he had wasted good money on bad advice.

Half an hour later, a coach pulled up, stopped in front. The driver settled the brake. The door slammed open, and the widow's attorney drew himself out. He was not a large fellow, but the driver was. Ezekiel watched as the attorney buttoned his coat, woven of cashmere. There was no turning back now; Ezekiel had to face down the inevitable. The grab in his stomach eased somewhat. This tardiness, this loud slamming of the coach door, this mad stomping of the attorney's feet was meant to gain the upper hand. The truth was, the attorney might not have shown up at all.

He waggled a paper at Ezekiel like a housewife waggles a rag at a cat. "What the hell is this?" His face was red and bloated. Ezekiel found this anger incredibly pleasing. If the attorney were not concerned, there would be no need for the display.

Fennet had said that with such a small share in the business, a court would likely not find in Ezekiel's favor, that it was likely Reading's estate would make some small offer to buy out Ezekiel's share to get rid of him. If it went to court, most likely a judge would find that Ezekiel's claim was merely holding up the estate, and that would be that. "It might take a while to get settled," Fennet had said.

"How long?"

Fennet shrugged. "Who knows, weeks, a couple months. Depends."

How Ezekiel's life had changed. So little time ago all he wanted was to hold on just long enough to get the diploma in his hand and board the next train to Nebraska. How trite it felt now, how toothless a goal. Having Bob here colored everything: he wanted the store, now, for his own. He pictured himself becoming a success in Bob's eye and that led to thumbing his nose at Totten and to proving himself to his ghost of a pa. He knew beyond certainty just how to fix the store. He knew beyond certainty how to make himself a success. And, given time, he would do it.

Ezekiel and the attorney planted themselves in a sort of stand-off at the door. The attorney shook the paper again in Ezekiel's face. In another time, Ezekiel would have found the attorney's frustration comedic. "Tell me, what the hell is this?"

"It appears to be a letter," Ezekiel said. "Who are you?" He knew well enough who this fellow was, had seen him half a dozen times in the store talking to Mr. Reading.

"Who am I?"

"That's what I asked."

The attorney's head jerked. Apparently, this was not what he had anticipated. "Edgars," he said. He held out the paper, slapped it with the back of his hand. "What is this?"

"I need to repeat myself?" Ezekiel said. "It appears to be a letter. Torn,

I'm afraid."

"You're holding up the estate. You can't do this," he said. His face puffed like a bladder. He was near shouting.

Ezekiel cupped his hands around his mouth, leaned in, and whispered, "People are going to hear you."

"You can't hold up the estate."

Ezekiel pulled the key from his pocket, waved it at the attorney, said low, "Oh, can't I?" He swung open the door, stood aside, waved the attorney in. "We'll discuss it inside my store."

———

He'd found Hainsworth's address from Mr. Reading's old address book and paid a courier one dollar to deliver a letter to him. If Ezekiel were someone who prayed, he would have asked the heavens that Hainsworth had not yet found work.

The widow's attorney had spent no more than two minutes screaming threats before he stormed out. Ezekiel knew he had not seen the last of him. Meanwhile, the two percent he owned meant the store was in his hands, even if his hold was fragile, but to have any chance to manage, he needed Hainsworth's engraving work to do it.

With just him in the store, his footsteps echoed. The dark windows sucked up the light. The workbench lay like a shadow, the engraver's stool tucked under, lonely, solitary. The water pump dripped in the workshop sink. He opened the grates for heat, and it took hours to dispel the damp. In the bin was coal enough for a few days, if he was lucky.

He had spent the last three years absolutely certain he would know how to bring the store around, if he had his hands on it. He had had a gullet full of courses at the university that told exactly how to run a business, how to make millions, how to grab success. His professors spouted figures and examples as if their cocksure dogma held all the answers. But reality? This was reality: Reading & Reading had once been a good business, but the brothers had not changed with the years. Now Wanamaker's sold everything the Readings' did, and they sold it cheaper and in better selection, not only stationery and calendars but everything else as well. Coats? They had racks and racks. Household items? They sold thousands: dishes, linens, rugs, China, sterling, something for every room in the house. Stationery? Puh, every color in the rainbow.

Ezekiel began to spend hours cramped at the old office desk. Long into the nights he pored over the books. He needed money. For a few days, maybe weeks, he could manipulate finances and keep the store open. For a time, bills would be forwarded to the estate. But the totals the store owed made him choke: nearly four hundred to A M Collins, Mfg., for cards and card boards, another eighty-seven to Molten and Munch for writing papers, a couple hundred to Smithers & Smithers for calendars now nearly two months out of date. He took inventory of the stock in the front of the store and the dusty stuff on the shelves in back. It would bring less than half what the old men had paid for it. He needed to sell it fast.

Ezekiel went outside in the prickle of cold rain and looked back into the store's windows: everything in the displays spoke defeat—the woods warped from a leak through the cracked window, cobwebs draped along the transoms, tarnished cardholders, blanks for wax seals no one fancied anymore, dusty bookends, and baby albums. Even the FOR SALE signs appeared exhausted. It was a mess. Across the street, a Syrian fellow ran a business selling rugs. The Syrian's windows danced with color and his door let in customers all day long. His business was prosperous and growing. Ezekiel had to capture some of that traffic—and it had to be soon.

———

The heavens seemed to open three days later, when Hainsworth showed up wanting to work again. In fifteen minutes, they had slid back to their old routines. Ezekiel paid him from whatever they took in at the end of each day. It was not enough, but Hainsworth asked for no more. If he had not had family to live with, if he'd had to pay for his own food and room, he would not have been able to stay.

Then, toward the end of their first week, Hainsworth brought in some of his own tools and a bit of copper and asked if he could sometimes work on designs of his own when he had no engraving and when the store was not busy. For hours at a time, he sat hunched over the workbench, fashioning jewelry for his sister, using the old engraving tools, the workbench, the burner, getting up only when the bell rang in a customer. He said it was to be a pin and earrings to match.

———

One day Ezekiel left Hainsworth in charge of the store. It was cold out, a misery of wind and sleet blowing sideways. Ezekiel wandered up Chestnut, down Walnut, to Market then Broad. He stood before storefronts. He cupped his hand and peered into windows. The banks, of course, announced their solid importance, but some other businesses shouted success as well, windows were full of their products, storefronts fresh-painted, doors swung open into interiors that beaconed people in with a warmth. Those shouted prosperity and abundance. Others lay empty and dark, a blight of failure.

He watched people venture into Lits, and Clothier & Strawberry and Wanamakers eager to shop at those stores in spite of the cold. A store selling Turkish bathrobes and towels teemed with people, more dinged through the door into Coxton and Wood whose specialty was ladies' shoes. Customers crowded into A. Colburn's to buy *The Finest Table Delicacies,* and G. S. Lovell's clocks and bronzes, and W.T. Tilden's *Wool, Hair, Noils.* The windows of Joseph M. Walsh's Teas and Dreer's Seeds were steamed up from the excitement of people spending money. In those stores, nary an owner stood still. Those stores bustled with movement, with the crush of customers and clerks. The registers rang and rang. The smaller, thriving establishments served some narrow, distinctive market the department stores did not.

Reading & Reading could not continue selling tired stationery, and obsolete calendars and pens. But what in hell *would* it sell?

Chapter 19

He gave up his room at the end of the month. He had to call for a cab to move him and his things: his suitcase, the trunk, and the cat. When the cat had come in the night before, he had quietly closed down while the cat licked up on his pillow. He placed a particularly good morsel of meat on a plate and set it in a wood box he had brought home from the store. He let the cat lick and lick until he feared it would not notice the meat in the box. Minutes later, it stopped, lifted its nose, and rose up. Its path to the meat became almost tangible, something concrete. Ezekiel had laid the box near his leg, and, when the cat climbed in, he slapped closed the door. The cat screeched and thumped and caused the box to shift and bounce. And, when it finally realized it was trapped, it lay quiet with the one good eye peering through a crack, watching.

At a second-hand store down on First Street, Ezekiel bartered for two riddled blankets and a used mattress. The mattress was stained on one side but fairly good on the other. He carried them to the store on his shoulder, laid himself a bed in back, on one of the empty storage racks. He bought himself a bowl of stew and two biscuits. Also bought two used bowls and carried one back to the store with a lump of good meat in it.

He set the bowl with the meat in front of the box that held the cat. He filled the other with water. He closed the door that led into the front of the store, checked the door that led out into the back alley, and let the cat out of its box. The cat darted into a crevice and hid under the shelves.

That night, Ezekiel washed in the frigid water at the sink. In the morning, with no mirror, he felt of his face in order to shave and cut himself on the chin and twice on the cheek. By the time Hainsworth came in the bleeding had let up.

They worked together in the pattern of silence they had eased into. Ezekiel said he had brought a cat and pointed to where it hid. Hainsworth stepped over there. "Kitty," he said, in a high pleading sort of voice. When the cat did not come out he said, "Ah, we could use a mascot."

The day was bleak, the streets heaped with a filthy snow, sidewalks worn through in a narrow path that made women heft their skirts and grab the arms of their men. The afternoon winds had whipped a hole in the awning and a long piece of it slapped. From the street, it made a terrible impression. Ezekiel went out with the ladder, took his knife to the rip and trimmed what he could of it. A rib showed through. The thing would need to be repaired soon. God only knew that cost of that.

He settled again at the ledgers. No matter how neat he had made them, no matter how precise, their news was not good. It struck him like a blow. He envied Mr. Reading's decline. In the end, the old man had not had sense enough to understand any of this. Ezekiel spent the day with the truth: He had gotten himself into more than he knew what to do with.

The doorbell dinged. It was late, near closing. Hainsworth had left a little early that day for some family function, a birthday, Ezekiel thought. When he was alone, the bell still could cause Ezekiel's gut to cramp; he had never conquered the timidity of dealing with a customer on his own. He only hoped he would not appear too needy or but too hopeful of a sale. He got up from the desk, expected to hear the thump of feet on the front floor. Instead, he heard a shout, "Easy, the chop-house in an hour." The door slammed shut and left the bell dinging.

The largest table in the chop-house was full. Ezekiel recognized most of the men here, rehearsed their names in his head before he sat down; the surly one was Calder, the ruffian Redfield, and the narrow, refined one

Hugh Breckenridge. One, a severe fellow with hair flying out like wings from a razor-straight part, Bob introduced as Grafly, a sculptor. Another fellow sat at the table, one Ezekiel not met before and whose name he did not catch. Scattered among the men were women—*women!!*—girls, really, about Ezekiel's age. The prospect of women put an uncomfortable bend on things. He had expected the guys, but women threw a wrench into it. For the few women who came into the store, he could muster some performance and chatter in order to make a sale, but that was it. Otherwise, he kept them and their confusion at an arm's distance. But the men were laughing and talking to these women as if they were equal. Women had no business in a low place like this, and, God, at night! Had they no grace? No refinement? Apparently not.

Redfield stood, took a chair from a nearby table, made room. Calder lit a cigarette. Breckenridge chatted with the woman sitting beside him. Two were of a conventional sort but a bit off proper in wrinkled shirtwaists and too animated the way they leaned on their elbows and talked as equals with the men, nodding, discussing paints, and each other's work. The third female sat next to Bob. She was a mess of a thing, quiet, a dark lump with a Medusa's snaking black hair and who wore a tight and dingy blouse missing a button. Ezekiel had an impulse to leave, but Bob waved him to take a seat.

The conversation had entirely to do with art, some new thought coming from France, and they spoke with total, bald-faced anger at the conservative drivel being taught to them here at the school. The crude woman sitting beside Bob did not join in but sat like a threat, dark as a thunderhead, her tangle of hair jerking as she rolled a cigarette from tobacco and paper Calder passed to her. She gave a practiced lick to the papers and leaned across Bob for a light. She held her hair away from the flame. On her arm was a bramble of rusted wires she must have thought made do for bracelets. "Tank you," she said, her voice rasping like a low note from an accordion. Her name was something long and complicated and from some strange foreign place. Ezekiel did not catch it when Bob made the introductions. Later, he thought he heard Bob call her Soap.

For a while they talked about the paucity of inspiration in their classes. "Anschutz sets out a plaster cast and tells us how we're supposed to do it," Redfield said. "Do *what* with it? Smash the damned thing?" The men laughed.

"Give him credit," Bob said. He turned his water glass in his long fingers.

Calder blew smoke from his nostrils like a bull. "For what?" He said. "They fire Eakins who gave us flesh and blood models and we get Anschutz and his plaster." He spat it out like a curse, as if Anschutz were the devil.

Bob said, "At least he can give us technique."

"Sure enough," said Grafly. He was serious, calm, focused; Ezekiel liked these things in him. The fellow they called Reddy—Ed Redfield—had sat all through dinner with his sleeves rolled up, his tie undone, his collar sloppy and loose. Grafly said he had signed up for advanced classes in sculpture. "You can make a few thousand dollars in sculpture, if you can sell it."

Bob turned on him. "You let yourself go for the greenback and you can't call yourself an artist."

"You have to go for the greenback or you don't eat." This pragmatism Ezekiel could understand.

But Bob was after his point. Ezekiel had never seen this side of him. In their youth, Bob had been the placator, friendly with everyone in town, joking, laughing, enlivening conversation and making peace, particularly with his own brooding pa. Bob's face was set now. "They want us to paint what everybody has always painted since forever." Ezekiel wondered what was so wrong with that. "They want us to paint the same old brown cows in their pastures, the same portraits of stiffs in tuxedos, the same ships and harbors, and children at picnics, and if we do that we might be able to make a go of it." He laid his hand on his middle, like he might be getting sick. "And where does that leave us?"

"Eating and paying the rent," Calder said.

"That what you want?"

Calder gave a tiny shake to his head, and Redfield said, "They want rote at the school. They want craft. Hell, a sawyer does craft, a stone mason does goddamn *craft*." Ezekiel looked at the women, expecting some embarrassment at Calder's language but saw none.

"Nothing wrong with a stone mason," Grafly said, more to break the tension, it seemed, than to make a worthy point. "Eakins painted what he saw, and look what it got him. I think with sculpture I could at least manage to feed myself."

"If that's all you want, we aren't talking the same thing," Bob said.

"What are we talking, then?" Grafly asked.

"We're talking something no one can see but us. We're talking essence."

"Essence," Calder said. "Now *that* puts food on the table." The fellows laughed and the women laughed, all but the dark one. Ezekiel was enjoying the banter and wished he could be part of it.

But Ezekiel *could* see the point: One had to make a living. One had to do the things that brought in money. Artists always starved, even he knew that trope. How could these fellows be so naïve? Bob had always been somewhere off in a private distance, even when they were boys. Bob could afford dreams. He had had a pa who, as mean as he was, had money enough to pay cash for forty-three thousand acres in Nebraska. Bob had his ma, from a known and prominent family in Virginia. He had always had more than enough to eat and clothes to wear and a roof to sleep under. "We can't let them stop us," Bob said.

Grafly pulled a pad and charcoal pencil from his gear. "In Europe," he said, taking up a pencil, "that fellow Rodin is incredible." And, as the others watched, Grafly's pencil flew across the paper. In seconds he had sketched the figure of a sinewy St. John the Baptist, right there in front of the women—totally nude. Ezekiel's ears burned.

Calder said, "It's France that's got the nod."

Grafly said, "Here we are stuck in the upchuck of the Academy, drawing plaster casts, and half a world away they're doing what we should be doing."

Their food came and, for a minute, they set to eating and losing themselves in their dinner, a community of frustration. Finally, Bob said, "I'm thinking about putting together a class for women." One of the women slapped the table and said, "When?" the one next to her said, "Sign me up." But the third woman, the rough number sitting beside him said nothing. Her coarse, dark eyes and her outrage of hair made Ezekiel seethe. By the end of the evening, he'd learned she was not even attending the school.

Chapter 20

The offer came three months after Mr. Reading's death. The days were growing longer, one day filled with robins and the glare of early sun, the following pounding with thunder that laid down skiffs of snow. As he waited, he had managed to keep the store open and he sometimes whispered thanks to himself that Hainsworth had stayed on. What sales they made largely hinged on Hainsworth's gift of the gab and the way women, particularly, took to his curling red bang, and his honey lashes, the full, wet, red of his mouth. He had a way with them, an ease that made them linger and spend a few cents more on items they might not have otherwise come in for.

Ezekiel had kept the cat inside since he moved and it had hidden in the shelves for a few weeks, then began coming out, snatching food from the plate, scowling one-eyed at him, then dashing back to its hole. The shop began to stink of urine and Hainsworth placed a box with ripped newspapers near the hole. In the night, Ezekiel heard the hiss of the cat's relieving itself and the grunt as it pushed, then the stink of its droppings. In the morning Ezekiel threw out the papers and Hainsworth filled it again with more from the ones he brought with him. Then it began to howl at the back door to go out. He finally relented, opened the door and never saw the cat again. He missed it.

Hainsworth had given his sister the pin and earrings he made. He told Ezekiel she had worn them every day since. Ezekiel knew the care Hainsworth had spent on them. They were quite lovely, though Hainsworth had had only the cheapest wire and quartz to work with. He made another set and asked if he could put them in the case for sale. Half in jest, Ezekiel said sure, if he got half of what Hainsworth brought in if they sold, and Hainsworth agreed. The pieces sold the same day. That afternoon, with his share of the sale in his pocket, Hainsworth went to a supply house and bought an amethyst stone, some tiny pearls and two small, clouded rubies with which to fashion a broach.

Hainsworth had sold two good-sized orders of stationery for weddings coming up in June. He drew up worksheets for the jobs, got them signed by the customers, then did the engraving and worked the press to fulfill them. He worked hard all day long, then he stayed evenings after hours to work on his jewelry designs. They worked together long into the nights, Ezekiel fussing at displays, or sweeping, or dusting, or in his office bent over his books, listening to the hush of his own pencils while the ticks of Hainsworth's happy pinging of metal as he hammered. It should have been a time of peace, if only Ezekiel could trust things as Hainsworth seemed to. Sometimes Hainsworth groaned as he worked, sometimes he hummed low in his throat and it became clear that this working on his own designs was what kept him there, no matter how desperate the place was.

That evening just after closing, someone slipped the Reading offer through the mail slot: a paltry fifteen dollars to buy out Ezekiel's partnership. The nerve of such an offer made Ezekiel gasp, then respect the audacity of it. If he took the offer, the space could be made available to him for rent of fifty dollars a month. Ezekiel shouted, "Hell!" and Hainsworth's tools went quiet. For this, Ezekiel had moved from his room! For this he had existed on one meal a day? For this he'd slept on a mattress that smelled of someone else's hair oil and feet? For this he had bathed from a frigid pump?

Hainsworth peered around the office door. "Anything I can do?" "Nothing," Ezekiel said, and Hainsworth went back to the bench and back to his infernal tapping. Fifteen dollars. Fifteen damned dollars.

The next morning, Ezekiel left Hainsworth in charge of the store and went up the five flights to Fennet's office. He laid the offer on the lawyer's desk and sat himself down in the chair. He did not say a word as Fennet read. And when Fennet was through he laid the letter down and said one word: Counter.

"Counter with what?" Ezekiel could smell the stench of tension on himself. Anger and fear clouded his thinking. This was just what he had spent the last nearly four years at the university believing he knew how things were done. Now he was in a corner, now that everything he wanted was in jeopardy, he had no brain to think with. "With what?" He knew it sounded rude.

"Half," Fennet said. "And ask for all past payables to be settled by the estate."

"God," Ezekiel said, "would they settle for that?"

"Probably not," Fennet said. And he began to strategize to himself out loud. He ticked ideas on his fingers. "There will be costs to rent it. The location is not great. It might not rent right away. There would be expenses to sell the stock."

"Old stock," Ezekiel said, beginning to pick up on Fennet's theme. "Out-of-date."

"There would be repairs," Fennet said, "whitewashing, cleaning, etcetera." Ezekiel thought of the awning, the leak around the water pump. He thought of the crack in the corner of one of the windows. "Ask the estate to come up with the cost of repairs. Tell them you will sue if they don't do as you want." Fennet leaned back, looked straight at Ezekiel and smiled. "Hell," he said, "maybe we can make them pay you to stay." And he laughed and Ezekiel surprised himself with a chuckle.

Fennet wrote the letter. Three days later the estate responded with a counter of its own, reducing the rent by fifteen dollars, but stipulating that all past outstanding bills and arrears be paid by Mr. Harrington, and demanding the remaining stock be purchased outright for two hundred dollars. The letter concluded, "This is an exceedingly generous proposal from Mrs. Nestor Reading as she wishes for Reading & Reading Stationers to continue in the same successful tradition as it has the past forty years. We have advised our client not to carry this discussion on any further. In order to not hold up settling of the estate, we demand a reply from Mr. Harrington by closing tomorrow or we will begin proceedings to prepare the business to be sold according to our client's wishes." And the letter was signed, Regards, M. John Edgars.

"I believe this is their last offer," Fennet said. "Can you make it with this?"

A pit in Ezekiel's gut said he did not know. "I'll find a way."

Before he left, Fennet handed him his bill.

Chapter 21

He was going broke. He had no one but himself to blame. As undemanding as Hainsworth was, he still needed to be paid, the gas needed to be kept on, coal to be brought in, ink and paper to be bought. He needed money.

He spent his next day's meal money for a train ticket to Chestnut Hill. The train screeched out of the station into a canyon of buildings drenched in the rain and of trees just beginning to bud.

It was warm in the train car and smelled the odor of damp wool coats. He had rehearsed his demands, the speech he would deliver, so many times that, once he started in on it, his mouth moved on its own.

By the time the train stopped at Chestnut Hill, the streetlights were lit. He had not been this way in the nearly four years. It had been summer then, the gardens in full bloom, the streets running with carriages, the walks filled with maids pushing prams. The trees were bare now, their branches fingering the dusk. Rain filled the gutters, slickened the slate walks. The shops on Germantown Avenue had already closed. He wrapped the muffler tighter around his throat, ducked into the wind wearing his best suit and a fresh shirt.

The Hume house was dark but for a bit of light that escaped around the prison of heavy drapes and an electric bulb in the porte-cochere. He stood at the bottom of the drive, allowed himself one last breath. Several carriages crowded the drive up by the house. The family carriage sat under the roof of the breezeway, the mare in her trace, the driver's seat empty. Behind the Hume coach was a smaller buggy and a hansom cab.

Ezekiel shuffled up to front doors sized for a cathedral. He pulled back the boar's-head knocker and let it drop. He waited and was about to bang it again when the maid opened the door, the same woman he remembered. He could no longer recall her name. "Yes?" She said. Apparently, she had forgotten his name as well.

"Ezekiel Harrington," he said.

"Oh," she said. "Mrs. Hume's nephew, isn't it?" He could hear voices inside, muffled, serious, and low. "Come in," she said and held the door as the wind swept him in.

Everything in the house had been moved, the center table, the excelsior chairs, the side tables, the footstools, even the rugs, all shoved aside, giving way to a hospital bed. In the bed lay Totten. A doctor leaned over him, listening to Totten's chest with a metal and tube contraption. Prune and a woman he did not know had positioned themselves out of the way and were holding hands. The woman, Ezekiel guessed, was Addie, Totten's sister.

He stood in the doorway, out of the drift of their attention, which was on Totten. The room had the same hushed feel as his mother's before she died, filled with whispered encouragements that things would get better.

The doctor told Totten to "Breathe out." The doctor was a slim man with dark hair and a fine suit. It seemed the room held its breath as he stood up straight, pulled the device from his ears, and folded it back into his case. "Well," he said, "it could be worse." As he said it, Ezekiel recognized the doctor was his cousin Oliver, the boy in the long-ago photograph. He knew it was Oliver by the bed and Cornelius standing behind his mother. The resemblances to their parents were obvious. Oliver looked down at his father, laid a hand on his shoulder. "Bed rest, Dad," he said, "or I'll see to it Mother ties you down." Prune blubbered a laugh and blew her nose.

Cornelius came to the foot of the bed, gave a little shake to his father's toes. "You going to listen to the doctor?" he said. Totten whispered something in response. He was withered, pale, his color blended with the white of the sheets. Ezekiel was not sure if had he come upon his uncle on the street, he would recognize him.

He must have made some little sound. Oliver looked up and said, "Wh…Ezekiel?" His aunt sprang from her chair. She patted her mouth with her fingers. "Dear," she said. "Dear." Four years ago, his aunt had been fat but was thinner now. Her jaw had no more of its ripple, only a small hammock of skin. It was her chin that nearly made Ezekiel gasp. Without the fat, it was pointed in the way his mother's had been, in the way his own was. She reached out to touch his arm. Her hand was soft and damp. She let it lie there longer than he found comfortable. When she finally let him go, she took a handkerchief from her sleeve and dabbed at her eyes.

Totten lay inert but for the soft rise of the coverlet. He raised his finger, then, and motioned Ezekiel to come closer. He licked a dry tongue over dry lips. "I know why," he whispered, "you've come." He took a breath and waited. Then he managed, "I heard," took another breath, waited again. "You are not in school." He closed his eyes as if waiting for the breath to take. When he opened them again, he said, "You'll get your money when you finish your education."

Ezekiel left the room with no more than a nod toward his aunt. He raged at Totten's sick-bed obduracy. The anger carried him out the door and, once out, bolstered him. After Totten's comment, he had stayed at the Humes only long enough to pluck himself from the clutches of his aunt. He had twice refused her offer to have their man Joseph drive him home. He had meant to give nothing of himself away, but, in the end, his aunt had extracted the name of the business where he worked.

Ezekiel hand-delivered his response to the Rawle Law Offices the next morning. By the end of the next day, a courier delivered the widow's answer: She accepted, even with no more money from him. *Could he have extracted even better terms for himself?* It was too late. The store, and every tired item in it, were his—and he had no idea how he was going to keep it.

Chapter 22

Hainsworth began to stay longer into the evenings to work on his jewelry designs. Each day, after the store closed, he went out for a bite to eat and, after he had eaten, let himself back in with the key Ezekiel had given him. Their habit grew into a quiet companionship. The pick-pick of Hainsworth's tools, the tang of his waxes, and the whir of his jeweler's drill spelled a kind of peace. They spoke little, but bit by bit Ezekiel learned he was a single fellow, no longer living with his family. He had taken a room and lived alone in it. It was a cheap room that provided nothing but a bed, no boarding, no laundry. His family, parents and two brothers, lived in Wilkes-Barre. The store was his first job since his job working for his family on their farm. He had not had time to make friends and had nowhere to go after work but to his miserable rented room, so he seemed to welcome Ezekiel's company, as reticent as it was.

Ezekiel admired the manner in which Hainsworth worked, particularly on his own designs. He concentrated with an intensity that seemed to involve his tongue, which flicked outside his mouth, planted itself in a corner and stayed there until his lip grew so chapped it bled. One evening he confessed he thought he might one day want to give up the engraving profession to make jewelry. It was the first Ezekiel had heard of this. The stationery sales and the engraving business remained the store's primary income. *What if Hainsworth no longer engraved? What then?*

Hainsworth showed his most recent piece to Ezekiel. "It's a pin for my ma," he said, "for her coat." It was quite a beautiful thing, a rounded shape set with red and green glass beads. Hainsworth had hammered the metal shim into the designs of flowers and vines. The next morning, after

Hainsworth gave it to her, he seemed more talkative than usual, and he said his ma cried when she opened it. He asked if Ezekiel minded if he began work on another broach. Of course, Ezekiel said—if working on his jewelry kept Hainsworth at the engraving and printing, he might have promised anything.

Hainsworth's next design turned out even more elegant than the first. When it was done, Hainsworth asked if he might put it for sale in one of the displays. The pin sold in a single day, and Hainsworth set to hammering out two more.

Chapter 23

A postcard came in care of the store. The note was scribbled with a hurried hand. *"Easy, you can call me professor now. I am teaching a class at the Academy. After hours. Why not join up?????"* The note was little more than scribbled, barely readable, words whipped out as if there had been no more than a second to get them down. It took Ezekiel a moment to see what they spelled out: the time and place of the class in the Academy and at the end a scratching that appeared to be Dobly. There was a sense of the old Bobby in the note—excitable, quick, silly, a side Ezekiel did not see him show now. It was as if, somehow, he felt safe enough to let this side out, but just now, and just with Ezekiel.

Bob was emerging as the artists' leader, and it seemed the weight of leadership and trying to make his own art was sometimes too heavy. To Ezekiel, this pursuit of art self-expressed, no matter the outcome, seemed arrogant and ill-conceived. If tradition had a chance of making a living, why do anything else? Some of the students were poor beyond penury, wearing patched clothes, pants with holes, shoes whose soles flapped. A lot of them worked twelve hours a day at the mills or on the docks or drawing for the newspapers, then dragged themselves up to class to spend hours at a mess of paints. Bob could afford this. He had his rich family behind him. What about the others? They looked to Bob to inspire them, just as Ezekiel had looked at Bob when they were boys.

Ezekiel had never sketched anything in his life, had only picked up a pencil to write numbers in an accounting book or a signature on a check. When they were boys, he had watched Bob ink drawings on the backs of broadsides, on the walls, even in the palm of his hand. It might be anything:

the head of a horse, a man's hat, a child's face, a foot. He had watched him churn the initials of his name into a tangle of whorls and loops and shadows. And he would draw comic figures in a diary and write page after page holding forth on the plans his pa had for the town, on certain people his pa did not like, on politics. He had long ago even come up with a silly newspaper he printed and passed around town. It was called *The Runty Papers* and included sophomoric pictures of Runty, a kind of ironic clown. If Bobby had done all this when he was a boy, how could sketching be so difficult for an adult that it required a class? Ezekiel had no idea. He had seen Hainsworth struggle with sketches of his own, scratches on paper, then on metal, which, to him, appeared nothing more than scribbles. How hard could that be? Ezekiel felt it was something he could do quite handily and doing it would put him in a place among Bob's group.

He asked Hainsworth what one needed for sketching and Hainsworth pulled sheets from his own folio, handed them to Ezekiel. "You can use these," he said, "And you'll need some soft leads, and probably some charcoal." Ezekiel went the next day to a shop Hainsworth recommended and he thought about how his drawings would impress Bob and all of them.

The evening of Bob's class, he made his way a mile in the wind to the school. The Academy building was a heavy structure of brick, stone, and white masonry. It took up a good part of the city block and was meant to appeal to staid and rich tastes. It was as if the architect had thrown everything at it, arches, porticoes, columns, dark stone, light stone, red brick, black brick, windows that appeared both Gothic and Oriental, a crown of fancy ironwork and, smack in the middle, a life-sized statue of some dignitary set high over two massive doors.

Inside, the place was as silent as a library. Its overwrought extravagance, its arches, its Moorish tiles, its marble precipices, and gilt woodwork made Ezekiel dizzy. Up the steps, the halls became darker, trimmed with elaborate moldings stained dark, hung with portraits and landscapes framed in gilt moldings. The artwork was somber, mostly, made one want to whisper.

He was early. He did not want to seem too eager, so he hung around the halls, viewing the art as if he knew what he was looking at. The halls smelled of floor wax. He sauntered them, hoping he appeared to belong here. The dark portraits, the faces of men and women, the pastoral scenes were the sort stiff Philadelphia society demanded and that spoke of the conservatism that made Bob and his artists rail. The paintings were—every one—as still as death. He understood the value of these images to the Academy; they represented the figures who endowed the school, the people the Academy existed upon. He soaked in the names. He searched until he found one of Totten Hume. He wanted to spit. He wanted to yell that the school had hung the portrait of a crook on its walls. None of Bob's cronies belonged in this place.

Ezekiel made his way down the marble stairway to the lower floors. He grasped his roll of sketching papers until the sweat of his hand made them wrinkle in. In a bag, he carried the charcoals and pencils he had bought that day. The building was even duller down there, even more somber and lightless than upstairs. The rooms smelled of solvents and sweat. A million feet had dulled the floors. Dust, part charcoal black, part the color of clay lay on the moldings, above transoms, and filled one's nostrils.

He found the studio where Bob had said the class would be. Gas lights hung from the ceiling and cast shadows under everything. The walls were messed with drips and slaps of paint, chairs sat everywhere in tumbles, filthy with a detritus of years suffering paint, pencils, and chalks.

Men were already there. Some had set up, some had already started, some were still assembling their easels around a small table set with a cloth, a book, and a lamp. Bob was walking around giving instruction to one who had begun, pointing out some aspect of light and shadow he might want to capture. Most of them seemed to have had some painting experience, but some gawped around looking as lost as Ezekiel felt. "Loosen up a bit, there

I think … Work fast … Get it down before you begin to think," Bob said. He looked up as Ezekiel entered. "Hello, Ezekiel," he said, his voice formal.

The students' seriousness suddenly made Ezekiel feel he had stepped into a place he had no business being. What idiocy that he came. Bob reached to shake hands as if they hadn't known each other for a decade. His manner was professional, his stance straight and upright, taking advantage of every inch of his height. Everything about him said he was in charge. His head was bare, his hair still wet from a bath and combed back. He was not wearing the stupid flat hat.

Ezekiel felt himself wither. "I didn't bring an easel."

"No matter," Bob said. "We can set you up somehow with chairs." Bob grabbed two, brought them over.

"I'll wait," Ezekiel said.

"No, no." And Bob continued to look for something for Ezekiel to draw upon.

"I said, 'I'll wait.'"

Bob turned back toward Ezekiel and grinned. "As you will."

The views of the lamp and the book on the table were beginning to emerge on some of the papers. Ezekiel took one of the chairs, checked to make sure the splotches on it were no longer wet. He envisioned sitting for a few minutes, for appearances, then slipping out. But before he could, Bob came over and stood beside him. The class had gone quiet but for the shifting of feet and the hiss of charcoals. Bob pointed at one of the students, a small, dark-haired boy, who seemed to be working faster than the rest, his arm sweeping as if he wanted to rip the paper to shreds. He was very young, his face clean of even a shadow of beard. His movements were bold, his fingers and wrists black with char dust. He was an odd boy, tiny as a runt, poorly dressed in pants that billowed at his waist and held on with only a string. He wore a sailor's hat large enough to swallow his face. He worked in a sort of fever. And as he worked, images began to emerge: the book and then the folds of the white cloth, the lamp. Everything he drew was not real, was not up to some ideal, yet everything he put down seemed to live. No other paper or canvas in the room was but drivel next to it.

Bob tipped his head, sighed. "You try to teach that and you'll find it damnably unteachable," he said. The youth was so odd, so set apart from the rest he seemed a spectacle. Yet even Ezekiel could tell that his work was somehow beyond the others. And he also knew that, if that which the odd boy did was the standard Bob measured by, Ezekiel would never measure up.

Bob moved away, circled the room, stood by each student, one by one. And, when Bob's back was turned, without setting pencil or coal to paper, Ezekiel let himself out.

Chapter 24

The note was slipped through the slot in the door.

Dearest Nephew,

Your uncle is much better, thanks be to God. We so appreciate your love and care in visiting during his illness.

Lovingly, Auntie Prune

God, after all these years his aunt finally knew where he was. He did not like it.

Chapter 25

The days grew longer, more temperamental, irascible and cold at times, coddlingly warm at others. The month passed in flurries of bills and threats for payment. Merchants, with whom the Readings had done business for decades, seeing there was a new proprietor, were calling in all their receivables, demanding payment on bills they had carried for ages for the Readings.

Ezekiel began to read the newspapers; he had never paid them much attention until now. He could not afford to buy at the newsstands, so he gathered leftovers from hotel lobbies late in the afternoons, before the hotel help had a chance to throw them out. He began to care about the news as never before; he cared about events, he cared about personages, families, markets, even banks. Everyone in business had to.

For hours, Ezekiel sat in the office, sifting through what was urgent and had to be paid and what he could let slide. Hainsworth had to be paid. The sellers of papers, and inks, and repairs on the balky press had to be paid. The engraving business had to be seen to because, if engraving was let go, he would have practically no income at all. He knew he had to make changes. He had to have some kind of plan. Bitterness at life's unfairness did not pay the bills. Rage, however, having to prove himself to his uncle, now *that* was another thing altogether.

Hainsworth's two new jewelry works sold within a week. The woman who bought the first brought in a friend to see the other piece, but by then it was gone. The friend asked Hainsworth to produce another like it.

"It won't be quite the same," he said. "I will not duplicate my work."

Ezekiel heard the woman say, "Oh," in a tone of real discouragement. He bolted from his desk, afraid Hainsworth was turning away business, and was about to set out trying to try rescuing the sale. He stood in the doorway, watched as Hainsworth took out a paper and began to scribble. The two women leaned in as his pencil shaded and crosshatched. Finally, he turned the paper their way. "I could do something like this?" The friend patted her cheek and said, "It is lovely." She then inquired as to the possibility of bringing in some of her own stones to be set in it. "An amethyst and two pearls."

"Of course," Hainsworth said.

"I think I would want them in gold," the friend said. All Hainsworth's previous work was done using copper and brass, the cheapest wire and sheets he could afford. Her face pinked. She seemed worried her amethyst and pearls might not be up to Hainsworth's high taste.

"Yes," he said, and the woman took her friend's hand. He turned the drawing back to himself and put a finger to his chin. "Rose gold with a touch of yellow would set it off nicely, I'd think." The woman gave out a little yip and laid some money on the counter.

Then one night, his ma came again. He still kept the tin by his mattress and, from habit now, gave it a pat each night before turning down the lamp. He no longer whispered her name, no longer invoked her as he had the months after she died. *Had he slept?* He did not know. He had been unable to truly sleep for years, only half sleep ever came anymore, where fears and troubles magnified endlessly in loops, and coils, and circles without end.

Just her face came to him, a floating oval, pale as an egg. There was no neck to it, no shoulder or thigh, only her face. She made some movement with her lips, but he could not hear it. He roused, tried to cling to her image. He tipped an ear toward her, but, as he tipped, she disappeared, and he could not bring her back.

He lay back then, and he slept a true sleep without thought.

He began stocking some small art supplies, more in an effort to bring in Bob and his friends than to make any sort of business of it. Hainsworth sold another stationery order for a wedding of decent size and set to work on it. He worked like an ox in harness on his etchings and at the press uncomplaining and methodical, though he had begun to rush through his engraving work, and it was at times getting a bit sloppy and hurried. Ezekiel would have spoken up had he not been taking half of what Hainsworth brought in from his jewelry, and his jewelry sales were coming close to the amount the engraving brought in. The moment Ezekiel turned the sign at the end of the day, Hainsworth rolled up his sleeves, loosened his tie, and bent over his workbench. He hummed when things went well, cursed quietly to himself when they did not.

One evening Bob came into the store again. "Isn't it about time for class?" Ezekiel asked.

"I guess it can wait a bit," Bob said. His complexion was blotchy, his hair plastered to a sheen of oil on his forehead. Had Ezekiel felt it was his business, he would have asked if Bob was feeling well.

Bob asked for a couple charcoals, and Ezekiel wrapped them in paper and waited for Bob to put a nickel on the counter. He didn't, just braced his elbows on the glass. He slumped his face into his hands and did not speak. His frame seemed to have no more substance than a stretch of wet paper. "So," he said, without energy, or focus, or strength. "I was wondering if you might want to come out and sit a spell."

Ezekiel said, "Sure." He turned before Bob could see the satisfaction it gave him to be asked.

They went out, walked the few blocks, found a bench at Washington Square. Bob dropped his paraphernalia at his feet. He took a deep breath, blew it out his cheeks. "I could sit here forever, never think again, never move, or," he huffed, "never pick up one more damned brush." His voice was liquid with exhaustion. Ezekiel could not have said what it meant to him to have Bob here, spent, spiritless in a way he never allowed himself to be with the others.

This was the same Bob whom Ezekiel had encountered so long ago, one hot night on the bank of the Platte River. The heat that night had made it impossible to sleep. Ezekiel had heard his ma's bed thump as she tossed against a night so close it sat on one. He finally had gotten up and dressed in pants and a shirt he did not bother to tuck in, and he left the house to make his way, in the dark, to the cool of the river. Only familiarity and the light of the stars and the moon were there to guide him across town.

The Platte's banks were summer-broad. The birds asleep for the most part, the sandhills high on their stilts of legs in the middle, surrounded by mallard and the thousands of Canadas like lumps in the moonlight along the far edge.

He had lain back, slapping at mosquitoes and listening to the seep-into-the-bones croaks of the bullfrogs and the coots' quarrelsome arguments, the water making a pipping when some creature moved.

The stars rested on his face. His backside grew damp. He let the cool damp soak away the heat and was about to fall asleep when he heard something, a cry, or some noise he could not make out. It was not a frog or a bird. The voice went quiet for a moment, and he thought he imagined it. Then it came again.

"Somebody there?" he said. His own voice was small and girly. He wished it were gruff. He listened, heard a rustling then a sniff. "Who's there?"

"Bobby."

"Bobby? What you doing down here?"

"Who's that?"

"Ezekiel Harrington. What you doing down here?"

"Nothing." Bob's voice cracked, went high, then low, on the verge of becoming a grown-up. "Cooling off, I guess."

There was the rustle of movement, then a blowing of a nose, then neither of them spoke. Ezekiel was good at silence. Bob snuffed again. "You ever think about stuff?" he said. It could have been a ghost talking, close and invisible.

"I don't know," Ezekiel said. "Like what?"

"Oh, like why everybody else seems to have everything settled, and you don't."

"Like who?"

"Oh, I don't know. Like your parents, I guess."

It had never occurred to Ezekiel. His ma was so tired from cooking all day at the hotel. She didn't seem to have anything settled and nothing on her mind but to feed him and to fall into bed. His pa, however, he had to think about: How did you know if your pa had everything settled, when he was not around for you to see it? As mean-spirited as Bobby's pa was, as bad his temper and sharp his tongue, Bobby's pa *was* around. Why did it sound like Bobby was crying?

"I guess I never thought of it," Ezekiel said.

They were men, now, sitting on a park bench in Philadelphia, in an evening that, to Ezekiel, had the same sweet intimacy as that night so long ago on the banks of the Platte River.

Bob rose, then slapped his gear onto his shoulders and said, "Well, back to the battle. Thanks." Ezekiel felt he was the one to give thanks.

Chapter 26

Charlie Grafly came in asking for sketch papers. Grafly, Redfield, Calder, and even some of Bob's students were making it into the store often now. Grafly pulled coins from his pocket, counted, and found he did not have enough. "Next time," Ezekiel said, knowing it would be a binding, a sort of contract that would bring the soft-spoken man into the store again to make good on his debt, maybe buy something more. In passing, Grafly said, "We're getting together at the studio tonight, Reddy shot a deer and is stewing it into some glop for the guys. We're going to paint some, but probably not much, because Reddy said ale and whiskey go real well with his deer soup."

Ezekiel arrived at the studio at half past six. The smell of onions and meat wafted down the stairway, a lid rattled over a pot on a burner. Reddy was trying to chop a carrot with a palette knife and not making much success of it. Calder was sketching on a canvas. Another fellow, who introduced himself as Brothers, was just smearing a palette with dabs of blue and green. At one end of the room sat a dais and, on the dais, an empty chair. Eight easels were set up around the dais, canvases, five empty but for streaks of preparatory paints, three showing pieces and parts of a young man—nude—painted from different angles.

Bob was not there, yet. Footsteps came from the hall, the sounds of voices, the cut of a loud joke, then naughty laughter. A couple fellows entered. They began unloading their paints and brushes, others pouring linseed and turpentine into cups, dipping knives and brushes into pigment. Reddy said Bob's women's class at the school was running late. "Yeh," Brothers said, "if I was teaching the girls, I'd be running late, too." It sent up a riffle of more laughs.

A slim fellow came in not long afterward. He carried no supplies but ambled into a closet in the back of the room and pulled closed the curtain. When he emerged, he was wearing nothing but a cloth the size of a tablecloth, which he had pulled around himself, Indian style. He climbed the dais, dropped the cloth and made a careful and naked arrangement of himself, assuming the same position as on the three canvases.

Ezekiel leaned against one wall, hands in his pockets, a foot braced up behind himself. The men settled in, the laughter dropped away, and there were only the sounds and smells of onions and deer meat and of art endeavoring to be made. Had they grown so serious in that time? They seemed tired now; gone was their chattiness and levity, every bit of their attention given over to paint and brush and canvas. They were tired, yet this seemed to lift them in some way. Every one of them, the model included, had worked a long day, they grunted about what they did, some in shops, others in menial work, but most illustrating for the dailies.

Bob did not come until a quarter hour later. When he did, a mood in the room changed. The men began to shift on their feet and to work with more vigor. Bob greeted Ezekiel with an even "Hello" that lacked intimacy. It piqued Ezekiel a little that Bob said nothing more to him but, instead, turned away and set to circling the room, ambling to each of the fellows, offering comment.

They painted for an hour. Being in that room, listening to the pot burble and with all the still and serious effort, Ezekiel forgot—for those moments—all his trouble.

When they broke, the nude model slumped from his pose, threw back his head, jerked his shoulders and wrapped himself in the cloth. While the rest cleaned up and rinsed cups to drink from, he went to the closet to dress, then joined in as they found bowls for Reddy's glop-stew and lit up their smokes and tipped back their beers. The drinks loosened their tongues, and they began to complain more profusely than ever about the school. The model was apparently a fellow student "doing time" as a model, and he joined in. Bob passed around cigars. By the time they lit up, any real discussion plummeted to full-out, loud anger at the Academy's director, Anschutz, "An-shits."

"Damn classics," Grafly said.

Ezekiel rinsed his bowl, went back to his place against the wall at the periphery. He was not one of them. He did not drink, he did not paint, did not study under Anschutz. He wondered how serious this discontent could be. *Wasn't the doing of art merely smearing shapes on paper and canvas?* They took it too seriously. How hard could it be?

The discussion went on for a few minutes, then turned serious. Redfield said, "Cameras are gonna take over. Halftones are going to kill us illustrators. We'll soon have no work." He took a drink of ale from the tin cup he had used to rinse his brushes. "The New York papers are already printing photographs. You just wait and you're gonna see photographs everywhere. I mean what paper's going to wait for some dumb illustrator to draw, then put up with the time it takes an engraver to screw up his work, when *pffffft*"—he snapped his fingers—"one click and you got a photograph that fast."

Redfield was on a rip. "And for artists, Jesus, who's going to want an oil or watercolor picture when they can have a photograph. Just wait. They're going to figure out some way to put color in a picture. What then? We can't even say we can do color without them saying, 'So?' Sooner or later you, me and the jerk down the street are gonna be out of work. None of us is gonna have any work, I tell you, none."

Bob crossed a long shin over his knee and took a drag on his cigar. "I think we can put photography to use."

"Yah," Calder said. "How?"

Bob blew smoke toward the ceiling. "Reference," he said. "For reference."

"Isn't that messing with inspiration?" Calder said. Ezekiel did not like Calder, his intensity, the sense he conveyed a sense of superiority.

"I don't see how," Bob said. "For god's sake, your sense of a thing is not in the photograph but in what you see and how you see it."

"I see a photograph," Calder said, a challenge.

"Then paint a photograph," Bob said, "and lose whatever you might bring to it."

Brothers leaned forward, stomped out what was left of his smoke with his boot. "What's gonna come of me if this painting stuff don't come through? I'm getting married in a couple months."

"All we have to do is paint what we see," Bob said. He patted his chest. "It's up to us to make it ours. No photograph can do that." He blew a breath. "Ain't I the one who knows everything?" He stood, then stretched, and the others stood with him.

Reddy yawned and said, "Getting too deep for me."

Calder took up his coat. "I sometimes think old Bobby steps too deep in it."

Chapter 27

Bob hadn't come in again, though every time the bell dinged, it brought in the hope. Ezekiel had not returned to the studio again for a few weeks, though he knew Bob and the men got together there every Tuesday and Friday. *The Inquirer* printed a story about an impromptu exhibition for students attending the Academy's antique and life classes. That would mean Bob and his fellows. A few days later, in *The Philadelphia Call,* Hainsworth pointed out a short review of the exhibition. "Say, isn't this your friend?" he said. The store had had another quiet week, and Hainsworth was relaxed, spending much of the time on his own work. The display held his four new jewelry designs. Customers had already put holds on two of them.

It was the end of May. The weather had turned warm. If Ezekiel allowed himself to think of it, he could mark his survival this long as some kind of success; he had made it through May. If he continued to eat near nothing, if he never felt sick, if he slept in the storeroom among the boxes, he could keep the doors open a few weeks longer. It was beginning to feel that everyone in his life but him was moving somewhere.

With all the struggle, all the push and drive he had put into his life, doubt galloped in and, with it, the thought maybe his route spelled nothing but failure. Maybe it, and he, had always been just as his pa said when he condemned him as useless, a runt, a loser.

He could remember only a fog of his earliest memories when his pa did not shout, when the strop was used only to sharpen the razor. His ma often reminded him about a time when his pa was gentle, how his pa had loved him, had been proud of him. He had a cloud of memory of it but could barely conjure a time when he was not scared, could barely bring forth a sense of peace about anything of his youth. Even if he could picture a corner of it, the gentle times with his pa had no shape, were never something he could quite grab onto.

The memories that sat clear and sharp as a blade were the ones that came later, after things went bad, after his pa's cattle froze in an early winter, when the dull thuds of his pa's fists on his ma filled their house, when the pain of his pa's strap left welts on his back and his buttocks until he could not sit or lie face up for a while. He had buried his boy's fear of then, but could not bury the fear, now, that maybe he was as his pa proclaimed: worthless, useless, a runt.

He had once, when he was old enough to handle a spade, found a hole some distance from the house. Thin fibers of fur from a hare blew in the grasses around it. He took his ma's spade and began digging, throwing the dirt high to spread into the air, lest a pile of it reveal his digging and the hole he made. And from the hole, he began watches for the sharp figure of a man on a horse. When the pinpoint of a silhouette appeared from the south, he would, before the figure spotted him, crouch low and run into the house so his pa would think him there. Then he would climb out the back window and run to the hole and let it swallow him until his ma whistled the signal that his pa was asleep.

One day, on an afternoon of low sun, the ground still holding warmth. Ezekiel was out watering and digging weeds in his ma's garden. He had not seen his pa until it was too late to run. His pa was riding sloppy and loose, tipped in the saddle, the horse plodding toward the farm, unguided. Ezekiel lay flat in the furrow between the rhubarbs. His ma came from the house, drifted over to where he lay and whispered, "Stay there." She positioned herself to block her husband's view of him.

She murmured behind herself, "Och. Ezekiel, come." Her voice was tight and urgent. "Stay behind me." She began backing toward the house, holding her skirt fanned out. "Keep down," she said. She sidled toward the cellar door with him behind, on his hands and knees. "Get into the keep."

He remained in the cellar until she came to get him. By then, his pa had passed out on the bed. "In the morn," she said, "tell him you were hunting."

Now, with the store floundering, he wondered: maybe his pa had been right. Maybe it would be easier to drink himself into a stupor. Maybe one did not have to feel when one drank. Maybe drink took the pain.

Chapter 28

By two o'clock in the afternoon, the shop was hot enough to parch lungs and humid enough to curl the stationery, an early portent of summer to come. During the winter, the awning had sprouted another hole and could not be let down for shade or people in the street to see its misery.

The few customers who came in now mostly came to see Hainsworth's designs. There was very little of the old Reading stock left. The store rang hollow. Ezekiel was only able to keep the doors open by paying pennies on bills, when dollars were owed, and by putting mirrors in the back of the displays so it appeared there was stock more than there was. He diddled along with Hainsworth's pay, day by day, never quite catching up, and Hainsworth too shy or unaware to ask about it.

Hainsworth laid *The Philadelphia Call* on the counter where Ezekiel had been arranging a cloth. He pointed to one small article on an exhibition. "Isn't this your friend?"

> *A number of marine and landscape studies by* R. E. *Henri show a rather labored attempt in both detail and color and lack the broadness of the surrounding work, but they are good subjects.*

Ezekiel handed the paper back to Hainsworth, who returned to the bench, where he was drawing out a new design for a lavaliere and was taking great pains with it. And Ezekiel swallowed at something sour rising in his throat. In someone else, he would have called it jealousy.

———

The evening was still bright, the shadows a dazzle on the walks, the breeze carrying a whisper of relief from the early heat of the day. Maybe it was not the soft evening that eased the eternal cramp in Ezekiel's gut, maybe it was that he was on the way to the studio for the distractions of the men and their shallow travails with paints.

He slung his jacket over his shoulder. It was not yet dusk, but the late spring afternoon had brought families out onto the streets. The spring gave the city a short moment of splendor in which mosquitoes had not yet hatched, when winter chimneys no longer belched smoke, and the trees in the parks were tender and clean. In a park, a man was lifting a toddling child over his head. The child screeched with glee. The father laughed and threw the child up again and together they yipped. Ezekiel had to look away.

He made it to the studio as the men were setting up, apparently beginning some new project. All but Redfield were laying down their preparatory slop of leftover paint, some on clean boards, some on canvases. Ezekiel never understood why a canvas had to be messed up before it was begun, why they had to muddy a perfectly clean, white canvas before they could start to "do art." Yet he had seen every one of them stand before an untouched canvas with a look of bewilderment akin to fear. The act of muddying, of setting their arms in motion and hushing their brushes on a clean surface seemed to allow them to begin.

The skinny, beaten runt he had seen some months ago was not there; he had not seen him again. Ezekiel surprised himself that he even noticed. Redfield's shoes were caked with dried mud, his shirt torn shoulder to elbow. Redfield was not poor, as some in the classes were, but spent so much time outdoors, on his own, he seemed only to care that something covered him. He was dabbing finish on a landscape of some farm outside town. It was a lovely image of hills, grasses, some trees in the distance.

The group had dwindled since the last time he was there, the forest of easels cut, now, to just five. A man new to Ezekiel came that night. His name was Luks. He had been a student at the Academy, then had spent the last couple years in Germany, living with a relative who was a lion-tamer, if that could be believed. He was a puggish sort with a stumped, red nose gone bumpy. He had been in town only for a few weeks because of some family matter and was going back to Europe in a few days. He was loud, short, stout, balding and had apparently stopped by a local saloon beforehand; his movements were clumsy and his face bloated.

The men had begun pooling a few coins to hire models. Apparently, the model they had counted on for that night was sick. Luks said, "Say. I know just the fella to take his place," and he staggered out of the studio. Five minutes later, he returned with a bottle in his hand. He swigged at it and said he had found someone to substitute, no doubt at a saloon. "Should be getting here any moment. I just left him down at Smitty's. Good man. Good man."

They were all done with their washes of muddy goo and ready to get into their painting. Luks squatted on a chair, gulped from his bottle, and took a great sniff at his can of turpentine.

Five minutes later came a shuffling outside the door and breathing that puffed like a dog's, panting and wheezing that sounded mortal, awful. Bob started toward the door just as an enormous man appeared in it. He was as tall as Bob but heavier by double. Fat. The fellow grabbed the jamb and stood there gulping formidable lungsful. Bob finally opened his mouth to speak, and at that moment the fellow caught his wind and managed, "Bull Chuffle here. George Luks sent me."

Luks staggered from his chair. "Ah," he said, "our hardy fellow well met." Luks teetered then grabbed the fellow's arm, and the two of them staggered toward the changing closet. Ezekiel wondered if the fellow would fit in it. Luks shoved Chuffle in like a sack of grain. When he was mostly behind the curtain, everyone in the room broke out laughing.

They went back to their preparation, heaping blobs of paint onto their palettes, sloshing brushes into solvent, shrugging into old stained shirts, tucking rags into their belts.

The dressing curtain turned alive with Chuffle's efforts, his grunts filled the room. The men giggled. Finally, he came out with a cloth draped half around him. "Where you want me?"

Bob said, "Up on the dais."

Redfield said, "If it'll hold."

Chuffle pulled himself up. The cloth split open to a tremendous, white tree-trunk of a thigh. "Y'ont me to keep the cloth?"

"Hah," Luks said. "I told you it was a whole figure job."

"Just thought...." He hiccoughed and dropped the cloth. He was huge, mostly gut.

Luks said, "You just stand there, let us admire your beauty."

Bob shook his head and let out a yelp.

Nude, Bull Chuffle was like a mountain of dough, white flesh drooping into breasts, gut draped over his thighs as if it had somehow flowed there. "Okay," he said, "get to paintin'." His weight shifted. The dais groaned and sent a hush over the room. But the box held.

Bob said, "Not so fast." He retrieved an old cavalry hat from the shelf of props and dug around until he found a walking stick. Chuffle plopped the hat on his own head. He seemed game.

Bob handed him the stick. "What you want me to do with this?" Chuffle asked.

"Pose," he said.

"Pose?"

"And step back, one step, for a bit more shadowing."

"Make it grand," Reddy said.

And Luks shouted, "Like a general."

Chuffle stepped back until Bob said, "That's good," then he shifted to one hip, put a hand on the ripple of his waist. His fat shifted as he moved.

"Something like this?" he said. Skin seemed to want to bury him, his knees, his neck, the lower regions. All but the dark tip of his manhood was lost to it.

"You'll give us a good chance to work on our values," Bob said. "We can always use work on values."

Ezekiel had to admire the man. He did have endurance. He stood like a statue, only his chest heaving as he breathed. For an hour, or more, the room was silent but for the hissing of brushes on canvas, the whap-whap on rags, the slaps of palette knives on the walls, the easels chattering under the pressure.

They had been working for a good long time when someone else came in: the small boy Ezekiel had seen at the studio once before. He wore the same bulky sailor's cap, the same ruined coat, the same huge-collared shirt, the same string-gathered pants. He carried a stretched canvas tethered in a strap to his back. The boy's face was a ravage of injury, scabs, and bruises as well as new, open wounds. His lip was split and bleeding, one eye purple and swollen near shut. He made barely a sound.

Bob nodded to him as he sidled in and took a place at the back of the room, behind the others. He took one of the easels folded against the wall and began to unfold his supplies behind everyone else, in the farthest place in back, as if wanting to hide. Bob was positioned so he was the only one able to see the boy's canvas.

The boy set to work with lightning speed, faster than any of the others, even Luks. His arm flew, laying down whites and browns and touches here and there of black, red, blue. The doing of it seemed to put him in a kind of trance, made his scabby, misshapen mouth loosen in the way a mouth relaxes in sleep. Now and then, he sniffed back drips of blood and snot and swallowed it. Ezekiel's stomach turned. From nothing, like an apparition, an image began to appear on his canvas. The boy would swipe up a glob from his palette and lay it on, seemingly without plan or purpose. There was an energy, an excitement, and anger in the way the boy painted. Bob came over once, mouthed a few soft words Ezekiel could not make out. Whatever Bob said was meant only for the boy to hear. The boy only nodded.

He kept swatting the canvas, struck it in an awful fury. It was as if the paint laid itself down with its own will; a mix of red, white and yellow *became* the fat man's gut. Another mix built the jelly globs of Chuffle's flesh, another glob became his swollen red nose and mouth and the near-buried brown of his eyes—and, in the very center, in the perfect middle, was the swollen, purple tip of his manhood.

Ezekiel left the room, once, for a visit to the water closet. When he came back, the boy, his canvas, easel, and paints were gone.

Chapter 29

The financial pages were the hardest to find, yet they were what Ezekiel wanted most. The men who bought the papers normally cast off everything but the financials to the trash bins; the financials they took on the trolley and train rides home tucked under their arms. When he came upon one, Ezekiel pored over it as if the news were nutrition.

There was a lot to read, bad and good. Some businesses were growing huge, particularly the steel businesses and the electric companies. The railroads continued to lay down thousands of miles of track, and the steel companies sold them the steel to do it. Some new businesses were making news, like this Standard Oil that had recently bought out a gas company and, with the sale, the exclusive rights to create and sell electricity. The papers screamed "monopoly." Names riddling the news grew familiar far beyond the abstract: Carnegie, Stanford, Gould, Morgan.

But it was not the huge businesses—unattainable and out of his reach—that caught his attention most. The vagaries of the smaller businesses made him take real note: a hotel on the seacoast in New Jersey, built just six years before at a cost of $90,000, went bankrupt for a debt of just $20,000. A small bank in Pennsauken and another in Haverford went under, leaving the bankers and their families publicly destitute. Those were the ones that stuck out. Those were the stories that caused him to lie awake most every night. How could he keep from becoming a shameful item in the newspapers such as this? How could he survive?

Chapter 30

It might have been just another miserable hot day, his shirt sticking to his ribs, his armpits chapped. He had started work while it was still dark but still cool. When Hainsworth came in, Ezekiel was behind the counters his head buried in the center display, as he rearranged cloths to distract from the paucity. The transoms were open, the sun just beginning to slant in, the air still somewhat fresh, the scent of green pouring in.

There came a banging on the door. Ezekiel jerked, knocked his head on the case. He tossed the rag on the floor. The hammering came again. He rubbed his head. "Damn," he whispered. "I'm coming."

Two people were standing on the stoop, silhouetted in the morning light: a man with long, spider's legs, a woman with an agitation of dark, uncaught hair. He knew, by the leaning-toward-things way he stood, it was Bob Henri and some woman.

Bob was smiling, he could see that now. The woman was small, came no higher than to Bob's chest. She was dark, her hair an uncombed ruckus, her skirts dirty and disheveled. He remembered her: the vile thing at the table that night at the restaurant, the one who had filth in the creases under her ears and oily strands of hair pasted to her forehead.

He slid back the bolt, turned the key. "Easy," Bob said. "Can we come in?" He was bright, now, smiling and calm. Ezekiel would have thought the wretched review of Bob's paintings in *The Philadelphia Call* might have set him back a little. Bob held the door for her. "You two met at the diner last winter. Easy Harrington," he said, introducing her, "Soap iya Mar…ka Dibr…ki," Once again, Ezekiel could not follow the name and its impossible syllables. She let off the tang of a body that had not been washed for too long. "Hullow," she said. Her voice was smoky, low, asthmatic. She had a scar on her lip and another on her cheek under her eye. How did Bob know her? God, she was awful.

She barely looked at Ezekiel, but stood gaping around the store as if ogling the place in order to return later and steal it bare. He had an impulse to usher her out, to send her back to the street where she obviously belonged.

"Did you see the review of my stuff in the *Ledger*?" Bob said.

"Afraid not," Ezekiel said.

Bob pulled a section of newspaper from his breast pocket. "Here," he said, "read it."

> *R. E. Henri shows several characteristic landscape sketches, which might be worked up into clever pictures.*

Ezekiel handed it back. It was hardly an endorsement, but Bob seemed pleased. "Could be worse," he said. He pointed at the thuggish girl. "Our girl here has come into some good news: Someone wants her to paint a portrait." *Her? Paint?* "A commission," Bob said, "and she is in need of a place to do it. I am going to spend the summer in Atlantic City. Since I'll be gone, I won't have my studio, or she could use it."

What is this, for God's sake? Ezekiel stood there in the light of morning just inside the door with a tramp, the store about ready to open. He wanted her out.

"I was wondering if she might be able to work in here."

"In *here*?"

"Yes," Bob said, "the light in here is extraordinary. Don't know why I never thought of it myself."

Hainsworth came up the steps. He saw the girl. He threw up his eyebrows, muttered, "Good morning."

Bob turned to her. "You think this would work?" he said, as if a deal were already struck.

Hainsworth tried to slip by her. She did not even have the courtesy, or the presence, to step aside. When he brushed by her, she huffed at him. "Ya," she said. She had a shifting way with her eyes. They were dark. Her mouth was full about the lips and puckered at the corner with the scar. She held it in a hard, dangerous manner. How could Bob bother himself with someone like this? Bob knew manners, had refinements. His own mother was a lady of breeding who taught manners to her sons back in Cozad when they were boys. There was no hint of the lady with this one. Under her dress, her figure was loose, uncorseted, her chest flat. But her grimy dress did nip in at the waist in a way that spelled either beauty or hunger. Ezekiel thought hunger.

"She is just starting out," Bob said, "and needs somewhere to set up a sort of studio. Tell him."

"You," she said. She had an odd way with English, riddled with dark accents. The smell of yesterday's cigars lingered on her.

Bob said, "She's pretty darned good with a brush." He elbowed her like she was one of the fellows. "Yes?" She shrugged and tipped her head like it meant nothing to her one way or another. But she kept her eye on Ezekiel as if his answer might mean more than she let on. He recognized the look of need.

"She has a job to paint a portrait of Broughton Pettygrove's daughter," Bob said.

"And the dog," she said. "I got to paint a dog. I never painted no dog before."

"You'll learn," Bob said and looked down at her. "The painting is for his daughter's birthday, and it has to be finished in a month because the family are leaving for Europe."

"So," Ezekiel said. "I am not sure I understand. She wants to paint a portrait of the Pettygrove girl and a dog"—he pointed to the floor—"*here*?" How in the hell did she even know Broughton Pettygrove? He had read about the Pettygroves in the *Register*, some of Philadelphia's elite. Pettygrove owned ships, for god's sake.

"Yup," Bob said. "It would be a big favor."

"What about my business?" Ezekiel said. How could Bob be so stupid as to think any sort of real business would want an association with filth like this?

"I come," she said, "now." She had no equipment with her, nothing, not even a handbag.

What little Ezekiel knew about painting, at least he knew it took brushes and such. "Now?" he said. He thought about what he had to do that day. It was not much. He had no appointments; the books were closed for the month. "I am busy. I am afraid there is too much to be done. I don't think so."

"Mornings," Bob said. "She'd come in the mornings before opening when the light is good, like it is now."

Ezekiel said, "Before I open. Only?"

"Yes," Bob said. And, as if to tenderize Ezekiel, to give him time to consider, or to wind him around his finger, Bob added, "By the way, us fellows are having the last session tomorrow evening before we all go our ways for the summer. Going out to the Chinaman's afterward. Come along. Last time for a while."

Ezekiel could not get his mind off this wretch named Soap. Why did Bob have anything to do with her, anyway? "She would be gone by the time anyone came in," Bob said, a confirmation that no one but Hainsworth and Ezekiel would catch sight of her. "Pettygrove said he would pay her. And she will pay you half for the use of the store." She looked sideways at Ezekiel, an expression that conveyed she had no intention to make anything good at all. "Won't you?" Bob asked.

Ezekiel began to think of a price so high it would quash the deal altogether: twenty dollars, maybe twenty-five.

As if anticipating his next question, Bob said, "You'd clear fifty." Lord, Ezekiel thought, Pettygrove was coming up with a hundred dollars? For a *painting*? "You'd get half the first week and the rest after it was all done. Bob stared down at her. She looked away. "I'd make sure of it," he said.

The day had begun to stir as if someone had taken a spoon to it, out of his control, first the tramp, now this. Bob and his *artist* had been gone no more than minutes. Ezekiel should have expected it, should have prepared somehow. It had been months, now, since the day he found his uncle ill but still obdurate. But for the scene at the sickbed, he had seen neither his aunt nor his uncle. He had dusted his hands of them; he would never have to deal with either of them again. And here she was, standing across the counter from him, cherry-cheeked, a ridiculous frilled summer bonnet squat on her head and the waistline of her dress ruched tight at her bosom.

"Nephew," she said. She peered around the store. He knew what she saw—dismal, empty shelves, the make-do spreading out of what little goods he had to sell. "This is *yours?*" she said as if nothing could make her prouder.

She chattered about "Tot," how his health was in such good hands under Cornelius' care and was gone back to work at the bank. As much as Ezekiel tried to hate her, he could not. He saw his ma in his aunt—the shared small mouth, the thick black hair, the sweet pointed chin. He heard the questioning, Irish rise in her voice, as he remembered his ma.

Before she left, she bought an odd, mismatched armload of detritus: address books, baby albums, old and curled children's stationery, eight lengths of ribbon, two boxes of greeting cards, and three wax seals.

Chapter 31

Humidity squatted on the city even at dawn. It sat on faces of workers trudging to jobs just after sunrise, left wet streams down their backs. That morning promised no let-up in misery. Thunder showers the day before had given a few hours' relief, but had blown over just after dawn. On days like this, the heat slowed speech, it mocked initiative. Curs festered in the alleys, panting among the trash and flies. Businesses cooked; their doors lay open, but no breath passed through nor did customers. Little traffic bothered the streets. Whoever had not abandoned the city spread out on blankets, collecting what they could of relief in the parks.

Bob had fled Philadelphia until fall; his leaving had sucked away hope and possibility. Ezekiel began to count the days until summer ended and classes began again and the boys at the studio got back together.

Hainsworth was moving through the heat in a slow stupor, though orders for his jewelry kept coming. It was solely on the back of Hainsworth's sales that Ezekiel had been able to pay his rent last month.

Ezekiel had just washed and shaved for the day, his hair was wet. He wished he could hold his head under the water pump for the rest of the day. He heard Hainsworth let himself in, heard him hang his hat on the tree, heard him grunt, "Hot today."

"Yuh," Ezekiel said.

Hainsworth plopped himself on his stool and wiped his forehead. There would likely be little business today. Anyone with any sense at all would find a bench in the park, or a rock on the river, and plant themselves there until fall.

Hainsworth had taken in a large order the week before for an elaborate necklace, earrings, and pin. It was his biggest order yet and included twenty-one emeralds. Hainsworth whistled when he saw the stones. The customer made a down payment of forty dollars to cover the cost of metals and supplies; Hainsworth would be paid the rest of the balance when the pieces were done. The stones were locked away in the safe. The store had not sold a wedding or a decent stationery order for weeks. The stationery business now was now down to nothing more than the unsold leavings of cheap cards, tired papers and even cheaper writing utensils.

It was an hour yet before opening. Ezekiel had begun opening yesterday's mail: a bill for the gas, another for water. His stomach had set up an appeal, but he had already eaten the biscuit he shoved in his pocket from the two-bit diner where he ate last night.

There came a slapping at the door, a flat palm on glass. It could be nothing but a collector or a salesman hawking something Ezekiel had no way to buy. Nothing good could come from answering it.

The slapping came again. Hainsworth looked at Ezekiel as if asking if he should answer. It came again, a hammering this time, and a woman shouting, "Hey!"

Ezekiel jumped. He peeked out, squinted through the store. She had an easel and a rucksack strapped on her back. In her hand she held a canvas stretched over boards. God. *Her,* the crude thug Bob dragged in. He had forgotten all about her. Her hands were cupped around her eyes, her face pressed to the pane. She had already smeared the glass. He would have to wash it. Again. "God," he muttered. This was the day she was supposed to set up to begin her painting. "Just a min-ute," he yelled back.

She drew back to hammer the pane again. "What?"

"I'm coming," he shouted.

Behind her, a trolley went by. The mare's withers ran in the heat. "What?' Soap shouted.

He blew a huff and went to the door to let her in.

She brought in a reek with her, the smell of onions, and she must have fallen, or run into something, for there was the huge crust of a new scab on her lip.

Hainsworth stood with his hands on his hips, a half grin on his face. She threw her head toward the corner where the sun shot in through the windows. "Over der good," she said, "Yah?" She was a total distraction, a wind, a tornado. She picked at the scab on her lip, waiting for Ezekiel to answer.

Ezekiel shrugged. She took it for consent and strutted to the corner, dropped her paraphernalia. *A portrait for Broughton Pettygrove. How in damnation did she even know Pettygrove?* She was nothing. And how in damnation did Bob know her? Ezekiel had agreed to this because of Bob and because he was desperate for money. But where was Bob now? She was scheduled to be around for the better part of a month. The next day Pettygrove would be here. What would a thing like this girl do to business? She turned to him, thrust her fists into her waist. He had to think of something. He had to get her and her reek of onions out of here. He opened his mouth to say something, he knew not what.

It was as if she picked up his thoughts. "Start today," she said, "zat's what me and Bobby agreed." She nodded once as if that were the end of it. If a creature could be the exact opposite of the sort he wanted seen in the store, this was it. Her skirt hadn't seen a washtub since the last century and had picked up soot and dust, horse leavings, and whatever else Philadelphia's streets could throw at it. Her blouse was clean, Ezekiel had to give her that, though it had been ripped at the neck and repaired clumsily. A tangle of wires hung with milk bottle caps, buckles, an assortment of buttons, and a fishhook that wrapped her wrist like a bracelet. How the hell did she come by a job with the likes of Pettygrove, especially one that would pay a hundred dollars? He would have jettisoned her on the spot had Bob not promised he'd make sure Ezekiel was paid. He knew if he took his eye off her, she would steal everything down to the shelves.

Hainsworth went back to work but seemed unable to keep himself from coming out now and then, taking peeks.

"Be out by the time we open," Ezekiel said.

"Yah," she said, "I know about dat."

He tried to busy himself as she began to lay her things out. "I don't want paint spattered everywhere when you're done," Ezekiel said. "You have to clean up."

"Yah," she said, "I know that, too."

She worked as if she were alone. She set up her easel, stepped back, tipped her head, moved it a quarter inch, then stepped back and tipped her head again. She gazed up at the window, assessed the light and moved the easel back where she'd had it in the first place.

She asked for a chair. Ezekiel told Hainsworth to get one for her, leaving no opening for her to be alone.

He brought out the dusty, useless old wreck of a chair shoved by the back shelves. The legs creaked and the seat rattled as he set it down. "Give her mine," Ezekiel said. Hainsworth went back with it, brought Ezekiel's desk chair, a bruised and scraped ladder-back nearly as ugly, but solid.

She took the chair without complaint, set it in the light. He realized then he could not even remember her name. It was a long one, Russian, or Slavic, something throaty and dark. Bob had called her Soap.

She unrolled an old rag of a blanket from her sack and laid it under the chair. It was nothing but a stained horse blanket, ripped and hole-damaged, something one would find at a dump. She made a fuss about it, toed it into folds and ripples she tried to make graceful. It had been washed, some of the greens and yellows retained in the stripes.

When she'd settled her trappings where she wanted she put the stretched canvas on the easel. The canvas had been treated, before she came in, in the way Bob and the others did with a slop of leftover paint that smelled of solvents. When she was done settling things, she grunted and slapped her hands on her thighs and said straight to Ezekiel, "No touch."

"You're not going to *leave* it there?" he said.

"Yah," she said. "What you think?"

He heard Hainsworth chuckle. God, it was a mess. "I can't have it there," he said.

"It's *me* you don't want no one to see." She lifted her skirts and stomped out the door just before it was time to open the store.

Came the splat of a palm on the front glass again, just as he lathered his face. Hainsworth was not yet in, would not be for another half hour. "Damn," he said. He started to wipe his face, then thought better of it; she was not worth the trouble.

She waited outside on the stoop. The sun had not cleared the transoms. He could see nothing of her out there but a dark blotch. *Let her damn well wait.* Then he realized keeping her there would mean more of her oily hands on his glass.

Gone were her filthy clothes, her wretched skirt and repaired blouse. Gone were her ripped shoes. Her hair was the same, though she seemed to have made some better attempt at collecting it in a wad at the top. She did not bother to say hello or good morning, when he let her in, and she made no more note of his indecent open-necked shirt or his lathered face than she would have a cur she passed on the street.

"You're early," he said, his tone gruff.

She chewed the inside of her cheek. "I got something to do," she said, "before he comes."

In appearance she was almost totally transformed. She wore a new dress, fitted, blue and white. The dress was fashioned of good silk fabric. In place of her useless shoes she wore proper brown ladies' shoes. But for the tumble of her hair and the scab on her lip, she might have made do for something other than street tramp.

With some apprehension, he went back to his ablutions but kept watch as she fiddled with the chair and easel. There seemed to be no end to what needed to be done with the arrangement. Her hands were nervous, her movements staccato and busy. She picked at the scab on her lip until it bled.

Hainsworth showed just before the Pettygroves were due. It was a relief to have him here. He gave her a long stare before he settled himself at his desk. Precisely at eight o'clock, a brougham drew up front of the store and a man in a straw boater and a white summer suit got out. He turned and handed down a blond, curly-headed girl and a small beagle dog.

With no greeting whatsoever, Mr. Pettygrove came in, stood by the cases with Hainsworth's jewelry. He seemed above making conversation and simply leaned on the counter as his daughter was arranged in the chair. The girl began to fuss. "You'll have to sit still, Millicent," he said. The girl slumped, already bored. He clicked his fingers at the beagle. "Sparky, come here." The dog's head drooped as if it had been caught at something. Mr. Pettygrove slid the dog, feet scraping, toward the girl's chair and said, "Sit." The dog peered up at him, confused, then started to get up. The girl squirmed. Mr. Pettygrove pushed the dog down again. Gone was the artistic "arrangement," the careful folds in the horse blanket. Ezekiel thought she would send up some kind of fuss about it, point her finger and shout, "No touch," but she did not. It was as if she were unaware of the fracas with the dog and the squirming of the girl. She took out a pallet and put it in the crook of her arm and began to dollop out paints with a crude knife.

Ten minutes before opening, they were gone, all of them, Soap, the girl, the dog and Mr. Pettygrove. The next day, exactly at a quarter to eight, she slapped the door window again. At eight o'clock, Pettygrove's coach drew up and spat out the girl, dog, and Pettygrove. The girl went to her chair, and Pettygrove took one Ezekiel had set out for him and lit up a pipe as the sun heated the store. Without greeting either of them, Soap began to paint.

At the end of three days, there was nothing to the canvas but smears of whites and browns, shadows and spots that added up to no more than a mess. Ezekiel could not see how anything would ever come of it. She was something to watch, though. Painting seemed to remove her, to take her somewhere else. Her face puckered, trance-like, her mouth gathered up like a flower bud, and, though it seemed to produce little that made sense, she continued to swipe paint on the canvas. Her movements seemed to transfix Pettygrove in some disquieting way, his eyes scanning every inch of her, watching each move she made.

Each day, after the Pettygroves were gone, after she had cleaned her brushes and made way to leave, she turned back to Ezekiel and said, "Don't touch." It rankled. *Wasn't this* his *store, after all?* He could barely wait until she was done and get what was owed him so Hainsworth and he could get back to their routines.

One evening five days into the morning painting, near closing, Ezekiel approached Hainsworth. "Say," he said, "I been giving it some thought about your designs. Could you maybe pick up the pace, get a few more ready for sale?"

"I'm getting faster," Hainsworth said. He was putting out designs as fast as anyone could expect. But Ezekiel also knew he had to do more to bring in business. It was obvious that Bob's experiment with Soap and the painting was going no place at all, though he had to hand it to Pettygrove for staying with it and with the little girl who sat through the time, diddling her fingers, thumping her feet on the chair. But all the while, Pettygrove leered at Soap through the smoke of his pipe, and, in some tiny increment, it made Ezekiel uncomfortable on Soap's behalf. "I was thinking maybe you know somebody to take in."

"Take in? Like another jeweler?" Hainsworth said.

"Like a helper."

"Helper," Hainsworth said.

"Perhaps."

"Not another jeweler?"

"Another jeweler would need to be paid," Ezekiel said. "I could pay only in space." He had plenty of that now. "And you could make use of some of the displays."

Hainsworth massaged his chin, screwed his mouth to the side. "I got a little brother," he said, "just out of school."

"He know anything about design?" Ezekiel knew about dock work, had seen workers sweating, filthy, boys not yet men with injuries, backs so pained they could not stand straight. It was awful. "Seems like design is better than some other work, like the docks, or something."

"He's fifteen." Hainsworth looked down at his feet, gave a little shake to his head. "Knows about as much about design as I did, which is nothing."

"I see," Ezekiel said.

Hainsworth rubbed his jaw. "He could live with me. I could teach him." He laid a finger against his chin, began talking to himself. "I sure do wish the place I'm living at put on a meal; he eats like a porker. The room's got a bed big enough, I guess, for the two of us. Got to feed him, though. That there's a feat." He looked back as if his work bench could give him answers. "Maybe could train him up some, maybe on the waxes, maybe have him do some cutting here and there. It would give me time for the finer work."

Chapter 32

Mid-day, another brougham coach pulled up at the curb. It bounced a bit then it leaned to one side, rocking like a cradle. It was a fine coach, like many crowding the streets in the Financial District. Ezekiel watched as the driver tethered the leathers, then put his hand to the small of his back and hobbled around the coach to open the door. Aunt Prune. She had come to the store twice since Totten's illness. Twice. Well, here she was again, smiling and adjusting the brim of her sun hat. Ezekiel felt spied on, caught out somehow.

The carriage swayed as she stepped off. She waited as her driver Joseph—the same driver Ezekiel remembered from his first day in Philadelphia—limped around to the far side to open the door for someone else. His aunt picked up her skirts in her great arms as Joseph handed her and another woman up the steps to the store. She had regained every pound lost during Totten's illness and stood for a moment to pat her chest before she swept into the store. She was dressed in her frills and ruffles, her hat tied by a ridiculous pink bow under her chins. "Ezekiel," she said, her voice high, chatty, "good afternoon." She leaned to him with her cheek, as if expecting a kiss.

The woman coming behind her was slim and wore a cloud of a dress made of soft, light fabric so fine and expensive that, in the days his mother sewed for the women in Cozad, she would have pressed her face into it. The woman patted her bonnet as she came in. He could smell wealth on her, the sense she had never doubted the lofty station given her the day she first breathed. She really was quite lovely.

His aunt set her fingers on her friend's arm. "Mildred," she said. "This is the nephew I spoke of, the stationer of the family." The woman gave him her hand. "Mrs. Quinn, this is my nephew Ezekiel Harrington. Ezekiel, Mrs. Padraig Quinn." Prune clapped her hands. "Isn't he as handsome as I told you?"

Mrs. Quinn smiled and nodded. And Ezekiel knew, in truth, she saw a young man who was not handsome at all, but ordinary, his collar pinned closed after the loss of a button and wearing his only suit, a winter wool, which needed a good press he could not afford. "We came to town for lunch and a little shopping," his aunt said. "I wanted to pick up some cards for…," and her voice trailed as if she didn't quite know why she wanted cards. "Well, anyway. I wanted Mrs. Quinn to see your new jewelry designs. They are so lovely."

She leaned around her toward the easel with the smeared canvas, ignoring the riddled horse blanket and the wretched, scarred chair the child sat on every morning. "What's *this*?" Prune said, her tone delighted. There seemed to be nothing false about her; she sounded as if the painting were the most interesting thing in the city. He told her that an artist was using the store as a studio in order to paint a portrait.

"Oh?" she said. "A portrait of *whom*?"

"The Broughton Pettygrove girl," he said.

"Little *Millicent*?" she said. "I thought they were in Europe."

"Not for two weeks, yet," he said. *A very long two weeks.*

His aunt scrunched her face into an impressed expression, gave a wink to Mrs. Quinn. "So, my handsome nephew is an art connoisseur now."

By the time his aunt and Mrs. Quinn had left the store, Prune had bought a box of tired and graying cards that had gone unsold for the last year. It was, he knew, her contribution to him, and Mrs. Quinn had placed an order for pearl earrings.

Chapter 33

Ezekiel still did not know what word to apply to her, could think of nothing more than "ruined." He'd overheard Mr. Pettygrove mention something about the dress she wore and added in a low, side-of-the-mouth manner, "I can have another made." Then he bumped her with his elbow in a way that made Ezekiel cringe, "if you're good." Even wearing the silk dress Pettygrove had obviously provided her, everything about her was coarse and, on inspection, filthy. The furrows of her ears were lined with grime, the roots of her lashes dark as coal dust. It was as if she lived in dirt and spent her life breathing smoke straight from a flue. Each morning when he unlocked for her, she came in with a huff as if disgusted that he had made her wait. Each day she wore the same dress, one Ezekiel finally guessed was meant to cover her in a manner Pettygrove thought suitable for his precious daughter. By now, the dress was becoming in need of pressing and, though she wore a smock over it, was collecting smears of paint on the cuffs.

After a few days, the dog had caught on to the routine and sat licking itself and sleeping away the hour, and the girl squirmed and fiddled with her fingers but stayed in the chair as more and more paint was gobbed onto the canvas. When the child whined, he quieted her with promises of sweets on the way home. Still Pettygrove leered. Ezekiel wished the man would at least buy something, but he seemed to have no interest at all in anything but the tramp painting his daughter. Meanwhile, paint went down, globule by globule, yielding little more than dull shadows and rough hillocks of lighter and darker tones. No matter how fast she laid down paint, the canvas was still devoid of either child or dog. Ezekiel feared the deal would be off if something didn't start to come of it—and soon. It had to be done in less than two weeks.

Then one day, just before the hour was up, she set down her board and wiped her brush on her smock. "You dun't need to come tomorrow, Mr. Pettygrove," she said. Her voice was as dusty as her knuckles. The child cheered and clapped her hands. *Didn't need to come? Was the painting done?* It was no more a painting that Ezekiel himself could have done. She was no artist. *What in heavens was Bob thinking?* There was nothing to it but muddle and vague outlines.

After the Pettygroves were gone, she sloshed her brush in solvent. When she was done stinking up the store, she clomped up to Ezekiel, dusting shelves behind the counter. He had opened all the transoms in an effort to rid the place of the stench before he opened the store. It promised to be cooler that day, the wind blowing dry from the west, the air clear and for that he was grateful. "I come same time tomorrow," she said.

Hainsworth came to work with a younger replica of himself in tow, a boy with straw-colored, butterfly lashes, and Hainsworth's tufts of blond hair. "Mr. Harrington," Hainsworth said. The formality made Ezekiel stifle a smile. "This is my baby brother, JJ."

JJ's face reddened. He was young, with no more than a shimmer of silk above his lip. But he was three inches taller than Hainsworth and thin as a broomstick. Hainsworth elbowed his baby brother. "Shake hands," he said. The boy's fingers were long, quiet, and damp.

Introductions done, the brothers went back to the engraving area where Ezekiel had added a board to lengthen the workbench and had bought another used stool. The brothers set to work on an order of pearl earrings for Prune's friend, Mrs. Quinn. Hainsworth also had another jewelry job in line, an order to design some pieces for Mrs. Finley Hill.

Ezekiel spent most of the afternoon on a ladder mending, as best he could, the rip in the awning. The wind began to blow, but the day was gloriously dry. The freshness brought people out and when people were out walking the streets, they peered into windows. As he worked on the awning, he began to notice people under him, peering into his store. He had never noticed so many people doing this before. They took some time at it, too, leaning into the glass. He bent down and saw what they saw: the painting, sitting there smack within view. He expected them to laugh, or shake their heads at it, but they did not. They tipped their heads side to side. Some of them pointed and leaned closer. Some of them folded their arms and stood back. But none of them laughed, not even a titter. It made him look at it differently. By god, there it was, just a hint mostly, but definitely the image of a dog and a girl in a blue summer dress.

Chapter 34

The next morning, Hainsworth began teaching his little brother the rudiments of the tools for making jewelry. They had long discussions about temperatures and wires and the properties of metals. After a couple days they began to relax into a routine, and to talk and tease, their voices carrying an Irish patois, the same as Ezekiel's ma and pa's, the same as Ezekiel's own once had been. He began to resent them and their intimacy, the sense they had one another to belong to. But for Bob, he had no one, and now Bob was not even here.

She came to work a little later than usual the next day and wore her old ragged skirt and the grimy white shirt with the ill-done repair. The scab had been picked off her lip and in its place was a baby's pink, new patch of skin. The brothers were already at work in the back. She did not bother to say hello, not even to nod. She simply went to her painting and began work. Without Pettygrove or the girl to deal with, her mouth was softer and her brows relaxed and she worked in a kind of catalepsy, a detached universe of her own.

The store was quiet, with only the murmurs and occasional laughs from the brothers in back and with the hiss and slip of her arm as she painted. And, for the first moment in years, with the promise of a deal of money to come from the painting, Ezekiel's shoulders did not ache, his head did not throb. He yawned. How long had it been since he had yawned?

He heard his aunt before he saw her. She stood outside the door like a dog, waiting to be let in. "Yoo-hoo," she said, her tone a proprietary yodel as if it were she, not her nephew, who owned the store. He gave out a huff, went to the door.

"I was in town to pick up some dresses from my dressmaker," she said.

"At this time of the morning?" he said.

"Wanted to get things done before the misery of the heat was on us." Soap did not look up. It was as if there were nothing in her world but the girl's face and the mess of her blond hair pulled up in its blue bow. "Where's Millicent?" Prune asked. "I thought I would come by to see her and Broughton. Millie must have grown, I haven't seen her for months."

Soap looked up, then, and as if coming through some foggy world. She said, "They don't come today."

Ezekiel thought his aunt would be repelled by the girl—any woman would be—but she drew out her spectacles and clomped over beside Soap. They stood together looking at the painting, side by side, almost chummy. How could his aunt not notice the musk coming from her, or the filth of her hem, the sleep-tangle of her black bear's hair? "Why," his aunt asked, "would you do one for me?"

Soap hesitated a moment. "Yah," she said.

Chapter 35

The shop sank into the drone of late summer. The streets bore little traffic, the sidewalks even less. Families left town for the shore to escape the heat. The trolleys were often empty as they jangled by, their drivers limp at their bells, their nags wet with perspiration, heads dangling. Flies convened on the droppings of the horses. Mosquitoes droned and made people flap their hands and slap themselves. There was not much in the news. But, for a few sales the Hainsworth's managed, business was dismal.

Soap made good on her promise. She came early the last day. Just before opening, she cleaned up her easel and paints and then stood around for two hours, like a shadow in the corner, waiting for Pettygrove. It was mid-morning by the time his driver came in. She had gathered her things into the blanket and propped the bundle against the counter on the floor. The image in the painting was complete, now, the dog, the girl with her blue dress and her flopping bow. The image would have been sweet as honey, but, somehow in the girl's ice-blue eyes, in the shine of her pink mouth, and the position of the sleeping dog, it revealed the child's spoiled, independent personality.

The driver looked at the painting. "This it?"

Soap ambled over in a casual way, as if she had not just spent weeks working at it. "Yah," she said. She snapped her fingers and held out her palm. He took a roll of dollars from his pocket, put it in her hand. She turned her back and began counting. He left with the purchase. She licked her thumb as she paged through the money, pulled several of the bills from the handful, and gave them to Ezekiel. She slung the easel and her pack over her shoulder, nodded once and left the store.

For a couple weeks he waited. As much as she put him off, he had begun to see her as potential income even more lucrative than Hainsworth. But, as summer steamed through the days, she did not return, and he ached that he had no way to find her again. He was beginning to see that, if his business were to survive, it would take more income than both of the Hainsworths could bring in. It was as hopeless as it was endless, his need for money. Was his pa right? He had once been so stupid as to believe he was one who seized circumstance, a full-bore opportunist who let nothing escape. Yet he had let a lucrative money crop escape: Soap was gone.

Long into the nights, he began to look back at her time in the store with longing. The store had seemed fuller when she was in it. He tried to blame his let-down on the heat, and on the vacancy Bob and his buddies left behind them. But it was *her* he thought of, the oiled scent of her hair, the clank of junk she wore on her wrist, her rude and windy language.

Chapter 36

Here and there at the Academy, the summer sessions were near done. In one hall, a summer class spun clay on wheels, another class in sculpture gave out the smell of pitch from wood chips, another the reek of a solvent, or two.

The clerk yawned as Ezekiel approached and did not bother to cover his mouth. "I'd like to reach three of your students," Ezekiel said.

The clerk smacked his lips and blinked at yawn-tears. He was a pale fellow, Ezekiel's age, with thin hair that could not be called blond or brown but a mouse's shade in between. Thick spectacles shrank his pupils to pinpoints.

"They aren't in class now," Ezekiel said. "Will be in the fall."

The clerk shrugged. "Can't help, then."

"They were here through spring," Ezekiel said.

The clerk shook his head as if to wake himself. His complexion was pale and gray, as if he had stood at this dark counter the entire summer. "Can't," he said, lifting the eyeglasses and fingering sleep from the corner of one eye.

"Can't what?"

"Can't do last year, only this one, only summer and this fall coming up."

"Well this fall, then," Ezekiel said.

The clerk slipped a paper across the counter. Someone down the hall yelped and a hammer went silent. Ezekiel scribbled Bob Henri and Edward Redfield, then, the third, only Grafly. He had no first name for Grafly; they had only called him that or Graf. The clerk carried the paper to a room in the back. Ezekiel heard a file drawer open and close, then another.

The clerk returned with a card with the addresses of Redfield and

Grafly. He tapped Grafly's name on the card and said, "His first name was *Charles*. Going into sculpture. We'll be in the same class, he and I."

"Where's the card for Bob Coz—Henri?"

"Didn't see one," the clerk said.

When Ezekiel returned, the store was as quiet as the Academy. But for the murmurs and grunts and taps of the Hainsworth brothers, there would have been no activity at all. Ezekiel wrote to Redfield and Grafly, saying he wondered if either of them had paintings, framed, they might want to display for sale in the store. He wanted to inquire about Bob but could not bring himself to, thinking they might sense how important Bob's return was.

Redfield and Grafly wrote back within days. They were eager to display their efforts. Grafly said he thought he had one or two paintings that were presentable but wondered if Ezekiel might want to think about a small bust he was working on. He did not say how big it was. He signed his letter "Graf." Redfield described, in minute specificity, three paintings he thought worth framing for the store: two landscapes of the country around his parents' farm and another of the docks on the Delaware.

At closing that day Hainsworth said, "Oh, I forgot to tell you, the girl came in this morning when you were gone."

"What girl?"

"Soap," he said.

Chapter 37

By the time the university started up again, Prune had gained so much weight Ezekiel found her nearly unrecognizable. Her face was a swath of flesh, the point of her chin totally lost in a pillow of jowl. Her ponderous girth made movement difficult.

He had pulled open the doors to the soft day and heard the wheeze of her breath before he saw her lumbering up the step. He was alone in the store then, the Hainsworths having gone out for a bite to eat at the lunch counter on Chestnut. Sales of their jewelry had begun picking up even more now as people came back from summer retreats.

The weather had finally begun to break. The days still held warmth, but the nights bequeathed cool relief through morning.

Prune made it through the door, dropped the hem of her skirts, and stood dabbing her face with a handkerchief she slipped from a frill at her sleeve. Ezekiel pulled out a chair, set it behind her, and she flopped in a heap on it. "Aunt Prune?"

She patted her chest, mouthed, "Just a moment."

The store had changed since his aunt was last here. He had removed all stationery from the counter in the middle store and had devoted the entire space to the Hainsworths' work. The display was the first thing to catch customers' eyes. Sales were making it hard for the brothers to keep the case stocked, and they often worked late into the nights. Sometimes pieces sold the day they put them out; their jewelry sales had paid Ezekiel's rent through the summer.

JJ seemed to have inherited his brother's eye and was beginning to hanker to design his own pieces. But Hainsworth was making his little brother wait and finish some more aspects of his apprenticeship first. JJ was beginning to chafe with his brother, and their struggle worried him. He needed them. The stationery business was all but dead except for an occasional engraving order that came through and that took Hainsworth away from the jewelry work. Ezekiel could not imagine the art business, such that it was, could ever hold much real promise. But he was surprised when, within the first week after he had hung Redfield's canvases, he sold one and another had gone home on approval with Mrs. Biddle. Grafly lugged in his bronze bust. It was of such a weight Ezekiel had to help him up the steps with it. It sat in the corner where the front and side windows met, atop a stack of wooden boxes Ezekiel covered with a white cloth. Grafly had sculpted the bust's expression with a glower that was supposed to spell justice and had put a price on it that would have paid two years of Ezekiel's bills—if it sold.

He left Prune sitting there like a princess. She had gathered herself, so her thighs and the volume of her skirts swallowed every bit of the chair. He left the room, telling her he would be right back with a glass of water. She smiled when he handed it to her and said thanks. He waited as she gulped it down. He went for a second glass and, as he came out with it, she was dabbing at her hairline and wiping her handkerchief on the flesh at the back of her neck. She drank down the second and held out the glass for more. He went back again and pumped her another. "Thank you, my dear," she said.

The wheeze was gone now, and her chest no longer heaved. She began to take in the store. Ezekiel squinted to see what she saw. What little of the old Reading stock he still had was heaped amid sales signs on an inconspicuous table off to the right. The case in the middle of the floor sparkled and shone with the Hainsworths' work. Redfield's two remaining landscapes gave the room depth and took one's eye right into the beauty of meadows and rivers. Even the sour bronze bust gave off a sense of richness and prosperity. But prosperity was nothing except a fool-the-eye lie. She asked about "that girl who painted the Pettygroves' daughter. Mildred said she and Broughton can't take her eyes off the portrait." Ezekiel could only say he had lost touch with her. His aunt bought a tarnished pen and pencil set, then gathered her skirts and tied the bonnet under her chins. She went to the door, then turned back, once more, to gape at the store. "I can't *wait* to bring in your uncle," she said.

Chapter 38

Only the Hainsworths knew Ezekiel had no true home, and that he slept just feet from where they worked every day. As the summer began to cool, he moved his mattress and blankets from the drafts of the cool floor and set them high on one of the empty shelves. But for the workbench and tools, jewelry required almost no space at all. The paintings, however, were beginning to become problematic. Word had spread through the Academy that Ezekiel had put up some students' work, and they were dragging in armloads of it for him to put up. Most of it was awful, even his untrained eye could tell it. But some caught a bit of light or color, and those he took on terms that, if they sold at all, would bring him eighty percent of the sale. He had not realized how good Redfield's pieces were until now, or the rarity of a portrait as good as the one Soap had done for Pettygrove.

He drew out plans to tear out the unused storage pallets—all but one for his bed—in order to replace them with slots to place paintings. Every night, he read and waited for sleep, but it rarely came. He had waited for fall like a child waits for the beginning of school. He had imagined nights at the studio with Bob and the boys, their rants at inane teachers, discussions with Bob, had even pictured delicious arguments of the sort Bob and he used to have back in Cozad over Dickens and Dickenson, Irving and Cooper.

He lifted the hatch to his old steamer trunk, took the top book from the tumble in it: *Nicholas Nickleby*, which he and Bob had discussed with such naïveté so long ago. He went to the free library, borrowed Crane and James, books he had to return in a week. But without the promise, the threat of Bob's challenges, the stories sputtered and he closed them.

———

Prune paid another visit. She said she wanted to see some of that beautiful jewelry her nephew sold and asked about buying a broach for herself. She came in alone, her driver parking in front. As Prune stood with Ezekiel at the counter, Joseph got down from his seat, put a feedbag on the patient mare, then pulled himself up onto his seat again to wait.

Prune made small talk about having luncheon with friends at her club in an hour, so Ezekiel passed her off to Hainsworth, and she set to looking at the pieces the brothers had on display. Unless the Hainsworths were working on a particular design for a customer, they designed items to sell on speculation. These things were bold, of stones with bright colors and mixes of golds, often with the shapes of unusual animals and insects. Under their hands, a June bug became a dazzling broach, frogs, sporting enameled greens the color of emeralds, linked together to form a necklace. Their designs shouted new and bold and elegant.

The Hainsworths fed on one another, a suggestion from Jasper was magnified and multiplied by JJ and edited by Jasper until they put themselves into a froth. Their noise filled and lifted the days. The designs that came from their bench were beginning to challenge the beauty of those of a new fellow named C. Tiffany, who was making a name for himself in New York.

That day, she bought a dramatic broach with a large and fiery opal that did not suit her. The broach was grossly expensive. As she left, Ezekiel felt as if she thought her purchase was little more than the price of admission to him.

Chapter 39

He was in the office paying bills due the first week of the month. Classes at the Academy were finally to start that day.

The front bell dinged. Hainsworth wiped his hands on his apron, then took it off and threw it aside. Of the two brothers, the elder Jasper was the social, outgoing one, JJ silent, uncomfortable with people in a way Ezekiel understood. JJ was, as well, the more ambitious, the more concrete in his attitude toward what he thought could sell and how much they could ask for it. It was as if the two brothers, no matter how much they resembled one another, had dropped from two different trees; Jasper, whom Ezekiel thought of as Hainsworth, was loquacious and sweet and JJ withdrawn and serious.

Hainsworth went out to greet the customer. For a moment, Ezekiel heard him talking, then he came back. "Someone for you."

God, not Prune again. He pulled himself from the chair, did not bother with his jacket. He did not know what to make of this business with his aunt. Her persistence was beginning to cleave how she made him feel about her. She was, after all, his ma's sister, and his ma had loved her dearly. She was a benign sort, seeing only light in everyone, even in him. Totten was the trouble. After all this time, he could see how her letters had lifted his ma when nothing else would, more even than the bright calicos, the ribbons, books, the China rug she sent. Nothing had brought as much color to his ma's face as one of Prune's long, chatty letters, pages loaded down with the frills of her script. His guard around her was dropping away. Yet she was in league with her thieving husband. Had it not been for that, he might grow to care for her.

It was not his aunt, after all, who set off the bell. Bob was back. Bob was back. Every lanky, raven's hair of him was here in the store again. Part of Ezekiel wanted to yip and jump like a child, part wanted to not care so much.

Bob was tanned, his complexion clear of fresh eruptions. He was standing by Grafly's bust, wearing a fat silk bow at his throat. It looked silly. "Hey, Ease," he said. His eyes went to Redfield's landscape. "Reddy said you were hanging a couple of his pieces. He's come along nicely this summer, I'd say." Then Bob uttered what Ezekiel had waited the whole summer for: "Want to go out for a bite?"

They went to a small bakery on Arch Street, just them, just the two of them. Bob was calm as he never was with the others. He pulled at a sweet bun with his thin fingers. His hands were stained, nails rimmed with blue pigment. Ezekiel said, "Did you do a lot of work this summer?"

Bob threw back his head, barked a laugh. "Depends on what you call work. Tried, anyways. I spent the whole summer in…" He looked away, sober now, as if searching for a story about where he had been. Then his face relaxed and he looked Ezekiel straight on. "I was in Atlantic City with my folks." It was the truth. The secret, the intimacy made Ezekiel feel like he was floating.

"Painting?" Ezekiel said.

"Yup." He tossed a piece of the bread into his mouth. "Seashells."

"Seashells?" He began to laugh.

"Clamshells, more precisely," Bob said. "Painted hundreds. Was planning to sell them for ten cents each to begin paying my own way as a full-blown *artiste.*" He waited for Ezekiel to quit laughing. It took a while. He chuckled as if he enjoyed this joke on himself. "You know how big a clam shell is?" He measured with his fingers. "Maybe I even painted a thousand of the damned things, painted the shore on them, painted starfish on them, painted the waves, even a cloud or two. Got pretty good at seagulls."

"God," Ezekiel said.

"Ma's still got a few hundred that didn't sell. She keeps them in a basket back of the house, downwind. Clamshells never quit smelling like clamshells." They laughed until the customers shot them sour looks. "Those clamshells are going to make her and Pa rich one of these days."

A man at the next table said, "Hey, keep it down."

Bob raised a peace hand in the man's direction.

For a minute, he and Ezekiel sat quiet. "You seen anything of Soap since you got back?" Ezekiel did not know why he asked, it seemed to blurt on its own out of his mouth. Bob shook his head. "Your folks doing well?" Ezekiel said. The levity cleared from Bob's face. He looked up at him with such a pointed and questioning intensity Ezekiel wished he had not asked it.

"Yeh," he finally said, "they are." As serious as he had become, he seemed relieved. The others would never even know of it. Then Bob said something odd: "Frank is good, too."

"Frank?"

A hive flared in the middle of Bob's forehead. He cleared his throat. "John R. calls himself Frank now," he said. "He wanted no more, association with the likes of what we left behind." His shoulders dropped, his mouth turned down. "It's hard," he said, "for all of us."

Chapter 40

Late summer bled into a gentle decline toward fall, days warm and dry at the first of the month, but toward the end of September, cloud and sky warred and sent the city drenchings.

The days at the store were settling. The Hainsworths' output increased as JJ could do more. Rarely did one of their designs linger in the case longer than a week. Ezekiel's income was crawling up, though it was barely enough to pay bills. In a few weeks, all of the old Reading stock would be gone, and he would be dependent totally on the Hainsworths and the bit of art he could sell. The thought cramped him, made him gulp gallons of soda water. The student paintings were not selling much, though another Redfield landscape sold for ten dollars. When Ezekiel had paid Reddy his two-dollar share, Redfield clapped his hands and gave a little jump. "God," he said. "I'm a *professional*."

The city gave itself over to celebrating the centenary of the signing of the Constitution. This required fracas. This required parades. This required flags and music. For days the voices of two thousand boys filled Chestnut Street with their rehearsals at Independence Hall. Ezekiel bowed to civic extortion and spent a week's income to buy bunting. He spent the better part of a day hanging it. By the time the parades began and the brasses blatted and the drums pounded, Chestnut Street and Market and Broad were almost hidden by the flutter of banners and flapping flags. Nothing worthwhile got done the day of the celebration. The Hainsworth's took the day off.

As winter approached, he found himself feeding on the news. He skipped the folderol about the Phillies and the bits about weddings and about the comings and goings of ships, the stories of high families returning home from summers away in Europe. He concentrated on the financial: the markets and mergers. He could no longer count on the rumpled papers in the hotel lobbies for information but had begun to lay out precious money for four or five different publications every day, which he read late into the night. Men like Astor, Carnegie, Cooke, Morgan, Fisk, Vanderbilt, Stanford, Harriman, were making millions. Reports of their dealings burrowed deep inside him.

Yet there was dark resistance to all this as well: labor. Laborers, miners, railroad men, steel men, dock workers, the very men whose existence depended on the industrialists, were beginning to nip at the hands that fed them. They were forming unions, calling themselves "knights." Authorities pushed back. Not long ago, the militia had gunned down two thousand Poles in Wisconsin who were striking for eight-hour workdays. In Chicago, a bombing had killed both workers and police at the McCormick Harvesting Machine Company. In Louisiana, Negro sugar workers were shot when they tried to form a union.

Ezekiel had paid little attention to it when it began, but now the very idea of labor inhibiting business posed a threat: What would happen to him if Hainsworth wanted more money? What would happen if JJ insisted he be paid like his older brother? What if they demanded a higher cut from their sales?

Ezekiel had worked hard and had spent his life feeling as if he would one day prove himself, that something would come of him, but that something was always out *there*, and he had always been waving his arms at it. The question was: How could he manage it? He needed money. Thanks to his uncle, he had none.

Chapter 41

He fixed a swag of green bows up over the door and the windows, letting tails of it drop down the sides. The Christmas holidays seemed to demand bows, and swags, and lights in the windows. The bows snuffed out a good bit of daylight from the showroom and he feared the lack of light would dampen sales. In the freeze of an afternoon, with the wind cutting the streets and the sky hardening for snow, he was atop the ladder, hammering up another branch. Other merchants up and down the street had already decorated their stores. Some had even put lit candles in their windows. The lights flickered happily among the displays. He would do without candles. With his luck, they would set fire to the place.

He blew on his fingers and slapped them under his arms. It was taking longer than he had planned—everything did—and he was beginning to chill. He had just finished with the last swag when his aunt came. Again. She had two other women in tow. He could hear the crescendo of her "Yoo-hoo, E-*zee*-kiel." *God, how can anyone be so relentlessly cheerful?*

The women went inside, waited for him to collapse the ladder. Prune's friends were stylish with fitted coats trimmed with beaver fur. Her clothes, however, were dark as a haymow, entirely purple. All. Everything. Gloves, hat, shoes, coat, even the ribbon at her throat. She turned her friends' way, then swept her arm at him. "Here he is," she said, "my nephew." Her voice was high, eager as if she had spent years telling her friends all about him. "Fannie," she said, "my nephew, Ezekiel Harrington. Ezekiel, Mrs. Paul." He dipped his chin. Lord, Mrs. Paul—born a *Drexel,* connected to half of Philadelphia and a good part of Europe who put their money in the banks owned by the Drexel's.

Mrs. Paul lifted a kid glove his way and he took it, wondering if he was expected to kiss it. He took the tips of her fingers and dipped again. He was relieved when she took back her hand.

"Mildred," said Prune, "this is my nephew Ezekiel Harrington. Ezekiel, meet Millicent's mother." *Millicent. Millicent. Who the hell is Millicent?* "Mrs. Pettygrove," she said. *Ah.*

Mrs. Pettygrove smiled. It was a sweet smile and passive. "Oh," she said, "I am so delighted with the portrait of my dear Millicent."

His aunt clapped her hands under her chins. The purple ribbon quivered. "Oh, you see," she said, "that's exactly why we're here. Isn't this just so exciting?"

He had no guess as to what this meant. "Why is that?"

"I said to my friends I would like a portrait done of my grandchildren by that wonderful artist who did Mildred's little Millicent, and I told them I was coming to see you. They *insisted* they come with me. You see, Fannie and I want portraits done of *our* grandbabies, too."

"I see," he said.

"By that wonderful young artist of yours. Do you suppose we might have them done by Christmas?"

"Christmas is a week away," he said.

"Fannie could go first," Prune said.

"It takes time."

"Oh! don't I know that," his aunt said. "That's why we're giving it a week."

"A month," he said.

"Oh, dear."

"Or more. Per painting."

His aunt commiserated a moment with her friends. "Then maybe in time for Easter?"

"Maybe," he said.

She began the ordeal of rolling her purple leather gloves over the flesh of her fingers. "The whole family," she said, "is coming for the holidays. Both Cornelius and Oliver will be here with their wives and the kids. We're inviting everybody to drop by." She pinched open her purple handbag and withdrew an envelope. She slid the envelope his way, across the counter. "Mr. and Mrs. Paul will be there, won't you Fannie?"

Mrs. Paul said, "Would not miss one of your affairs, Prudence."

Prune looked back at him, clapped her gloves at her chin. "Just everyone is coming, darling. You must come. And you're to be with us for dinner Christmas day as well." She turned and waggled her fingers over her shoulder and began leading the other two women out of the store. "You'll talk to that lovely artist of yours, then?"

"If I see her again." And he did not allow himself the thought how many times each day he longed she would walk through his door, and did not allow the thought that it was not only for the money she could bring him.

Classes at the Academy would let out next day to begin the holiday. Ezekiel had not gone to the studio since the beginning of fall. He longed to be among, to belong somewhere. But to be "one of the boys" one needed to paint, and one needed to rail at convention, and to wail about art done for no reason other than to be "art." The studio was not a place for anyone but The Misunderstood.

It was cold out, dark falling now two hours before closing. Ezekiel was hungry. He made his way to the diner Bob had taken him to several months ago, hoping the boys would be there. It was closed until the first of the year. He turned up Arch Street, beginning to feel stupid to be out in the weather. He thought to turn back. He trudged in the direction of the Chinaman's chop house. He did not particularly like the food, but was hungry enough to eat whatever was laid before him. If he did not find Bob there, he would eat alone. It was nothing new.

He turned the corner at Twelfth, anticipating the Chinaman would be closed, but the lights were on and at the big table in the window sat Bob, surrounded by others. Some of them Ezekiel knew, some he did not. He watched a moment, taking a pulse, expecting levity with next week's reprieve. He found the opposite: All of them were hunched over like lumps, their faces dark. Calder was hammering on the table with his fist. They had already eaten, their plates wiped as if they had been licked.

Ezekiel went in, brought himself a chair and sat down. Bob managed a brother's nod toward Ezekiel and a fingered greeting to his forehead, but turned back to Calder. "Paris," he said. The others muttered "Yahs" and "Hey, heys." Paris was in the conversation last time Ezekiel had been in the studio as well. It seemed to have taken on a mystical power. "Over there they work eight hours a day," Bob said. "And what do we do here?" He picked up his gear, stood. "We could do better, all of us. All of us," he said. They clattered out with their gear banging on their backs and left Ezekiel to order a dinner alone.

Chapter 42

Smoke billowed from the Humes' chimney. The drive up to the house was banked in snow and filled with coaches. Drivers hugged themselves on top of their coaches, or got down and stamped their feet, and nipped from flasks they pulled from their pockets. Ezekiel had not intended to come, had not sent an answer to his aunt's request. But, in the end, he had finally convinced himself he could deign to show, it would be in the name of getting his hands on connections; coming was all in the name of business.

The windowpanes gleamed with light. The drapes had been pulled back, giving the interior a sense of smiling. His fat aunt fluttered about in a green dress, thick as a toad, and talking first to one guest then another, leaving each with a laugh and an affectionate pat on the arm. The house lit the night, welcoming as a sun: candles in every window, the gas turned high in the crystal chandeliers. Inside, people laughed, the women sat in their finery, talking, sipping at China cups, the rich silks of their dresses like bright flowers.

He would have gone in right then had his uncle not circulated into view. The last time Ezekiel saw his uncle, Totten had been extremely ill, which had given Ezekiel a brief upper hand. Now, Totten was dressed in a frock coat that gapped open over his gut in a stout show of health. Totten mingled among the social register, men who practically wrote the columns in the financial papers, men who leaned toward one another, nodded, threw back laughs, their faces red from the heat and the nip in their drinks. Every important name in the city crowded into the Hume house: the Paul's, a Biddle or two, the Pepper's, the Cadwalader's, the Hollingsworth's and, of course, the Pettygrove's. Ezekiel held his hand over his stomach, swallowed the urge to be sick.

He lifted his hand toward the boar's-head knocker, took up the ring, but could not force his hand to drop it. Muffled voices bled through the heavy oak: the ladies' chatterings, the roars of the men's laughter. He held the ring until the frozen cold bled through his glove. He could not do it. As much as he needed what his uncle could give him, he could not allow the man to know it.

Silently, he laid down the knocker and faced the cold.

The next mail delivery carried an envelope. It was formal, on the richest linen stock and engraved with the return *Philadelphia National Bank & Trust.* The letter was written by a thick, commanding hand:

> *Nephew,*
> *You did not come. Your aunt was disappointed. I believe you shoot yourself in the foot.*
> *TH*

Chapter 43

She huddled in the doorway wearing a frayed man's coat that floated on her like a tent. Her hair bore no indication it had seen a brush since he last saw her. She was shivering, thinner, her arms crossed over. He opened. She came just inside. She gawked as if surprised she had ended up where she was. "Yes?" Ezekiel said.

The winter had turned soft, warm, unnatural. Though calendars were still turned to February, people were out, shopping, strolling as though it were spring. Easter was almost a month away. In the time since he last saw her, his image of her had softened, he no longer thought of her as a tramp, yet she now appeared more derelict than ever. He did not know what he thought she was, now, did not know how to this peg this downfall in her. He was unsettled by it. He had once pinned too much hope on her, had been pathetic in his waiting and watching. But time had softened the urgency of it and left behind a longing he had tried to turn away from. He thought he had finally come to grips about her.

She looked away. Every strand of hair, every thread of clothes spoke of squalor. And, though she wore the same patched blouse under her coat, it was filthy and had another rip in front that made it quite immodest.

He said, "Come in."

She threw her hands into her armpits and began to lurch forward. She smelled of dank smoke and even danker breath and there was a yellow smear of old bruises on her cheek and jaw. She opened her mouth to say something, then closed it again. Where was her bluster? The old confidence?

"Are you ill?" he said.

She lifted her chin and looked straight at him and the gesture gave out a bit of her old haughtiness. "There was this lady," she said, "wanted a picture painted." Prune. His aunt.

"This lady," he repeated.

"Yuh," she said.

"Stay there," he said and went back to tell Hainsworth he'd be gone for a while and to take over the front of the store until he returned. Despite her filth, she represented the thin possibility of income and he made himself believe the chance of business, not some other sense, impelled him to do something with her now. He took up his coat, a heavy one he'd bought used and had had enough cash to have tailored. It fit well. He shrugged into it and said to her, "I think you need something to eat."

The dinner house was two streets away. She kept herself half a step ahead as they walked, her eyes scanning every fellow who approached. Ezekiel began to regret bringing her. What would others see? A businessman out with a woman who belonged in the gutter? He slowed, put some distance between them.

He ordered stew for her and half a loaf of bread. He told the waiter to bring extra jelly and lard. She grasped the spoon in her fist and leaned over the bowl. Her hair fell into it. The noises of her eating were animal, slurping, piggish. And when the bowl was near empty she picked it up and drank down the rest.

"Another?"

"Yah," she said.

She came back the next day, and the next, asking about "that lady." She had not cleaned up, had not gained a bit of color, even with the meal he had fed her. He regretted seeing her now, much less having encouraged her by feeding her. He almost convinced himself she was, indeed, nothing. He could not allow his aunt to see her now. She was in no shape to paint, or do anything else. She belonged back on the street. Ezekiel could not afford a silk dress to clean her up, as Pettygrove had. Any money he risked on her would certainly be for naught He gave her no encouragement. He told her she didn't need to come back. Yet she persisted, again and again. Lord, how had Bob ever known her?

He finally lied, told her the lady did not want a picture, after all.

Chapter 44

When the rains began, Ezekiel was cooped in his office, writing out a list of things needing done. The roar outside took over, filled the store, filled his head, filled the store, with its relentless dark. Hissing, drumming took away thought. Mid-March was not the season for the warmth that had brought such a deluge, but it had stuck long enough that people had been seduced and were already planting gardens. Ezekiel had not seen Soap for two weeks. He hoped she had finally given up, and he tried to feel relieved but could not.

The skies turned ugly, nearly black, in the middle of the afternoon. The Hainsworths at the workbench had lit several lights against the dark to finish a particularly complicated matched set of women's necklace and earrings. They had fashioned the set with gold and rubies laid out as salamanders. By four o'clock, rain gushed from the awning and pummeled the front windows. Throughout the store, lights flickered from drafts carried in on the wind.

The brothers began putting away their tools and getting their coats to leave early. JJ said, "Damn, we'll get soaked."

The gaslights flickered again, a reminder that the store needed *electricity*. Successful establishments had it, now. A merchant had to show he had means, and the glitter of electrical bulbs spelled means. But he could not afford electricity, as "electrifying" was tremendously expensive. He had done everything he could think of to obscure scarcity in the store, had learned to hide the rot in the front window, had learned the fine art of patching the awning when it ripped. He patched and cleaned and arranged and spread his stock until he could spread it no further. He could hide the fact that the owner could not afford a place to live and was forced to sleep on a mattress on a shelf among boxes. He could hide the fact he washed and shaved and relieved himself in the utility sink and that he could afford no more than one suitable garment in which to present himself. He could cover the fact that, though he dealt in jewelry, he had only one piece of it himself, a ring fashioned in bronze from a chipped intaglio stone Hainsworth had removed from another piece a customer brought in, then decided to discard it. But electricity, that was something he could not hide; either a store had it or it did not. All up the streets, storefronts were beginning to glow with electric lights, and those without them grew darker and duller by contrast.

Outside, the sky had gone black. The brothers said good-bye and let themselves out into the torrent. Ezekiel locked the door, went to bed, and tried to sleep as the wind pounded. Blasts threw themselves against the store and the windows swayed. The violence took his breath. He pulled himself up, tied the sash of his robe, took a lamp, and trudged through the showroom to look out. He had put up a new section of awning only weeks ago. The wind had ripped it, one half of it was gone, the skirts of the piece remaining now flapped so hard they were near shreds.

In the wretched, wet glow of the streetlamps, the figures of renters in the upstairs rooms across the street peered out the windows, their faces like ghosts. In just moments, the warmth from the drafts at his feet had turned cold as the devil and down came a torrent so loud it seemed to take over creation. The gutters along the street were filled with scraps of food, clothes, horse excrement, and, lord, a baby? Its round white face, its lifeless arms, legs, fingers floated by. He choked down sickness, tried to convince himself it was nothing more than a doll.

He turned to the safety of his office and books and, when he did, the wind suddenly went silent. His ears hushed with the silence. It was momentary. The hammered picked up again, but in the quiet he had heard something outside, a groan and a rattle against the front door, a threatening sound, as if someone getting ready to break in. He went out, cupped his hands against the dark. He saw nothing. As he turned to go, he looked down and thought he saw a foot on the stoop. He nearly shrieked. The foot pulled back as if to locate the body it belonged to. The wind hammered again and, the world blinked, the streetlights went black. The world disappeared. "Eeeeeee!" he thought it was the cat come home, but it came from the stoop, piercing, sharp, awful like an injured bird's.

He slid back the bolt, turned the knob, and the body of a woman rolled onto the floor: drenched, blinking up with eyes wet and sightless: Soap. Her hair was plastered over her mouth, her skirt stuck to her thighs. Her shoes were so worn her toes were exposed.

He had no words; the misery, the wind, the night had taken them from him. She closed her eyes, as if sealing them against something he could not imagine. She began to shiver. She raised a leg to kick him. He stepped back, out of reach. Her leg struck at the rain. How would it look, a tramp at his door? "Go home," he shouted. She drew her leg back under the sop of her skirt, then lay there shivering with such ferocity he could almost feel it. She did not open her eyes.

She took in a huge gasp, her leg dropped, her arms fell away, and every bit of her went flaccid. He thought she had died. He leaned down. Rain ran down the rent in the awning, through his hair, onto her. If she were not dead, she surely would drown, right here on his doorstep. He bent down, managed to get his arms under her to drag her inside. He wrestled her into his arms. Water streamed off her, her head and her arm flopping loose as a mop. He carried her, stumbling, through the store, edged her beyond his office, beyond the Hainsworths' workbench, laid her at his feet and stripped off her coat and skirt. She had, at least, the decency to be wearing an underskirt, though it, too, was sopped. He brought her in, and he tossed the coat and the skirt aside and grabbed a clean rag, began patting her off.

She was so small, her hipbones rising sharp and wooden. Through her underskirt she smelled like a cat. He patted her forehead, her shoulders. He thought to remove her wet blouse, but could not allow the immodesty.

He balanced her against himself, best as he could, turned her to the side. She moaned as he toweled her back. He wrung the hem of the underskirt onto the floor. When he had her as dry as he could make her, he pulled back the sheets and the blankets and lifted her onto the shelf with his bed.

Chapter 45

If life were nothing more than a sum of its pieces, its fates, its days, and happenstance, he might have understood the turn his took. He had only begun to whisper to himself he might know where he was actually going. In the last week, he had had a sign painter remove the old Reading & Reading Stationers lettering from the windows and replace it with fancy gold script: *Harrington Fine Art and Jewelry*. The gleam of the gold leaf was grand, and the lettering sometimes caught his eye, but the snap of pride it bequeathed was illusory, something he had yet to truly believe. The storm was threatening everything. And now, there was *her* to deal with.

He wrapped Soap in everything he could find to warm her: rags, blankets, his coat, cloths from the displays. He would later recall the confusion this caused him with the memories of his mother's fevered last days when he took care of her. He thought the storm would soon blow itself out, and that the building's furnace would last. But none of that happened. The rain turned to snow and would not abate. For days, wind threw ice and snow higher and higher until they covered the windows and took away sky and light. Snow soon became a warden locking him in. He inventoried what he had worthwhile on hand: to eat, two slices of bread dried stiff in his pocket; to see with, lamp fluid enough for a few days; for warmth, a bit of wood, if the furnace failed; water, if the pump did not freeze. He had never spent to buy a clock for the wall nor even a watch. Time relied on signs, the sun, the night, the ding of the doorbell, someone expected. As hours crept on, he was not even sure of the date.

She slept hours, lying on his bed still as death but for the hungry rumble of her stomach. She groaned, now and then, letting out a sound that could have come from a ghost. Nothing woke her. At times her breath grew so quiet he thought she had gone the way of his mother. At some time in the dark, he had knocked against the Hainsworths' workbench and sent a hammer clattering to the floor. She did not move even in the racket. She did not wake to relieve herself, did not cry out for water or food. Yet, when he brought the lamp to shine on her, he could see color returning to her cheeks.

In the next three days, the heavens pounded. Later, he would learn the extent of it: the cold froze dogs to the ground and heaped drifts so deep they obscured three-story buildings. The storm spread all the way from Chesapeake Bay to Maine. It did not discriminate; nothing was immune to its force. Telegraphy was lost, fire wagons could not leave their stations, ships were trapped in ice. Four hundred people would die, many frozen in their homes.

By the second day, the furnace quit, and, by the third, he had burned all the wood and was shivering with such force he chipped a tooth. And still she slept. He pulled himself near as he could to the mattress where there was a bit of her warmth. Several times he held her up in his arm and forced open her mouth. He poured water down her from a pitcher and forced her to swallow. He finally covered himself with the edge of the blankets and lost himself to trembling exhaustion.

He would not have known he had closed his eyes but for the sense he was being touched. He lay for a moment, remembering the storm, and thought he must have frozen to death. He felt the warmth of breath on the back of his neck. Was this heaven? He could see nothing. It was dark as coal, no light. Nothing. He felt warmth of a body pressing against his back, heat along his spine, his backside, his thighs and calves.

Chapter 46

In slow, crusted sounds, the city woke. Through the dark, through their muffled imprisonment came the scrapes of shovels, the hammering of picks, the police calling, "Police. Anyone in there?" Ezekiel called out but had no idea if he could be heard.

He wished he had a hole to crawl into, a place to hide and wait. He lit an oil lamp, turned back the wick. Soap sat up in the dim light, pulled the blankets to her neck. She blinked as if in a daze, her stomach growling ferociously. His own gut had set up its own howling. Days ago he had eaten what was in his pockets. He had found two rocks of old biscuits in one of the Hainsworths' work aprons. He handed one to her, kept one for himself, and together they chipped at them with their teeth.

The doors front and back were welded shut with walls of snow. The quiet inside the store continued to give way to the promise of outside sounds, the crackle of the ice melting in the flue, a drip from the sills, the groans and thumps of heavy equipment, picks slamming at ice.

Hunger rendered movement a slow, aching dance. He had to figure out a way to get out. The front door had been frozen shut since the first day. He took the lamp and a chisel and began tapping at the cracks around it. It finally gave and then opened to a sheer wall of ice shaped precisely like the door handle and slot for the mail.

He took a hammer and pick and began swinging at the ice like a miner. It was heavy at first and hopelessly dark, like night. Slowly, he hacked out an indentation, then a larger one. As the hole deepened it grew brighter and then brighter, until there came a rabbit's hole of daylight. He swung again and again until the hole grew large enough to crawl through. From inside, she said, "You ain't leaving me here." He reached back in and waited until she took hold of his hand.

His store, and those on his side of the street, had fared worse than the establishments on the other side. Though nothing in the city was spared the storm—no street, no walk, no building. The winds had driven snow against some buildings in great and fickle drifts, while leaving others clear.

The city had already opened some narrow paths in the streets, barely wide enough for one or two people and a horse. Soap followed as they worked their ways around telegraph lines, through canyons of snow where men sold ten-cent buckets of coal for a dollar, and where dark women peddled baskets of stolen oranges. Reading station was locked, people being turned away by signs that read *No Trains Until Further Notice.* Ships listed to their sides in the river, some revealing hulls that had cracked in the crush of ice. In the end, two dozen marine vessels would be destroyed.

They came finally to a shop that had opened its doors just minutes before. It served food. It was already filled with people, thirty more huddled in a line out front. He and Soap waited with the rest, she standing against him as the lines moved ahead toenail by toenail. The smells of breads and peppered soup made Ezekiel's gut roar. They sat with others, bumping legs at a table. He bought them both stew and paid for half a dozen biscuits, which they began to eat dry then to soak in the broth when the soup came.

They ate in silence. He paid and they went out again into the white world. He turned in the direction of the store. She followed. He stopped, turned to face her. "You can't stay."

"That lady," she said, "wants a painting."

Was this the sole reason she had come to the door of his shop the day he found her? He realized he had hoped it was for more than just that. "I'll tell her," he said. "If I see her."

"Yah," she said as if she didn't believe him. She picked her way past him in her ruined shoes and disappeared beyond a pile of snow.

The city turned toward survival. Shopkeepers pushed water out their doors with brooms. Men in suits joined men in overalls, repairing their stores, looking for something to eat. Food was scarce. Preserves, carted in from the farms, sold for ten times what they were worth, bread for a dollar a loaf. Ezekiel believed he had dodged the worst—but for the pump, which had finally frozen the last night, and the shreds of the awning that flapped in the breeze, and a large new crack in a front window, the store remained dry.

The sign in his door still read "Closed." The shades were still pulled over the windows. He could smell himself. He had not bathed since the storm began. But for the wooden dinner rolls and the soup and biscuits with Soap, he had not eaten a full meal since the storm hit. He was a mess, his face covered with stubble, and he wore a disgrace of old clothes, torn slacks, three shirts piled on for warmth, which made him appear suited more for a coal mine than to be the owner of a store selling fine art.

When it was all done, one sound he would remember above everything else; it came when the worst was past, it came like a crack of lightning, or like rock hitting ground from a bluff. He was in the back when it happened. After the impact came the tinkling of glass, then one horrendous pounding that shook the store. He shouted, "God almighty!" He stumbled from the storeroom as a huge wall of sodden snow, broken through the largest show window, settled like a dirty white hill onto the showroom floor.

Chapter 47

The avalanche consumed everything in its way. It had lasted a mere second, yet that one second had destroyed half the front of the store. And then came the water, rivulets of snowmelt, the store running with streams as though off a mountain.

Alarm turned to hysteria, then to a frantic kind of calm. He grabbed rags, he grabbed mops, he threw his bedding at the river. With the snow drift gone, the store had light in it again, the cold, blue, light of winter.

He took a shovel and began to dig.

———

In the end, he lost two paintings, which had been on easels in the window. He tried to force himself to remember that it could have been worse. He had not lost any of the paintings on the walls or the two bronzes he had taken in just days before the storm.

He ripped boards from the back shelves and hammered them over the opening. He shoveled mounds of snow onto the street. He swore that the Hainsworths were not here to help out. *Where were they?* He needed them here.

For hours he mopped, wrung out his blankets and rags, and waited to see what damage was done to the floor. He did not know how he would pay for repairs. He did not know what liability he had to the paintings that had been destroyed. But not for a moment did he think to abandon the store altogether. The store was still his.

———

When he opened again three days later, the floors were rippled and pulling away, the air filled with the smell of mildew. The Hainsworths returned that day—not to work but to gather their tools, their powders, and their small locked safe. Hainsworth stood aside, his face pale, as his little brother JJ told Ezekiel they had found a place three blocks away, vacated after the storm, and had decided to open their own shop in it. They were gone by noon, and they sucked the air from the place as they left.

Chapter 48

Ezekiel hired a new man. He had been two weeks without income, with nothing to put on the books but expenses and now he had to hire someone.

The fellow had seen the notice Ezekiel put in the window offering a position to someone who was familiar with fine art. He was a pleasant sort, slow moving, but willing to work for little money. He smiled often, promoting a view of full, white, perfect teeth. He seemed to have means of support beyond the wage Ezekiel would pay him. His name was George Smith. and he said he was a shirttail relative of the Brills, who had made fortunes in streetcars.

One thing endeared George to him and did so tremendously: He did not seem to have ambition. Ambition, Ezekiel had come to understand, was something to be wary of in others. JJ Hainsworth had ambition. Ambition in others flummoxed things, caused things to get out of hand, to threaten what Ezekiel saw as his. He liked this lack in George.

George said he had been educated at Yale and had spent some years traveling in France and England where he learned an appreciation of art. He wore rumpled suits that were well-tailored but looked as if he had slept in them half his life. From the first day, he spoke to anyone entering the store as if he had known them for centuries.

Chapter 49

The city breathed a collective sigh as March died away. Spring came gently, on tiptoe, and it blessed Philadelphia with soft breezes and crystalline skies. The new man, George, knew a great deal about art. Each day, he went out for what he called mid-day meetings. By the second week, the "meetings" had become habit. Ezekiel suspected they always took place at a saloon.

He heard the mail drop through the slot. It had turned beautiful out, warm enough to open a window and to hear the noise from the street. The city had nearly returned to normal from the storm, though the streetcar schedules were still somewhat uncertain, and the prices for food were double what they had been before it.

Ezekiel was sore and favoring an arm due to a sprain to his shoulder that had occurred while he hammered down new wood to the front floor. He had hammered and sanded, painted and scraped long into the nights. He had had to hire someone to replace the front windows, and they shone, now, as they had not before. He tried to hold onto the idea that the new window and the new floor were a start, and he often found himself stopping what he was doing and peering through the shine of new glass and wishing Soap on the other side of it.

The mails were coming again, regular as before. He heard the thump and slush of it through the slot. He went out, took up what had come in: three bills for repairs, circulars with advertisements promoting Anderson and Son Photographers, Otterson's kidney and liver medicine, La Sciencia cigars, and a sheet announcing a hundred items on sale at Wanamaker's. He tossed the advertisements in the trash. A letter was slipped among the bills. It had the return address of the Rawle Law Offices. He opened it while standing there in the doorway.

Dear Mr. Harrington,
Mrs. Reading has made arrangements to sell the building in which your business is located. You have thirty days to make arrangements. After that, my client will put the property into the hands of a real estate establishment May 1, 1888.
Respectfully Yours,
M. John Edgars, Attorney at Law

Ezekiel folded the letter, pressed the creases, slipped it back into the envelope, and slammed it in his office drawer, out of sight.

Chapter 50

Easy. Bob had nicknamed him Easy, he said, not because of his given name but because things came easy for him. *Hah.* Easy. He forced himself to concentrate on parts, now, never allowing a look at the enormous whole. Dusting, rearranging, organizing paintings bequeathed a certain grace, however fleeting. A certain rhythm, an ugly drumming had set up shop in his head: chump, chump, chump. *What a chump. What a chump. What a chump.* He could not shake it, no matter how much he dusted, or cleaned, or planned. Was it all for naught? Was it folly? Totten would be laughing, if he knew, and this, more than even wanting Bob's admiration drove him. Totten.

George had set about shuffling some of the drawings and paintings. "Just a little fuss to make it fresh," he said. He brought in some art "pieces" he said he "caged" from the trash bins of some of his friends who were modernizing or moving to new homes. The paintings were all framed, small works most of them, a variety of flowers or quick sketches of Philadelphia streets.

"Where did you get them?" Ezekiel asked. They were light, fetching, each with some sense he thought of elegance and joy that for a moment lifted even his trouble.

A few days ago, the cat came again. It just showed up thin and an ear half gone. Ezekiel found scraps of gristle from some meat, put it down on a plate and the cat ate then left. It came again the next day and the next. It would howl and spit if Ezekiel closed the back door, so Ezekiel took to keeping it cracked open. It began sleeping on Ezekiel's bed. He was surprised at how much he was glad the animal was there, how much he had missed it; it was a good cat, quiet unless the door was closed, asking for little but food. Ezekiel decided he might cut a small opening in the door so it could come and go.

He could not help but admire the fact that the widow had waited to sell the building until he had fixed it, painted it, and made repairs. The debt he had incurred for the repairs alone would take years to crawl out of, at the rate things were going. He knew he could not block a sale. He knew there was no tiny point of law a lawyer could pull out on his behalf.

Meanwhile, George continued to bring in more paintings to sell, and they were beautiful. He would not say where he got some of them, only that he had an old aunt with whom he was close. His face went reflective for a moment, then he said, "She died and left them to me. She had a carriage house full of them. I'm keeping the best. The store," he said, "can have the overflow for a hundred dollars."

They were worth well more than a hundred dollars, even Ezekiel could tell that. He had just spent the most ever on repairs from the storm. The new window had cost more than three months' rent. "It will take time to come up with it," he said.

"Take time, then," George said.

When he had hung them all up, the store seemed to exhale.

Chapter 51

The bell dinged. George was not back yet from his noon meeting. George's meetings were taking longer and longer. God, where *was* he? Ezekiel's office chair squawked as he stood. He smoothed his hair and straightened his tie. He went out, pulled his face into a smile.

A young woman, fashionably dressed, stood at the counter looking somewhat confused.

"May I help you?" he said.

Her clothes were expensive, muted silks expertly fitted. "I thought you carried jewelry," she said. Another woman had come in with her but stood at the door. The other woman was rather plain, dressed in a servant's dull shirtwaist and holding a spaniel on a leash. The spaniel's owner peered into the showcases where Ezekiel had arranged the detritus of what he still had of the Readings' old stock. There was nothing of jewelry in the store, not a broach or a necklace, since the Hainsworths pulled all their things. "I had heard the establishment carried fine jewelry."

"Yes," he said, "we do."

She peered at him, confused. The dog began to whine. "Keep her quiet, Bernadette," she said. The woman patted the dog and muttered, "Quiet." The dog yipped, threw its head in the air, winding up for a good squall. "Bernadette, take him out. I won't be long." The servant woman took the dog out to stand beside a coach, which was waiting in front. The customer turned back to Ezekiel, her expression one of privilege and of one used to being in command. "I understood I could have a pearl necklace made for my niece here."

The Hainsworths' store was on Locust, a five-minute walk away.

"Certainly," he said. On the spot, he envisioned referring business to the Hainsworths and getting a cut from it. He cleared his throat. "I could arrange for a special string to be made for her," he said and realized how stilted he sounded.

He heard George let himself in the back door. He had carved out a routine of coming in the back way, reeking of whiskey, unwrapping a mint, putting it in his mouth and sucking it half down before beginning work. *God, George, hurry up.* "We can arrange any quality, any color, pink, perhaps?" *Did pearls come in pink? God.* Her neck arched a little but did not need to utter a word to convey derision, his clumsiness, his lack of knowledge echoed. Ezekiel was losing the woman; she must think him an imbecile. He could see she was about to leave and take the potential sale with her.

He heard the *tink* of the mint as George threw it into the barrel, heard the tap of his shoes and felt the heat of embarrassment; he knew George was about to observe his incapacity with a customer.

"Good Lord, Ruthie," George said. "I haven't seen you since your wedding. You look *wonderful.*" Her face reddened and she smiled, obviously pleased. "George," she said, "hello."

He said, "Coming in to find something to hang in the parlor of the new house?"

"Something for my husband's niece," she said.

"How is Henry now that he's an old married man?" It had the tone of an old saw, worn out, yet she was clearly enjoying it.

"He can't complain."

"Well, you came to the right place," George said.

"A necklace."

"I mentioned we still had access to fine jewelry," Ezekiel blurted.

"Why yes," George said. "By the way, Ruth," he put his arm around Ezekiel's shoulders, "Let me introduce Mr. Ezekiel Harrington. Ezekiel, Mrs. Henry Coxe."

Ezekiel managed to mutter, “Pleased to meet you.” *Coxe. Coxe.* They owned half of Pennsylvania, for God’s sake. His ears began to hiss.

“Which niece?” George said. She told him a name Ezekiel did not quite hear. “Aren’t they leaving soon for the Continent?”

“Next week, in fact,” she said.

“What about a portrait?” George asked. “Something they could all enjoy.”

“A portrait?”

“After they return,” he said.

Mrs. Coxe clapped her hands and gave a small gasp. “Yes.”

George said to Ezekiel, “But who to paint it?”

“I have,” Ezekiel said, “a connection to one of the best artists.” *Where the hell was Soap*? He hadn’t seen her since the storm. “She has been away…in France,” he said. The lie escaped without thought. *France?*

She said, “When will she be home?” as if going to France were as common as ordering supper.

“Soon,” Ezekiel said. “Could I take your card and contact you when she arrives? She did a wonderful likeness of the Pettygrove girl.”

They both looked at Ezekiel. George said, “You know the artist who painted Millicent?”

Ezekiel hesitated. Who *didn’t* the Pettygroves know? Who didn’t *George* know? “Yes,” he said.

Chapter 52

He was sleeping, but barely. He could blame the heat for the trouble and the letter of eviction in the desk—but it was not only that. How could he be so dependent on someone as poor as she was, yet who would surely shirk away what he offered? It was not custom. Custom dictated that a woman needed a man to keep her, and provide for her. No matter what panned out, he could offer her that, yet she seemed not to want what he could do for her, seemed always to avoid it, to dodge him, to leave him spitting her dust.

At the end of the day, when he had pulled the chains over the windows, closed the books, opened every window to catch the feeble breeze, he laid himself down and walled his skull from thoughts of her. But, just at the cusp of slumber, in the snap of moment when his defenses lulled, the vision came, almost a dream: the vision of her, turning from some canvas, or some joke, or from some rough intake of smoke from a cigar. And she would see him, and her face would soften. She would make some little gasp and begin running toward him, arms out, and take him to her and whisper how she wanted him. He would waken and find himself longing for it with such power he wept.

He still had not retrieved the attorney's letter from the drawer where he put it. Yet it seemed to pulse there. He had a month to make up his mind. Even with the help of Sebastian Fennet, there would not be a way to hold up the sale of the property.

The business George brought in was compounding as the days grew longer. He had sold nearly half the small works from his aunt, and their sales had allowed Ezekiel to pay George what was owed him. George was relegating space on the walls to less and less of the student art Ezekiel had taken in; since a couple sales of Redfield's, nothing more had sold for months.

Ezekiel could not make sense of why George worked at the store, other than for the transparent joy he seemed to have in dealing with art. Ezekiel once thought to ask him, decided to leave well enough alone. He would use George for as long as he had him.

Every day, now, George asked something about the artist who painted the Pettygrove girl. "Where was she trained?" "How did you come to know her?" "What was her name again?" All Ezekiel could tell him was that her name was something like Soap. Before George left that day, he said, "Good day, Mr. Harrington," and patted Ezekiel on the shoulder. "She's certainly worth finding. I didn't know anyone around Philadelphia was doing that kind of work."

Chapter 53

Bob came at closing time. Half a dozen of George's paintings hung on the front walls, a couple behind the counter, another on an easel in the window, each splat of color and movement that made the store glow.

It was the first Ezekiel had seen of Bob since winter. Summer was not far off, the light already long on the days. The Academy would soon spit out Bob and all the students for the summer. Ezekiel dreaded the coming months that took the chance of a conversation with him or a maybe a dinner, seldom as these were anymore.

Bob had apparently been out painting. He smelled of linseed and solvent, and his hands were stained with pigments. He dropped his pack and massaged one shoulder as he gawped around the store. "Lord, man," he said, "where did you *get* these?"

"A fellow who works for me had them," Ezekiel said. "Wanted to sell."

Bob went to each one and inspected it, tipped his head, stepped nose-close, then back away. "So where did he get them?"

Ezekiel could only say, "From his dead aunt."

Bob laughed. "They're killers, Easy. God. Where they from?"

"France, mostly," Ezekiel said.

"That's the place," he said. "That's the place all right."

He leaned toward each one again as if studying. He was sunburned and tired, his hair lank, his breath full of sighs. Ezekiel would have kept him in the store forever if he could. Finally, Bob was ready to let go of the paintings, said he didn't have to teach class that night. "Night off."

"Want to go out somewhere?" Ezekiel asked.

"Someplace close, maybe, to just sit. You figure it out."

Ezekiel locked up. They went out to the park at Washington Square. The afternoon had turned pleasant, after a few days of thunderstorms and cool rains. The trees were yet to leaf, but tulips and daffodils fluttered and caught the light in the flowerbeds.

Bob dropped his paraphernalia beside a bench. They sat side by side. Ezekiel wanted to ask one question but didn't know how. He took a breath "Say, I wonder…" He paused.

Bob said, "Well, that's a long wonder." Ezekiel laughed, and it bled away some of his uncertainty. "You know where that girl went?"

Bob's paraphernalia fell over, in a clatter, at his feet. He did not bother to straighten it. "What girl would that be?" He snuffed, sneezed, then said, "I got a couple dozen girls in my class." He took out a handkerchief, blew into it. A breeze took up a sheen of yellow pollen and blew it by. Bob sneezed again. He seemed spent.

Ezekiel mumbled, "Soap," mashing her name because he knew he did not have it quite right.

"Yeh," Bob said, "our girl." It perked him a bit, and he leaned back as if settling in for a spell. "She's someone to keep up with." Businesses were closing for the day, shop girls walking by in shirtwaists and tired bonnets, nursemaids pushed children in strollers. Two curs picked a fight in the grass; a man in a business suit yelled and tossed a stone until one went yipping away. It was the time of year when sightseers were beginning to jam the streets, wandering the grounds at Independence Hall and around the old bank, out-of-towners mostly, looking in Ezekiel's windows but rarely coming in to buy. Bob said, "But I don't know where she is. I'd like to know, too."

He began chattering about his frustration with his work, his voice slowing, and his hands going quiet. It was as if had sought Ezekiel him out for no other reason than to let go of himself. It felt good.

Bob took a breath, turned his head directly toward Ezekiel. "What gets you up in the morning, Ease?"

No one had ever asked such a thing of him. What could he say? He felt he needed to come up with something, and it had to be worthy, but there was nothing noble in his motives. "I don't know," he said. But he did know. He knew all that mattered was about to slip from his hands, the building was to be sold, the doors locked to him, and his vision of success and proving himself, losing hold of retribution for his uncle's cruelty, everything that had held him together. He could not confess, could not admit that the store had become home, the only place he felt safe and like someone who might matter one day. "What about you?" he asked to take Bob's attention from him. "What gets you up in the morning?"

"Sometimes I don't know. And then suddenly I do know, and I wonder how I could ever have doubted it. I know there is something, some…" he waved his hands in front of himself, "*thing* that wants to be told. And God, Ease, I don't know how to tell it. I want to know how to tell it. I want someone to show me how." He looked Ezekiel straight on. "You ever felt like that?"

Bob's openness made Ezekiel uncomfortable; the intimacy seemed too deep. Bob had always been the one Ezekiel looked up to, the one he had gone to, had looked up to, just like the fellows at the studio did. But this time Bob was coming to *him*, and he wanted to meet Bob's truth with his own, but his own truth seemed hollow. And so, he sat and watched the play of his own fingers in his lap.

Bob straightened, threw back his shoulders. "Everything always comes easy for you," he said. "I wish I could say the same for myself." He bent down, began to gather his things, and the moment was over.

When he had strapped himself into his gear again, he said, "Oh, I almost forgot." He drew a letter from his pocket, handed it to Ezekiel. "For you," he said. "Sam didn't know where else to send it."

"Sam?" Ezekiel said.

"Schooley."

God, Sam Schooley. "You in touch with Sam Schooley?"

"Pa is."

It was as if a hot, hissing wind began to blow, evil and dry through the grasses. The mention of Sam Schooley put him back where he could smell dropseed and the dung of coyotes. Sam's betrayal still bled like a wound. Hadn't it been Sam who shipped Ezekiel and his trunk off to Philadelphia into the arms of Totten Hume? And now this: *Sam knew where Bob and his family were all along.*

Here was a letter addressed to Ezekiel in care of Mr. Richard Lee in Atlantic City, New Jersey. "You said Sam wrote your pa?" Ezekiel asked. "It says Mr. Richard Lee."

"That's Pa's name now," Bob said.

"Lee? Not Henri, like yours?"

"It's complicated, I guess, even for me." He gave a minute shake to his head. "They thought we should make it appear my brother and I were adopted, to throw off whoever was hunting Pa, maybe confuse them, so I took one name and Frank took something else."

After the shooting, the town of Cozad threatened to hang Mr. Cozad for murder. "But your dad was cleared. Did he still have to change his name?"

"You probably know how much Pa trusts the law."

Bob stood, patted Ezekiel on the shoulder, his touch without vigor. He gathered his canvas and his pack and his quiver of brushes and slung them on his back. "It's still between the two of us?" he said.

"Sure," Ezekiel said.

Bob turned, looked back. "See you, Easy," he said and headed off in the direction of the studio.

Chapter 54

Lightning flashed and left a ghost's glow on the backs of his eyes. Thunder pounded and the skies washed the city until Ezekiel feared a return to the torrent of March. But the rain turned soft by morning. He had not slept. The letter from Mrs. Reading's attorney had taken him by the scruff and dangled him, helpless as a kitten. Bills waited to be paid, yet he had had no stomach to open the books for days. He knew what they spelled: the end. Trouble was something he donned, now every morning, and never took off.

The letter was pleasant, written in pencil in Sam's awkward hand. He was well, and Cozad had begun to prosper and grow since Ezekiel's time there. Sam asked about Ezekiel's health and made some small talk. He wrote that he no longer roomed with the Claypools but had built a small house of his own at the edge of town. The true reason for the letter he saved for the end:

> *Ezekiel,*
>
> *Greetings from your old friend. I am not sure you rec'd the letter I sent through Totten Hume, tho I have never heard from you back, so I am writing through Bob's people as he wrote he has seen you. What I have to pass on may not be important but I think you should know. Here is my news.*
>
> *A couple years ago a fellow calling himself your pa was in town. He was traveling through with another fellow. He did not seem like a sort you would like to call your pa and now it is confirmed. He came through again yesterday. David Claypool says he learned this fellow*

calling himself Edmund Harrington had spent time in the prison up by Lincoln for murder and attempted robbery.

I know your ma believed she was a widow. But if this fellow is your pa I think you ought to know it.

Write if you have the time. I would like to know what has come of you.

Your Old Friend,

Sam Schooley

So, his pa was still alive. How could mention of his father bring up the bile, even after all these years? Ezekiel had seen him once when he was eight years old. It had been three years since he abandoned his ma and him. By then, Ezekiel was big enough to be some good at work. After school, he had jobs cleaning stalls at the livery and occasionally one at the emigrant hotel where his ma did the cooking. It was the same year Mr. Cozad had moved finally moved his family to town. They were living at the hotel while Mr. Cozad was laying out plans to build them a grand homemade of brick.

It was a Sunday. Ezekiel would always remember it was a Sunday. He had spent the afternoon carrying wood for the stove in the hotel, and Mrs. Gatewood had paid him a dime. He had just made some acquaintance with the younger Cozad boy, Bobby, three years older than he. He had encountered Bobby the day before, and they'd spoken about books they had read, particularly *Nicholas Nickleby*. It was the first serious discussion Ezekiel had ever entered into with anyone but his ma, and she rarely had time for discussion at all. He craved more of it. He craved more from his friendship with Bobby.

Had it been evening, or night, or morning before the roosters set up, someone might have heard the rumbling in the distance long before the herd made it so close to town. But it was Sunday, farm wagons were rattling into town with their families, townspeople were coming out of their houses on their way to church. The Lutherans had already rung their bell, but the Evangelicals were running a bit late and had just banged their first clangor. The weather was cold and dry. The women's skirts whipped in the wind, the men's hats blew, ribbons flailed in the girls' hair.

Ezekiel was outside town half a mile, hunting rabbit. He could hear the faint hammering of the bells, see the distant wagons collecting at the churches. From the south, a bruise of dust rose up. The cloud shifted, began to press toward town and brought with it animals' cries, bellowing high and hungry. It was the second herd to come through in two months, wild longhorns, rounded up in Texas and driven north to the markets in Omaha, Denver, Kansas City, and Chicago. The drovers customarily pushed the cattle through everything they came upon, farms, hay fields, cornfields, chicken sheds, hog sties, and straight into town. It was as if towns like Cozad were a challenge, a plaything to the drovers' guns and the cattle's hooves. The cattlemen claimed everything as theirs: towns, crops, wheat, corn, tomatoes in the gardens, even flower boxes on the porches.

The drovers' yips poked at the morning. Snow would cover town by the end of the day, but so far the day was bright and dry. Five drovers pushed the herd. Wind whipped their tails, their heads bobbed, dust rose from a thousand hooves, their movement making dull cracks of horn against horn, their cries filling the air.

The Evangelicals' bell went silent. People ran into their homes disappeared with their children into the churches, the livery, the hotel, anywhere to get out of the way of the cows.

Ezekiel ran into town, stood behind the first house on Meridian, away from the animals and their bellows and horns, his hand gripping a borrowed rifle and the hare he had shot for dinner. Bobby Cozad bolted out of the livery on his gelding. Farmers held their horses as their wives pulled their children into shelter.

Mr. Cozad came running from the hotel, yelling, "Bob! Bob! Get them the hell out of here!"

Bobby shaded his eyes. "Yes, Pa." He spurred the gelding. It jumped, then bolted—the two of them alone—toward the drovers and their rifles and the screams of cattle in the dust.

Mr. Cozad disappeared into the livery, bellowing, "Get my horse, get my horse."

Bobby galloped past Ezekiel, a boy eleven years old heading out to face the drovers entirely by himself. His eyes were white with fright, but his jaw jutting as if a jut could buck away fear.

Ezekiel began to run behind, as if pulled in the updraft of Bobby's horse. Bobby galloped directly into the herd, shouting, "Who is in charge?" He stopped then, his gelding sidling, blowing, throwing its head. A river of cattle surrounded him, their clattering horns, the blinding dust. "Who," he yelled, his voice gaining depth as if at that moment he was a man, not a boy. "Who's the head of this mess?"

"Who wants to know?" It was a short rider, wide and muscular. He held his rifle across himself, his hand on it, a Spencer. His fingers massaged the trigger.

"John Jackson Cozad," Bob said.

"You the Cozad who owns this place?" the fellow shouted. "You don't look old enough to be out of breeches."

Bobby did not look away. "You better be gone before he gets here."

"Who says?" the fellow yelled.

"His son, Robert Henry Cozad."

"Oh, I see John Jackson Cozad has to send his son to do his work." The herd milled. "Barely old enough to carry a gun." Two other drovers pressed around, two others rounding up strays, cutting them back into the herd. The herd was beginning to scatter along the railroad track, to pick at the little forage there; they were brittle-bone animals, starving. "Well, we just better be getting on into this little town, see what we can find."

Bob held up his hand. "You aren't going anywhere."

Mr. Cozad, rode up, then, followed by Mr. Atkinson, Traber Gatewood, David Claypool, Johnny Cozad, and Sam Schooley. They pressed in and stood beside Robert. All of them but Mr. Schooley carried rifles. Behind came the farm wagons for support, men dressed for church, hats brushed, suits pressed, some carrying rifles of their own.

Only one man tended the herd, now, one as thin as the cattle. Ezekiel stood away at the edge of the herd. The rider pushed into the cows coming Ezekiel's way. He was lost in dust for a moment, then reappeared. He rode loose, with easy grace as if part of his horse, his horse part of him. He drew closer, looking neither left nor right but only at Ezekiel. He seemed to have no more intent than to close the distance. The man's shoulders, his ears, the brim of his hat seemed to wash away the hard memory Ezekiel had clung to for so long. In its place the tenderness of a past where his ma hummed in the garden, where his pa whittled a stick and made a whistle for his son that tooted off tune, where strong arms lifted and threw him up and caught him again and together they laughed.

The rider rode straight toward him, sober.

There was no other being in the world, then; nothing or no one but remembrance of a time of soft summers and plenty and his parents' dim evenings, rides with his pa, the two of them sharing the saddle, his pa's arms around him trusted and trusting.

The rider made it through the herd, stopped half a foot from Ezekiel. The horse blew, threw its head.

Ezekiel had no voice, no words. His pa nodded, and Ezekiel willed him to lean down and scoop him up into the saddle. He did not think of the beltings that came later, the cruel rants. He did not smell the breath of whiskey. He imagined his pa as he once was, his warm strength as he leaned his son against his chest, as his arms wrapped around Ezekiel, and Ezekiel sat there happy, in spite of the discomfort of the saddle horn. It was not smoke, this figure, not a dream, and it was not Pa he became, the pa with the strop, the pa with the whiskey screams, the voice spitting out, "You're no good, nothing but a runt." This was his father, come back, he would see Ezekiel had grown, was stronger, able. He would see he had become a son he was proud of.

A whorl of dust covered them, got into Ezekiel's eyes. He coughed.

His pa raised up his lip, showed a disgusted scraggle of brown teeth. When the dust cleared out, his father leaned forward and spit and growled out, "Runt. Nothing but a runt." He touched the brim of his hat, then, clicked the horse and rode back to the herd.

Chapter 55

She came again, barefoot. He would never be able to describe how it was to have her there, how he had waited for it, how she jumbled his mind, how unable to think a clear thought, now that she was here.

The city was letting go of one season and tiptoeing into another. Some days rode in on humid mists, others in torrents blown on thunderheads. The rain was coming down in sheets. She carried her coat like a tent over her head. Her skirts swatted her calves, muddy and soaked. The streets ran wet, the cobbles shiny as fish scales, yet here she was, barefoot.

Her feet left wet prints as she slapped into the store. George had gone out to view a couple pieces from an artists' representative his family knew. In desperation, Ezekiel had sent a letter to Mrs. Reading's attorney saying that he wanted to meet with Mrs. Reading soon and that he was considering buying the building. The offer was no more than bluster, a delaying tactic. There were days when he could not even manage to eat.

Just that morning, George had swept a dramatic arm around the store and said, "We could use a bit of something fresh on the walls, something *today*." Ezekiel had not mentioned the letter about the sale to anyone, had not even hinted that the building, the rooms upstairs, the store, everything would soon be sold. He was failing, just as Totten knew he would. "Something Paris," George said.

Ezekiel's response was simple: "Don't promise terms."

She left a wet trail across the new wood floor. She leaned against the counter. "You don't look so good."

"Neither do you," he said.

"What's it to you, what I look like?" He pulled his mouth in. "You skinny," she said. Her bluntness, her quick gibe, left him wordless. He needed her, he knew that. But how ever could he deal with her? Her portraits could spell money, but association with her could just as well disaster. *He was afraid of her!*

Without good-bye or any other word, she left the store. He thought he had lost her again and the thought made him lightheaded. George came back half hour later, was working with a woman who had flounced in. She was well-dressed, with green stones at her throat Ezekiel knew were of quality. She had come in alone, unusual for women of her apparent class.

The sun had pushed through and the rain stopped, Ezekiel had opened the transoms to the air. Outside, pigeons had set up some pigeon chatter under the overhang of the roof, and Ezekiel was about to close up to quiet the noise. He took up the stick to reach the window hook just as the door banged open: Soap, this time carrying a dented bucket.

George's customer wore a huge, tilting green hat and a silk dress a color of pink so bright it made one blink. Everything about her attested to the fact she was not from Philadelphia's plain, conservative Quaker stock.

George did not know the woman, and Ezekiel had been listening to the manner in which he engaged her and brought her out. It was obvious she was someone whom George *should* know. When Soap thumped into the store, the conversation came to a sudden halt. They could not miss the crude violence of her entry or the smell of onions and spices wafting in from her bucket. Until then, the conversation had been lively. She said she had been recently to South America, where she had family in Argentina. George began guiding the conversation toward a painting on an easel by the door, an image of a girl and her red setter dog sitting under a summer tree. The girl wore a dress of aquamarine and was reading a book in her lap. The painter had caught the sun just as it was beginning to hit on the girl; it set a flush on the girl's face, the setter looked as if it were about to rise up and come for a petting. The customer went to it as George launched into some interesting history about the artist, who lived in Brittany.

It was there, in the magical light of the afternoon, with George making his light talk and grand gestures, that the customer introduced herself as Mrs. Wymberley Jones De Renne. Her diction was slow, drawn-out, rich, and very southern.

"From *Savannah*?" he asked.

She patted the ruffle at her throat. "Why yes."

"I heard you were in town."

"My heavens how?" Her delight was obvious.

"George Smith," he said and took the gloved fingers she offered. "Winthrop and I dined last evening with *Mr.* De Renne."

"I'll be," she said.

Ezekiel went to Soap, pulled her to a far wall as far away from George and his customer as he could take her. "What do you want?" Ezekiel whispered. He would have pulled her into the back, out of sight, if there did not seem to be something improper about it.

She set the bucket on the counter. "I brought you *food*," she said, "to eat. I pay you back, what you did."

He came around from behind the counter and gripped her elbow. "I don't…." The slop in her bucket sloshed. Mrs. De Renne tipped her head, amused. She said, "Well I must be off." And, as if feeling her comment too abrupt, she drawled out, "I did not re-alahz it was getting so late."

As she made her way out the door, Ezekiel opened his mouth to tell Soap to leave. But George blurted, "God, what delight is that filling my nose? Is it *bigos?* Why, I believe that might be *bigos*?"

"You know *bigos*?" Soap said. Where did she get *food? How* did she get it? It had to be stolen.

"Do I know *bigos!*" George said. She tugged against Ezekiel's grasp on the bucket. More of it slopped. "I had the best *bigos* in my life in *Vashava*."

"You know Warsaw?" She pronounced it heavily. *Where did the smile come from?* Ezekiel had never seen her smile. It lit her face. It was lovely. She would not let go the bucket. With her free hand, she pointed at her chest. "Me," she said, "Mariska Sophia Dibrowski, from Warsaw."

"You are from *Poland?*" George said as if this were the most intriguing news of the year.

"Yah, Polska." She thumbed her chest "Me."

Ezekiel laid his hand on Soap's back, gave some force to it. He wanted her, but he did not want her this way; this way embarrassed him. He wanted a different version of her, a cleaned up, decently dressed version. "Wait outside," he said.

She jerked away. "I go," she said and began skulking streetward, holding the bucket in two hands as if it had suddenly gotten heavier.

"Don't let me interrupt," George said. "It's about time for me to get myself home." He stepped around Ezekiel, came back with his hat. He put it on his head, patted it down. The sun was just slipping behind Independence Hall. "You take care of that *bigos*."

Ezekiel could feel the heat rise from her.

And then, as if from some divine cue, Prune rustled in.

George said, "Mrs. Hume."

Prune answered, "George."

"That lady," Soap said. To Ezekiel's dismay, Soap held out a filthy hand to Prune. "You still want that pitcher painted?"

Chapter 56

Things were happening so fast he could not grasp any of it. He was certain now that his aunt had been keeping an eye on the store. She swept Soap into her arms, causing soup to leap from the bucket. When Prune finally pulled back, Soap's eyes were wet. "Oh, dear," his aunt said, "I wondered if I would ever see you again."

"Me, too, lady," Soap said.

His aunt seemed to gain her composure and took Soap's hand. "Oh my," she said, "I do gush. I don't think I have ever heard your name, dear. I'm Prudence Hume."

Soap wiped her palm on her skirt, then, as if suddenly shy, just gave a little nod. An introduction seemed inevitable. "Aunt Prune," Ezekiel said. "This is Mariska Sophia Dibrowski."

"Soap," she said. She threw her head his way. "He calls me Soap."

Prune barked out a laugh as open as a mare's. "Soap," she said, "how lovely. He calls me Prune."

Soap looked at Ezekiel, her eyes glittering in a way he had never seen.

"I have so admired your painting of Mr. and Mrs. Pettygrove's sweet daughter," Prune said.

"You seen it?"

"Why yes," Prune said. "It is in their home, you know."

"You been in their place?"

"Of course, dear." As if it were the most natural thing in the world. "Often I have asked my nephew and Mrs. Pettygrove where you went, but neither of them seemed to know. And I could never make Mr. Pettygrove divulge where he found you."

The cherries bled from Soap's face. She squinted as if some part of his aunt were suspect, all of a sudden. It was a wicked squint, prepared to strike if something came up lacking.

"I suppose," Prune said, "he wanted to keep you and your talent all to himself."

"Yah," Soap said, all hint of warmth gone. Her tone had turned hard, rough as a rasp and her face dark again. "You got a kid need painting?"

Prune held up three delighted fingers. "Three."

Chapter 57

Summer came with a glee that mocked the blizzard three months ago. It was as if the storm had never existed. The breezes whispered. The park elms grew luscious. The farmers' carts along Chestnut sold straight and perfect rhubarb, tender lettuces, radishes, carrots, and enormous beetroot. The fish monger's stand swelled with sardines, and lobsters writhed in his tank. Ezekiel should have been happy—or at least relieved.

His fears about Prune and Soap had been toothless. She wanted three paintings and did not seem to even notice the girl's grimy disarray, only tittered on about her precious grandchildren and how to get their portraits done while the children spent a few weeks with her. The paintings were to be a surprise. Totten was not supposed to find out. Her plans to keep him in the dark were convoluted: She wanted the sittings to be at their house and done while he was gone during the day. She held Soap's hand as she extracted the promise of secrecy, then fell apart when she wondered how to keep the children from letting it out.

Soap had wanted to be in on the negotiation, but Ezekiel insisted things would go better if he spoke to his aunt alone, particularly since he was a businessman and knew best how this kind of discussion went. When Soap was finally gone, Ezekiel and his aunt discussed price. In the end, she offered double what he would have thought to ask, and George insisted the paintings be hung in the store, on loan and display for a time, once they were done.

But, as lucrative as his aunt's deal was, Ezekiel was not happy or even relieved. A sense of desperation sidled in the quiet of night when dawn had yet to bring out the nags and the trolley. The nights sometimes carried his mother to him, and she carried on her what he was missing. She had always felt life was sustained on soil—not of the sort that got itself under one's nails or the filth at the hem of a skirt but the kind of turned, weeded, wetted, fertile stuff she planted in her garden. His ma's soil had been a place of wet perfumes where seeds flourished and took root and produced. She had believed in soil, had cared for it, and had known it would take care of them. There was no soil in his life, now, but for a few meager parks a city had little of it, and its fecundity was buried and barren under structures, cobblestones, and boardwalks and never thought of other than dirt. His mother saw hope in dirt, she saw life and succor. His mother would have taken to Soap.

He thought he had slept but could not be sure of it. He opened his eyes to the blind night, spread his hands before his face but could not see them. No sound came to him but the rustle of his own movement. It was then, in the absence, that clarity came.

He crawled from his mattress, grappled for his robe. He struck a match, held it to the lamp. And he took himself in the shimmering shadow to the office. He pulled up the old chair and opened the books.

Chapter 58

Sebastian Fennet sat at the same homely desk, in front of the same homely window that looked onto the clutter of an iron fire ladder. But one thing was clear: Fennet's law business seemed to be doing better. He was wearing a new suit, modest but new. Near the door was a new desk at which a clerk sat tapping away at a writing machine.

Ezekiel told Fennet what he wanted: a deal to buy the building from the Reading widow. He knew it was a very long chance. Less than a few hours before, he had sat in his moldering office reviewing figures he could recite and now as if they were tattooed onto his palm. He had read the books countless times yet never *truly* saw what was in them until before sunrise this morning. He had known there was the store, of course, but upstairs there were also the rooms, three stories of them, twenty-one rooms in all, filled with tenants, each paying rent that the Readings had not adjusted for a decade.

"I want you to write a letter offering to buy the building." He told Fennet what he was willing to pay and Fennet's eyebrows shot up. It was low, Ezekiel knew that, but not unreasonable. "The letter should say something about the property's needing vast modernization, like electrification, before it could be sold to anyone else. I also want to say that the property is decrepit, and, because of the improvements I made when I repaired the damage done by the storm, I will not pay anything up front."

"Do you have anything to put down, if they do not agree?"

"No," Ezekiel said.

"In the agreement you signed when you leased, you were responsible for repairs."

"I know, but say it anyway, and say I want an answer immediately."

"How immediately?"

"In the next two days."

Since leaving Fennet's office, he had not been able to eat nor even think of food. He knew, with every hour that passed, how hopeless it was and how much anyone would see him the fool for even thinking of the deal. He finally thought he had armed himself with the inevitability of the situation; there was no chance the widow would take his offer, that he put too much hope in the outcome. But still, if he were someone who prayed, he would be praying right now.

When George came in later, he asked, "You all right, old man? You look like you had a bit too much of the dog last night."

"The dog?"

"The joyful nectar." Ezekiel knew what George meant. "You know what I do for a remedy?" He didn't wait for Ezekiel's response. "I take myself out to O'Doherty's just up the street and sip some of their good proof. It always works for me."

"I have work," Ezekiel said. He had never even sipped whiskey; he had seen what it had done to his pa.

The widow's response came by courier. He took it to his office, closed the door. He laid it on the desk and wiped his palms on his pants. He knew what was in it: some lawyer's smarmy language saying Ezekiel should go to hell. But, until he opened it, the store was still his. When the store was no longer his, he had no idea what would come of him; he had no other plan but to take himself down to the docks and get himself work if he could find it.

He wiped his brow. He could not stand still, so he marched in place. He had an urge to soil himself.

He must have moaned and George had heard it. "You all right in there, Ezekiel?" It was the first George had called him by his given name.

"Yes," he said. It had been two days since he had eaten. He felt sick, but there was nothing to come up. Yet he had to put his hand over his mouth.

Then came the calm and the peace in abject hopelessness. He slipped his finger under the flap and tore open the letter.

> *Dear Mr. Harrington,*
>
> *Enclosed please find documents pertaining to your offer of the twenty-fifth. In them you will find they require you to forgo all and any interest, partnership, claim you made previously with Mr. Nestor Reading.*
>
> *If you do not agree to the terms detailed herein, you must vacate the property on, or before, one week from today.*
>
> *Since there will be no intermediate lender, if sums are not received as agreed at any time until the terms are satisfied, you will immediately forfeit any and all previous agreements, as well as forfeit any claim, partnership, or ownership in the property or its contents.*
>
> *If you agree to these terms, the enclosed agreement must be signed and in my hands by close of the business day tomorrow.*
>
> *M. John Edgars, Attorney at Law*

His legs no longer held. He slid down the wall, collapsed onto the floor and began rifling the pages. When he could calm the rattling in his skull, he began to make sense of it. In fine, squinting print, the pages spelled out "Agreement Purchase and Sale of Real Property."

The building was his.

Chapter 59

The Hume coach pulled up, consuming the north window as if it owned it. Ezekiel watched as the driver knotted the rein, got down from his seat, came around, and opened the door. His aunt took the driver's hand, and they labored, together, up the stairs.

The morning was clear, and George would not likely be in for some time. His hours at the store were becoming irregular, an irregularity that seemed to depend on what had been going on in his life the night before. Ezekiel knew little about George, other than the time they spent together at work and that he was one of the Smiths. One day, in passing, he had mentioned he was seeing someone, but Ezekiel did not ask for details, for details were too personal, and closeness might have clouded their working habit.

His aunt leaned on the arm of her driver. She could easily have been the one escorting him, for his face was an old man's face, eyes hammocked, face pulled down like a hound's. When they came in, Prune was giddy, giggling, chirping like a bird. "Oh, our girl is supposed to meet me here in a few minutes. Joseph will drive us out to get her settled for her stay," she clapped her hands at her chins, "while she begins painting the children." Her face shone like a gaslight. She said she had found a room, somewhere near their house, where Soap could stay and use as a studio for the month she was painting. It was a complicated arrangement: The grandchildren were staying with their grandmother and grandfather while their parents went on holiday to a summer home the Hume's had recently built in Wyncote.

The grandchildren's portraits were to be set in the gardens in back of the Humes' house. In the mornings, after Totten left for work, Soap would come to the house, set up the children in a hidden part of the garden, out of Totten's sight. And she would paint. Ezekiel's ears rang with the chatter and made him dizzy.

For all this, she was to be paid one hundred and fifty dollars and Ezekiel would garner three hundred and fifty. It was a terribly high price. He'd expected his aunt to counter when he asked for it. How, Ezekiel wondered, could his aunt hide such an enormous amount from her husband?

Prune seemed more than her usual excited. She sang out to Joseph that he could go and wait by the coach; she would wave him in when it was time to go. Her face flamed as if she were hot, though the morning was cool, heat yet only a potential. "Oh, I am so excited," she said. "I just can't believe how fortunate we are to have this girl come into our lives. Aren't we, sweetheart?" *Sweetheart?* She was calling him sweetheart. It embarrassed him, yet there was a small salve to it he would not acknowledge.

Soap came in, then, smelling of jitters and sweats. She wore an ancient brown sweater with pockets crammed so full, the sweater was beginning to rip. She was laden like a mule with an easel, rags, a duffel, a drawstring sack tied to her belt. In her hand she carried a bristle of brushes. "Oh, my," Prune said. "I'll get Joseph to help." She went to the door and yoo-hooed, "Jo-seph."

Soap seemed to have made some effort to clean up. Her hair was neat and knotted in a band tight enough to pull back her face. Under the sweater, she wore a clean skirt that had no holes in it but was too long and dragged on the floor so she had to splay her legs and tick-tick side to side, to walk.

His aunt came back with Joseph, who took an armload of Soap's stuff and jangled out the door with it. Prune pecked Ezekiel a good-bye then opened a beaded purse tied onto her wrist. She laid a roll of money on the counter—her down payment. Soap and Joseph loaded into the coach and

Prune rustled out of the store and they were off.

Chapter 60

With the change in the weather, business began to pick up, though not enough to cover all his expenses, now that he was paying on the building. He raised the rents upstairs and lost three tenants because of it. It took nearly a month to fill the rooms. He had not only George to pay now but a housekeeper for the upkeep on the upstairs. She had begun complaining there was too much work and that he should hire her daughter to work as well.

He was getting to know George but only in meted bits. He seemed to belong to every social list in the city—the Rittenhouse Club, the Philadelphia Club, even the Cricket and Barge Clubs. He spoke rarely of his own family, and only then if he had been out late the night before and was still somewhat tipsy when he came in. He had grown up in a three-story house in Rittenhouse Square and had spent most of his youth in England, Germany, and France, schooled by a succession of nannies and tutors. He had never been married and still lived by himself somewhere not far from the store. He seemed to know everyone in the city who counted: Edwin H. Fitler, the mayor, the Bodine family, the Ingersoll's, the Drexel's, anyone in the social register.

It was odd for someone like George to work as an employee. The sorts of families that sprouted men like George did not need to work. Something else drove him, something Ezekiel could not quite understand. Because of George, the store had undergone a complete change; its shelves were bare of stationery, there wasn't a calendar in sight, nor did the old press in back ever shrug off its covering. He could use the space the press took up but sometimes worried he might need it again. If he could hold on, in another three years, he could wave his success under the nose of his uncle.

The store had been open an hour. He was alone when the bell dinged. He got up from his desk, straightened his tie and took a deep breath. He went out. It was Bob, his composure lost in an excitement Ezekiel could feel. "Hey, Easy old man. He trotted to the counter, slapped a paper on it. "You got to come!" He gave the paper a tap. *Grand Exhibition. Grand paintings. Excellent sculptures. Best in the world.* "Tomorrow. Academy," he blurted and turned toward the door. "Sorry, Ease, have to get these to the papers. Big news. See you there."

In the overwrought Academy building, laughter brought the place some heart. The merriment was high and loud, coming in waves, nervous and forced. A great deal of work and thought had gone into the art displays, the walls were filled with it. But the paintings were hung inexpertly, most too high and clustered in ragged, disheveled groups. Sculptures were put in an ill-lit section in back that patrons had to walk some distances to see. He wondered what George would have done with all of it. Would George even have come to an event like this one? Probably not. George would have found the art too staid, too predictable, too unpretty.

Bob came up from behind. "Good to see you, Ease," he said, as if he had been waiting. Redfield joined in and, together, they ushered Ezekiel around the room, discussing the merits of every piece. "Great show, isn't it?" Bob said. But to Ezekiel's eye the things here seemed dim and premature. Ezekiel nodded, but knew it was perfunctory. He stopped before a painting of Redfield's, a gentle and appealing landscape.

Had Bob's hand not been laid on Ezekiel's shoulder, he might have moved on. "Wissahickon Creek. I did them this spring." Ezekiel felt the weight of expectation, the burden of his response. He cleared his throat. "Good work," he said.

"Golly, Ease. From you, that's something."

The exhibition made it to the newspapers—most with critical and tepid reviews. *The Public Ledger* wrote of Bob, "R. E Henri shows several characteristic landscape sketches, which might be worked up into clever pictures." Bob must have seen them. How would he take the reports? Before Ezekiel could find out, classes let out, and Bob fled town for the summer.

Chapter 61

One morning, George did not show. He sent no word.

It was a heavy day: dark, thundering, pouring one minute, sun blaring on wet streets the next. George had taken in several high-priced pieces: an engraving by Thomas Cole, a painting by Jasper Cropsey, another by an English painter by the name of John George Brown, whom George had met some time ago in New York.

Mr. John Dahlgren came in, said he wanted to view the Brown painting on George's recommendation. Dahlgren was a thin-necked fellow who wore thick spectacles, and whose hair was fashioned with such precision it seemed glued on his head. He huffed when Ezekiel told him George Smith was not there. "He said he would be. Where is he?"

The price on the painting was hefty, nearly six hundred dollars, and showed the image of several tattered boys clustered together, talking. Ezekiel had paid a hundred and fifty for it outright, on George's recommendation. The sum nearly made him choke. The painting was a bit precious, George said, even with the rough boys portrayed in it. "But someone'll go for it. This kind of thing always has someone willing to put down a few hundred. The sale will be a good one." Then he added, "If it sells."

Here was a good mark, and damn it, George wasn't here. Ezekiel said, "George said you might be in and asked if I might show it to you." It was a lie, the best he could come up with at that moment. "We may have a sale on this already, a family was here earlier." Another lie. "They stepped out just minutes ago."

It seemed to spur Dahlgren. "Who?"

"I wouldn't be able to divulge that, certainly," Ezekiel said.

"Let me see it again."

Ezekiel pulled the painting from the wall, placed it on the easel by the window. Dahlgren stood with his hands in his pockets, chest out, and making pup-pups with his lips. "Well, I think George Smith is a little bit pickled," he said. "Let the somebody else have it."

He left the store. Ezekiel was certain George would have closed the sale and would have had Dahlgren dancing out with the painting. But, God, where was he?

As the day went on, it started to weigh on him that George had never been this late coming in, and, as the hours crept by, he began to image he might never see George again, that George had disappeared like everybody in his life seemed to. If George left, what would he do? His stomach went sour, his jaws ached. He began to realize how much he leaned on George, just as he had counted on the Hainsworths—and where were the Hainsworths now? Gone.

But then, the next morning, George appeared again, his face was bloated, his nose swollen, his breath reeking and sour. He said nothing about the previous day's absence.

As summer wore on, George's absences became more frequent. They normally came on Mondays. He would come in Tuesday, bleary and out of sorts, and would go to the back of the store, retrieve a flask from an inside pocket of his suit and drink it dry. He would then suck mints until customers began coming in.

Even as the city sweated, Ezekiel's business continued to creep up. But he could not trust it. He often left the shop to George for a bit, to wander and take in new storefronts and construction. Sometimes he passed by clusters of dark people along the streets. Their clothes would be rough, soiled, patched sometimes, left torn other times. They would be speaking—shouting really—in some tongue full of hisses and wet mists. He stood looking among them until they turned away or raised their fists at him. Were these her people? Would their hovels smell of stale meats and cabbage?

The Fourth of July came on a Thursday. By the following Monday, there seemed to be no one left in town. In the space of three days, the city died; every last picnic swag of bunting and blat from the parades was history. Families sailed to Europe, or drifted out to summer homes, or to the shore leaving the limp city to fry without them. If the building was "his," why was he beginning to feel otherwise? Where was the solid comfort he should have by now, knowing he was eking his way, making a success in the world, no matter how illusory? Where was the heady pride? How had he been so naïve? Had Totten ever felt the same ponderous doubt? Ezekiel thought not; Totten had come from a family of some wealth. Had Bob ever felt this? Bob whose father was rich enough to buy up forty-three thousand acres of Nebraska? *Forty-thee thousand acres!* Whom did Ezekiel come from? A pa who failed at everything he dreamed of, a ma who died holding things together. He envied and hated others for the ease of their lives. He had no one but himself.

The city squatted in sodden heat. As the summer went on, Ezekiel scraped his pen on checks to pay his bills and hunkered under the vagaries of weeks without sales and doubts about George.

He knew he had to do something to bolster sales. So many paintings came in bare and unframed. He began thinking he could cadge a high enough price to make a good margin on frames. He decided to set up a frame shop in back and hire a framer.

He spent money to advertise and hired a carpenter two days a week. The carpenter came in early and did his sawing and hammering, then turned to sanding and applying of solvents. Everything affected the store's potential to make a sale: the light in which a picture was displayed, the level at which one viewed it, and now the frame in which it was set. He learned to listen when George dictated which molding and what decoration would enhance or kill a painting's potential. He came to understand that a frame was not simply a frame, something to put around a painting, but an extension of the art itself. And, if it were done right, a frame could sell a mediocre piece, but done wrong it could kill the sale of a masterpiece. When George said a molding would not do for a work, that it needed plaster and to be leafed with gold, Ezekiel sent out to have one made of plaster and gold-leafed.

The back room was being consumed by lumber and tools and dustings of oak, pine, rosewood, and maple. It grew almost impossible to breathe. Ezekiel slept in the dust, his nostrils filled with fine shavings and sandings. He wheezed all night, sucking for each whistling breath. He knew he had to find somewhere else to sleep.

Chapter 62

Ezekiel saw neither his aunt nor Soap until mid-July. The city was suffering, overtaken most afternoons by showers that brought a few minutes' relief and left in their wake hot, steaming misery.

The Humes' brougham carriage seemed to appear nearly everywhere. Its tired driver, its too-red color, its gilded doors, its too-heavy lace curtains showed up among the stores, sat for hours in front of the bank, at the Philadelphia Club, in the line of assorted carriages at Wanamaker's, at Strawbridge and Clothier. It was here now, pulled in front, with Joseph handing Prune down. The wind whipped Prune's bonnet, and she grabbed it. When she was safely planted aground, she shoved the bonnet back and, as the wind brought it to life, struggled to tighten the bow under her chins.

Joseph reached up to take the hand of another passenger, a small woman wearing a light and fitted coat. She wore no bonnet. *Where was Soap?* Her dark hair was swept high in a lump at the crown of her head. Her skirts whipped against her hips and her thighs. She was very small, with a wasp's tiny middle.

Joseph crawled onto coach and began to untie something from the rack on top. He tucked the package under his arm and followed Prune up the steps. Her girth had grown so she obscured most of the doorway. She stuck her head in and trilled, "Yoo-hoo," as if Ezekiel weren't standing ten feet away. Joseph wrestled the flat package through the door. The other woman had not made it in, yet, and was having trouble keeping her skirt at bay with the wind. Joseph laid the package on the counter.

Prune leaned forward, cupped her mouth. "Oh hurry, Joseph, I can't wait for my nephew to see." The other woman was just then making her way in. The wind caught the door and it flew out of her hand, banged the wall, sent the glass rattling. She reached for it. The wind whipped her hair, pulled strands from the pins. She managed to close the door as a whorl of detritus blew up from the street. Soap.

It caught him, then, seeing her as if for the first time. Had he seen her on the street, he might even have taken a second look. Her fine dress didn't suit her. And as much as he had condemned the mess of the earlier her, he was not sure he liked this change at all; it and its acceptability took something from her, dimmed her. He nodded to her, she did not nod back,

Joseph made a racket with the wrappings, revealed first the contents of one painting, then made more commotion as he undid another. Ezekiel could smell the residue of fresh solvent off the canvas, the soft wafting up of linseed. He could also smell the honey sweet of a horehound on George's breath.

George took the canvas, an image of a baby in a white wicker perambulator surrounded by yellow and red and white roses. The child bore a sweet expression. Ezekiel could not recall the child's name.

No one spoke. Prune stood patting her brow; even she was uncommonly silent. George held the painting at arm's length, made a click with his tongue. He set it on a shelf behind the counter. Joseph unwrapped the second painting, depicting Cornelius' older boy, nearly seven. George took it, set it beside the first. The last was of a baby, three years old. George put it with the others, each facing toward the afternoon light.

Finally, Prune erupted. "Aren't they just," she clapped her hands under her chins, "*beautiful?*"

No one would have described them as anything but beautiful. They seemed nearly magic, done rough in places, a rose not much more than a splat of color, a garden bench merely suggested, done as if with no thought to any part of them. But the children's faces were not rough, each lip, each eye, ear and lash a finished study and highlighted with whites so clear life seemed to throb from them.

"God," George blurted. Another woman might have taken offense. Prune did not. She stood with her hands under her chins, as in prayer, her face oiled and pink. Soap had worked some kind of magic. In all three canvases, the children's expressions and a chemistry of their poses and colors seemed to shout the kind of people they would grow up to be. One *knew* each child. The middle child, the three-year-old, spoke intelligence, caution, and intensity. A *three-year-old*, for God's sake. That child would grow up to be a man exactly like Ezekiel and probably one whom he would not trust. The older boy was dressed in a stylish suit, an imitation of a man's. He stood with his hand on his hip, his flank flat and lean, and his hair combed in a sweep to the side. The image shouted that he would grow into someone entitled, selfish, and beautiful. And the baby in her white buggy, would be loved, trusting and sweetly deserving.

"You did good, little sister," George said.

Prune put her arm around Soap's shoulder, pulled her in. "Isn't she something?"

"Lord," George said. "Soap, my dear, where did you come from?"

She blushed. "Ain't funny," she said.

Ezekiel said, "We have just the frames."

Chapter 63

It had been months since Redfield was in the store. He was wearing a summer suit of cotton worn thin. Humidity hung in the air so dense it was visible. The collar was stained, and he toted a satchel that obviously carried canvases. He and Ezekiel shook hands and made small talk, though neither was particularly good at it. Ezekiel wished George were here to break the ice. But he'd gone out to look at some work at an art representative's he knew. The representative had said the works were from France.

Bob had been gone all summer. Ezekiel wanted to ask Redfield about him, but pride kept him from it. It could not be long before Bob was back; classes would begin in another week.

Redfield said he had taken a room near the Academy for the year. He seemed nervous, his handshake damp and cool, in spite of the heat. Where he was usually rough-spoken, tactless with his honesty, leaving niceties to others, now he was making a try at holding up his end of the conversation. He set his satchel on the floor and began to unwrap what he had brought. "It's not much," he said. "Was hoping you'd take a look at them." He chattered, anxious. It was not like him. "Nothing much but Bucks County where my family lives." A damp shank of bang stuck to his forehead. "Am afraid I'm going to have to do a hell of a lot of work to get anybody to look at it."

One by one he held the canvases up. They were large landscapes of farms, hills, and trees, and they were lovely. "It's all from around home," he said. He broke a laugh. "I don't get around much." He carried on as if afraid of Ezekiel's judgment. "I don't know if any of them's worth putting up."

Ezekiel said, "All."

Redfield put his hand to his mouth and coughed. "Didn't think so."

"I'll make room for all," Ezekiel said.

"Golly, you would?" was all Redfield could come up with.

Ezekiel began discussing terms. He would not buy them but offered consignment. Redfield bargained well. As eager as he was, he was not willing to give his work away. Others from the Academy would practically pay to have their work displayed. It made Ezekiel respect Redfield.

"They need to be framed," Ezekiel said and told him a price.

Redfield said, "Lord, Easy at that rate, I'd do them myself if I had the time. Damn, I should be in the gallery business." He laughed, and Ezekiel laughed with him.

Ezekiel brought the canvases behind the counter, leaned them against the wall. "You hear anything from Bob lately?"

"Just did," Redfield said. "You'll never guess." He paused, then said, "He's leaving."

"Leaving?"

"For Europe."

"Europe?"

"A bunch of them went already, you know. I'm planning to head over there myself if I can manage it."

Ezekiel blurted, "He's getting back in time for class, of course."

Redfield shook his head. "Henri, Haefeker, Finney, Fisher, and Grafly, all those creeps sailed yesterday. Going to study in Pairee the whole next year."

"The whole next year," Ezekiel said.

Chapter 64

As summer ended, families returned to the city. Ezekiel had not seen Soap again since the day with Prune. He had asked her where he could get in touch with her, and she had replied only, "Around."

The month Prune had agreed to let him display the paintings was up. Someone would be picking them up tomorrow. George had hung them in the windows, each with a SOLD sign. They had drawn people in like nothing else ever had. Sometimes people waited in line to inquire about them, wanting something painted for themselves. Ezekiel had had to dodge and dance around answers, could only take cards, and make up a list, saying he would get back to them later.

George was out touring the artists' studios and speaking with "his people." He brought in some promising pieces but constantly asked if Ezekiel had seen Soap again.

Ezekiel searched the streets for her, ambled through the neighborhoods where the tenements, immigrants, whores, and Negroes lived, and where filthy women stood in front of doorways smoking cigars and eyeing him as he passed by. Some made comments, some made kisses and gestured with their hips.

———

In the fall, a card came from France. It bore a fancy stamp of a rooster crowing. The image on the card was a colored photo of a wide boulevard lined with trees. People strolled on that boulevard, men in dandies' suits and women in fancy dresses and parasols. Bob's writing on the back was scratched in a hurry:

Paint every morning. Class with Bougereau (more damn plaster busts). Out on our own till 3. Back in studio until dark. Grafly getting some good sketches. I continue to dirty fingers with charcoal. Paris salons show some strange stuff by the fellas Van Gogh, Pissaro, Cezanne. They won't last. The French call me Ro-bear On-hree. Hold down old Philly for me.

Bobby

Ezekiel was at his desk. The doors would not open for business for another hour. The wheezing had not gotten better; lately, he was finding it even harder to catch a breath. The framer was out, had gone to the lumberman's to order a fine grade of walnut in which to carve a frame for a work the Ingersoll's had ordered, a work on paper by a painter named Achille Emperaire. The study had been sent to George by a friend in Paris, and he had sold it to the Charles Ingersolls the day it came in.

Ezekiel's quiet moments at his desk were few now; the carpenter's din started before the doors opened, then George usually sauntered in and put up his hubba hubba throughout the rest of the day. Even when there was no one in the store but him, a constant trail of painters and sculptors and glassblowers came in, bringing in their stuff to show.

Ezekiel knew sawdust and sanding grit were causing the problem with his lungs. He had to sleep somewhere else, even if it meant evicting a paying tenant upstairs in order to take himself away from the dust. Some days, he yearned for the way it used to be, when he worked for a steady, predictable paycheck. He envied the framer's carefree life, his going home every evening with a day's pay in his pocket and carrying none of the weight and responsibility of holding things together.

He heard the key in the front lock, expected the framer to wander in. He had worked a couple months, and Ezekiel still was having difficulty remembering the fellow's name. Was it Hansell Steven or Steven Hansell? He was a colorless fellow, hair light brown, complexion sallow, and he wore a yellow-beige suit that rendered him nearly invisible. Hansell, that was it, Hansell Steven, alphabetical.

The door jingled closed, the bolt clicked. Ezekiel could tell who it was by cough and the rattle of phlegm. Why so early? George normally did not come through the door until near noon. He coughed again. "Hail, fellow," he said. It sounded as if he were holding his hands around his mouth. Why such heartiness? Normally George's joviality was reserved for the occasional male patron he knew from one of his clubs.

He came right into the office, dropped himself into the extra chair. His voice was liquid, his top lip puffy. "I have some great"—he belched—"news." His breath bore the sour taint of last night's liquor. Ezekiel laid down his pen, closed the checkbook. George leaned back in his chair, wove his fingers behind his head. "I'm going to France," George said. Ezekiel's gut felt as if it had been punched. "With a friend, for a couple of months."

Ezekiel collapsed forward, threw his elbows onto his desk. "When?"

"Have booked passage on the *Caland* in two weeks. You and I have some work to do before I go." George loosened his collar, let out his debauchery of chins. "You have to circulate while I'm gone."

"Circulate?"

"We have to get you into the clubs." *Clubs? Him?* George could have been speaking Chinese or African for the sense it made. "I made us reservations at the Rittenhouse. Couldn't get them to let you in down at the Philadelphia."

Circulate. God. "When?"

"Tomorrow."

Their reservations were for eleven-fifteen. The framer would be in at his regular time, then keep the doors open until Ezekiel and George returned.

Ezekiel had barely slept, wondering what kind of a fool he would make of himself at the club. He had no idea how to circulate, and the thought of trying to converse, it had made his skin prickle and sweat the entire night.

They left half an hour early. Ezekiel wore the coat he had bought the day before, special for today. It was second-hand but of good quality and very close to a good fit. He wore a muffler and a hat, though George went bare-headed. The winds picked up bits in the streets and thrust them between his teeth and into his eyes. In the parks, the trunks of the trees swayed and their branches flailed. The nights had grown cool, though real cold was yet to come. George had broken out his lightweight wool suit. a gabardine that once might have been dashing but that shone slick at the seat and elbows. It still had last year's spot on the lapel. It was rumpled, needed pressing, and a good cleaning, the sort of careless dress only the old rich could get away with. Under the suit he wore a fresh shirt.

They had worked together for a bit more than two years now. Despite it all, the partnership had been good. George could not have survived in business on his own, could not have balanced accounts, could never have kept a job or operated a business and made a go of it. Ezekiel was aware he could not have stayed in business without George and had come to suspect George's family had cut him off. He also suspected George spent every nickel Ezekiel paid him on drink and craps. He liked craps, he said, and used the word often as if he enjoyed the crude sound of it. Ezekiel also suspected that the friend George was traveling with was from a wealthy New York family George had spoken of recently and was paying for them both to go to France.

In the months that had passed since summer, Ezekiel tried not to think of Soap, but often found himself catching a shadow in dark doorways, or a woman in filthy skirts, or a wisp of dark hair. He never envisioned her as he had seen her last, in the tailored suit his aunt had bought her. The suit had seemed more a costume, just like the dress Pettygrove gave her, something she donned because it conformed to what someone else thought she should be.

The newspapers were awash with the elections: Cleveland against Harrison. All season the illustrators and pundits on each side had accused each other of fraud. Fuel was added to the fire when Harrison won the electoral vote and Cleveland the popular. The papers were also filled with the gruesome murders of a killer they labeled "Jack the Ripper." Newsboys could not keep stocked, the gore, the illustrations of women dying in agony from slit throats, half-dressed, blood gushing sold the papers before the ink was dry. Just that day, London police thought they might have another victim on their hands; her name was Mary Jane Kelly.

Bob was still in Europe. Ezekiel heard from him now and then, a card that told nothing but how the light fell on Marseilles, or how the gardens of Paris practically begged to be painted. Sometimes he exclaimed about artists whose work he found "fantastic"; sometimes he complained angrily about his current instructor, the fellow named Bouguereau who, Bob had come to see, was "trapped" in the conventions as much as anyone back there at the Academy. Redfield had left town in the fall and had joined Bob in Paris. The latest card from Bob said he and Redfield were heading out to Monte Carlo, then would see what there was to see in Rome and Florence. Ezekiel was beginning to detest the very idea of Europe.

He'd finally moved his mattress to a space upstairs that had once served as a maid's closet. He could not make himself take over a room bringing in cash. His mattress took up the entire floor, the closet had no windows, and for his clothes three nails he pounded up on which to hang them. Someone else may have found such a place hard to breathe in, let alone sleep, but its walled-in closeness felt safe.

He was going to miss George. George's influence on the store had been good; Ezekiel was beginning to accumulate a small reserve of cash. He had even allowed the door to open to the dream he might own the building outright in a few years and had begun to dream of buying a house for himself someday, even opening another gallery in Chestnut Hill, right under his uncle's nose. *Hah.* He took a pencil to it; opening another store would be expensive, would need a signed lease. He could not be in two places at once; he would need to pay someone to run it. He ached for what it would show his uncle. The ache kept him awake night after night.

Nothing would come of his dreams if this store didn't grow. The piddling amount he was laying away was too little, even if he continued to get by on one meal a day and to cramp himself and his mattress in the maid's closet, and dress in second-hand clothes from the church bins. *What if George went to Europe and never came back? What then?* It hinged on George. He could do it if George returned and if he could find some way to bring in more money. *What if George left and didn't come back?*

George hailed a cab to the club; he didn't want to walk, though it would have done him good. He looked as if he had had no sleep, his nose a strawberry, his face puffy, and his hands, eyes, and chin bloated. He said he had spent the night before with his new friend, the fellow who would accompany him to Europe. Ezekiel reached into his pocket to pay for the cab, but George laid his hand on Ezekiel's and shook his head. "A trotter paid out last night," he said. "Let me."

As the hansom made it through traffic, George spoke of the club warmly, as if it were home. It might as well have been: George's family, his father, grandfather and three brothers had belonged since it began. Sometimes he still called it the "Social," though it had been called the "Rittenhouse" for a decade and a half.

Ezekiel grew more and more nervous as they proceeded, needed to think of something else. "Where will you stay in Paris?" The question was perhaps the most intimate he had ever put to George, and it served merely as a self-serving distraction now.

George cleared his throat. "My old friend Jackie," he said, "wants to introduce me to someone who owns a home on Boulevard Des Capucines." He cleared his throat again as if uncomfortable. Ezekiel had thought George was going to Paris with someone he knew in New York but now he was not sure; people seemed to come and go in George's life by the day or the week. "The building is one of the glorious Baron Haussmanns," he said, as if Ezekiel had any idea what that meant, and he looked out the window and went quiet. George had mentioned Jackie before. They had known each other for most of their lives. She was responsible for sending him the artwork from France that George sold at the store.

They were coming on to the neighborhood that lay between Broad Street and the Schuylkill, the homes spelling the addresses of the richest and oldest families in the city, names that spilled out of George's mouth like poetry. Ezekiel felt as if he were somewhere else looking in on himself, seeing the poor, small man he was, a man who, in truth, desired nothing more than stability from others, people he could trust, predictable sorts whom he could count on one day to the next. Mingle. He had no idea how one mingled. George was right; he needed to learn to hobnob. The prospect made him want to vomit.

The cab pulled into Rittenhouse Square, rounded it and joined the lineup of coaches and broughams in front of the club. Ezekiel had walked by the club over the years; everyone, it seemed, did. Tourists and the lower class openly ogled its protrusions, bays and porticoes that set it apart and whispered *not allowed.*

George paid the cab driver, slouched toward the stairway half a step ahead of Ezekiel. A doorman held open the door, saying, "Good afternoon, Mr. Smith."

"Louis," George said.

Louis said, "Vincent will have your table ready"—he pulled a watch from his vest—"in fifteen minutes."

Ezekiel's throat constricted: a crowd, particularly this one where everyone expected certain behaviors, certain pasts, certain connections, and smiles and conversation would expect the same from him.

George meandered in as calm and composed as if he had spent every day of his life here. People greeted him by name, people who shared his liquid greetings, his hearty, particular smooth way. Ezekiel had learned how to perform in the manner required of a merchant at the store, had come to some terms with greetings and flatteries, to put into his mouth bits of the right language he copied from George and old Mr. Reading. *But this?* George had dragged him here because he knew the importance of the relationships with these people.

George led him past a library, a heavy, dark room full of deep and somber chairs covered in leather. Its walls were filled with bookshelves floor to ceiling and niches that holding a community of statues. Ezekiel yearned to go into that dark, quiet place, to join the carved figures and avoid the mob George was leading him to.

The entire club was fitted with manly blacks and browns. It was odd to see George in this dark cave. Some time ago he had hinted, then persisted, then fought with Ezekiel to get rid of clutter, even to remove the store's old wood shelves to make space to hang paintings. Once the walls were bare and patched, he insisted everything in the store be painted white, even the moldings and trim woods. In the end, Ezekiel did what George wanted—and sales multiplied.

George called out greetings and drew Ezekiel into introductions. "Sam," he said, "meet Mr. Ezekiel Harrington of *Harrington Fine Art*." He pulled Ezekiel's elbow. "Mr. Samuel Bodine," George said. "Sam, you need to go right home and tell Eleanor to bring herself into the gallery tomorrow. We have a Homer, a nice little piece of a young man and woman in colors I know Eleanor would be keen on, for the parlor."

George pulled a calling card from his vest pocket, slid it into Mr.

Bodine's hand and said, "Either you tell her, or I will."

Mr. Bodine threw back his head and laughed. "Extortion!"

George wagged his finger. "It's either you, or me. She should have it. That piece won't last the week."

The names George mumbled as they made their way through the room could have filled a year's issues of the *Intelligencer.* Ezekiel caught bits of conversation, tips on the stock market, the Phillies and their chances. "Oh," he said, "there's Widener." He ambled toward a fellow standing off and somewhat alone. George leaned in, covered his mouth and whispered in Ezekiel's ear, "They let him in," he said, "the Philadelphia wouldn't. *Nouveau*, you know, richer than half the country, and the Philadelphia Club *spurns* him, for God's sake."

Widener watched them approach. He was bald, stood straight as a rod, his shoulders pulled back and defensive. He was not a bad-looking fellow, but there was an aspect of suspicion on him. George went straight to him. "Silas," he said. "How is Hannah? I haven't seen her since George and Eleanor were married. How is your son finding wedded life?"

Widener's face softened then, and his mouth split into a shy grin. "I think well," he said. "I got a cable from them in France just yesterday." The newspapers spent columns on Widener when he bought and took over all the streetcar lines in the city, made headlines of it when he named the business Philadelphia Traction Company, then again when he brought his son George into business. Ezekiel knew the man belonged to most every board in Philadelphia, including Philadelphia National Bank & Trust, Totten's bank.

George said, "I heard you are building a new home for Hannah in Elkins Park."

"How did you hear about *that*? I haven't even signed papers yet."

"I have my ways," George said. "That's why I wanted you to meet my associate Ezekiel Harrington." George pressed Ezekiel's arm. "Of

Harrington Gallery. I am going to Paris in the next few days and will be shipping new stuff home as I find it. Important works, *essential* I'd say, for your new place. I understand you are planning more than a hundred rooms."

"Is nothing secret?"

George tipped his cheek, a bit of a flirt. "Important works," he repeated.

Ezekiel came away that day dreading George's absence even more. How would he carry on without George? How?

The mail came just after Ezekiel returned from the "mingle." There was a note from Bob.

> *Leaving Paris for Brolles. Sometimes I think I am on to something. But the minute I look away, it's gone. Some of the other fellas doing good work, though, so that is something.*
>
> *Keep home fires burning. Bobby*

Bob had sketched the skyline of Paris with a bum in the foreground holding his hands over a fire.

Chapter 65

George left on a day of skies heavy with rain that weighed on Ezekiel and pressed him further into doubt and depression. He had hired a young man, whom George knew, to stand in for George while he was gone. He was, in George's words, "quiet and perhaps a bit of an effete but comes from a good and entrenched New York family." He also said the young man had a lisp, then added, "You'll find it endearing." He would live in George's room while he was gone.

Ezekiel circled the day George would return and set to bearing down until then. Doubt prickled: George said he would return—*but would he*? Ezekiel felt helpless before his own inadequacies.

The boy pronounced his name on the back of his tongue. It sounded like Hyam, but was spelled Chaim. He was timid, in the beginning, spoke little and stood back when patrons entered, his thin fingers knotted in front of himself. His tongue flicked, nervous, over his lower lip.

Two days later, Ezekiel's framer quit. Ezekiel scrambled to hire yet another one and did, but the fellow seemed to grow impatient within the first week, muttering that he had found a new job at the shipyards and the pay would be half again what he was getting here, hinting for Ezekiel to match the amount. Ezekiel prepared to hang another sign in the window.

For a week, the boy Chaim did nothing but stand back, even when Ezekiel told him he needed to earn his keep. Then, as if he had read from the page of some book of behavior, the second Monday of his employment, he entered the store wearing a new suit and a custom shirt and carrying himself with an entirely different, more confident demeanor. "Good morning," he said, "Mithter Harrington."

Chapter 66

The new boy was punctual, as George never had been, but reticent and of little words until he began discussing the art for sale. Then, he was transformed. He had been exposed to the museums and galleries of New York. He knew art and loved it with perhaps even more passion than George. Though he never claimed to be an artist, art seemed to release him of his timid misery, even to lift a bit of his lisp. He could toss artists' names around like men at the club tossed the names of the Phillies. He could discuss in detail the merits of each piece and compare them with some of the best-known works, works by artists everyone seemed to know. He was turning out to be reliable, and, as odd as he was, people took to him. Chaim began to make sales.

Ezekiel started to understand fully how much he himself had learned from George. He had some vague notions now what art was good, what was not so good, and he was beginning to be able to peg what might sell and what, for certain, would not. So much coming in from the artists' representatives was dark and detailed, perfect representations of landscapes, oceans, properly detailed and flattering portraits, and, as dense and dark as some of it was, it often sold. It would have sent Bob, and George, into apoplexy.

When George left for Europe, he had taken two thousand dollars from Ezekiel's coffers to spend. It was meant to last, but two weeks after he hit Paris, he wired that he needed more. Ezekiel sent everything he could, holding back only what he needed to make the month's payment on his loan. He could jockey every creditor but the widow; her he had to pay. He only hoped sales and rents would keep him afloat until George returned.

And *what if he came back and could sell none of what he'd bought? What then?*

It was a Sunday in November. Winter had come on in batterings of wind, sleet, rain, ice. The church bells had finished their battling hours ago. The city was quiet now; the silence amplified the streetcars' screeches, the clanks of conductors' bells. He rose from his desk, put on a wool cap, slung a scarf at his throat, and shrugged on his coat. The stores were closed, the streets clear but for a lone carriage, or two. The quiet left room for unbidden thoughts, for fears and doubts and visions that did him no good. He sought noise, or movement, or some other thing to distract from the misery. He headed out, turned toward Dock Street; Dock Street never really went quiet.

He walked toward the river, took Dock's curve. It was cold. He sank his hands into his pockets, pulled his head into his shoulders. He felt out of place down here, a dandy in his coat and his polished shoes, among the roughs. Life there was hard, a cacophony of carts heaped with produce, laborers screaming, toting fish by hand from boats to the mongers' stands, lugging whole cow carcasses on their backs, hanging them high on butchers' hooks, the butchers whacking the haunches, slicing the soft briskets, the tongues, and the brains, throwing meat into wrappers. He knew that, before his parents moved to Nebraska, his pa had briefly worked down on Dock. It smelled of rot, of produce gone off, of slops, of sweat, of offal.

Some of the farmers' stands were loaded with pumpkins and squashes, others with potatoes, beets, carrots, parsnips. Apples were already gone; soon it would be too late even for squash, and, for a few short weeks, the shanties would lie quiet but for the freezing carcasses of hogs and chickens and cows.

He made his way along the cobbles. Now and then one of the laborers would look up and give him a once-over. He knew what the laborer saw: a young pale fellow, whose hands were uncalloused and fine and whose shoes were polished, someone to resent, someone with airs who endeavored to make himself appear better than he was.

A cluster of a dozen children played among the wagons and shanties. They had split themselves into two teams and were tossing a rock, shouting, running, now and then calling out a score in a game that made sense only to them. Three and four-story brick tenements with flat, blank windows peered over the street, ignoring the rude game. Along the walks rippled ugly overhangs, unmatched from one to the other, some made of tin, some of wood, some of fabric. A trollop sauntered to the edge of the game, leaned against a support a few feet from the children, hand on her hip, murmuring to men as they passed by.

A dark figure caught his eye, a lump of a woman sitting on a straw bale. She faced away from him. She could have been an old woman—one of the children's grandmothers watching her grandchild—for the position she had taken at the edge of the children's game. Her skirts were lifted indecently to her knees and her legs splayed, unladylike, around canvas leaning against a box labeled *Darragh Farms*. Only her arm moved, dabbing at some puddle of color on a palette she held on her hand, then slashing and patting at the canvas. A dog barked and began to chase the stone chattering along the cobbles. A boy, whose pants were torn at the seat, screamed "Blackie!" and caught the dog by its ear. It let out a yip and dropped the stone, and the boy threw the stone back into the game.

Ezekiel stepped closer, stood a few feet behind the woman as she brushed on color. She was capturing the children. They were rendered in dark and somber tones, their knees poking from ripped knickers, the girls' outgrown dresses too small to be decent, feet with no shoes, noses dripping. The image was painted without romance or prettiness.

She wore a shawl, a slack and stringy thing that fell off her shoulder and flopped into her paints. She muttered something sharp in a language wet with spit. When she flopped the shawl over her shoulder again, her face turned to profile. She looked up then, as if she had sensed him standing there. She nodded once, then went back to her painting, as if to excuse him. He returned the next Sunday; he would approach her, talk with her, ask her where she lived. But she was not there. He returned the next week, and the next after that, and never saw her there again.

1893

Chapter 67

It had been three years since George's first trip to Europe. In May, eight months from now, Ezekiel would turn twenty-five, the age when his uncle could no longer keep him from his inheritance.

Fortune had finally begun to turn Ezekiel's way. The store was doing well, paintings filled the walls, floor to ceiling, more of them—dozens—were slipped into slots in the storeroom, a half-dozen sculptures, some worth thousands, sat on pedestals in the windows. His displays were full of expensive bric-a-brac: leaded crystal goblets, sterling trays, ivory photographic frames. Every month, sales gave him more quantities of cash to put into his safe.

He did not trust it, but if he let his feeling in, he *might* consider himself lucky. But he had never been lucky. He had always been a plodder, an ox in harness. Luck came to everyone else; he could not allow himself to be seduced into believing in it now.

He came down from his room upstairs, early as always. He still slept up there, though finally had taken one of the regular rooms for himself, a small one with only a single window. The cat no longer showed; Ezekiel had not seen it for over a year, and he was surprised how much he missed it.

He bought two new suits not long ago and some shirts, and he took things to a proper laundry instead of to the washer woman down the street. He'd finally given up shaving his own face, went to the barber every day now, before the store opened. He spent little more on himself than that, still washed in the sink by the workbench, still filled his pocket with a biscuit from the diner every night to eat for his breakfast in the morning, and he clung to the comfort of habit; changelessness was expectable, changelessness was trustworthy.

After his first trip to Europe, George had returned to Paris a year ago and would be going back again in a few weeks. The first year he had bought thirty-seven paintings. He had been giddy when he returned, the artists' names rolling from his lips like music: Bonnard, Boudin, Vuillard, Serusier, Morisot. After an excruciating wait, the paintings arrived by ship a month later, and Ezekiel had spent the last five dollars he had in the world to have a sign made for the front windows, *Grand Opening Paintings from Paris.*

Ezekiel hired another framer. Mr. Weir. A large man with a fine hand and had spent a good part of his life doing heavy carpentry work framing houses only to have someone else do the fine finishing work. He lost an arm in a fall from a roof, an injury that put an end to building and made him infinitely grateful for the job Ezekiel offered, which paid less than carpentry but which he could manage with one arm.

George hung the paintings and called in every contact he knew. They were beautiful, bright, in colors that lit the shop as if they called in the sun. By the time the store opened that morning, three carriages were waiting out front. Half the works George had bought had sold within two weeks. The rest—but two—sold within the month, and Ezekiel bought a safe and put his first stack of dollar bills in it.

He had not seen his aunt for over three years. She had come in a few times after the summer Soap finished the portraits of her grandchildren; then, her visits trickled off, and he had not heard from her since.

George returned to France again and stayed with his old friend Jackie, who Ezekiel eventually learned was a wealthy woman whose full name was Jacqueline Fournier and who lived in the middle of the city. She kept her eye on the art in Paris and helped George winnow and cull pieces. Customers were willing to pay hundreds, sometimes thousands, for what

George brought back.

After two years, the art sales allowed Ezekiel to open a second gallery a half block off Rittenhouse Square. He was finally beginning to negotiate for what he thought of as his *piece de resistance,* the storefront property in Chestnut Hill, only blocks from the Humes' home. The store in Chestnut Hill was, he knew, a vanity. He planned the design of it with doors that opened right onto the street, with an elegance that would shout his success right under the nose of his uncle. It would be finished and open within weeks of his twenty-fifth birthday.

———

It was nearing the end of September, the lovely season, a time of energy, beginnings, dry leaves crackling in the breezes, the days clear, the evenings crisp. Everything about the store had changed markedly in three years, not just the preponderance of art, and the quality items he had in the displays. Rugs he had bought from the Syrian across the street spread three-thick on the showroom floor. The awnings spread across the face of the building, broad and fresh, and had been built to adjust in order for the best light. The Hainsworths had approached him to take some of their new line of enameled and gilded boxes on a decent consignment, and he displayed them in a case lined with beveled mirrors and embroidered Chinese silks.

He had spent the day getting his books ready to close for the month. He had hired a new fellow, Covington Supplee, someone George knew through a new friend in New York. Supplee would manage the new gallery near Rittenhouse Square. The Rittenhouse gallery was smaller than the main store, but gave *Harrington Fine Art* a presence nearer the wealthy; it had turned profitable not long after opening. He would use its profits to help open the store in Chestnut Hill.

George spent a good deal of time in New York, always seemed to have many acquaintances in that city and would talk of this one or that one for a while, then quit and fall into a kind of torpor, until, once again, his mood would lift when he found another whom he called *tres jolie.*

Ezekiel closed the ledgers, gave them a fond pat, and picked up the evening paper. He held it up into the lamp on his desk. His lights were electric now, installed by an electrician who charged a dollar an hour for the labor. When Ezekiel complained about the rate, the fellow said, "You can take it to the union. We got one now, you know."

He shook open the *Bulletin,* poured himself some tea, and leaned back. The newspapers were full of the menace caused by Labor and its demands, demands that were partly the cause of the failure of some businesses. Labor and its demands were causing costs to rise to such a degree that some businesses were borrowing more than they should to stay open. Labor's high salaries were blamed, in part, for the worrisome finances of the railroads, as they could not get men to work at reasonable rates. Yet the city seemed to be exploding with work, the streets torn up for the new sewers, the curbs ripped apart for poles for telephony. A new mint was in the works a few blocks away on Walnut, and the city was buying up buildings—more than three dozen addresses—to build it.

The stock market was down a bit, though seemed mostly stable, though Jay Gould was apparently manipulating it to his own benefit. How could one man shake things so? Ezekiel felt a ping of envy at that sort of power. Jay Gould was greatly responsible that Reading Railroad stocks had plummeted, though things for the company were made worse when the public became aware the railroad had bilked Philadelphia out of a huge grain business by diverting shipments to Baltimore.

Even *women* were causing problems. If Labor wasn't stirring up enough trouble, women's badgering and snits about their rights were making up for it. Loud, raucous women seemed to be everywhere marching and raising their fists, waving placards and screaming speeches. Could nothing ever stay as it was?

The men at the Rittenhouse debated endlessly about the mess women raised. Women wanted the vote; the men shook their fists at the thought of Pennsylvania falling for that. But some states had already succumbed, Westerners mostly. Sometime ago, Utah and Colorado had made women's vote legal. When Wyoming became a state last year, right off, it granted its women the vote. Some women were even getting themselves elected, and a woman in Iowa was allowed to become a lawyer. In Chicago, Jane Addams, whom the men at the club called a loud-mouth, had set up a settlement house for the poor—women, of course. Women were the subject of much speculation, and the men called it falderol and travesty.

Newspaper articles said women did not know when they had it good, called equal rights balderdash. Women did not have the ability to think like a man, they were hysterical, could handle no more than making homes and taking care of their children. Giving them rights would be the ruination of America's greatness. But sometimes Ezekiel was not so sure women were so helpless; after all, hadn't his ma done a pretty fine job on her own?

A knock came to the front door. He folded the *Daily News*, laid it on the desk. The knock was gentle, at first, as if apologetic. He pulled his watch from his pocket. He had a gold watch now, with an eighteen-karat fob the Hainsworths had designed for him. The Hainsworths' success showed now in Jasper's bit of a paunch, and the heavy watch and fob JJ sported on fine-tailored gabardines. As young as JJ was, still not over twenty, he was accumulating a web of crow's feet that did not spell mirth—but ambition.

The knocking grew louder. Ezekiel grunted, rose from his desk, made his way through the store in the dim early light. Through the door was the ghost of a man's face and a pale hand waving a greeting—the face he had been waiting three years to see. He pulled open the door to the cool morning humidity.

"Easy!"

Ezekiel wanted to throw his arms in the air and shout hooray. Bob was thinner, no more than a stick. He still wore a black suit, and it made him appear tall as a tree. He had aged in the last three years. It was this moment, having Bob here, that had carried him through the last three years. Ezekiel turned up the lights to highlight what he had achieved. Bob's eyes went to the paintings, then to the sculptures near the windows.

"This *yours*?"

"Yes," Ezekiel said and could not swallow the pride.

"All of it?"

Ezekiel shrugged; he could have said yes, but he let this be enough.

Bob gawped, his eyes stopping on every canvas. He seemed more serious, now, more subdued. "It makes me feel like I'm back in Paris."

"I hear you have been working a lot," Ezekiel said.

Bob shrugged. "I've been going through a whole lot of paint, but not making much of a living on it." He stood back, folded his arms, looked at Ezekiel in an assessing manner. "The little brother from back home made it," he said. "I knew you would." Ezekiel had to turn away, or Bob would see he was about to tear up.

They talked awhile about Bob's "fellas." Redfield was still in Europe, had had a snow scene accepted in the Paris Salon. A piece of Grafly's he called "Daedalus" had been exhibited in the Salon as well. Grafly was back in town, the last few weeks, teaching sculpture. Calder had remained in Europe, and Bob thought there was a chance he would never come back to the States. Bob sang the praises of everyone but himself. "All of us are still at it, but none of us making a living."

At one point, Ezekiel inquired about Bob's family, and Bob's attention roved through the gallery to the door. "Are we alone?" Ezekiel nodded. "We had a little scare," he said. "It's why I came back. Pa got into a bit of a scuffle with someone." Ezekiel could imagine, Mr. Cozad had never been shy about a scuffle "And Ma said I should come home. Pa's disagreement was settled before my ship landed." The slant of Bob's shoulders, his resigned manner made Ezekiel think Bob would still be in Europe but for the situation with his pa. "Was a horrible trip, too, me sick as a chicken all the way."

Ezekiel felt a distance creep between them. "How is Johnny?" he said, He corrected himself, "I mean Frank."

Bob squeezed his eyes near closed like he might be assessing some problem. He looked down at his hands, seemed to gain some comfort in them. "Good," he said. "My brother's a doctor now." He looked up, then, tipped his head as if weighing a thought. "Doctor Frank Southern, my pa's proud older son." He wove his fingers in front of himself, spun his thumbs. "He got married to a girl named Jennie. I'm going to live with them, over on 16th Street, until I find a studio. I'd like very much to find myself someone like Frank's Jennie." He fingered back a hank of black hair. "But first I have to find a place to paint."

The thought of painting, something he knew, seemed to calm Bob's thumbs, and they settled. "It's nasty finding someplace with good light in the fall. The good cheap places around the Academy are taken, mostly." Bob prattled on, and his presence sat on Ezekiel like a warm touch. He said he was planning to enroll at the Academy come winter, though he did not seem to look forward to the prospect. "Maybe try to get them to let me teach a class." That seemed to please him. Suddenly he blurted, "You seen Soph?" The question sounded intimate, somehow, and made Ezekiel look away. He shook his head no.

Bob rambled on. "The guys are getting together tonight," he said. "The last minute of freedom before we turn over our lives to the halls of the Academy." He mentioned the name of a diner and, with both hands, slapped Ezekiel on the shoulders. "Six o'clock. See you there."

As Bob put on his hat to leave, Ezekiel said, "I'd have a place for yours." Bob turned, confused. "I'd put up some of yours." Ezekiel realized, in that instant, that this was why his life was playing out as it was, why he had come the way he had, why the store was what it was, why he was who he was: All to be able to say to Bob, "I'll make room. I'll put up some of yours."

"Mine?" He was obviously pleased. "You haven't seen anything I've painted since, since...forever."

"I know it's good."

"How you know that?"

"It has to be."

The diner was small, cheap, with one big round table, a counter, and a line of stools. The menu on the wall featured salt fish, pear pudding, ham hocks, and potatoes—mashed or boiled.

Earlier in the day, Bob had dropped off three paintings, rolled. He was nervous, stripped of bluster, his movement quick and breathless. He slapped the roll on the counter and made some disparaging, nonchalant remark. He did not wait for Ezekiel to unroll them, but mumbled he could not stay, that he had to run to the school immediately. But his eyes shifted to the roll, his expression uncertain, his shoulders held high like a boy about to be judged. It pained Ezekiel.

Two of the paintings were quite dark, one of looming rain clouds over a somber river and bridge, the other of a misty busy Paris street. The third was of a bright day with rusty fall trees on a broad boulevard with one carriage in the distance. He knew how much of himself Bob had put into them. He wondered how George would think.

Six people sat the big table. Ezekiel pulled up a chair at a space between a couple of new fellows he had never met. One of them they called Butts, a gentle sort with pooling eyes that reflected strange lights. Butts' name was William Glackens, but, for some fond reason, the fellows called the quiet fellow Butts. He looked so much like Jasper Hainsworth they could have been brothers, and it made Ezekiel warm to him.

Ezekiel had not caught the name of the other new fellow, an intense sort with restless hands that fluttered around as if playing the keys of a piano. He had a rage of red hair that stood away from his head like orange cotton. The orange-headed fellow did up illustrations at the *Philadelphia Press with* Glackens.

Reddy was back in town and Grafly as well. Ezekiel had not seen Redfield for years. It was good to see him.

Everyone was rested, sitting loose. The regulars—Grafly, Bob, and Redfield—talked among themselves as the new men listened and observed, laughed at jokes, kept smiles glued their faces, and nodding like sycophants at whatever any of the guys uttered about Paris.

The redhead sitting beside Bob was the most animated, nodding as the "royalty" spoke. At mention of France, Soap's name came up. Bob said last he knew, she was already painting in the style they were "over there." He asked if anyone knew where she was. Ezekiel leaned forward, squinted to better hear, then sat back again when no one seemed to know.

They all launched again into their miseries, of the letdown of coming home again only to return to getting work out on deadline, returning to the damned Academy's grind of studying "from the antique." As the night wore on, the redhead grew more vocal, then nosy. He asked Butts Glackens some personal question Ezekiel did not hear. "From Philadelphia," Glackens said. The redhead's hair was the shade of a Rhode Island hen's, his hands, chin, nose, and forehead speckled with run-on freckles. "Your family still here?" he said.

"Yup," Glackens said, too polite to rebuff the fellow's meddling.

The fellow made inquiries around the table, his questions probing and curious; Ezekiel learned more than he had ever known about Redfield, who had apparently just met someone named Elise. He learned Redfield was born in Delaware but raised near Philadelphia and that he had started painting when he was a boy. "Slow learner," he said.

He skipped inquiries with Ezekiel, merely mumbling hello and then moving to the next man, as if, by not being a painter, Ezekiel was of no account.

The interview nudged toward Bob. Ezekiel wondered what Bob would reveal of himself. As the redhead faced him, Bob grabbed the sides of his chair and hopped it back, away from the table, a remove, a shuffle to safety. He pulled a panatela from his jacket, braced an ankle over his knee; the ankle lay there, solid as a guard gate.

The redhead said, "Mr. Henri, what about you?"

Bob rolled the half cigar in this mouth until it turned swamp brown. When it was sufficiently wetted, he turned it and rolled the other half. The redhead waited, patient. Ezekiel waited as well. *What would Bob say?* Glackens and Redfield listened, as if neither of them knew Bob's truth but wanted to.

Bob struck the match, held it for a moment to heighten the flame. A dish smashed in the kitchen, someone hollered. The match burned half down. He brought it up and, cross-eyed, lit the smoke. Behind the murk, his eyes flickered at Ezekiel and stayed there a century, querying the security of their pact. The redhead waited. Bob blew toward the ceiling. "Like," he said, "everyone here..." he sucked at the smoke again. "...the past was what it was."

In January, classes began again. Bob's paintings had not been stretched when he brought them in, Ezekiel had had them framed, then hung them himself clustered on a wall at eye-level in the prime area of the showroom. In spite of the light, they dimmed next to George's French paintings. The first day he saw them, George stood in front of the arrangement, tipped his head to one side and said only, "Your friend's?" Ezekiel said yes, George said nothing more.

A week later Bob ambled into the store. He went to his paintings. "Look good, Easy." They did look good, Ezekiel thought, the frames touched with gold leaf. Around the store, a good number of George's paintings had tags on them saying sold; he left the pieces hung like that until the buyers came to pick them up. "Helps sales," he said, "seeing some already spoken for." Tags hung on none of Bob's pieces.

Bob stayed a few moments, and in those moments, if Ezekiel were a praying man, he would have sent up a request for some high Philadelphia nob walk into the store and lay down a couple hundred dollars for one of Bob's paintings. Bob said he had begun teaching at the Academy's School of Design for Women.

"Women?" Ezekiel said.

"Don't sound surprised, little brother, women do some pretty good stuff these days, and they don't complain so much as the guys."

Two women conservatively and expensively dressed came in then. They toured the room, stopping at several of the French works. George came out from the back, greeted them, recognized one from some garden party he had attended. They stayed for several minutes, and, as George blithered, they discussed aspects of most all of what was on the walls. They did not pause at any of Bob's.

They left, then, and Bob touched two fingers to his forehead, waved off and said he had to get to the school.

Two weeks into the year, a trail of young women began to come in. They came in clutches and gave perfunctory glances around, then clustered at Bob's works as if his paintings were something holy. At first, George engaged them until he learned they were Bob's students and had come in solely to see the sage man's work. It appeared they might all be, to a one, in love with Bob.

His paintings had hung in the store nearly two weeks when Ezekiel finally asked what George thought of them. George had been out the night before. His eyes were thick, shot. He screwed up his face, closed one eye then the other before he shook his spectacles open and put them on. A candy clicked in his teeth. "What they seem to want to say isn't clear. I think they will be a hard sell. People want pretty. People want Paris. People want light. People want chimera, castles in the air. They want something to take themselves away from their lives." He took the eyeglasses off, ground his eyes with his palms. "These images don't do that."

"I want you to write up a sales slip on one of them," Ezekiel said.

"Which one?"

"It doesn't matt...," Ezekiel pointed at the misty street scene. "That one."

"Made out to who, Ingmar Frabbitz?"

"That'll do," Ezekiel said.

George looked straight at Ezekiel. "You have something going with Henri?"

"Friend," Ezekiel said. The question was curious. "Old friend," he added.

George polished his glasses with a kerchief. His expression was fallen, with a sense of being let down somehow. "Ah," he said. "Friend."

Two of Bob's paintings made it into the Academy's exhibition that year. They were in the rough and bold-stroke manner of the three he had brought for Ezekiel to hang in the store. The school had put Bob's paintings in a section near three done by a Frenchman, works the Academy had borrowed for the exhibition. The Frenchman's name was Monet. The newspapers railed at the Frenchman's art, called his works painful to the eye. *The Philadelphia Times* called Bob's works "faulty exaggerations of an extreme mannerism in color."

Chapter 68

Ezekiel took his meals mostly at the club now. He had been a full-fledged member a couple of years. He would never be good at mingling. Mingling was merely a thing to be endured. He made conversation because business required chat. He mingled because it was what one had to do. He knew from the Rittenhouse's roster that his uncle belonged, though he was never there, apparently spending his time at the more rarefied Philadelphia Club.

At least now Ezekiel knew how to *pretend* to be what he was not, George having also seen to that. He could force the smiles, could join into the talk, could banter about stocks, about the implied investments that had made them millions. He made it appear that he, himself, had "sunk" some of his own money into "The Market" and had done well. The men at the Club would have found him peculiar for holding on only to cash. Cash did not grow unless one added to it. But cash was certain, and cash was what he kept, and each month he was keeping more and more of it. He would never have set foot in the Rittenhouse, with its yakking, cigar-smoking braggarts, had he not needed it for his business. But a meal in a rude diner with Bob and the fellows, some dim place with its tang of whiskey and its eye-tearing smoke, that he ached for every day.

Ezekiel had not seen Bob since the day he came into the store, weeks after George had put "sold" on Bob's painting. George was already gone for the day, the framer had swept his shavings and cleaned up his bench two hours ago. It had been a dark, thunderous afternoon. Ezekiel was at his desk, about to go out and lock the door when he heard the bell ding, then a clattering of a quiver full of brushes.

He heard Bob whoop then shout, "Easy!!" He clattered through the store, stomped into through the door to the office. "One SOLD!" Why did he sound so surprised? Joy pulsed on him, so tangible Ezekiel could almost grab it. "Who?"

"Who, what?"

"Who bought it?"

"George sold it," Ezekiel said.

"I must thank them. Tell me who it was." He was nearly shouting in his excitement.

Ezekiel put a finger to his mouth, as if remembering. "Someone from out of town," he said, "left no address." He let out his breath and sent up a little thank you that George was not there to hear the lie.

He had always believed things moved along when one had funds, a place to live, associates. It appeared so, when he viewed others, the men at the club, Bob, his uncle. So, he thought, *if I have what they have, why am I not happy*? He knew what happiness appeared to be, could see it in others, the heel-tapping when they got what they wanted, a family's quiet murmurs and pats when things did not go as planned. He did not have what they had, someone to catch him, to buck him up, other men like him. He had had that once in Bob, when they were boys, but Bob had other fellows now: his artists. Ezekiel felt like some sort of beetle who worked alone boring at a rotten tree, fixed on its hole, pinching, cutting, riddling. But eventually even a beetle reached wherever beetles reached: it produced its young, or slept through the winter, or woke to couple with another of its kind. Even a beetle had somewhere to go, somewhere else to make it happy. Ezekiel had his so-far success and could not make himself believe in it. The only thing solid in his life was disdain for his uncle—*that* was something he could hang his hat on. But he had no one to make him happy.

Chapter 69

A man who spent time wandering was viewed as shameful. Men at the club spoke of direction. They spoke of plans. They spoke of aims. Yet wandering was what he was doing. He had not really slept for weeks. He tired of throwing himself on the bed, hearing the hiss of his sheet and his breath, rising again and again into the emptiness.

One night he finally rose, gave into the sleeplessness. He dressed and stepped out into the dark. The city, at least the respectable part of it, lay dark, quiet but for the sound of a ship's horn on the river. Had someone seen him and greeted him, he would have said he had worked late and was out, now, simply catching some air.

Fall had stripped away color. The trees in the parks were stripped of their greens and reds and yellows, the roses their pinks and blinking whites. In their place, the dull browns the color of madder. Winds cut through the city. Thunderstorms replaced the oiled humidity of summer and left the streets slick, the curbs running and frigid. People no longer strolled but trotted, holding onto their hats, disappearing into the stores that now displayed winter coats, mufflers, and gloves lined with fur. Across the street from his store, the Syrian had taken down his rugs of summer: the lighter blues, the peaches, and the yellows and had filled his windows with reds, browns, and tans. His display shone under two electric lamps, the only warmth on the street.

The stores were closed, their windows shuttered behind gates. Life was left to a few rough eateries and the saloons and the scattered and sloppy noise of men's voices, their laughter and drooling threats that bled out through chocked-open doors.

It was after midnight. He wandered around the Academy, then made his way over to Walnut. He had not been to the studio at 806 Walnut nor had he seen Bob for months.

The wind whipped his cap, blew it off before he could anchor it. It landed in the gutter and cupped up water. He swore, dumped the water, slapped it against his thigh. He turned, then, ready in his misery to finally go back. In the window of an ugly diner stood a dark man, wrapped in a soiled apron, shaving bits of meat from the bones of what had been a whole roasted pig. Little was left of it but bits and the head.

Men leaned against the bar, downing whiskeys. Three women milled around the men. The bartender filled glasses from the bottles the men had brought, then poured for the women after the men whacked coins onto the counter.

Seven or eight men sat at the sole table, napkins tucked into their collars. Ezekiel recognized only Grafly and Bob, sitting with his back to the door. Ezekiel whispered, "Ah," and went in. He stood for a moment by the door.

Bob was leaning in to Grafly, listening. Before he left Paris, Grafly had won an award in Paris for one of his busts and was home to begin teaching the Academy and a new college named Drexel. Bob nodded.

The aproned man, an Albanian Ezekiel thought, brought the platter to the table, then went out a door in back. The next day's pig was already stretched out on a second spit over a low fire in the alley. The aproned man gave the spit's handle a half turn, and the meat juices dripped and sent a cloud of smoke into the room. Grafly flapped his hand.

Grafly saw Ezekiel, then. "Easy, my man, pull up a chair," he said.

Bob turned, then his face pulled back in a grin meant for some place behind Ezekiel. Bob blurted, "Soph."

He had not seen her for three years. Her blouse flew open as she seated herself and revealed a cleft of bare skin. She lifted her skirts and laid her hand on Bob's arm.

"Long time," he said to her.

"Yah," she said, "long time."

The Albanian kept pushing through the back door, turning the pig, and, when he came back, he set a loaf of cut bread in the middle of the table. He went back to the picked over bones and took up a cleaver. He cracked off the pig's head, put it on another platter, and set it in front of Soap. Remnants of what had been eyes, black-leathered pupils, stared through burnt lashes, the eyelids crisp and brown. She threw back her head and gave out a raucous laugh. She picked up the head with a fork and a bare hand and dropped it into her bowl. She smacked and licked her thumb. With a knife she lifted the nose, braced it with a spoon and cracked open the jaw joint. The soft throat steamed. She knifed into it, brought out bits, put the tender meat into Bob's bowl. Her movement toward him was proprietary, more than friendly.

Grafly muttered, "Save some for the rest," and Bob laughed. They began passing the platter, and, as they did, she tipped up the top of the skull and began digging into the brains with the spoon.

Bob and Grafly talked as if continuing conversation. Bob said he was impressed with some of the women he was teaching at the Academy.

Soap snorted. "Wimmin. What you want with *wimmin*?"

Bob laid his hand on her shoulder. "You're not the only girl who paints," he said. Ezekiel could not see her in a place like the Academy, could not see her in Bob's classes, or at the Plastic Club, or any of the normal places women learned to paint. Yet she must have had some training. *How had she learned?*

She made a drama of sucking the last drop from the pig skull, opened her mouth, slithered out her tongue, soft, pink, a jagged crack down the middle. She seemed to lose herself in the slow licking, first her thumb, then her palm, then the juicy rivulet along the side of her arm. She offered Bob a slick finger, and he laughed. Ezekiel felt a heat.

Grafly pulled the cloth from under his chin, slapped it into his bowl. "Got to see to the necessities," he said. He pulled himself up from the table. He wavered there a moment. "I say," belched, "you otta see what our girl's been working on lately, Bobby." And he tottered off toward the water closet.

Soap made a show of ignoring Grafly, sticking a finger into the skull, licking off last bits of brain. She turned to Ezekiel for the first time since she had come in. "You auntie still doing good?"

Ezekiel did not know how Prune was doing. He nodded for no other reason than to remove the weight of her eyes from him. "Maybe I come in, see you some day." The urge to yell out "Yes!" filled him, but he sat quiet. He had learned he could not count on anything from her.

A couple of nights later he went to the studio again. Once, Redfield asked him why he came, since he never brought anything to work on. Redfield had taken Ezekiel by surprise and he stumbled and spurted. He finally said, "Keeps me up on what's going on," a feeble excuse, the best he could do. How could he admit that the men at the studio were all he had? And knowing it, he realized how pathetic.

It was cold out, not bitter but nearly so. Most of the regulars were there: Davis, Redfield, Grafly, Schofield, Glackens.

Schofield and Redfield were working on winter scenes, Schofield on a sketch of a barn and some trees that grew along a muddy creek. Redfield was still working on landscapes "plein air" they all called it as if the term was a code of brotherhood.

Redfield normally kept himself clean and sorted out, but he looked like a bear, now, his hair grown too long, his face covered with a beard he had not cut for a couple months. He had been out working that day in the wind and could not seem to get warm, though they had stoked the fire high. He had brought in a near-finished scene of a creek iced over with rolling snow banks set among winter-bare trees. His face was red and cracked, his lip bleeding from the cold. His gear sat in a heap in a corner of the studio: gloves, caps, rags he wrapped around his boots for warmth, his filthy plaid coat.

The rest of the men were still dressed in their suits from work, ties loosened, collars open, their arms through the sleeves of old shirts—the bigger the better—they turned backward to serve as smocks.

A new fellow named Shinn came that night, late. He was younger than the rest, no more than sixteen or seventeen and so thin his large head sat on his neck like a weight. He was already working as an illustrator at *The Press*. Ezekiel found him inscrutable, large head, pale face with dark brows, his hair nearly as black as Bob's. He tried to cover his outsized forehead with it and it gave an odd tilt to his expression, as if he had something to hide. He smoked ceaselessly, lighting a new smoke with the next that he pulled from a silver case. He stood at his easel squinting and snorting as smoke wound into his eyes.

Men slid Shinn's way as he painted. The scene Shinn worked was of a dark alley with little light; a tired nag hung its head in it, a cigarette vendor shouted his goods, three men were tangled in a cruel fight. He drew quickly with a confidence. Ezekiel wanted to dislike the sketch but could not. Apparently, Shinn had been at the studio only twice before and already earned the nickname "The Baby," and Ezekiel disliked Shin for that, too.

Near midnight, the men stepped back from their easels and began cleaning their brushes, and they chattered about doing some party, a "soiree" to celebrate the holidays.

Chapter 70

She came on a day of snow melt. The eaves dripped, the dirt from the streets heaped a grime of old snow to the curbs, shoe prints wore paths through the slush and filth. The *soiree* at Grafly's was the next night. Ezekiel had already had a suit pressed; it hung on a peg in his room.

The store would open in a few minutes; until then, he had been hiding in the office. A pounding came at the front door, a rough voice calling out, "Hey, you der?"

He sprang from his chair, then sat back, would not give into the impulse to rush out. He knew her knock, knew her rude tone. He thought of her nearly every day, sometimes saw her face in some stranger's, heard her in the rasp of a foreign tongue, glimpsed her in the wave of an arm, the flip of a skirt hem. The sense of her always was of turned soil, pungent and damp; which, as hard as he tried to make it so, he could not think of filth. But, now she was here, he had no idea what to think of her. Let her wait, as she had forever made him wait.

The store had had a good year, and when the calendar turned, in a few days, his books promised another. George's friend in Paris had sent another shipment a month before the holidays. Ezekiel had intended most of them to fill the new gallery near Rittenhouse Square but had sold almost half before they had a chance to hang on a wall. He was putting cash in the safe by the hundreds of dollars a month even as more new art poured in from Europe.

Bob's two paintings had not sold; he had come for them not long ago saying he planned to use them for some show soon. The store felt, somehow, remote when they were gone from it, but the two pieces George hung in their place sold within days.

She pounded again, shouting, "Hey!"

He settled his vest, ran a hand through his hair, as if she counted.

She was standing there dark as lint. He turned the bolt, opened the door a crack. "Yes," he said, not a question but something else. She pushed through and swept her skirts and her thick scent in with her. It happened George came in just then, starting early that day for an appointment to show one of the Corots to Mr. Biddle.

She stood between them. "Hey there," George said.

"Hey der to you."

"When do I get to taste some more of that *bigos* of yours?"

She threw back her head and yowled a satisfied laugh.

"Are you still putting paint on canvas?" he said.

"Do fishes swims?"

"Bring them in."

"It's why I come in today," she said.

That night, Ezekiel dreamed of winds so powerful they picked him up and dangled him, helpless to their whims. He woke and listened to his breath hiss from the confines of the walls and then wrestled until he could endure the blanket no more. She said she would be back soon but did not say when "soon" happened to be.

Chapter 71

Nearly forty men crowded into Grafly's studio. As soon as Ezekiel came in, Grafly fuffled up to him wearing a huge pair of bear-hair chaps. *Was it to be a costume party?* Grafly slapped Ezekiel on the back. "Easy, great. I didn't know you were coming." It was then that Ezekiel learned he had not been invited; he had come on assumption. Grafly did his best to cover, motioned Ezekiel in. "The place needs a little decorum."

The room sweltered. The regulars milled around in ridiculous costumes with no theme whatever: chaps, top hats, fake face hair, guns, togas. Every seat was taken, the overflow sitting knee-to-knee, Indian-style, on the floor. A table filled with whiskey bottles was pushed against one wall. Another held a platter heaped with roast and piles of bread.

Redfield wore sandals and a garb apparently meant to be primitive. He wore a nose ring the size of a bracelet, a serape scarf around his neck and bells at both of his ankles. The nose ring must have bothered him because his nose ran, and he kept fiddling with it.

Bob wore a top hat and a vest of some zebra stripe. He smoked a long, drooping pipe that banged his chest and held it clamped in his teeth as he talked to someone Ezekiel had never seen before. The fellow was dressed in a tweed jacket and slacks. The new fellow was smoking a pipe as well—a traditional chimney. The other fellow was apparently new, a student perhaps who was not in on the news he should have worn a costume. Ezekiel took some comfort in him.

He sidled through the heat of bodies and drink to where Bob and the fellow talked. Bob side-talked around the pipe as he introduced Ezekiel to the new man. "Easy," he said, "John Sloan." Sloan was about Ezekiel's age, handsome, jut-jawed, and wore thick spectacles. He reached to shake hands and as he did Bob said, "Ezekiel owns Harrington's," and Sloan raised his brows.

In unison, as if Ezekiel were not there, they went back to their conversation, a discussion of Whitman and the themes of his poetic accessibility to the beauty he saw in the individual. *Blither.*

A photograph was taken that night. Ezekiel saw it months later pinned to the wall in Bob's studio. It showed a pile of raucousness; Bob in the front with Redfield, Preston, Breckenridge and Grafly, Grafly's huge fur chaps prominent. Ezekiel was not in the photograph. By the time it was taken, he had been gone hours.

Chapter 72

He had not seen Soap again, since the day she was in the store saying she would be back "soon." It had been over two weeks. He should have been on the six o'clock for Chestnut Hill with his architect's drawings. The carpenters were putting the finish to the showcases. He had taken a lease a month ago on the storefront a few blocks from the Humes. He planned niches for sculptures, high arched windows, display cases twelve feet long to hold crystals, bibelots, and palettes of the Hainsworths' designs.

But he was not in Chestnut Hill. He was here, at the store. Waiting. She had come in the day before, but neither he nor George was there. The framer had said she would be here at ten o'clock. George had come in that morning, special to see her. It was quarter 'til. He would not wait; if ten o'clock came and she was not here, he would be gone.

She came just as the clock marked the hour. It had begun to rain. Hearing the bell ding, George said from the back of the store, "Is that our girl?" Ezekiel tightened his necktie.

She toted stretched canvases, uncovered and four thick, on her head like a Nubian, face up to the weather. Rain dripped off them, ran down her back, and soaked the arm that held them. More unstretched canvases she carried, rolled, under the other arm. George was sick with a cold; he was coughing and tooting into a handkerchief and taking swigs from his flask.

She did not have the decency to dip or shake water off the stuff on her head. A trail of water dripped behind her. She smelled of wind and rain and of laundry fresh from the line. She put the paintings on the counter. The rolls she threw on the floor and began toeing open with her foot.

George came out then. "Could id be our girl? God, id is." He stuck his handkerchief into one nostril. It hung there like some limp appendage, as he began pulling up her canvases, one after the other. He took them to the window for more light. "Somb of these," he said, "are incredible."

George had filled the store with paintings everywhere they could be put. The walls were cheek by jowl with stuff, floor to the highest spaces near the ceiling. When he ran out of space, he propped paintings on the floor, leaned them against the feet of easels, shoved them behind the counter, and filled the racks in back. They had ordered heavily, getting ready for the new opening. Ezekiel had had to hire on another framer to help Mr. Weir, and they were working ten hours a day. Paintings came in from everywhere, a shipment of fifteen from Germany, another ten from France, and five from a contact of George's in Japan. He was selling them nearly as fast as the stores took them in. Yet, he insisted they make room for Soap's.

George and Soap were still going on about her paintings when Ezekiel left. He finally made it to Chestnut Hill late in the afternoon. When he returned, the low winter light was coming full into the store. George was working in shirtsleeves, his face red and shining from fever. The framer had finished half of Soap's stretched canvases, and George had hung three of them. Her scenes from around the city raged on the wall: images of streets filled with people, done up in gypsy reds, purples, cobalt blues, swashes of color under bilious skies. On first glance, they seemed gay, energized. But, on a closer look, they took on a heavier weight; in one, the children running in the purple light were filthy, perhaps chasing in play, perhaps fleeing some unseen danger. Another depicted women standing, hips out, smoking logs of cigars, squinting, their faces lined and tough, telling of experience one could only imagine. A third was of a butcher's done on Dock Street, carcasses, their fats colored blue, the meats bloody red, hung in the background, as the butcher wrapped a piece from a large rump for a smiling customer. They sold in a day. The rest, but one, sold before Mr. Weir had a chance to mount them and hammer up frames. By the end of the month all eight were gone.

A few days later, at the end of the day, she came again, not bearing paintings but a palm held out. She snapped her fingers. "Pay," she said. It was the end of the day. He counted the money, put it in her hand. She wadded it into a pocket hidden in the waist of her skirt without saying thank you or even good day. She left, then, and took the air with her.

He locked the door and reached to pull down the gate on one window. She was standing there looking in. He unlocked. He opened the door. "You forget something?" he said.

She shrugged. "Mebe," she said. "Mebe not."

She put her hand to his chest and pushed. She brought her face close. Her eyes held his. Her breath joined his. Her hand was warm, its pressure relentless. Her hand drove him through the store, into the storeroom. When his leg pressed against the worktable, she reached down and cupped him in her hand. He gasped.

He had no words.

Chapter 73

By sunrise she was gone. He wanted her again; he wanted what he had had. She did not laugh that night, though she could have. He had fumbled. She had not.

Nights came again, one after another. She had made sleep impossible. *Damn her.* He was sleeping in the workroom again where he could hear her if she came. He bought a new mattress, laid it on the floor near the shelves where he had once slept. He had the housekeeper make it up with fresh linens and blankets and cover it with a spread against the dust. All night long, he listened for a rustle outside, a splat of hand on door, the low rasp of her call. As the nights grew long, and rustle and splat did not come, he dressed again and went out, into the dark that held her somewhere.

In daylight, he found distraction, could fill the hours with bills and plans. In the months since the party, Bob and the new man John Sloan had grown close. The few times Ezekiel saw Bob, now, he spoke of Sloan more than any of the others. Sloan worked long hours at the paper, work he despised. He attended class at the Academy, which he despised even more than the paper and was talking about starting a club at the studio where men would pay to come to draw from a live model and be supported and critiqued by Bob. He would call it The Charcoal Club. Sloan's angers and enthusiasms seemed to glue Bob and him together and to leave little room for anyone else.

Through Redfield, Ezekiel heard that Sloan's Charcoal Club hired its first model and opened its doors in March on "The Ides." Twenty men came that night.

The store in Chestnut Hill was opening in two months, timed just before Ezekiel's birthday. After dreaming so long, of the opening anticipation of it did not fill him like he thought it would. It had once been The Thing, his obsession. Delicious. He barely thought of it now; only the nights had any meaning.

At some level, his wanderings carried shame; others of his kind, the sort who membered the clubs, did not do it. But there he was, in the shadows like any other slouch, any other transient or miscreant with nothing better to occupy him than to cast about, hands in pockets, cap tipped low, collar turned high. He was like a gambler who wanders and pays a price but wins nothing. For months, he wandered only to return to his empty bed and to roam again the next night.

Then, in the frigid end of March, he saw her.

Chapter 74

The establishment was in bad shape, one window covered with a sheet of wood, an odorous downspout spitting out a gray rat that set out running along the foot of the building. The place catered to men of a sort who called the footings of a bridge their home. The saloon paid its rent from the coins of laborers who smelled of meat gone rancid, of bodies unacquainted with shower or bath, men who spent what they earned doing grunt labor work, on whiskey and spirits.

He saw the tangle of her hair first, the way her skirt hung loose on her hip. She leaned against the bar, as if she were a slut. A bottle sat between her and another woman. The other woman was so small, she could have been taken for a young girl but for her woman's shape and her dusting of a mustache. It was obvious they were together, the only women in this place. The small one swigged a drink, turned, and began laughing with a man at her side. She swayed as she laughed, drunken and rocking. Soap reached out to steady her.

For half an hour he watched. Men came and went. Men talked with the two women. Men strutted and teased, mostly with the girl-woman but with Soap as well. A dark man with a stained cap came in, his mouth filled with pink gums. He went directly to Soap. She talked with him, gave him her attention. Ezekiel heard the smoke of her laugh through the pane. Once, she swatted the fellow away.

Ezekiel might have mustered the courage, might have gone in. But what would he do? Would he say, "Fancy you're here, my dear…?" So, he brooded, lewd and cold. He watched the tiny woman sort out a particular fellow who laid some money on the counter. He watched her guzzle the drink his money bought. He bought her two more. Ezekiel watched her lean against him, and, when she did, he felt the warmth. She staggered toward the door. The fellow followed her out.

Soap was left there alone. She threw on the rag she called a coat, a man's coat, thick, dark as coal and huge. She drew a scarf around her neck that had apparently shared life with moths. A fellow strode up to her with a bottle in his hand, positioned himself against her. He was drunk, his face bloated red. She shook her head no. He began to rub himself against her. She shoved him back. His arms flailed. He caught himself in the back of a chair. He pulled himself straight, shouted something Ezekiel could read, "Slut," and made to come at her. Ezekiel grabbed for the door handle, but she pulled away and rushed out as the bartender grabbed the fellow. "Let her be," the bartender said. "She ain't worth a fight."

Ezekiel flattened himself against a shadow. She ran-walked into the night. He followed, half a block back. Her coat blew in the wind. He could feel the cold against her. She wore boots, he saw, fairly new ones that had lost their shine and were covered with a scrim of dirt as if she had walked miles in them. She drew her shoulders up around her ears, pulled the scarf over her head. As she made her way, she looked ahead, careless, inattentive, as if she did this every night.

On Market, she turned toward the river. Like a lecher, he followed. The wind took his breath. A woman had no business being out late at night. At Third she turned. Another woman would have cast glances. She did not; instead, she leaned forward, huddled into her coat like a turtle. He pulled up his scarf, hid half his face.

She was approaching the corner where his store sat and, as she did, she slowed. She rounded the corner. He rushed so as not to lose her. Through the corner of his display windows he could see her there on the stoop, gazing inside, her cupped hands against the glass. She could not have seen a thing, the store was dark, the display windows dimmed by chains.

She stayed long enough that he wondered if she would knock—or break in. A part of him wanted her that homeless again, sick, needy when he had the power to nurse her, feed her, to indebt her. But why would she be penniless? George had sold every one of her paintings, and Ezekiel had paid her enough to live on a good long while. Surely, she had money. What did she want here? He willed her to stay on his stoop. He willed her to rap on the door, to follow him in, and to the mattress. But as soon as he thought it, she threw her head back and clomped back down the steps.

She headed toward the river, where small live things moved in the gutters. She turned onto Front Street, continued past the sewer chutes on Lombard, past the unlit cobbles of South Street. She began to run, not in a manner of fear but of expectation, her posture straight, the scarf flying. She grabbed the scarf as she ran. She turned onto a street Ezekiel did not know the name of. She dodged and turned. He lost her in the alleyways of Montrose Street.

Chapter 75

He knew pretense. He lived pretense. He dressed his windows to pretend what they showed was better than it was. He dressed himself in a fakery of good suits and gold watches. The gallery in Chestnut Hill was becoming more than a pretense; in two months it had become a liability. Money was suddenly a problem; the markets in Philadelphia and New York were wavering downward, businesses beginning to run sales, men were losing their jobs. The newspapers salivated with the news of bank failures, and the banks had stopped giving out credit. *Where did this leave his uncle?* Ezekiel could only delight in the image of his uncle's wretched worry. *Hah.*

The city bathed in its own style of pretense; in spite of the economic changes, progress *appeared* to go on. Half the city was under construction. The city choked with grit that crackled in one's teeth, made one squint and sneer-eyed. What was not being built or expanded was being torn down. The streets were dizzy with the clanking, belching. What work there was seemed to be only with the city. Crews laid pipe, built filters and dug sluices for water, ripped up streets to plant ever more electrical towers for telephony and electricity and for the gaggle of new electrical trolleys. The city's cacophony surrendered only at night.

With economics as they were, even with the work in the city, opening the new gallery was turning into a canard. He was turning twenty-five in May, the month the store opened. Twenty-five, the magic number that would release Totten's hold on what was his. Ezekiel had not graduated, as his uncle required, but what had he done? Better. Better. He could thumb his nose at the traitor, could spit at him; his uncle would have no more control of him, or his mother's estate, if he had not squandered every cent.

Whatever was in it would be *his*.

He knew going through with the opening was not a sound business decision now, and yet, for or the sake of winning, of one-upping his uncle, it would be done. Then what? What came after *pre*tense? He did not know.

The main street of Chestnut Hill catered to wealth, was filled with useless, pretentious shops that were running sales of their own and beginning to close their doors. "Going under" was the vernacular for shutting doors, for being declared insolvent. The stores' closings, particularly in the heights of Chestnut Hill, scripted testament to an owner's shame, to the disgrace it brought to his family.

Dozens of banks were "going under." Ezekiel read the papers, watched, and he waited, but Totten Hume had yet to be included in the financial gossip. Ezekiel imagined his uncle escaping the troubles; from Ezekiel's view, it seemed Totten basked in success, wallowed in prosperity; hardship never knocked at the door of someone like Totten Hume. Ezekiel imagined his uncle in his mahogany office, smug, secure, arrogant.

Through it all, Ezekiel remained solvent, though the expense of the Chestnut Hill opening had depleted his reserves by three quarters. The businesses that ran on credit were closing. Ezekiel had never borrowed for anything. Even with the Chestnut Hill expenses, he had gold stashed in his safe, yet sales were beginning to turn down.

Even the dollar was in jeopardy. For the last couple of years, Europe had been going steadily downhill, while Philadelphia had done nothing about it but twiddle and ponder. Gold in Europe had had a run on it, stocks of European gold were gone and English, and German, Norwegian, and Swedish investors had grabbed a good part of America's gold before Americans caught on to the threat, and the country's bank run caught fire. Now, there was no more gold to back the dollar.

At the club, there had been a sort of smugness, a sense that the Europeans did not know how to manage their money. Yet America's railroads—every one of them—were begging for money, stocks were plummeting, particularly silver. Ezekiel understood all this, and he understood the folly of making his point with Chestnut Hill.

The gallery at Chestnut Hill was his birthday present to himself. On May twenty-first, he would turn twenty-five years old. That day he could sue if Totten did not turn over Ezekiel's money. His mother's estate had not been much, just over two hundred dollars, but the amount was not the point. Whatever was left, if there was even a penny, was his.

Chapter 76

Chicago opened its World's Fair the first of May. Ezekiel opened the store in Chestnut Hill that same day. George had designed freestanding walls and hung dozens of paintings on them. A special decorator had filled the displays with jewelry and trinkets, and caterers served up petite-fours and punches; spiked for the men, sweetened for the women. People milled and shook hands and clustered in circles to gossip. Prune came, dressed in something the color of daffodils, set off with a purple ruffle. Totten did not show up.

Four days later, on a morning of glorious sun and soft breezes, National Cordage's stock crashed. It had been the golden stock that filled shareholders' coffers. It bought them trips to Europe and summer homes in Maine. Ezekiel knew men who had spent fortunes buying it. Sales swamped the markets and shut them down. Guards stood with guns in front of the exchange.

Chapter 77

May 21, Ezekiel spent the morning in his office, working on his columns, adjusting plans. The day had begun like a whim or a portent. The city woke to thunder and lightning, then a downpour. By midmorning, the clouds had given way to sun, and the streets had begun to steam.

Ezekiel had let the young framer go and was keeping Mr. Weir, only as needed. It had been almost a month since George's last sale, though he was doing some small sales in jewelry. Down the street, the Hainsworths had closed their shop, and JJ had gone back to work on the family farm. Ezekiel had consigned what was left of their stock to put in the cases at the new store. As much as his income had fallen, he was not, he knew for certain, in as dire straits as men in the market or the high-powered men in the banks. *And what was happening with Totten?*

Ezekiel had not set foot in the Philadelphia National Bank & Trust for the better part of a decade. He waited until late that afternoon to pull open the door. He had planned this day for so long; he could recite the way it would unfold. He choked down a flutter in his gut. No matter how he had planned for this, no matter how he had practiced and bucked himself, he had to wipe his palms on his trousers.

The door was heavy as a church's. He held it as lieutenant William P. Biddle came in. Biddle nodded at him, and Ezekiel took some comfort in Biddle's acknowledgment. The bank had changed. Intimidation still lay on the rise of the ceilings, the high balconies, and the cold stone floors. A decade ago, it had been filled with earnest clerks in dark suits, wearing fine shoes, and talking in muffled voices. The sounds were different, now, angry and pleading. The desks reserved for patrons of import were empty. Lines twenty deep waited at the counters to be served by clerks who shook their heads no.

The men in fine suits and heavy watch fobs were gone. In their place, the bank was crowded with men in altered and re-sewn suits, patched at the elbows, and women in home-fashioned bonnets and dresses that had seen many Sundays. These were people one saw every day on the street, people who owned small vegetable carts, butchers and barbers, or those who worked on the docks, or delivered the mail. No longer was the bank filled with the types who had wads of money to invest, but the sort who were on their last penny and had come to the bank to seek loans.

Ezekiel approached a fellow sitting at a desk with a sign saying "See Clerk at Counter for Assistance." A nameplate said his name was Mr. Clarke. He was in his middle twenties, the same age as Ezekiel. His fingers were narrow and looked as if his handshake would be cold and unpleasant. Ezekiel stood before the desk until the fellow finally looked up. "Yes?"

"I am here to see Totten Hume." On purpose Ezekiel had not said "Mister."

The clerk assessed Ezekiel's direct gaze, his trim, expensive suit, the heavy chain across the vest and his fresh-barbered face. Mr. Clarke's tongue worked at a rim of chap round his mouth. "Mr. Hume cannot be reached."

"Where is he then?"

Mr. Clarke's tongue disappeared. "I am not privy."

"Tell him I want to see him."

The tongue made another round, slipped back. "Who should I say is calling?"

"Ezekiel Harrington."

The clerk pulled a speaking tube from somewhere in back of the counter. He told it Ezekiel's message. As he listened, his eyes flickered down to his pen. His tongue peeped out again, then back in. "Oh. Oh," he said. He laid the speaker piece on the counter. "Mr. Hume was expecting you first thing this morning."

Totten *expecting* him? "I'm here *now.*"

"He said to convey his hope you could see him at his home."

It was another trick, another of Totten's games.

For years, Ezekiel had envisioned this day; in his head it had already played out just so, and it played out at the bank with him taking the superior position, standing, hovering over Totten while he demanded his money. In his staging, Totten blushed when he saw his foe, his face purpling when Ezekiel insisted on an exact account and a cashier's check, "Every cent."

Totten was setting him up. The scene had shifted. The man was hoping Ezekiel had given up, but that would not, repeat, would *not*, happen. He would not be put off.

The train to Chestnut Hill took an hour; an hour to conjure another scene, but he could not get his mind to it, could not focus. The miles clicked away, and as he got closer he felt unhinged. He could not see this day taking place anywhere but the bank. At the Chestnut Hill Station, he hailed a cab. By the time the driver pulled up to the Hume house, his scene at the bank was fading a bit. At the Humes, he told the driver to wait and that he would not be more than a quarter hour.

He marched up the steps to the door, stood at it. He lifted his shoulders, took breaths. He put his hand on the boar's-head knocker and let his fingers lie there a moment on the cold metal. Finally, he lifted the ring and slammed it down.

At first there was silence. He feared Totten might not be here at all. He did not know what he would do if only his aunt were at home. He had no script for her. He heard rustling.

The door opened, and their maid peered at him, drying her hands on her apron. She opened her mouth as if about to turn away a salesman, then realized who it was. "Ezekiel," she said. "I'm afraid Mrs. Prudence is out."

"I'm here to see Totten."

Her eyes went to the coach Ezekiel had come in. The driver had already settled in, head back, arms crossed, eyes shut. The mare shifted weight.

The maid's brows lifted. "Your aunt should be home soon."

"I won't be staying," he said. "It's Totten I want to see."

She seemed confused, then stepped aside. "Would you like me to take your coat, then?"

He gripped the coat. It gave him cover. He hated this weakness. He handed over the coat; it was what one did on entering a house. He laid the scarf on her arm and waited in the entrance like a broom salesman while she went for Totten.

The house was dim. A drape covered the parlor window. The room had been cleared of gewgaws. The tables held only lamps now, sitting on laces, and the floors mostly bare. What rugs remaining were small and of little consequence. Soap's portraits of the children hung on the far wall. In the new simplicity they were even more startling and beautiful.

He heard the maid's voice down the hall: "Should I bring him here?" He could not remember her name. He seized on recalling it, now, as if her name were important: Phoebe.

He heard Totten mumble, "No," as if in some sort of pain. *Pain.* Totten deserved every bit. "The den."

"I know where the den is," Ezekiel said when she came back. Phoebe left him, still wringing her hands on the apron.

Trunks and boxes lined the hallway, more were stacked against the walls in the children's playroom and the two downstair's bedrooms. The Humes were, apparently, getting ready to move. He had heard nothing of this, but then of course he wouldn't. The state of their house was illuminating, spelled some decline. The thought sat in the back of his throat like good food. It was right in front of him: Totten's bank had suffered with the rest;

this picked-apart diminishing was proof of it.

He heard the screech of the chair in Totten's office, an exhalation of pain.

Totten was sitting at his desk dressed in a business suit he must have worn earlier that day. The shirt underneath was rumpled as if he had napped in it and the tie was askew. He seemed to have shriveled, his neck shrunken into his collar, yet his face was bloated.

"Totten," Ezekiel said. He tried to make it sound flat, unperturbed. He was not sure he succeeded.

Totten motioned for him to take a seat. "I'll stand," Ezekiel said. At least he could hold onto that part of the script.

"As you wish," Totten said. He turned to one side, opened a drawer, pulled out a file, and laid it down. It was the same folder as had been there a decade before, the same one on which was written simply, "Mary."

Mary.

The desk was as cluttered, piles of papers, some in a heap to sort, others sorted and wrapped with string. Against one wall stacks of boxes were labeled with clients' names and instructions for movers.

Totten opened the file, drew out what appeared to be a bank document. He slipped it toward Ezekiel. "I believe," he said, "this is why you came." The document likely held a paltry check, if it held anything at all.

Ezekiel let it lie there between them. If there was a check in it, he would not give Totten the pleasure of looking for the amount on it. He should just grab it right up and leave. Everything he had done the last years was in service of proving himself to this man, the struggling, the plodding, scraping, hating, the lying awake wondering how to manage to come up with money to eat, to pay rents, to pay wages, living in penury in order to scratch out enough for the store. *Why didn't he just take it and go?* But he did not.

He took up the paper. There was no check in it. The document was a receipt articulating the contents of a safe box in Totten's bank: nearly ten thousand dollars' worth in gold.

"What is this?" he said. It was a fortune. *Surely a joke.*

"It is," Totten said, "what has come of what your mother left you."

Chapter 78

Bob once said he thought there were times when the ground seemed to shift, when earth and the heavens slipped, and in the slipping took you with them and threw you down in a place so foreign and strange as to change you forever. He had, of course, said this with regard to some aspect of discovery or insight into his art, and he had seemed delighted with the concept; trusting that the Fates would take him someplace beautiful and grand. Ezekiel had not comprehended any part of it; the mere hint of turning himself over to some vagary of the stars left him without footing, and he turned away from it, to his own pragmatic idea, grounded in books, and columns, and paying bills.

Ezekiel left Totten's office without saying good-bye. The receipt was folded in his pocket. Phoebe heard him and came through the parlor with his coat.

He put it on, stepped out into the late afternoon. The sun was low, lighting only the tops of the trees. Summer would not take hold for another few weeks. At some level he was aware the greens were fresh, new and translucent. He felt a pulling on him and turned, expecting someone to be there, but there was nothing but the stone face of the house.

The cab driver was asleep, slouched low on his seat, his head tipped back onto the body of the carriage. Ezekiel stood for a few moments listening to the fellow's snores. The mare turned her long head toward him, then swung it back and resumed her waiting. High in one of the maples, a breeze riffled the trees, a robin began an evening warble.

Ezekiel touched the driver's thigh. The driver jerked. He looked down at Ezekiel. "Sir," he said and wiped at some drool with the back of his sleeve, "Ready, Sir?"

"No," Ezekiel said. "I need you a few minutes more. I won't be long."

"You'll pay," the driver said.

"I'll pay."

He stomped back up the front steps and did not knock. He went in, around the center table, past the kitchen. The thunder of his own feet reassured him. Phoebe was stooped over the oven, putting in two loaves of bread. She stood, gave a start. "May I help?"

"No," he said. There was no hiding his anger.

Totten was in the second bedroom by then, lying on the bed. He was still dressed in the suit. He lay there, eyes closed in his bloated face, Apparently, he could no longer make it up the stairs to their grand bedroom.

"I am not done," Ezekiel said.

Totten's eyes opened. "I see that."

Ezekiel hovered over his uncle. He yanked the paper from his pocket, shook it.

"What?" Totten said and left the word *now* unspoken. "Isn't it enough?" It was enough, all right, enough to demonstrate Totten's success managing his mother's estate, enough to show his superiority. As well as Ezekiel had done in his own business, it was not nearly *this* well. He could not abide it, could not leave it unchecked. "Take it," Ezekiel said.

"It's yours."

The old anger flamed again, hot, damp. "I know it's mine," he said, "it's been mine all along."

Totten pulled himself up on his elbows. "So, what do you want then?"

"More."

"More what?"

"I want to see what you were doing with Mother's money," Ezekiel said.

"You want to audit what I did with your mother's money?" He tipped back his head. Even lying prostrate, his head on a pillow, Totten's expression was dominant, superior, and defiant. "The paper I gave you should show you well enough." *How did Totten maintain this supremacy?* He was a sick and shriveled man. His bank could not be doing well. Philadelphia National Bank & Trust had not yet made it into the papers, but if the gossip got hold of the state of the Humes' lives, it would be delicious on society's tongues.

Totten reached up. "Pull me," he said. Ezekiel took his uncle's hot hand and pulled. Totten grabbed walls and shuffled out; a slow, turtle's padding to his office. He began to topple near the chair, caught himself, dropped into it. He wheezed, then, gathered himself for a moment. Nothing moved but his shoulders and his eyelids.

A glass and pitcher of water sat by his elbow. He took a drink, then another. He laid the glass down. "I have two sons," he said. He held up two fingers. "Two chances one of them would ask just what you have asked, two chances one of them might have had even an inkling of interest in business. They are both good boys. They are smart. They are responsible. Their mother and I are proud of them. But neither of them has ever stood where you are standing. Neither of them has ever asked what you have asked. I dreamed of it, but it remained a dream."

Ezekiel had no sense of anything. Every tidbit his uncle had thrown him the last ten years, he had dined on: Rage. Injustice. Theft. But now? Now? This had to be a ploy. *Hah.* He clicked his fingers. "I want to see Mother's account; you must have a copy of the bank's books here."

Totten's finger jabbed toward a ledger in the corner of his desk. "Get it."

The old stone was back in Ezekiel's gut.

He took the book to a table in the corner. He thumbed through the columns, tracing not only the flow of his mother's money but the bank's.

The bank was indeed in poor shape. It had experienced the same run on money as had the others. It was depleted, going under like the rest. Apparently, Totten was endeavoring to hold it together by selling whatever he could sell: some land, the summer house, even some jewelry he had inherited. Prune was mustering as well, had already sold most of her precious things: the furnishings, the Oriental rugs, the sterling, her china place settings. The house was to be sold next.

In order to stanch losses, other banks were claiming bankruptcy, even though they still held onto cash; they had money, they just were not extending it in credit. Yet here it was, Totten was still extending loans. There was a list of requests for money, three hundred lines long. Nearly fifty names had been underlined. To the bank's oldest customers, the bank was still granting money so its customers could keep running, but to do it, Totten was feeding Philadelphia National Bank & Trust from his own pockets. Was it generosity? Ezekiel thought not. Was it wile? If his mother's estate was any clue, it was good business.

Ezekiel closed the book. He let the acre of space between them lie there. "Give me a share," he said.

"A share in what?"

"The bank."

Totten blinked, then blinked again. "You want a share in my *bank*?"

"That's what I said."

"Do you have any idea what you're asking?"

"A partnership."

"Have you read the newspapers?"

"Of course."

"Did you understand what you were reading?"

"I am in business," Ezekiel said.

"A very *small* partnership," Totten said as if beginning negotiations. He turned his chair to the side, a sham signal he could end this right now.

"We'll see how small," Ezekiel said.

Totten did not get up but sat looking down at his feet. He threw his head back, looked up at Ezekiel and laughed. "'We'll see,'" he says." Totten pulled a handkerchief from his pocket, swept it over his brows. "'We'll see,' he says. 'We'll see.'"

Two days after the meeting with Totten, Ezekiel received a letter and a fancy, flowered card from his aunt:

> *Dearest Ezekiel*
> *Darling, your uncle told me what you have done. It means we will be able to keep the house. Your uncle is recovering remarkably since your visit, you have lifted the world off his shoulders. I am so unhappy to have missed seeing you. Why didn't you tell me you were coming? On your birthday as well?*
> *We are ever grateful for your immense generosity.*
> *Your loving auntie, Prune*

He had bought fifteen percent in Totten's bank and had not taken home a penny of his mother's estate.

Chapter 79

The country's economics did not improve. To rein in expenses, in July, Ezekiel closed the store near Rittenhouse Square and, soon after that, the gallery on Chestnut Hill. He settled, once again, back into the original store. He had taken a hit, had lost money in the sales, but he still had some gold to carry him, at least for a while. He moved himself out of his upstairs' room and rented it. He slept, now, where he once slept: in the storeroom. He rented his room upstairs to three men who paid three dollars a month and shared the bed. The three men missed paying their rent one month, and he threw their belongings onto the curb. He rented the room to four men, then, who paid four dollars a month. He did not know how they managed to sleep in the space and did not ask.

He had waited before, he would wait again.

All summer, George would be in Europe. He had gone on his own this time, to see his friend; Ezekiel could not afford to send him. The store was changing. Art sold in the good times, but this was not the good times. Nearly twenty percent of men were unemployed. He knew that people at the club were losing fortunes. Banks continued to shut their doors, and Ezekiel no longer took pleasure in this; bank failure was personal now in a way it had not been before. He found the anger at his uncle dimmed somewhat; that he could see him in another light: an aging man in fragile health, a man he could not like but no longer hated. He wondered what his mother would think of his handling of the money she had left him; every cent of it had gone into Philadelphia National Bank & Trust. Sometimes he could not shake the thought he had squandered it.

He gambled. Pride and braggadocio toward Totten had made him gamble his mother's estate. But, now, his gamble was on the economy; he was no different now than the men at the club who had gambled in the markets and lost. It kept him awake long into the nights. But he assumed the economic ills would one day subside, and, when it did, people would be ringing his door to buy the sort of merchandise the store carried.

He began buying items worth hundreds for pennies from sellers going bankrupt or closing their doors. He filled his showcases with items from the best homes: crystals, sterling, eighteen-karat snuff boxes, jewelry boxes set with gems.

He bought the entire stock of the Hainsworth brothers' store. They were the most beautiful pieces, necklaces, broaches, earrings. They would have sold in days only a few months ago, now little of it sold. And still he stocked up: handmade laces and silks from a merchant on Broad Street, two-hundred-year-old chests from an importer in Europe, hair ornaments inlaid with pearls and gems from an agent who bought and resold items from the wealthiest homes, rugs from the Syrian across the street. He bought a three-hundred-piece silver service for ten dollars from a relative of the Pettygroves.

He hoarded beautiful things yet lived again as a miser as the cash in his safe shrank.

Chapter 80

Mania drove him night and day. He could not make himself sit, could not sleep, could not even be still. When one of the fellows struggled at the studio, Bob would say, "Don't think about it." The usual reply was, "How do you *not* think about it?" Indeed. Sometimes a thought of Soap settled on him, unbidden, and she left her dark sense he had yet to understand.

He was alone, again, or almost so, working the store by himself. It was not for lack of men to employ. Every day a stream of them came in asking for work. George finally made it back from Europe and several days a week would come in and try to work. He was having no luck stirring up sales, and Ezekiel had little to pay him with, but still he came. He seemed to like Ezekiel's company and to need to be among things he saw as beautiful. He would fidget, would move things around, rehang canvases and mutter about some new friend or another. One day he did make a sale, two in fact: a Decamp and a small Ingres to a fellow and his wife from Austria visiting one of the Biddles.

Bob had spent the summer in Europe, had sent two cards marked Concarneau, France. Not long ago, Ezekiel had heard he was back in the city and had taken a studio with Butts Glackens up toward the Schuylkill.

As summer went on, everything from factories to shops closed up. Hotels and rooming houses were boarding up and locking their doors for lack of paying business. Men waited in lines at the churches and soup kitchens. No one was spared the trouble. Wheat and cotton prices tumbled, and farmers had to abandon their farms. Silver mines and railroads continued to go under. Men who filled the ranks of the unions were becoming obstreperous; the newspapers filled with stories of labor marches, rallies and threats. Yet all over the country men went on strike as wages plummeted.

On a particularly restless warm night, at the closing edge of the summer, Ezekiel pulled on his clothes at midnight and went out. He had not wandered for months. The state of everything had distracted him enough he had not thought much of Soap. He did not know what made him think of her now. Once again, the dark liberated.

He strode past Girard Bank, The Bank of North America, Mariner and Merchant, Independence National. The pinpricks of the streetlamps exaggerated the direness in their darkened windows; their grand, soot-stained entrances shouted their impotence. No matter how grand their appearance, they were barely hanging on just as Totten's was and Ezekiel swallowed the thought *fool*. If Totten failed, he had squandered his ma's estate. *Fool*.

He ambled toward the park. A man was laid out on a bench snoring, another curled nearby on a walk. Ezekiel looked away. It could be anyone there. It could be him one day.

Some aspect of the streetlight on the forehead of the man on the walk shot him with the image of the last time he had seen this same flat square forehead, the forehead that had bred his own, the forehead that rippled with a worm of blue vein, the forehead that accused.

His pa held the rifle that day and a satchel that clinked with the glass of empty bottles, and he breathed the mean fumes of whiskey.

Ezekiel was pressed behind his ma. She splayed out her skirt in a weak protection. "Git out of the way," he screeched. A drunken drool streamed down his chin as he raised the rifle to bring it down on Ezekiel's ma, but the gun caught in the low ceiling and brought down a cliff's worth of dust. "Now look what you made me do! Git the strop. The runt, five years old and worthless, worth nothing but the strop."

"Edmund," she said, low and in a tone meant to soothe. She did not move. Ezekiel clung to her. She pushed him away, shouted for him to climb out the far window and run.

Ezekiel hid. When he saw his pa waver through the door and ride off, he returned to the house. His ma put her hands on his shoulders; they were cold and damp. She said, "It's all right, now. He is gone. He'll be better when we see him again." But he was never better.

They did not see him again but for once, when he was driving a herd of cattle through town three years later.

He had not thought of his pa for a long time. *Could his father be like these men? What if Pa was here in Philadelphia? What if Pa saw me now?* In that moment, he knew it had always been his *pa*—never *Totten*—he had had to prove himself to. It was his pa.

He turned onto Sixth, strolling at first but picking up his pace as he neared South Street. A streetcar rattled by. But for the car, the only animation came from the saloons, lights punctuating the night, voices sliding across the walks. The establishments had propped open their doors; the smells of smoke and drink swept out. The drinking houses ran contrary to the rest of the country. Their rooms were full, their tables filled with men, leaning on elbows tossing cards. Men's shoulders filled the bars. Men argued and fought and swatted one another on the back. Their faces shone, their mouths barked, and they cursed and laughed a loud hilarity in a sort of fluid companionship.

He took the same direction he had taken the night he followed Soap so long ago. On South, he came onto another saloon, longer and narrower and louder than the others, glasses clinking, the same forced and piercing laughter. He saw her, then, her and her cloud of impossible hair.

She stood at the bar, a man a head taller next to her. She threw back her head and laughed at something he said, though she kept him in the corner of her eye. The tiny female the size of a child slouched against her.

The fellow flopped his arm around Soap's shoulder, reached down into the neck of her blouse. She threw her arm up and swept his hand away. It was a perfected move, a practiced choreography. She mouthed, "No." The man flared, shouted something Ezekiel could not make out and reached to grab her again. She stepped back. Unpinned, the child-woman slumped to the floor, lay inert at their feet. The fellow brought up a hand as he would to slap the rump of a horse, brought it down toward Soap. She ducked. He raised a fist, then, and before he had a chance to bring it down, Ezekiel was on him. He grabbed the drunkard's arm, pulled him away. "No!"

He carried the tiny woman away. Sawdust clung to her from the floor. But for a clopping arm, she did not stir. Soap said her name was Dolly. She was as light as a girl of ten. He followed Soap, turned where she told him to turn, crossed streets where she told him to cross. The streets grew narrower, streetlights rarer until there were none at all. After a while, the woman grew heavy and his arms began to cramp. He tossed her in the air to resettle her. There seemed to be nothing solid about her; she rode like a rag, her head loose, her arm flopping. She groaned once and stiffened as if in some dream, then went limp again.

Soap spoke nothing but directions and even those gave way to finger points. She was not inebriated, though he had seen her drink from the fellow's bottle. Her friend, however, stank of it. Had it not been for Soap, Ezekiel might have laid the woman somewhere safe and gone on his way.

Soap turned into the narrow stairway of a brick tenement. He had to sidestep in order to make it up with his load. She pointed to a step tread that was broken and another that was missing; he double-stepped over them.

The room was barely big enough to move about in. There was not much to it: two mattresses on the floor, some clothing on pegs on the wall. It was neat, blankets folded, a water bowl that had water in it sitting on a stool, a hair comb, brush and a cracked mirror on a splintered table in the corner. One thing was out of place: an easel, which stood in front of the one window. It held a canvas. On the floor beside it lay a pallet and a quiver of brushes. The only light came from a streetlight. "You can put her," Soap pointed to the far mattress, "on dat one over der."

He laid Dolly on the mattress, began to loosen the neck of her dress, as he had loosened Soap's the night of the blizzard. "I do dat," Soap said. His hands flew up. He swallowed embarrassment.

He made to leave.

"I going to see you again?" Soap said.

He did not know his answer. "I guess," he said.

"Puh," she said and drew down her mouth, "'I guess,' he says."

"Good night," he said and waited for her to say something else, but she did not.

Chapter 81

He would not remember what night it was, only that it was not Tuesday, because he was in the store. Since Bob was back from Europe again, Ezekiel had started making his way to the studio on Tuesdays when Bob and the fellows critiqued one another. When the critiquing was done, they cooked themselves something to eat and drank whiskey and smoked cigars and talked about art and politics and poetry and the taint they saw in society.

So, it could not have been Tuesday.

The day had been unremarkable. George had dropped in to say hello and that he had canceled another trip to France. Ezekiel paid some bills, had served the few people who came in—merchants mostly, peddling everything from napkins to cures. He had evicted a family that day, living in a room on the third floor, for not paying their rent, had put up a sign in the window saying "Room for Rent."

He had spent most of the afternoon rearranging a display of French porcelain, his last purchase until things turned. He paid fifteen dollars on it from a broker needing money and was beginning to worry it had been a mistake. A year ago, he could have sold an item like it for hundreds. It was beautiful, decorated with ornate vines and blue flowers, an opulence incongruent with the times. His safe held a mere eighty dollars' worth of gold, now. It worried him, for, if things did not turn, he did not know how he could keep afloat. The rent from upstairs was barely enough to pay his loan and heat the store, and he still had to eat.

He polished the displays, tossed the rag in back, and went to the door to turn the sign for the night. He pulled the gate over one window, settled a cloth to cover a sterling punchbowl and a pair of crystal candlesticks.

He was reaching for a pallet of ruby jewelry to put into the safe for the night, when he noticed someone looking in: a man, ogling the rubies. The man's square forehead, his jaw, his left ear was bleached in the streetlight. He could have been any vagrant, rough, no coat, no hat. His eyes searched the window like the eyes of a starving cur. He was skeleton-cheeked, his lips pulled in where there were no teeth to plump them. The eyes were bright, iced over, sunken into their sockets.

He understood in that moment that he had lived every other moment in that moment's service. He had known it would come and, when it did, knew all his wondering would be answered. Every toss in the night, every question would be answered and his life would have meaning. All along, he had spent every part of himself in service of this man. Always. Always.

One could fool oneself that he was done with the past, could convince himself he had finished with *ago,* could refuse to allow thought of *then*, or *was*, and in the not thinking one could believe he was finished with *past.* If one looked at it long enough, the sun could blind. But one did not need to look at the sun; one could close one's eyes. One could cover his ears and hear no more than a whisper. One could pretend *then* was then, *ago* was ago. But neither *then* nor *ago* could ever be *never.*

His pa took his eyes from the rubies, looked straight up at Ezekiel. He mouthed, "It's your pa." Time had not taken away the knowing, after all. His father laid his hands on the window, cupped his mouth and yell-said, "Ain't you gonna let your old man in?"

Ezekiel's heart quivered, his bowels moved inside him. He had unlocked this door hundreds of times, as many as he had locked it. The bolt was smooth, its mechanism like silk. His head jerked once to say no, then caught. He made himself go still.

"I ain't gonna hurt you."

Would not hurt him? Then his pa *did* know; he *did* remember. He did remember the strop, the pain of Ezekiel's screams. This non-stranger stood before him, eye to eye now; his shoulders stooped, changed by time, his neck no longer roped in anger, his shoulders no longer thrown back in abject disappointment with his son.

Time did not exist. Philadelphia did not exist. Whatever had been—the evening, the wind, the blown leaves, the bolt, his breath—ceased to be. Ezekiel considered pulling down the second gate, turning off the light and shutting him out. The clock ticked, the bolt clicked and the door flew into his hand. His father grabbed Ezekiel's hand in a vice of a grip and said, "'Tis my boy. 'Tis him." His father squared his frame, as if emerging from some swamp. "I been up to where your aunt and uncle live," he said. Ezekiel still had not uttered a word. His father did not appear to notice the silence, but then he never had. "I didn't go in, a course, but saw your aunt inside. Almost didn't recognize her, she's so fat."

Ezekiel let him talk, and, as he did, his father's manner changed, seemed to feed on Ezekiel's silence. He tipped his head farther back until he was looking down his nose. "I see here my boy did real good." He set his hand on the glass counter with the pallets of the Hainworths' jewelry. "All this yours?"

"Yes." Ezekiel's first word. He had waited so long.

His father laid a hand on Ezekiel's shoulder. His hand was warm; Ezekiel expected ice. His father gawped. "Well." His eyes took in the art, the crystals, the jewelry. "You couldn't a done this yourself. Your uncle must have had a piece in it," he said.

Ezekiel barked, "No," with a force that made it sound like a lie. His father gave him a glance sideways. Ezekiel felt caught. He felt five years old again. He almost felt the drunken whack of the belt.

"I see," his father said, an accusation. "Well, no matter." His hand drifted over the glass then sat inert over the palette of necklaces. "Mary would have liked this."

I know. "Why?"

"Why?" His father looked and for the first time seemed not in control.

Why did you leave? "Why are you here?"

His father gestured toward the floor. "Why am I here?"

"In Philadelphia."

"I been places," he said, "all over."

Everywhere but…

"Ran cows for a while until it petered out."

"I know."

"It *was* you that day of the drive. I knew it."

It was me he spat at.

"Broke ground awhile in the Dakota country, thought I might try to farm again. Didn't work out. Worked silver in Colorado until the mines went bad. Your old pa," he said, "has had it hard." His eyes glistened as if he were the victim and Ezekiel were to blame.

Did you ever think of us after you left Ma and me?

"I can tell you, your pa's had it hard."

Are you sorry?

"I could have done different," his pa said. Ezekiel's throat cramped as if making to cry. Maybe, maybe what came next would set things right. In that one moment, that one flash, the world could have been one thing and, in a snap, could have turned.

"Your mother and me had a future, but she left me high and dry." Pity-tears welled in his eyes. "She up and left." He leaned on the counter, appeared to use it for support. His shoulders pulled up along the sides of his head. He took Ezekiel in a long and straight gaze. His eyes ran over. He sniffed, wiped his nose on the back of his wrist. "I went back," he said. "There wasn't anything there. She took everything. She left me with nothing."

"*She* left *you?*"

"Like I was nothing."

"It was you…," Ezekiel said, but choked and could not continue. *Was his pa telling a lie? Was it the way drink worked on him so he did not remember?* He could not sort this, could make no sense of it.

His pa put his hat on his head, settled it to the side, jaunty. He tipped his head back and said, "Looks like you grew up like your ma, too good for the likes of some." He sniffed as if he were hurt, then let his eyes sweep the goods laid out in the counters like one would take in the spark in a clear and cold midnight sky.

Chapter 82

The days drifted toward winter, days of rain turning to snow, turning slush, lightning bolts splitting the city, thunder, then silence—a breath—until the tempers flared again. Nearly a month had gone by since his pa came to the store; he had not shown again. Days, Ezekiel could pass by thoughts of his pa, but in the evening they came, and acid poured into his gut, his breath grew sick.

He had begun to live for Tuesday nights and the distraction of the men at the studio. He'd begun to view Tuesday nights in the manner of someone clinging to a log in a river. They gave him some *thing*, fellowship, something to think on besides the disorder his pa caused in his head. The old nightmares from his boyhood had returned, black and cracking, dreams he could not remember the content of, only the terror. They twisted him and wrung him dry.

The studio was full that night. Luks was back from Europe, had brought a bottle and was filling the place with his drunk and crazy energy. By the end of the night, he had shed his shirt and was taking sloppy jabs at Redfield to perpetuate some fantasy that he was a notorious boxer.

Sloan brought up the subject of cameras; the men saw cameras as a great threat, and the fellows lingered that night debating the contraption. Sloan did not have one yet, said he could not afford one. But now that a camera was no longer the size of a room and could be carried under one's arm, Bob and Reddy had begun using them. Davis was thinking of buying one.

Ezekiel could see the threat to illustrators, how photographs would take away the need for illustrators and could put them out of business altogether.

He also saw how, when photographs could be colored, they would threaten painters as well. The fellows seemed to need to convince themselves that artwork like theirs, with thick "impasto" and free stroke could not be done by a camera. They spent most of the night trying to convince themselves a camera was no curse, but Redfield argued it had some use.

Luks lifted his bottle toward Redfield like it was an invective. "For what?" he said.

"For reference."

"We got eyes for reference," Luks said and tapped his head. "And memory."

Sloan said, "Amazing you remember anything, Luks."

Luks tipped back the bottle, raised it in a sort of salute. "Trusht me," he said.

Bob groused that a photographic image made some decisions the artist should be making.

Davis said, "Like what? Looks like a photograph does a good job making decisions."

"Like values," Bob said. "Like depth. Everything in a photograph is flatter than it should be. It might look real, but there's no spirit to it."

"Getting sherious on us, old man?" Luks said.

Bob ignored him, "It's tempting to lose out on what we see as artists and to give up the spirit of the thing we want to capture. The sense of a thing isn't necessarily real."

"You mean you make it up?" It was one of the rare times Ezekiel had said anything.

"I mean *it* makes it up. It is what you hear, if you listen. I mean it's what your brush wants, your green or your red, or violet."

"I still see the camera killing illustrators," Sloan said. He took up his pipe, puffed it alive. He took on the aspect of a professor, the shape of the pipe's shank and bowl marking the jut of his jaw. He dragged on it, let the filament of smoke snake from his mouth as he waited for one of the men to counter.

"Never," Luks shook his head, what was left of the whiskey sloshed. "Kill illustrators? Not me. I ain't going nowhere." He had taken off his shirt and draped it over his shoulders, like a boxer's robe. His gut hanging loose over his pants.

Sloan ignored him. "The papers are going to figure out how to make half tones, no more doing the trick with a little scratching and cross-hatching. Then what?"

"Won't happen," Luks said. "The papers"—he belched, thumped his chest—"like us too much."

Sloan was modest, had always downplayed his own art, had never carried on about being able to paint anything worth selling, particularly sufficient to make a living on. "When they figure out how to print photographs, *pffft* we're out of work."

Bob badgered Sloan, "I keep telling you, you got something worth doing."

"Paint?"

"What else?"

"My sisters have to eat," Sloan said. "I have to eat. My mother has to eat, and we have to pay the rent. It's my illustrating that comes up with the money for that. I have to work, man. Paint? You tell me how it's going to make me a living and I'll believe in it."

"Until you do," Redfield said, "you're just a dabbler."

"I guess I'll have to dabble, then, until the newspaper kicks me off my stool."

It was near midnight when they broke. The moon was a cold prick that turned the city to metal.

Ezekiel had left a dim electric bulb on in the store, a token illumination covered by an amber glass, meant only to break the dark. He let himself in, turned the lock. The store was frigid inside, though the radiators crackled and popped. He saw it then: The back alley door was open, cold air rushing in. He had checked everything before he left. He always checked. The glass display, the one with the silver, was shattered, the shelf bare but for the glitter of glass.

It was then he saw the safe, its door slit open ever so slightly. He could not make himself move, had no command of any piece of himself, not an arm, not a leg. A warm, wet stream ran down his leg.

Chapter 83

Hissing, hissing. "SSSS, wh, wh, ssss…." Another, lower, hossing. "Hossss, osssss, hoss." Then the hissing once more. "SSSSS, sss, ssssss-s—sssss." Curious, he looked: two faces, one framed in a dire black cloud. That face hissed some more. The other, pocked, hossed something back. His eyes closed and left the faces to their hissing and hossing.

———

go…nothing…go…close…breathththth. Oh.

Shivers. Sibilant, soft, nonsenses. Non…none…nnnnno…nothhhh…noth-hing…nev…nev-ver…there…there…there… Time. No time. Day. No day. Hushes, whispers, sourceless.

Ice. Hands on his head, ice hands. His teeth. No stopping the teeth. "Cold," the teeth said.

———

"Ma." Like a whisper in a muff, soft and redeeming. "Ma," he whispered. "Ma."

"Thinks I'm his ma." The words came, muttered somewhere from behind him, knees behind, stomach, arm and shoulder draped over. The warmth moved, then drew back. His eyes shut. He returned to where he had been.

———

Smells, food. Suffocating. Suff-o-cating. Blankets, legs, arms captive. He threw them off. And he knew. Everything.

There came the shuffling of feet, the rustle of clothes, a spoon ticking in a pot. His mouth watered, his scalp leaked. Was it still winter?

He was in his bed in his store. Onions. Potatoes. Sounds of boiling liquid not familiar here. The hard things, shelves, workbenches, racks, the trunk, those were familiar. Cooking was strange.

He tried to stand, but the rafters turned to the floor, the window slid down with them. He rolled back onto the bed.

"Stay," she said, her tone sharp, like she would use on a dog.

"Soap," he said.

Chapter 84

The days wove one to another, bent to nights again and to the moon in the high window, white with winter sky. Soap's breath, her hand on his thigh, baskets filled with pears and apples Bob brought, a blanket scrounged from somewhere when the wind wheezed through the windows. The blanket smelled like cellar.

Bob and George repaired the door. The lock had been broken, the door kicked in. It was George who'd found him and deduced he had lain there three days and nights as snow drifted in from the alley. George crowed that, had his friend in France not broken off with him, he might not have been there and Ezekiel might not have thawed out until spring.

The day George discovered him, George had managed to cover the gap in the door, then had hailed a cab to the Academy and wrestled information from "a rather attractive young man at the reception" as to which room Bob taught his class from. He said he had waited, "in that dim mausoleum they call a school for art," until Bob's class let out. It was Bob who went for Soap.

Mr. Clohessy, who lived in one of the upstairs rooms with his wife and five children, had heard the hammering on the door that night. "Ay," Mr. Clohessy said. "'Twas two," He held up two fingers as if Ezekiel did not understand. "Two of them fellas, a skinny sort and big one who was kicking at the door when I seen them. We was sleeping. It woke me and the missus and two of the young ones. They wasn't in there long enough for me to dress proper and see to them. I tried, Mr. Harrington," he said, "but it was all too quick. They was rushing up the alley, stuffing their pockets before anyone coulda done anything."

So, he hadn't been alone. Ezekiel did not think his father would have been the one to work the safe, but then he would never know.

Soap stayed. Winter bit. Sleet etched the windows. The walls breathed with the wind.

She began to paint. In the dim winter light, under inconsistent electric bulbs, she dabbed at a canvas: an image of the basket with Bob's fruits. The doing of it seemed to remove her. As she worked, her face grew soft, her motions fluid.

Ezekiel lay on the bed and watched, then slept, and, by the time he woke again, she would have quit painting and have put something on the stove.

One evening, George yoo-hooed himself in, shouted, "Everyone decent?" He shook snow from his coat. "God, it's not fit for the devil." He saw the canvas with its dabs of pippin greens and blanched reds, and said nothing more.

He returned the next day, and the next. When she finally put the painting aside, George took it and hung it in the store.

She painted no more for two days. The third day, she grabbed her paraphernalia and barked, "Gotta go."

It threw a jab under Ezekiel's ribs. "You leaving?"

"Yah."

"Where?"

"Out," she said.

"Why?" His voice was raspy, but not truly as bad as he made it sound. He tried to think, to gather an excuse to keep her here. But she had slung on her coat. His question lay like an echo after she had gone.

Chapter 85

He dragged himself from the mattress. He was weak, his legs shivered but held. She had left something on the stove for him, but he was not hungry. He caught the reflection of himself in the mirror. For a while, she had shaved him and bathed him with warmed rags. But three days ago, she had quit. The face he saw now was shrunken; his jaw, cheeks and chin were covered in a fringe of drab whiskers. He looked like his father.

It had been nearly two weeks since the robbery. He went to the police, reported that it was gold that had been stolen, and that he knew the name of one of the people who took it. Lieutenant Mahoney was a gentle fellow, soft-spoken, slow in his manner, bald but with nostrils aflame with brambles of red hair. When Ezekiel told Mahoney the name of one of the men was likely Edmund Harrington, Mahoney said "You Harrington, the art guy?" Ezekiel nodded, tried to take pride in the recognition, but was too knotted to do it. "Any relation to the suspect?" Ezekiel said, "Very distant." The policeman said there was little to go on with gold hard to trace and since Mr. Harrington had no known address.

He was bent over the books in his office, running figures with a pencil when she came back. He nearly collapsed with gratitude. He asked where she had been, but she did not answer. She took off her coat and lit the burner to begin cooking something to eat.

George began coming to work every day again. He would check with Soap, dither nicely over Ezekiel, then would down some of her soup and diddle around with things in the store. His arrivals were no longer spotty.

He made it every morning to open the store. Ezekiel would hear the front lock, hear the rattle of the chains opening the windows, and George would stay and serve whoever came in. Every day he closed the store mid-day for an hour and returned, unsteady, catching himself on the counters, leaning against the shelves, eyes pink, watery, nose swollen like a berm in his face.

Soap began working on three canvases, scenes of the city. She left every day with a pack of brushes, bottles, and pallets strapped to her back. There was no question where she went, or where she had been; her images told that story. She painted the winter, the wind, the scrims of rain and snow. She was close to finishing one that held a dim image of people rushing somewhere down by the river, holding onto bonnets and caps in the wind, their coats and skirts whipping. She had begun another of a dark afternoon in a dim alley, tenement houses on each side, a canyon of laundry hanging from windows, children playing amid slop pails and garbage bins, their faces blanched from the cold, noses chapped and running. The image should have been grim, the poverty and filth making one want to turn away. Yet there seemed to be a sort of redemption, a joy in one of the faces, a hint of humor and fun racing up the filth and cobblestones. Whenever George saw her begin one of her paintings. "I want a peek." She would mutter, "Yah," and he would stand in front of her easel as if it were an altar and eat some of her soup and his ears would redden, and he would shake his head and say, "When do you think you'll be done with it?"

"When I'm done with it."

Chapter 86

He read every paper that reported anything but fluff, though fluff was coming in short supply with money as it was. Nearly half the workforce had no jobs. Men who did have them clung on, sweating against the day something might happen; a locomotive might run them down, or they would fall to tuberculosis or pneumonia, or the hole they were digging would swallow them, or a crane knock them crazy, or the business they worked for would fold and jettison them into the streets.

Unions gained strength on the misery. Strikes were making it into the newspapers nearly every day. Miners, railroad workers, tailors, and whoever else, all wanted the government to bail them out—or to give them more money. In late March, a vulgar contingent of the unemployed, calling themselves the Commonweal in Christ, began a march toward Washington wanting the government to hand out jobs. A fellow named Jacob Coxey started the ruckus.

The march began in Ohio with a hundred men and picked up sympathizers until their numbers spread like mange. As they went, they fished the rivers and camped in sympathetic farmers' fields. They shouted their rants along the way, stirring up the citizens in towns and cities as they gained more marchers. There were six thousand of them by the time federal agents arrested them for stomping on the fine grasses of the capital grounds.

Ezekiel grappled with figures again. He had lost his gold, little as it was, and had nothing to spend, yet George kept coming in every day. His pa had taken the three pallets of jewelry, most of it Hainsworths' designs taken on consignment. At the end of the month, Hainsworth would be in to see if anything had sold, and Ezekiel did not know what he would tell him.

At least he ate. But he did not know where Soap got the funds to pay for the stringy chickens she cooked or for the potatoes and carrots and biscuits. He made a guess: Bob. The thought sat slantwise in him. *What relationship did Bob have with her? How did he know her?* The food, no matter the wealth of spices she put in it, tasted flat.

The newspapers fed on the nation's troubles. Everyone wanted a handout, laborers and women alike. Women were stirring up more trouble, as if the country did not have enough already. They marched. They paraded. They shouted about equal rights with men, rights to vote and work, and Lord, forbid contraception. They ranted and roared and raised American flags and shook scepters shaped like the flame on the new statue called Liberty. But the country sank farther into the hole until finally the Democrats and Populists were becoming as fashionable as the plague.

Ice and wind gave way to spring once again. Snow melted. Eves dripped. Grit washed into the gutters. Businesses began to stabilize, if not exactly prosper. A third of the windows along Market remained shuttered, the doorways posted with bankruptcy notices. But it seemed the panic might at least be passing from roar to rumble. Cash was still scarce, gold even scarcer. But the banks had begun to work a scheme to extend loans again by issuing, and honoring, clearing-house certificates. Ezekiel knew, from his time at the university, that this was an old scheme and not entirely legal, a desperate move to get things going again. The government turned a blind eye and did begin to release some credit, giving banks some way to cover money—even paychecks—again. He wondered how his uncle's bank, *his* bank. was managing.

Though people were beginning to walk the streets and to peek into windows, they spent little. *Harrington Fine Art &Jewelry* was not making it; George sold at best a couple paintings a month. But the rest of the inventory languished on the walls and in the racks in back, even two pieces of Soap's.

For the past two months, he had not been able to pay the mortgage on the store.

Tuesday nights at 806, the discussions veered away from the abstract and unintelligible follies of making art and took up discussions of Shakespeare, Zola, and Baudelaire. These Ezekiel could at least make sense of. He craved those nights, wished they could last forever. But the last time he was there, they were on a kick discussing the peculiarities and observations of Moore in his *Modern Painting*, and they were planning to put on a play for themselves in the studio. They were calling it *The Poison Gumdrop*.

Bob continued to study under Anshutz and to teach at the School of Design for Women. He was exhausted. He was painting little. He barely had time for it. He came to the store every few weeks and gave Ezekiel a tired and cursory hello, then checked to see what Soap was doing. He might give some critique of her work. He might even dip a spoon into her goulash before he dragged himself out to another class.

One day he came in with a canvas he called *Street Corner*. Ezekiel had not seen it in the studio. The image was done in thin purples and blues, painted from the window of Bob's own studio looking down onto the street, overlooking the awnings, and the people walking. It was lovely, Bob's best work ever. One could almost hear the cacophony of horses and streetcars. Ezekiel said he wanted to put it up for sale, but Bob thought he might try to enter it in some competitive exhibition.

Because of some contact George made, he sold three canvases and Ezekiel managed to make up the payments on his mortgage. Perhaps it was testament to the dire state of the economy that the widow's attorneys had not badgered him for payment. George sold another canvas, and Ezekiel used the money to pay the Hainsworth's what he owed for the jewelry lost in the robbery. If he could hold on, *if, if, if,* he would retire his loan in a year.

He went to the club two times a week, only to sit and listen. As if the rooms were buried in a pillow, quiet held onto it. No longer was it filled with laughing, few men made it in, now. No longer were the rooms crowded with men whose faces were bloated and smug. It was as if the club had turned to lead. He could not afford to eat in the dining room, so he sat in one of the high library chairs, holding a newspaper, taking some consolation in what he heard. He was not the only one. Conversation, what there was of it, was low, head-to-head, mumbles of deals that had gone wrong, businesses going under, the death of someone they knew, dying of an ailment of the heart or suicide.

He spent near nothing on his own living. Soap required little, asked for nothing, expected less. He thought of going to Totten, thought of selling back his partnership in the bank but did not; pride would not allow it.

Rents from upstairs trickled in. He raised rents one more dollar a month. He cut the middleman expense of buying anything from brokers and agents and began to bid against them himself at the auctions for stuff he could get for pennies. His shelves tumbled with the wreckage of the wealthy: crystals, rolls of rugs from Persia, trunks filled with silks and pearls. The store began to look like the stash of a madman.

As the light began to crawl back into the days, the scramble of goods dazzling in the windows attracted more people in, and the door at *Harrington's* swung open for business more often.

Spring turned to summer, and for a few days the summer lay soft on the city. Soon it turned hot. Soap still filled him with her cheese pierogi and cabbage and her sausages and potatoes. He began to gain a little weight. He had his best slacks let out. His suit jackets were about to need some easing under the arms.

After a day so dense with heat one could see the air, Ezekiel said he was going out. She said, "Where?" He said, "To the studio, if you need to know." She asked to go with him. He laughed, told her no. "It's stag, just for the fellows."

She stomped and threw up her fists. "Fellows! Fellows! What is wrong with you?"

"Wrong with me?"

"You fellows scared of a *woman*?" He threw the word at him, full of breath, full of something he did not understand.

"I take care of you," he said. "What else do you want?"

"Vell you voudn't know," she said. He did not know what was happening.

She grabbed a red, leaded Czechoslovakian decanter on the counter. She swung back her arm and heaved it at him. He ducked. It whizzed past and smashed into a million rubies on the floor.

She pushed around him, through the door to the storeroom. He waited, heard her bracelets knock against wood, heard her shout something in Polish, a sound spat in rage that needed no translation. She came out, shoved her shoulder at him and blasted out the door.

Soap was not there when Ezekiel returned from 806. She had no key; he had not given her one. He had been gone for hours. As he put his key into the lock, he heard the tap-tap of a woman's steps behind him. He turned. He'd thought she was done with her nighttime wanderings. He bellowed, "Where have *you* been?" She went in, but gave him no answer.

Chapter 87

On the last day of July, George came in wiping his face on his handkerchief and blowing at the heat. He had news: Julia Berwind, a friend of his, wanted "three," he held up three fingers, "count them, *three* portraits, some nieces and nephews apparently. And she wants 'the girl' who painted the Pettygroves' daughter to paint them."

Was there *anybody* George did not know? Julia Berwind was one of the Berwind's. It was as if Mining-Magnates was their middle name. They owned half of the world. If Soap agreed to paint them, it could mean a good deal of money. But she seemed to be slipping out of his life, seemed only to use the store as some place to sleep. Gone were her stews and any touch in the night. Only a barren space lay between them on the mattress as she slept. She left each day just after sunrise with her brushes and sketchbooks and sometimes with boards and canvases strapped onto her back, and she did not drag herself back until well after dark. She worked all day in the heat, and, by the time she made it back, she was barely able to stand. She was out, now, painting railroad tracks and steaming allies, curs and tattered children.

He told her about that Julia Berwind wanted three paintings done. "Wull, good for her," she said.

Ezekiel's palms sweated; a commission for three portraits would mean Ezekiel could pay most of his bills and have some to put away.

She dropped her gear on the clean floor, looked away. "I don't do pitchers of people no more."

"You do them all the time," Ezekiel said.

She shook her head. "Not that way, I don't."

"You did it before."

"Yah," she said, "when there wasn't nothing to eat."

Ezekiel nearly screamed, "Can't you see I need money?" After all he had done for her, why didn't she do what he wanted? "It's three damned paintings, for God's sake."

"So, you don't like the damned pitchers I already paint."

He said through his teeth, "Can't make a living on street trash."

"Then what you want?" She waved her hips and slapped her groin. "I give you a little," she slapped her groin, "of this?"

"Stop it," he said.

"What else you want?" Her face grew dark, her pupils taking on what looked like hatred.

"Three paintings," he said and then added, "for your keep." The words hung there.

She bolted to the door, whacked it open, and was gone.

She stayed away three days. The day she returned, only George was in the store. Perhaps she had waited somewhere watching, Ezekiel would not know. When he returned, all her things were gone.

Chapter 88

His wanderings began again, nights that turned real only when he went into them. George continued to come in most days, but he stood listless, his chins draped over his collar. Neither Ezekiel nor George mentioned Soap, nor did they mention Bob or the others. A semblance of the old 806 fellows still gathered on Tuesday nights, but Ezekiel no longer attended.

He had received a card from his aunt on his birthday in May, but that was months ago. As a partner in the bank, he received a monthly accounting and knew it was still struggling, but he also saw it making a glacier's crawl toward solvency.

The store crept along as well though held afloat mostly on the rent from the rooms upstairs. The store, in spite of its paintings and the spark of light on the sterlings and crystals, was barely more than a showpiece for the little business it did. *What happened?* He felt punctured, deflated. He yearned to find the old sense of peace in his columns of the store's books.

———

The days ruptured into the city's interpretation of late summer: lightning bolts, thunderhead bombs, rain. Days, the streets steamed. By evening, the storms passed, and the nights grew still as held breath.

The city had been asleep for hours when he took the umbrella and went out. The rains had let up, but the streets shined wet. Droplets pipped from awnings. Cats fought in the distance. A trolley rattled by, then left silence behind it. A killdeer called. He had not heard a killdeer since the nights in the fields along the Platte River. The bird flew closer. He tried to see it, but it sped along, unseen, a mere reminder, then went away and took its dolorous song with it.

He often came this way at night, the direction having grown to habit. The upstairs apartment windows were all open, but dark, the smells of cabbages from dinner bled out, the stink of diapers, the tang of men's sweat after a day's labor. A baby squalled. A mosquito whined. The rain had washed away the odors of horse urine and the usual smells of the rendering plant, but the air pressed down.

He passed the sailors' hall near the sluice of the new sewer. And, as he had done time and again, he stopped, looked into the long, smoky saloon where he had once found Soap and Dolly. Why did he think he would find her there again? *Why did he even want to?* Nothing but the names of the drunks in a place like this ever changed, but their voices, their noises, their elbows on the tables, their same fetid stink was always the same.

And there she was.

She was standing just where she had before, a bum standing too close to her. As before, the tiny Dolly was there, though she was sitting near the end of the counter beside an empty stool.

Ezekiel pushed through the smoke, through the loud voices, through the stench of breath sickened with drink. The fellow beside Soap draped an arm over her and Ezekiel felt the possession in it. She laughed—or faked a laugh. The fellow was the sort who spent his days on the docks, or the stockyards, when there was work. He must have come to the saloon direct from work for he still wore coveralls and a shirt filthy with excrement. He pulled a coin from his pocket and waggled it at her, and she grimaced another laugh.

Ezekiel was repulsed, feeling something he could not name. He was about to turn and get out before, but she saw him. As he turned, he was pushed with such force it threw him toward the door. His feet slipped in the shavings. He nearly went down. He turned to fight.

It was her. "So," she said—a scold, "you come back."

She half walked, half ran, her skirt gathered up in her hand like a fishwife's. He kept a step behind her. They did not speak. She stopped suddenly; he nearly butted into her. "You still think I should paint them three pitchers?"

The pictures. The portraits. He had all but forgotten them.

"They still want them pictures?"

What could he say?

"You think yes, you think no?"

"I don't know," he said.

"George, he still working in your place?"

"Yes."

"You want them, or don't you?"

"Whatever you want," he said.

"My way."

"Your way."

"My way," she repeated. "Then I guess I'm gonna paint them pitchers."

Chapter 89

They called the paintings *The Julias*. Julia Berwind's three nieces were to pose in a garden on her summer estate northeast of the city. The portraits had to be done by the time school started in barely a month and were to hang in their aunt's home.

George had known the three Berwinds for years—all of them, Julia and both her brothers, Edward and Charles. Ezekiel knew them through the newspapers, knew they had made a fortune and that their wealth put them on the rosters of every club in town, organizations Sloan would have called "everything social and antisocial." George talked about Julia Berwind in a way he might talk about a favorite aunt.

George began to dictate what needed to be done before the painting began. He said Soap would need a studio with good light. Ezekiel asked, "Where?" and George said somewhere with good northern light. Ezekiel would not go to the expense of renting a studio for her; it would be cheaper to forfeit rent from upstairs. He removed a family of renters from one of the top-floor rooms, a room with three windows, two of them facing north. George said it was not enough. Ezekiel did not know why she needed a studio anyway if she was going to paint the damned things in the Berwind garden. George insisted Ezekiel poke a hole in the roof and put in a window for more light. He could not argue; he knew Bob had "poked" a hole in the studio at 806. "Why? She's working *outside* and in the light of day, anyway," Ezekiel said.

"A painter needs a studio," George said. "She's got to have one. It's clear you've never been a painter."

The room was high, in a corner off to itself. It shared only one wall with a room that housed a family of six. To get out required climbing three flights, then managing the long hall to the last door.

He envisioned the summer playing out like an idyll: Soap escaping to the quiet surrounds of a garden, painting the children while some housemaid served refreshments and the birds chirped away. He pictured her returning every evening, making her way back to town on the trolley, cooking him something to eat before she moseyed up the stairs to her studio to dab at whatever she needed to dab at.

The building took on a sort of mania. Everything began to move: George, carpenters, window glaziers. What little money Ezekiel had scraped up was flying out the door. He could not sleep, but he did not wander, either; there was no need for that now.

George could not shut up. He talked constantly about possibilities. He came in early each day, blinking as if surprised at the hour, and Ezekiel forked over money for everything George dictated she would need: sheaves of papers, erasers, charcoals, paints in colors she normally used, linseed, turpentine, canvases the size Miss Berwind wanted. Ezekiel groused at the cost. George said one did not quibble with a master—"or is it a mistress?" Ezekiel did not find the joke particularly amusing.

Soap was supposed to begin work on the portraits in three days; they had to be finished in a little over a month and a half, by the middle of September. "A hell of a short time," George said. She replied, "Puh, ain't nothing." Miss Berwind made a quarter down payment, the balance to be paid in installments as things went along. So much weighed on this. A good part of the first of the money had already been spent on supplies and the ceiling hole the carpenters were cutting. Bits of the roof rained down into the alley all one day. Carpenters sawed through the timbers, through the beam, and hammered up only the roughest bracing. They would install glass the next day.

By nightfall, the air bled down from the upstairs hall, snaked down the stairs as he went up to see the destruction. There was nothing but a gap between the sky and him, a hole the size of a tabletop.

The room was cluttered with sawhorses, a ladder, and tools. The newspapers said the weather was to stay clear, but how often were they wrong? What if it rained? The men had put a canvas over the opening when they left, but a canvas was nothing against a storm.

Ezekiel braced the ladder against the hole, climbed up, folded an opening in the canvas, and pulled himself out onto his roof. He stretched back against the slope. Gravity pulled him down. His pants crept up, creased into his crotch. He put his hands over his chest and rested there alone, his face pressed against the city's dimmed stars.

It became imperative that the studio be perfect—not just for the three paintings but for the future as well. The studio would be a place he could hold her and keep her.

When the roof window was finished and glazed, he had the room whitewashed and the windows polished until the studio was squinting bright. But in the afternoons the room sweltered. By one o'clock, it was hot enough to take one's breath. He called the carpenters back to put in a hinge to open the roof window. He bought a new-fangled electric fan, then had to have wiring run up through the floors for it and for special Welsbach lamps George said she would need.

The day before she was to start, carpenters and electric technicians were still hammering. They would be done barely in time, but everything—everything would be perfect.

He should have known.

Chapter 90

The note from Julia Berwind was delivered by courier. Miss Berwind had had a change in plans; she wanted to discuss details with George immediately because she was leaving in three hours for New York City. She said for him to meet her within the hour at her home at Rittenhouse Square.

George told Ezekiel they should both go. Why? Ezekiel already knew how this would turn out: the deal was off. He had evicted his best renters. He had spent all of what Miss Berwind had paid. He had let himself believe that this time maybe things would go right for him. *Hah.*

She lived in a three-story building. Outside, it was disappointingly modest. He had expected something a bit grander, more flamboyant. But what did he know?

They were shown into the vestibule by a man in a waistcoat. George handed the fellow his hat. Ezekiel waved him off and held onto his own hat, knowing they would not be here long. Meanwhile, as George made himself comfortable in a high, carved chair, Ezekiel gawped. As plain as the house was outside, inside it was quite magnificent. A stairway swept up from the entry in a grace of curves. The walls were filled—corner to corner, floor to ceiling—by incredible collections: portraits, fine tapestries, works with scenes of forests and streams. The floors were layered with silk Persians. He knew of these things of this quality, had seen a few this fine in the hands of the bankruptcy agents, but they had been too rich for him, even at liquidation prices. He ran a business now, preying on the once-wealthies' destitution, but had never found anything like this: carved jades so fine they appeared lit, shimmering crystals that caught every window and light.

She came from a doorway behind the stairs. He and George stood. She was not a large woman but was solid and sure in the same way Ezekiel remembered old Mrs. Gatewood, the woman his mother once worked for in Nebraska. George took Miss Berwind in an embrace and peck-kissed the air each side of her face. "George," she said. Her skirts rustled.

She was plain of face and beyond an age likely to marry, yet she carried herself as if spinsterhood did not matter a whit. She was corseted, but loosely, and her breasts rippled softly. Her dress was simple and unpretentious, but over it she wore yards of black pearls. George pulled Ezekiel toward an introduction as his friend and the owner of *Harrington's Fine Art.* She nodded, said nothing, not even hello; it seemed not an affront but more a matter of time and efficiency.

She pulled a cord hanging beside what he knew was a three-hundred-year-old tapestry featuring women playing lutes in a field. A young maid in a pinafore entered as if she had been waiting for the call. The maid was young, no more than seventeen and had unfortunate protruding front teeth. Miss Berwind ordered her to bring tea and a tray of sweets, then she led George and Ezekiel into the parlor. She motioned for them to sit in chairs covered in leathers the color of peaches. Julia Berwind was someone who, if passed on the street, would not command immediate attention. But on her breast, under the perfect black pearls, was the largest ruby Ezekiel had ever seen.

The servant girl came in with two different teapots. She set them on a marquetry table. She left and, in a moment, returned with a tray of pastries. Ezekiel wiped his palms on his slacks; the shoe was about to drop, the ax to fall. He knew how a man felt when he was about to be lynched. He did not know for sure if he would be able to manage to sip the tea, much less eat.

Julia Berwind leaned forward, settled cups and saucers before Ezekiel and George. She pointed at the pot on the left. "Tea from India", she laid her hand on the other, "or China."

"No sherry?" George said. How could he be so forward?

A smiled flickered on her mouth. "You'll have the Darjeeling," she said.

She poured then sat back holding her saucer and cup. The cup chattered. "I want to see if your artist is willing to change her plans." She sipped, took a century to swallow. *Soap change her plans?*

George sipped his own tea. "I don't know. She is busy." He wore a long necktie that he straightened and patted as if the tie were more important than the discussion. He settled the tie straight. "You may lose her." George knew as well as Ezekiel that Soap had no more painting to do than to dab at her ugly streets.

"I am leaving for New York this afternoon," Miss Berwind said, "and am taking my nieces with me." She handed the tray of sweets to Ezekiel. "A pastry, Mr. Harrington?"

"Yes," he managed. He had to clear his throat or else choke. "Please." He had no idea why he should be nervous. Nervousness bespoke hope. There was no hope. The entire plan was dashed.

George draped an arm over the back of his chair and revealed, without embarrassment, his paunch. "Artists are independent, you know." He chuffed a laugh. "At least *she* is."

"I have," she took one of the pastries from the tray, set it on her saucer, "a place for her. The rooms are adequate, you can tell her that." She took a bite of pastry. Sugar powder speckled her blouse. She swept her hand at it, spread the sugar farther. "I will, of course, pay."

Pay?

George wagged his finger at her. "She's not just inde*pen*dent, she is ec*cen*tric." George made a sing-song of this. He was walking the edge. "You can't toy with someone like that."

"I'm not toying," Miss Berwind said. George was risking the whole thing. *Doesn't he know it? God.*

"You have to understand: she may be the most talented painter on the

East Coast," he said. "Look what she gave the Pettygroves and Humes." He clicked his tongue. "But she goes her own way."

She took the last bite of the pastry, fingered a linen napkin. "Everything will be covered," she said, "her transportation, upkeep, any supplies she might need." Had she not heard George?

"You know how artists can be."

"This sounds like extortion," she said.

George laughed. "Well, Mr. Harrington and I both know she is busy."

"Another thousand," Julia Berwind said. And George shook his head as if there were still some doubt the artist would agree.

When they were done, in the cab driving back to the store, George said, "I could have made her cough up more if she had not been in such a rush."

George worked his magic. Soap agreed to the changes. Ezekiel asked how George managed to do it. George only said she has family. "Family?" Ezekiel said.

"You know, brothers, sisters, that sort of thing." He would say no more than that.

She was to leave for New York that day on the train. She was tired, her eyes lined with dark circles, her movements jerky and nervous. She spoke little, her face shining. Ezekiel had always thought her fearless. It touched him to think she was not. She wore a clean shirt buttoned high at the neck and a skirt that may have passed for good had it not had a burn hole at the shin. She carried a satchel and clung to a sketch pad as if it would somehow save her. As for the rest of the stuff George said she needed, Julia Berwind's *people* had arranged for it to be sent along on the same train. She would be met in New York by more of these people.

The conductor hollered, "All aboard," and Ezekiel reached to hand her up the first step. His hand could have been invisible for the notice she took of it. She was nearly swallowed by the door when she turned and shouted over the noise, "You still gonna be here when I done with this?"

They were the sweetest words he had ever heard. He cupped his mouth with his hands, shouting, "Yes!"

Chapter 91

By midsummer, Bob was in Brittany. Butts Glackens, Shinn, and the rest of the illustrators were busy sketching candidates for the coming elections and dramatizing the fracas Labor drummed up. All but Sloan were laying in plans to leave for Europe soon. Sloan had won recognition for some of his magazine work and was staying in town. "Can't afford to go anywhere," he said.

Even George was heading back to "La Belle France." He said he would stop one night in New York, "to check on our girl, before crossing the puddle." Ezekiel was beginning to hate France; France took people away.

He rented the studio upstairs to another family who refused to pay extra for the electricity and special lighting. He brought the fan down, set it in a corner of the store, and let it whir impressively in the heat.

The country had begun a slow tiptoe toward recovery. The store was selling some of the cheaper items and beginning to show pennies of profit each week. For the first time in months, the books closed with a few dollars in columns without brackets.

As the summer ground on, he heard nothing from Soap nor from Julia Berwind, and the sweet tang of Soap's parting words at the train began to turn doubtful. He grew certain she would be swallowed up by New York as had dozens of the "serious" artists Bob knew who had escaped to the city of art. Ezekiel feared he would never see her again.

Then, late in the summer, on an evening with the city sweltering in horseshit and sweat, he dragged himself back to 806. He had been there only once since Bob abandoned it. It was as if a giant hen were pecking 806 apart, crumb by crumb. There were only two men there that night: Sloan and a new fellow whom Ezekiel did not know. The fellow was a student of sculpture, and Sloan had tried to make some worthy conversation with him, but seemed to have no heart for it. Ezekiel bid them good-bye and headed back to the store.

Chapter 92

He was in the workshop in back, polishing a huge and grossly ornate bronze epergne he had just taken in. The bowl was held up by the form of a seated nude, braiding her hair. It was three feet tall and three centuries old. He laid his hand on the smooth metal of her flank, the curve at the small of her back. Her bronzed skin made him sweat.

He had heard nothing from Soap. He had not expected her to write; he suspected she did not know how to. But he hadn't heard from Julia Berwind nor George. He knew if she did not finish by the time Julia Berwind sailed, there would be no more money.

The bell dinged. He removed his hand from the sculpture, composed a breath, tossed aside the rag.

She was standing at the counter. She had nothing with her but the satchel she'd left with. She wore a smock that was clean but for some spots of red and blue. She stood there like a rag, shoulders drooped, hair undone and flattened on one side, where she must have slept while on the train. She said, "Easy." It was the first time she had called him this; he did not know whether it was said with affection or exhaustion. Her voice was thick. She started to shake. He came around and took her elbow. She jerked it away. "I came for my money."

"You'll get it," he said and reached for her elbow again. She let him take it. He led her back to the bed, settled her on it. He pulled up the sheet and, as he went back to the rags and the nude girl with the braid, she began to snore.

Chapter 93

The telegram said, "Back by the first. Geo." Ezekiel wanted to pump his fist and cry out. There was a chance George would not have come back. The day George departed he had made an off-hand remark that he had gone to meet someone whom his friends had introduced him to while he was in New York.

Soap had been back nearly a week. She was still pale, her color yellow. She hardly spoke. She rose late in the day and stayed out all night until dawn. When she returned in the mornings, she reeked of cigars. Every day she reminded him of the money he owed her. The first day she had asked for it, he asked if she had finished the paintings, and she said, "What you think?"

"All three?"

"Where's the money?"

"All three?"

She did not answer.

Then, on a day of dry heat that baked the city in one last go at summer, the check arrived from Julia Berwind for the complete amount. The figure was dazzling. George had extorted enough from Berwind to pay what was left of Ezekiel's loan on the building, enough even to by a small house.

He locked the check in his safe. When Soap dragged herself in the next morning and asked about her money, he said he would have something soon.

"How soon?"

"I said 'soon.'"

"You better."

That day, he closed the store for the afternoon. He saw a real estate man and bought a modest two-story house near the gracious homes lining Fitler Square.

Chapter 94

George returned the first part of October. Bob had left for Europe with Glackens in June, heading directly for Holland. Grafly got married and left for France the same month. Seaton was there. Calder was there. It was as if a giant vacuum sucked the life out of artistic Philadelphia. Even Sloan would have gone, had he had the money.

The heat finally broke. Lightning bleached the city, thunderheads opened the maws of their god-mouths, and rains drowned all. For two days, the streets ran like rivers. Then, on the third, came sweet, clean fall.

She was flopped on the bed, sleeping off the night. It had been nearly two weeks since she had come back from New York. She had not cooked for him since, had not painted, and each night when she knocked at the door in the dark of the morning and he let her in, she came to the bed and she stroked his back and moved her hands down him and led him where he wanted to go, but she left again the following night.

George had been back a few days. The liaison with whoever he met in Paris had not worked out. He was quiet, almost sullen, his eyes sorrowful, bleary. He left the store more often than ever and came back staggering. He found an apartment not far from the store and said he was never going to trust his heart to anyone again.

Ezekiel waited for him that morning. When he came, he told him he wanted to step out awhile.

"How long do you want me?" George asked.

"No more than an hour."

He went to where Soap lay under the covers, one foot and an ankle thrust out. He flicked her toe. Her eyes fluttered, mucked with sleep. They unstuck and flipped open.

She rolled over, turned her back to him. "What?"

"Get dressed," he said.

"My money?"

"Something better."

She sat up, her hair tangled over half her face. She was still wearing the ratty blouse she had had on the day before and a grimy underskirt. He took a clean blouse from the hook and a thin blue tunic the color of the sky and he handed them to her.

"This better be good," she said.

At a diner, he fed her a meal that she shoveled in with a spoon. When they were done eating, he led her on toward the square. He pulled her to a stop in front of the house facing the square. It was small, two-story, five stairs letting up to it, a small porch bracketed by tall bay windows. Together they would make it a lovely home. He saw his future with her in it, paintings on a wall, each framing some piece of their lives, her knitting, as he sat in a chair smoking, or reading, her in the kitchen cooking, with three children pulling at her skirts. Each image took place in a somber, safe setting: details of flowers on the center table, fine things on shelves and stands, platters of food, impressive statues in the corner, velvets at the windows, and at night all coddled electric illumination. She was in each picture he envisioned and each one a reflection of the life he saw for them.

He put his hand on her arm. "Here it is."

She gaped one way then the other, turned around, found nothing. "I don't see nothing."

He stepped behind her then, took her shoulders, and pointed her at the brick house. "This is *ours*."

"Ain't mine."

"It will be."

"Why would I want that?"

"It's what a woman wants," he said.

"Not *this* woman," she said. "You spend your money however you vant." She held out her hand. "Now give me mine."

"But…"

"But you give me my money." Her money had gone toward paying for this house. She snapped her fingers. "Now."

"I don't have it." He heard his voice crumble.

She thumbed over her shoulder. "You spent my money on *dis*?"

"For us," he said. "I want to marry you." He had not realized it until that moment.

"Puh," she said. "Me marry you? If I marry you, I don't have *nothin'*."

"Anything," he said.

"Anyting, nothing," she said.

"You have the house."

She shook her head so violently her lips flapped. "I marry you, or anybody and, *pfffft,* I got nothin'. A married woman don't have right to nothin', not even her own shoes."

"I'd see to it," he said, but he knew she had a point. He remembered the troubles in Nebraska after his pa disappeared. His mother had experienced a married woman's rights: none. A wife had no right to anything. In order to sell the homestead land that was in her name, she had declared herself a widow through the court. Only widowhood gave her the right to what was hers. He had heard the men at the club deride the laws that loosened a husband's grip on his wife since then, but the laws were anything but clear.

"See to it? Yah! You and who else gonna see to it?"

"What do you want from me?" he said.

"I want my money."

"You'll get it," he said. He would have to borrow.

"When?"

"Tomorrow." He felt the end of things with her, the realization that he had lost her. He had nothing more to lose, and it gave him courage. "What do you want besides your money?"

She looked away and sniffed, and he thought he could see her eyes tear up. "I want what Bobby and them has," she said. "I want to go to France. I want to paint my pitchers in France."

"Then," he said, "I'll take you to France." *What was he saying?*

"Fine then," she said, "after you give me my money."

He moved himself into the miserable house as the tips of the trees were beginning to turn color. He had bought himself a bed, the first real bed since he lived at Mrs. Hanson's rooming house. The proximity to those simple days brought him some consolation now.

He had borrowed heavily to pay Soap her share of the Berwind money. As he counted it into her palm, she said, "When we going to France?"

"Soon."

"When?"

God, does she ever quit? "After the first of the year."

Chapter 95

Her things were in the house. He had brought them there. She did not have much, six items of clothes, a box with brushes and knives, two pallets, three tins, a bottle and a half of oil, a half dozen rags, and some painted canvases rolled with a string. Now, amid the whacks of the park gardeners' pruners across the street and under the tint of the trees growing yellow and orange, movers were bringing in bits of used furniture he had spent more money on.

Their upcoming trip to France seemed to revive George, as if he himself were going. He said leave it up to me and Ezekiel did. As if George needed a clear head to get Soap to France, he had quit drinking but could not stop talking about what this trip to Paris would do for "his girl."

He sent telegrams by the dozens to "his people over there." His friend Paul Durand-Ruel had a gallery "in the heart of things," and George had jotted down the address. "Then there's my friend Georges Petit." He scribbled a street name but did not have the address. "Oh, and Josse and Gaston, you *must* drop by. You *must* go. *Must, must, must.*" He said none of these friends spoke English, "or not much of it anyway," but his friend Jackie Fournier spoke it "beautifully." Jackie would see to it Soap and Ezekiel were taken care of. George sent a telegraph exaggerating Ezekiel's status, telling Jackie that Ezekiel Harrington was "the premier collector of art" on the eastern seaboard and was bringing his "discovery" over, leaving for France in two weeks.

Ezekiel finally learned her full name, Mademoiselle Jacqueline Fournier. George emphasized that *mademoiselle* meant not married. "She might be a little this side of stern but rich as hell. She loves me, and she will love you and our girl."

Ice covered the streets the day they left. Wind blew sleet and snow the entire way into New York. As the train slowed, every part of Soap began to rock and jerk, *every* part: elbows, feet, hands, even her head swung forward and back. She began to pant like a dog. "I don't like this," she said. He had not known how much coming to New York for the Berwind paintings had taken from her until this moment. "I ain't gonna do any more just because somebody wants money or says I ought to," and she shot him a look.

They were sailing on the *Bretagne.* It would have them in Havre in just under two weeks. After they landed, they would have another three-hour train trip before Bob met them in Paris. Ezekiel had never sailed before, had never even seen the ocean.

Their room was delightfully too small to move inside of without bumping. It had one window, a tiny round pinpoint that looked out on a lumpy sky. Mornings, a porter came to change linen and to swing up the bed on its hinges. He came again in the evenings to pull it down and tidy the blanket.

From the first day, Soap was sick. She stayed out on the deck long after dark. Everything about the ship hummed and vibrated: the floor, the bed, the wall, until it numbed the soles of his feet. For days, Soap was too sick to manage food. If she ate, which she wanted to do because Ezekiel was paying, she could not keep it down. Finally, by the third day, she kept down a bouillon, then a biscuit, and her green pallor began to pink up a bit and allow her to take the hand off her gut. "Was like this, only worse, when I come before." He had never thought about her coming, had never realized until then that this was how she had gotten from Poland to Philadelphia. It were these details he would probe, when they were settled one day. Until then, he felt asking such was improper, merely the stuff of a busybody. He was certain she would not have answered at any rate.

She had brought a sketch pad, a brush, and a box of six watercolors with her. She took to staying out on the deck in one of the slatted chairs with the pad braced on the rail. She drew and she painted: strollers, crying babies, men in white hats wrapped in blankets, women in corsets and bonnets they held down with their hands in the wind, a servant girl walking a hound.

As the days slipped by, an undeniable dread set in, something he could not identify. Bob had written that he would arrange for a small hotel not far from his studio and apartment. He wrote that he taught evening classes at his studio as well as painted there. The neighborhood where he lived was called Montparnasse. He would meet them at the train station and see them to their hotel.

The skies of Paris were as gray and full of gloom as those they had left in Philadelphia. They had taken a cab to the train station in Havre. Neither of them had much to transfer; Ezekiel was glad they were not staying long. They had slept for three hours as the small European locomotive clinked along.

At the Paris station, they stood with their bags, gawping through the crowds, through the umbrellas, through the scarves that women waved. They heard him shouting. "EEEEEasy! E-*zee*-kiel! So-FEEE-Yah." Soap saw him first. She lifted her skirt and bolted, leaving Ezekiel scrambling with the bags as she ran straight into Bob Henri's arms.

Chapter 96

Afternoon had begun to darken toward evening. As they drove through the city, Bob chattered, calling out places they passed, remarking on things he was working on. He looked a bit debauched, had not had a haircut for too long, had grown a black goatee that did not suit him. But his complexion was clear, gone were the weals and white-headed infections that marked his cheeks in Philadelphia. He chattered about Glackens and their work together. He stretched his legs. He rambled, said he had finished painting a Spaniard, and a gypsy woman he found in the neighborhood. He said he and Glackens had taken themselves up to the old Julian school with good intentions of studying there again, but neither had enrolled. "It reminded us of The Academy, and we just couldn't do it anymore." The thought of the school seemed to make him nervous, holding himself still one moment, shifting the next, sometimes rubbing his hands together, sometimes wiping them on his pants.

Along the streets, the people of Paris seemed to be making the best of a dreary day strolling about in the pan-gray afternoon.

Bob truly needed a haircut. This changed Bob bothered Ezekiel.

They came upon a cathedral situated smack in the middle of the street, "Saint Madeleine," he said. He played with the goatee and seemed to relax a bit. He began calling out places like a guide—the names of the churches, the streets. They clattered to a broad plaza with two huge ornate and dripping fountains he said was called the Place de la Concorde. They drove through dense gardens he called were *twee-lurees*.

They turned, went over an ancient bridge. Paris fell into disarray after that, arabesqued into a nonsense of wasted space and knotted alleys, as if it had no idea of a straight line or organization. The names of the streets went on for short stretches then changed to something else willy-nilly. Streets curved, then flew off at any bizarre angle, narrowed, crossed—some ten at a time. Paris was definitely not practical Philadelphia.

Soap could have broken her neck for staring. She said nothing as they went; Ezekiel might as well not have been there. Bob kept up his prattle as streets wound, dizzy and un-squared, as if none of them had ever never seen the wonders of a planner's compass. Ezekiel could not fathom how people ever knew where they were here.

Bob seemed to relax as they went. "Dinkbot is doing some pretty nice work," he said. Ezekiel struggled to remember who Dinkbot was: Glackens, AKA Butts, the quiet fellow the men were fond enough of to give two monikers. Bob began to ramble on about painting in general, though he did not speak of his own work much. Ezekiel sensed an insecurity.

The coach bumped away from the main boulevards through a tangle of ever smaller streets. Bob said the hotel was a five-minute walk from his studio and his apartment. The stores were getting tinier, the streets narrowing. Lights were coming on in the shop, most specializing on one single thing: plucked chickens that hung on lines in the windows, gentlemen's hats on pegs, shaving creams in pots, women's stockings hung on lines. One even displayed a disgrace of corsets.

The streets grew too narrow for two carriages to pass. The driver had to manage the traces with a vigilance as pedestrians smashed themselves against the buildings to let the coach by. Businesses were closing, the streets growing quiet, people slogging home, women carrying carrots and chards and packages of meats. A ragpicker passed by, pulling a cart stacked with rags in bales. A dog lifted its leg, left a stain on a shopfront.

The electric streetlights had already come on along the main boulevards, but here in the alley ways, lamplighters, carrying their poles and their lighted wicks, lit the oil lamps by hand. By the time the coach slowed at the hotel, there was nothing left of the day but the warm, curried-yellow light of the lamps. Here it was, nearly night, and Paris' women were still out, laughing, walking brazenly, some alone, some with several men at a time. It was indecent.

Bob said, "Here we are."

The coach pulled up to a sign that read Le Cher Mouche. The hotel was so small and narrow, it could hardly be called a hotel. The building tipped slightly to the right and aslant to the street without either plumb line or the benefit of a surveyor's pin or chain. There were three floors to it, two windows to a floor. The two windows in the second story were lit, those in the third were dark. As he got out, Bob said, "It's not far from the Ecole."

They went inside. Bob babbled at a small woman at a tiny desk, then turned and said breakfast would be brought to their room in the morning. He waited in the entry as the petite, narrow-waisted woman led Ezekiel and Soap up two flights of stairs, through a dim hallway, two doors on each side. Her hair arranged in a complicated twist high on her head. As she unlocked one door and handed Ezekiel the key, she sing-songed, "Bon soir, monsieur, madame." And she made a little dip with her chin and went back down the stairs.

Soap dropped her bag just inside the door. The room was ancient with a needlepoint rug worn to canvas at the door, a sagged bed, night tables on each side. Against one wall, a chest covered by a rose-colored lace was missing a drawer. The room had one high, arched window with two pegs on each side. Ezekiel put his suitcase on the chest and opened it to air.

They went to a small café Bob knew of. It was filled with smoke. They ate in that hot place as their eyes teared and the rain began to pelt down outside. The meal was served in pieces, brought in small dishes, unlike the usual way food was dished up at home. The newness of it: oysters in shells, potatoes roasted in a rock oven built into a wall; mutton from a steaming carcass; tiny pears swimming in liquor, made Ezekiel shift uncomfortably in his chair. Soap ate as if starved, fisting up the food with her spoon, barely speaking, shoving pieces of bread into her pocket as if this were the last meal of her life.

Bob had launched into a tirade on how the schools squelched the spirit of art, how what one learned in them was merely pretty dabbings, a perfection of brushwork, color, fantasies of composition measured with yardsticks. He shook his head. "There's spirit in none of it, but it's what they are hanging in the salon, and the painters who paint it are getting rich." Then he said, "The new ones, the ones who have not been working in the schools, those who paint with real life in them, they are getting nothing but a lot of gawps and laughs."

He cut a lemon, sprayed an oyster in a shell with it. He tipped the oyster into his mouth and slid the wet gray thing into it. He wiped his mouth on a cloth. "But some of the salon's rejects," he said, "Sisley and Pissaro, maybe even Caillebotte, I think are on to something. I ask: How can the academies deny it?" He did not wait for an answer. "Here and there they get some play, but no sales. The salon won't touch them, the established galleries won't hang them."

He laid his hand on the table in a soft, reverent manner. "These guys have something, Easy." Bob seemed to need to convince Ezekiel of something he could not quite understand. "They do have something," he said. "They do."

That night, Ezekiel slept as if in a stupor. His chin itched with dried drool when he woke once in the night to use the pot. Soap slept in the glow from the streetlight. She had not moved since she had flopped under the covers.

A rap at the door woke him, then a woman's voice trilling, "*Bon jour, monsieur, madame. J'apporte le petit dejeuner.*"

The aroma of coffee wafted under the door. It was morning, the window letting in a slit of light from a dim sun. He heard the tinkle of glass and the sound of a tray being laid at the door. He turned to bid Soap good morning. The bed was empty. The place where she had slept was cold.

Chapter 97

The window looked out the back onto other buildings, apartments he thought, as cracked and crooked as the hotel. Three stories below, the walls formed a small stone square that made do as a courtyard. A cluster of wintering flowerpots sat in a corner, a wrought-iron table with two chairs tipped. He had eaten his morning pastry, drunk the hot, bitter-sweet drink. Soap's portion of the breakfast still sat on the tray when the clerk came in to make up the bed. She motioned to it. *"Avez-vous fini, monsieur?"* she said and motioned as if to pick up the tray. He nodded and she took it out.

Ezekiel stayed in the room, glaring through the dismal window most of the morning. When he could bear it no longer, he took himself downstairs, stood in the sodden day with his hands in his pockets, peering one way up the street then the other, willing her to come into view. He felt abandoned. He hated this weakness. *Where could she go?* He knew she had no money. She never had it; money seemed to fly from her fingers. He had once asked her what happened to all the money from Julia Berwind, and she simply shrugged and raised her hands helplessly in the air.

He stumbled back up the narrow stairs, lay on the bed watching the window turn dark, then light, then dark again as it began to rain. He rose, after some time, and sat on Soap's edge of the bed. He eyed the case she had brought her things in. It lay open beside his on the table by the wash basin. He began sorting through her poor underwear, her two woolen socks, her laddered stockings, her comb and brush. None of her artist's paraphernalia was in the room, he realized she must have taken it.

At the bottom of the case he found a tissue paper folded around some small object the size of his thumb. It was the sole item in all her kit that seemed cared for. He laid it on the bed and pulled open the tissue with the tips of his fingers. Inside was a small, soiled rag doll. It had been roughly fashioned, a string pulled at the neck to make a head, two arms sewn on the body, two legs with strings at the ankles for feet. The crown of the head was covered with hairs, sewn into it with a needle. The hairs were fine, blond, and curling. It had been used, or played with, and bore a stain in the middle and grime at the edges. He wrapped the doll back in the tissue, arranged it and her other belongings as they had been.

Late in the afternoon a door slammed in a room across the courtyard, a man shouted and a woman screamed. Ezekiel heard what could be nothing but a slap and the woman's scream again. It could have been Ezekiel himself delivering the blow he thought Soap deserved. He had brought her all this way, had spent handfuls of borrowed money on her, and she had the temerity to abandon him.

As dusk coated the miserable windows, he heard footfalls on the steps. He lay back on the bed and closed his eyes as if he had nothing better to do than to rest after touring the city all day. He readied himself to leap at her, to lash out the blow of his punishment. When she walked in, he would make his move; she would never repeat what she had done today.

He heard the rustle of her skirts, her hand on the doorknob. She came through in a dim shine of light, her art contraption strapped to her back, papers in her hand, tied in a roll.

Bob Henri followed her in.

Ezekiel sat up from the bed. "Get up," she said, "I am hungry."

Bob took them to a different place for dinner, a place not far from the hotel and on the way toward wherever it was that Bob lived. He said he and Soap had met just a moment ago at the hotel before they made it up to the room. Ezekiel was not sure he believed the coincidence. At dinner, Soap ate with all her appetite again, then grew sleepy. He had managed to get her to say that she had been out all day drawing. When he asked drawing *what,* she had said nothing much. He pressed her and she shrugged and said people, simply that: people. Her evasion only added to his anger.

There had been a delivery to the hotel while they were gone: two envelopes slipped under the door, one marked *télégramme*, the other simply bearing their names, M. Harrington, Mlle. Dibrouski. Soap stepped on the envelopes as if they were not there, then fell, face down, onto the bed. He stooped to pick up the papers and had the familiar sense that he was, once again, bending to her. The letter was of heavy linen stock. He gave it an assessor's toss, let its weight settle in his hand.

He read the telegram first, its simple economical language:

> *Mlle. Fournier to contact soon. Hope your trip good. Things swimming along fine in Phla. Geo*

The envelope's engraving was deep, the die perfect. The envelope was smeared and crumpled where Soap had stepped on it and it was unstamped. The engraving bore the name *Jacqueline Fournier* and gave an address on Rue Saint Honoré.

He turned the heavy paper in his hand, pressed his finger under the flap, tore the paper at the seal. The note inside was on the heaviest linen stock, engraved with her name and her seal. She had written:

> *Dear M. Harrington and Mlle. Dibrouski*
>
> *Please accept my invitation of your company four days from now, on Tuesday next 1400hr. My driver will arrive outside your hotel at 1000 hours to bring you to my*

> *apartment. He will return tomorrow to retrieve your answer.*
>
> *It would please me greatly to see any of Mlle. Dibrouski's work if she bothered to bring any of it. Our friend George has had no end of praise for it.*
>
> *J. Fournier*

Inside was a smaller, stamped envelope containing another engraved card for their response.

Chapter 98

Their first three days began to carve themselves into small habits. Soap had not disappeared again since the first night. Mornings, they would wait for the hotel clerk to place their tray outside the door and to announce "*Le petit.*" Soap would gather her gear for the day and he would follow her to wherever caught her interest: the river, or a bridge, or a park where she would sit on some bench for hours and draw.

The weather had caught what must have been Parisian spring. On the face of it, the season, the sweep of clouds, the threat of storms, the sudden glare of sun was no different from the season at home. But it *was* different here, impossible to predict. When Philadelphians came out of their winter confinement, they rode to the parks in the trolleys, and they walked the streets, but as they walked they made their ways with purpose and resolve. Parisians poured from their doors laughing, bringing out not the serious and practical air of Philadelphians but boisterous laughter, and they wore not sensible greys and browns done in woolens but stripes and florid satins the colors of tulips. They spread their blankets in the broad parks, and they sat themselves in an extravagant manner, opening their baskets, tearing at crusted breads, and pouring their wines while making a carnival of themselves.

It was this living of life that Soap seemed to want to capture, and her pale chalks allowed him to see what he could not see on his own: He found it beautiful.

They had not seen Bob for a few days. He had said he and Glackens would be on a brief project that would keep them out of town from early in the morning until late at night. Then, last evening he had come to the hotel again, this time with Glackens in tow. Glackens had changed in the time he had been here, had grown a dark beard, and, instead of his neat tweeds, he wore a corduroy suit that was sprung at the elbows and knees. He was still the same quiet fellow, his eyes still bright with their strange lights. His reserved grace almost brought back the good times at 806. Ezekiel was gladdened.

They were to meet Ms. Fournier the next day. Ezekiel dreaded the encounter, wished George were here to help him through it. He would be glad to get it done with.

That night, early, they went to a small restaurant that served first a plate of roasted pear with cucumber, then a cheese that smelled like piss. This was followed by a slab of fish Ezekiel could not identify and a liver of some sort they spread on thin wafers that Bob, Glackens, and Soap washed down with a tankard of wine the color of mud.

Bob and Butts Glackens talked about the coming of spring light as if light were an altar to some god. Before they all left the restaurant, Bob drew a crooked map to his studio so Soap could join his class the next day, after the visit to Mlle. Fournier's. Bob turned an intense eye toward Ezekiel. "She'll be the only woman." He seemed to be asking permission. "It'll be just her with the guys." And, though Ezekiel said nothing, this did make a difference.

They rose that morning before the hotel woman brought their food. Ezekiel was itchy, uneasy, unsure. The coach arrived at exactly the specified time. It was huge, the size of a cottage, taking up the entire breadth of the street plus some of the walk.

The coachman was standing by its open door as Ezekiel and Soap stepped out of the hotel. He lifted his hat and bent forward at their approach. Ezekiel guessed the man was five years younger than he, and dark, apparently from some country other than France. He wore a long, fine-fitting blue overcoat and black leather gaiters.

He shut the door after they were seated and, with it, muted every whisper of the city's noise. Inside, the coach was as big as a room. It was a lovely thing, its fittings as fine and tight as Hainsworth's jewelry. As the horses pulled the thing forward, Ezekiel felt the sense he would prove, once again, insufficient. The things he wore, his best suit, his coat, his elegant gold watch, had given him weight in Philadelphia. Here, it only made him feel diminished.

Soap sat in her ill-fitting dress, holding her roll of wrinkled papers. She seemed unaware and uncaring that the sleeve of her coat was frayed or that the hem of her skirt was dark with grime. She sat as she always sat, in her crude posture, her knees loose and improper, no more ill at ease than ever. At the edge of the hotel's modest neighborhood, they came upon a woman leaning against a dark stair. She smoked a brown tobacco cigar. She pulled up her skirt as they passed, bared an indecent ankle. Ezekiel felt heat in his face, turned to see what Soap made of the woman. Soap only nodded to her as if in greeting and the woman watched as the coach passed by.

They crept through the silent city. They observed a dog barking but did not hear it, a butcher mutely calling out specials in front of his store. Everything about the coach seemed meant to cushion one from the world: the thick carpet the color of burgundy wine, the seats upholstered with horsehair dyed the light tint of summer sky. No refinement seemed to have been overlooked—roses filled crystal vases on each side, door handles and window fittings had all been plated with gold.

George had said Mlle. Fournier spoke English well. Her note two days ago had borne that out. Knowing this should have given Ezekiel some comfort, but, as they drew closer, nothing George had said made him feel at ease.

They teetered from one neighborhood to another, then another, each more elaborate than the last. The boulevards grew broad then narrowed again at the river, squeezing into a bridge named Pont Royal. They had not been on this side of the city since the day they came. They drove past a palace set back from the street, and the *twee-lurees*. Women pushed babies through the gardens in prams decorated with ruffled umbrellas. Couples strolled arm in arm. The gardens were full of people and children and dogs, yet the trees were nearly bare but for scrims of blossoms and tender buds.

Here, on this side of Paris, the buildings rose five stories high, structures whose extravagant faces were plastered with gargoyles and flourishes. Above the shops, behind the tall, arched windows, people made their lives and their homes. Ezekiel could not comprehend the variety of the shops as they swept by: china, baby carriages, flowers, men's undergarments next to a shop with women's stockings.

The coach turned, entered an alleyway that was nothing more than a narrow canyon fitted behind elaborate buildings. The driver pulled to a stop in front of two doors as wide and tall as a Philadelphia bank's. He whistled and the doors pulled open. The coach lurched onto rough stone and pulled into a courtyard that let onto fancy marble doors bracketed by sculpted trees in pots.

The coach shook as the driver stepped down, the horses threw their heads. He went to the doors and pounded the knocker. The doors swung open. A young woman in a white cap and maid's pinafore stepped out. She was pretty, her complexion white, her cheeks pink as if she had recently pinched them. She curtsied and muttered, *"Bon jour, monsieur, mademoiselle."* Soap waved her hand at the girl, and Ezekiel was embarrassed at her ignorance of the girl's low position.

The coachman opened Soap's door, waited as she gathered her role of sketches and her skirt. Ezekiel got out, patted down his hair as the maid led them into a marble entry with a grand staircase two stories high. George had said this was Mlle. Fournier's home in the city. He had described it in an offhand manner and added that she had another home in the country that was a magnificent place.

But for the stairway, the entry was as broad and open as a field. Around it, statues of five women, unabashedly naked and half again larger than life, displayed themselves on pedestals. The maid led them to an alcove beside the staircase, stopped at a gate positioned in it. The gate was made of iron wrought in the fanciful shapes of herons and skunks. It opened to a well and a series of looping chains.

Soap stood back, suddenly tentative. The maid rotated a brass arm beside the gate, an electric motor whirred, and the looping chains began to move down. Soap chuffed in a breath when a floor drew down and a space the size of a closet slipped in front of them. She stepped back into him and stayed there. Ezekiel had experienced an electric elevator in Wanamaker's, apparently Soap had no idea what it was.

The room's walls were covered with mirrors. As the gate rattled open, her reflection in them was one of abject fright. She crushed her drawings to her chest and looked like a rabbit about to bolt. He put his hand on her back and she gasped. He pushed harder until her feet gave way, and she was in. As the gate closed behind them, and the floor pushed up, he was afraid she would scream. She grabbed his elbow when the room finally jerked to a stop. He took strength from her and the sense that, for the first time since they had left home, he had some use.

The maid took them to a huge room as great as the ballroom at the Rittenhouse Club. Sun streamed in through a half dozen windows rising floor to ceiling nearly fifteen feet. Drapes, heavy golden silks, framed the view of a broad plaza; a high column poked from the middle of it, topped by the ridiculous statue of some Roman emperor.

The sun disappeared behind clouds for the snap of a finger then blazed again onto an Aubusson carpet large enough for a game of cricket. The maid led them to a cluster of chairs and sofas covered in brocades, motioned for them to sit. This room was like no room Ezekiel had ever imagined, the walls covered with silks the colors of apricots, and cherries, and dark purple plums. It was as if someone wanted the room to conjure the image of a basket of fruits. The floors were set with marquetry patterns of birds and vines. Along the walls hung huge portraits set in carved gold frames half a yard wide. There was, he knew, nothing like this in all of Pennsylvania.

And then she came. She was tall. As she swept in, her manner, her dress, her carriage took over the room. She was erect, her hair graying and heaped somewhat messily high on the crown of her head. Her dress was dull, unassuming: gray skirts, modest pearls, white tailored shirt, clothes that would have blended into the streets back home, but here in this fanciful city were outstanding.

Ezekiel stood as she came in but Soap remained in her seat. "Welcome to Paris," Mlle. Fournier said. He reached to pull Soap up from the sofa and Mlle. Fournier patted her hands down in a leave-her-be.

"Thank you," Ezekiel managed.

She reached first for Soap's hand. "Mlle. Dibrouski?" Soap's mouth was open, her arms still strangling her papers. Mlle. Fournier continued to hold out her hand, waiting for Soap to take it. And, when she didn't respond, Ezekiel pressed her hand toward the woman. God, why hadn't he drilled Soap on these things? Mlle. Fournier gave a small grin as Soap gave her the tips of her fingers. "I am so glad to meet you," she said, her English touched with the soft accent of the French. "George has been eager for us to meet."

She reached for Ezekiel's hand, and, as she did, her eyes slid toward the papers Soap clutched. "I see," she said. "You have brought some of your work." Ezekiel could not know Mlle. Fournier, nor could he have ever seen her before, but he liked her; she felt familiar.

Soap nodded. "Yah," she said and pushed the papers at Mlle. Fournier.

Mlle. Fournier stifled another grin and took them. "We'll have something to eat first. Then I would like to see what you've brought."

Mlle. Fournier turned, put two fingers into her mouth and blew a shrieking whistle. It made Ezekiel jump. A scramble of noise came from the hall, scratching, thumping, scrambling sounds, and around the corner bounded two huge hounds, long-haired, long-legged, long-nosed creatures rippling in like two horses.

The dogs leaped up, put their paws on Mlle. Fournier's chest. They were tremendous, stretched up as they were, taller even than she. *"Allors,"* she said, "down, girls." And the dogs turned their attention on Ezekiel, began sniffing his ankles and between his legs. He pushed them gently away, and they transferred their noses to Soap.

One of the dogs was red with long hair the color of rust, the other white with patches of black. Mlle. Fournier motioned toward the red hound. "This is Roselyn. The other is my Fantine." She made a little giggle, some joke she shared with herself. "I suppose I should have named them Natasha and Ulya, or something the Czar might appreciate, but the tongue is so much gentler with the French, don't you think?" The dogs wagged. They seemed to know they were the center of things, and they set their muzzles down in Soap's lap and she laughed.

Ezekiel knew, then, whom Mlle. Fournier reminded him of: Julia Berwind. They were both strong women, confident in a way that made a cramp at the base of his skull. George had said Mlle. Fournier was not married and never had been; neither had Julia Berwind. What was it with these women who had no men in their lives to take care of them? What made them so certain, so complete? *Let a woman have money, let her have her way, and she would own the world.*

Two maids brought in ornate trays, one with pastries glistening with cherries and creams and molding cheeses, the other with tea in a silver pot, and a bottle of bubbling wine. Mlle. Fournier took the tray with the food. The dogs' eyes followed as she offered it first to Soap, then Ezekiel, then she took bits of the cheese and offered each dog a lick.

As they ate, they chatted, Mlle. Fournier asked about Philadelphia and George and Ezekiel's business. Ezekiel had a sip of the wine and began to let down a bit. The day was developing into a lovely afternoon, warm, the sun spreading the colors of the carpet. Mlle. Fournier's confidence was mesmerizing, her lack of fuss, the sprays of graying hair springing from her forehead, the certainty with which she spoke, her long arms, the length of her crossed legs, the sense about her that all was right, that no thought, no occurrence, mishap, or problem was beyond her ability to deal with. Ezekiel felt his bones loosen and give way.

When they were finished with the food, she produced a gilded leather box, held it open. Rows of thin brown cigars lined it. She held the box toward Soap, who slapped her own thigh with a glee. "My God!" Her tone was raspy, thick, and coarse as ever. She plucked one, licked it and drew it obscenely in and out of her mouth. Ezekiel wanted to disappear.

Mlle. Fournier held the box toward him, motioned for him to choose one for himself. He shook his head no. She herself took one and licked it, then hummed a satisfied drone back in her throat. She held a light for Soap, then crossed her eyes and lit her own. She took a long drag from it and watched Soap as the blue smoke drifted from her mouth. "Well," she said. "Let's see what you brought, Mlle. Dibrouski."

———

Ezekiel pulled himself up from the sofa, went to the table where the crumpled papers lay. He spread them as Mlle. Fournier leaned over. There were four, the first a sketch of men fishing from the ramparts of the Seine, the second a colored chalk of a woman strolling with a baby, in a park, under dark and barren trees. Soap had done it just yesterday. The last was one she must have kept hidden. He did not know what the image was at first, only that it was of a woman standing in front of a poor and narrow stairway. As he finished laying it out, he knew: the slut in the street they had seen the first day they came into the city. He rushed to hide it before Mlle.

Fournier would see it.

"No," she said. She opened it, pressed it smooth, and stood before it like someone at an altar. "Ah," she whispered and began dabbing her eyes with a handkerchief. "Our George was right." She looked up at Ezekiel and blinked. "Wasn't he?"

"Yes," Ezekiel said.

She turned to Soap. "George said you paint as well as draw, Mlle. Dibrouski."

"Not here," Soap said.

"Could I ask why?"

"Yah," Soap said.

"Why?"

"Didn't bring no paints."

"No paints? An artist in Paris with no paints?"

Why was Mlle. Fournier not incensed by Soap's rough rudeness? Ezekiel said, "I told her they were too much to bring and for her to leave them home." It was true, all of her things; her pallets, her lengths of untouched canvases, her knives, brushes, tins of solvents and oil, were stored in a closed bedroom at the house in Philadelphia. He could have arranged to bring them, somehow, but had wanted them to anchor her there in the Philadelphia house.

He said "home" as if it were *her* home as well. He had asked if she wanted to leave more of her things before they set out for New York, but all she said was, "No."

Mlle. Fournier clasped her hands under her chin. "Well," she said. "How can you do my portrait, then?"

Ezekiel looked down at Soap; her lower lids were drawn up as if she were hard in thought. "She has decided that portraits are no longer for her," he said.

"Let *her* tell me." It might have been a reprimand, a warning, though her tone was gentle. She leaned toward Soap, her head tipped and curious.

"If I had those paints I left back there, I would do it." She looked down at the dogs, which were stretched flat and elegant in a rectangle of sun.

Mlle. Fournier's attention went to the dogs as well. It was as if their lazy beauty were somehow merging the two women. "How long did you say you would be in Paris?"

"Another three weeks," Ezekiel said. He had been counting the days.

"Not long," Mlle. Fournier said.

"Yah," Soap said.

"Yes what, dear?" Mlle. Fournier said.

"If had those paints, I would do it."

"But you don't," Ezekiel said.

Mlle. Fournier's carriage took them back to the hotel before they left for Bob's.

His studio was on the highest floor of the building. Like sprouts, artists and their studios always seemed to be reaching higher for light. Bob held class there once a week in the late afternoon, presumably after he had spent the day out, slathering paints on his canvases and boards. It was, Bob had said, a chance to share and to critique each other's work. The room was warm with the cozy heat of a day that had seen sun. Though the sun was nearly spent by then, the room still collected what light was left.

Ezekiel and Soap arrived early. Bob was just cleaning a handful of brushes. The room smelled of his paints and of the heady vapors of turpentine. "Hey," he said as they walked in. The canvas he was working on sat on an easel turned to face the windows, its back to the door. Soap stepped around, squinted at it. "That some place out of town?" she said. "You been there this week?" Bob said yes. "Must be a nice sorta place," she said. And Ezekiel waited for her to comment on the piece. She was grasping her hands behind her back leaning close as if to stick her nose in it. "You use dem square bristle now?" Bob wiped his brushes on a rag, held them up. "You didn't use a square bristle before."

A table and a chaise sofa were pulled up against one wall. The table was covered with a cloth that had caught swipes of excess paint and the drips of a thousand stains. On the table were Bob's tins and boxes of paints, the plaster cast of a head, the vase he must have used for a model, and his easel. The room was also large enough for five or six more easels to be set up for students. A shelf held models: a vase, the skull of some small animal, a cloth, candlesticks, gloves, slippers, books, even a clock. The chaise against the wall was draped with a cover that might have been a blanket or something to use as a model's drape.

The sounds of feet, of labored breathing, came up the stairs and men began to drag themselves in just as the men had done back at 806. Glackens was the first, nodding at Soap. "Sophia." He had shared this studio with Bob for a time but had not long ago taken another for himself nearby.

The men came that night—not to paint, but to critique. One by one they propped their pieces on Bob's easel and stood back as the others commented on composition, color, and whatever else they could think of. Soap stood aside and shuffled one foot to the other, thunking her teeth into her fingernails.

Chapter 99

They had not finished the morning's *petite* when a knock came at the door and the hotel clerk's chirping, "Monsieur? Mademoiselle?" Ezekiel was still indecent, without a jacket, his shirt hanging out, not yet buttoned. Soap still propped in bed, the morning's tray in her lap, the froth of her café steaming in the light.

Ezekiel was wrestling with his shirttail as another knock came, a bit louder and more insistent. "Monsieur?"

He opened the door a crack. "Yes?" The clerk stood holding a large box and a long cloth bag drawn closed. An envelope with their names on it, written in Mlle. Fournier's slanting hand, was slipped under a string on the box. The hotel clerk said something in rapid French that Ezekiel could not understand. She pushed the box and the bag at him and left.

He laid the things on the foot of the bed: brushes, pallets, canvases, solvents, ten different pallet knives, a box of paints that weighed twenty pounds. He opened the envelope, read it, and handed it to Soap. "You read it," she said. Inside was a note embossed with Mlle. Fournier's seal and a calling card with her name:

Mlle. Dibrouski,

Now you have no excuse. We can begin tomorrow. I will send my coach in the morning at 1000 hours. I will be heart-broken if you are not on it when it returns.
Fantine and Roselyn and I will be waiting.

Yours, Jacqueline Forunier

PS

If you have nothing more today, I insist M. Harrington escort you to 97 Rue Laffitte. You will find there a gallery owned by my friend Ambroise Vollard. Give him my card.

He wondered why it was addressed to Soap; it was he who had been the one to get her here.

They made their way through streets that were becoming familiar. The day had turned the color of mud, the skies a tired gray. It had rained that night, after the previous day's whimsy of sun.

The door to Bob's studio was open, inviting. He was at the windows, working on a canvas. He wore a huge stained smock over his clothes, lifted his brush as they walked in. "Hello."

"Don't stop on account of us," Ezekiel said.

Bob slumped, gave a perfunctory dab at the canvas, then wiped the brush on his smock. "There's not much coming of it, I'm afraid." Ezekiel was not sure he had ever seen Bob seem so empty.

Soap went around the easel, stood with her hands behind her back like an inspector. As she did, Bob took up a pallet knife and began scraping away what was on it. "Tsk," she said. He swiped lumps of oil onto a rag, jabbed the knife at the canvas again. Canvas after canvas, board after board of his art was tacked on the walls, leaning against the floorboards, against the chaise lined with dozens of sketches, now, stacked on a shelf. Yet he swiped at this canvas as if it would be his last, a sure disaster, as if he were an abject failure.

Soap set her hand on Bob's shoulder. "I think," she said, "you gonna come with *us* this time, Bobby."

He looked down at her and blushed. "Anywhere."

Ezekiel gave Bob the name of Mlle. Fournier's friend's gallery and said an acquaintance insisted they see it. The gallery was halfway across town in a district harboring many galleries. Bob knew where it was, had already been there many times. "It will be interesting to see what you think of the things in it," he said. He said had seen works there by Manet, "who might be the best of them all. But there's some others I don't know about." George had brought home a small sketch by Manet, a loose water color of a rose, two or three years ago, had sold it to a fellow named Albert Barnes, a young chemist with little money. Barnes had gone to school with Butts Glackens and had an eye for art that George said was superior.

The gallery's walls were covered, floor to ceiling, with framed works, harsh and experimental some of them, soft and elegant others. All—every one—seemed to vie for one's eye, and each one seemed like an incredible accomplishment. Soap gasped as she saw them. "Gott," she said. "Gott." Bob began his own tour, leaning forward, finding one here and there that caught him. Each had a small card wedged in the frame, and the cards bore the artists' names: Paul Pissarro, Alfred Sisley, Edouard Manet, Paul Cezanne, Edgar Degas.

Soap began to hiccup, which she did not cover nor apologize for. Several times she turned to Ezekiel and shook her head. "Does that lady think I can paint good like this, that rich lady?" Ezekiel shrugged. What could he say? But standing among these things hit him with the depth of what Soap herself could do, the challenges she made with distance and color, the spirit revealed in the people she painted, their anger, their humor and tenderness; her paintings seemed to tell stories.

Had he seen this all along? He did not think so. Only now was it slapping him in the face. Soap's things belonged in this place, and he knew Mlle. Fournier had seen it, even in Soap's rough and unfinished sketches.

Bob was standing by himself, his hands grasping behind. Now and then he would give his head a confused shake. A stout fellow came out from the back of the shop. The floor seemed to tremble as he walked. He was not tall, but solid, thick-necked, balding, and heavy in the brow. He wore a fine suit and a goatee, but even his finery could not quell the sense he was a bull. He eyed Soap, then Ezekiel. "Bon jour." He blurted, his greeting like some kind of challenge. Ezekiel would not want to be on the wrong side of this man.

"Bon jour," Ezekiel replied, hoping beyond anything that it was the correct thing to say. "Monsieur Vollard?" The fellow dipped his head but did not smile or soften a bit. Ezekiel pulled Mlle. Fournier's card from his pocket, held it toward the fellow. The jut of his chin thawed a little. "Oui," he said and gave the briefest indication the line of his mouth might smile.

Vollard garbled out more French, then, and Bob stepped forward. Ezekiel could understand nothing of the exchange, but he could tell Bob's French was rough and his comprehension challenged. He often said "Pardon?" and M. Vollard was made to repeat. Bob endeavored to translate. The fellow seemed to be going on about the artwork, pitching a possible sale. He asked some question and understood when Bob pointed at Soap and answered, "Artiste."

The conversation came to an end as soon as Vollard understood they would not be buying.

Soap nosed into a large painting of a tree. In the distance, the image showed a buff-colored expanse and a foreground riddled with brushwork in blues and lavenders and purples. Here and there was a mere hint of the tree's true green. The painting seemed to affect Soap in some profound way, and she started snorting and dabbing her eyes on the hem of her skirt. Ezekiel reached down to cover an indecent slice of her exposed ankle and he could feel heat rise from her. The work was wonderful, George would be in all manner of paroxysms were he here.

Bob thrust his hands into his pockets and tipped himself up and back onto his heels. "What do you make of it, Soph?"

She blew into her hem. "I think it is the best thing I ever seen."

Bob looked confused. "Not much of this fellow Cezanne's work makes sense to me," he said. Ezekiel knew the painting did not make sense but sense did not seem to be the point of it. "The colors are not proper, the perspective pretty much ignored."

Soap snuffed and swallowed. "I don't tink it's sense he makes."

"Why would he ignore some semblance of right color?" Bob said. "I don't understand it."

"I think," Soap said, "dat dose colors he puts on is what makes here *here*"—she brought her hand to herself, then pushed it away—"and..." She took a breath as if to make what she wanted to say seem sensible. "Those colors is how he says here is here and there is there." Ezekiel could see what she saw and understood.

"Perspective?" Bob asked and leaned closer.

She looked up at Bob, then, like a child to a parent. "If you had to choose, either make a painting like this fella who makes it his own way, or make it right, like the colors is supposed to be and like everybody knows is in real life, what kind of choice you make? This or that?"

"This," Bob said. "This."

The cold rains continued. Soap barely said a word after the visit to the Vollard shop, but her face shone, pink as a child's. Ezekiel realized how long he had yearned for this.

Their hotel smelled of the baking of tomorrow's crescent roll. As they came to their room, their wool coats let off the odor of wet dogs. He held the door. By the time he had turned from closing it, she had shrugged out of her coat and dropped it in a puddle at her feet. She looked straight at him, as she began unbuttoning her dress. Her eyes stayed on him. She unlaced one shoe, threw it aside, unlaced the next, kicked out of it.

She did not remove her eyes from him as she rolled down one stocking then the next, or when she unbuttoned her blouse and dropped it with the shoes. When there was nothing more left but the bracelets, she came to him and slipped his coat from his shoulders. He felt her breath as she undid his vest, his shirt, his pants. She then knelt at his feet and unlaced his shoes and held them as he stepped out of them. When he was as naked as she, when his groin ached for relief, she motioned for him to lie on the bed, and she spread oil on him that smelled of lavender. She missed nothing, his legs, the arches of his feet, his thighs, stomach, chest. She missed no part of him, no muscle, no crevice, nothing.

Chapter 100

Each morning the coach came, and each morning it bore them through streets in which merchants threw buckets of water to clean off the piss of dogs and as women shook blankets from windows upstairs. The dogs came out and to pee again on the clear walks.

The first day, Mlle. Fournier had had the canvas stretched that Soap was to work on. It was sitting at the west windows overlooking the plaza. The canvas was huge, as big as a door. She had put one of the bright settees in front of the windows and had commanded her hounds to lie at her feet as she arranged herself as she wanted. Soap moved the easel a half dozen times, commanded Mlle. Fournier to reposition an arm or a leg, which she did. The second day, Soap pointed and adjusted Mlle. Fournier and positioned both dogs, and without whimper or comment they obeyed. It happened like this the next day as well and the next.

The days grew clear, beautiful, skies like crystal, the shadows creeping across the Aubusson carpet and lighting Mlle. Fournier's upsweep of hair. The light set the dogs' coats afire. The portrait would show the woman leaning elegantly on one arm, her head tipped onto her knuckles, the length of her legs brought up beside her, and, at her feet, the dogs stretched long.

As Soap worked, an electricity pulsed between the two women; a current that excluded Ezekiel. Day after day he sat there like nothing more than another piece of furniture. Soap's spark and glow were spent by the evening, and she did not bring out her lavender oil again.

By the third day, he grew grindingly bored and went out in the middle of the day. He had never in his life had a time like this when there was nothing expected of him, when he had no one to be responsible for, nothing to accomplish. He felt useless.

He walked the plaza. Its name, he learned, was Place Vendome. Merchants waited until the middle of the day to raise their shades and take the chains from their doors. All along the four sides of the square rose buildings attached wall to wall, floors, windows carved with fancy columns topped with frills of Corinthian capitals—all of it, every palatial residence, built side by side chummily together. Some pompous government building rose on one side of the plaza; on another side construction had begun on what Mlle. Fournier said was to become The Ritz hotel. The odd column in the middle was somewhat rude for such grandeur, he thought, ugly as a thumb. Along the streets sat shops that, in spite of their apparent laziness, seemed prosperous and every one of them bracketed by more Roman columns.

It was the businesses that caught him, the small storefronts selling specialized offerings: opulent hats on wooden heads, a shop displaying custom shirts, a dressmaker's: *Mme. Auberée's Robes & Manteaux.* And, off to the side, the clinic and office of a doctor named Heitz Boyer. There was nothing as modern as a department store, and he envisioned that as something to think about.

With the shopkeepers' opening so late in the day, he could not understand how they managed to stay in business. By noon, people began strutting the plaza dressed in their garish costumes, a sense of revelry carried on them. He could see the seduction such life was for artists, the displays people made of themselves, all the light, color, everything oversized, over-colored, overwrought, reveling in the sense of the gaudy: fuchsia-pink cravats for the men, women thundering about in huge hats and bold, nipped-in coats of broad stripes in gaudy blues, and oranges, and gold.

After three days' work, Soap's painting had developed into nothing more than a babble of blotches and streaks that added up to something only

Soap could make sense of. Ezekiel knew this was the way she worked. He had asked her once how she made sense of it, and she responded that she didn't. "I will know it when it wants me to know it."

He returned that afternoon in time to ride back to the hotel with her. As they made their way through the city, she leaned her head against the seat and sighed. She did not speak except to ask if they were seeing Bob for dinner that night. He said that Bob would not be back, from wherever he and Glackens had gone, until the next day.

He took her to a nearby *charcuterie* where they could point to stews and fat sausages cooked in earthenware dishes. After supper, she flopped into the bed and was asleep before she took off her shoes.

The next morning, he sent her off alone in Mlle. Fournier's coach. He told her he would meet her later that afternoon when she was finished.

He made his way up the four flights to Bob's studio. The door was closed, and a note had been thrust into its lock. "Butts," it said. "Gone to the Tuileries." He knew no one in the city but Bob and Glackens and Mlle. Fournier, and he could not shake the feeling he was of no more use in this city than teats on a boar. He counted the days; in less than three weeks, he would leave for home. He would settle Soap into the house, and he would, once again, be master of his life.

He guessed at the name on Bob's note: *twee-lurees:* the gardens. The morning had begun with a glistening light over the rooftops, but now a breeze had set in and brought with it a creep of clouds and sudden cold. By noon, the skies clotted with thunderheads. Within minutes it began to rain then pour.

He ducked into a shop with a sign that said "Bibelots." The window was filled with products that spoke of wit and humor and that gave him ideas for his own store: jeweled boxes and figurines of animals: frogs, roosters, a ceramic Russian hound, which he thought he might purchase to give Mlle.

Fournier. The shopkeeper came over and said something, perhaps a greeting. Ezekiel would have liked to explain that he wanted to wait until the rain let up, but, wordless, he tipped his hat and left out into the torrent.

He was late getting back to Mlle. Fournier's, and he was soaked. He secretly hoped for a bit of sympathy. The door was opened by a housekeeper, who handed him a note.

> *Mr. Harrington, the light impossible this afternoon for painting. So, I sent our girl home. I have gone to spend the rest of the day with a friend. My driver will return you to your hotel. Hope for sun and light tomorrow.*
>
> *Yours,*
> *Jacqueline*

But Soap was not in the hotel room, had not been there all day. The bed was still smooth, her brush and comb lay on the bedside table where she had tossed them.

He set out for Bob's. In his heart, he had always known what he would find.

He had always, always known.

1929

Chapter 101

The telephone call came at the end of a Friday. The new clerk, a girl, was busy closing the gates for the day and turning around the sign. He had given her a summer job as a favor to Jim Fisher, after he bought several pieces of art. George had moved to Paris years ago. Ezekiel made do, these days, with a series of clerks and salesmen who ambled in, worked a while, then left.

For the summer, in addition to his regulars, he had taken on this girl. Her name was Candace, but she called herself Candy. She had just spent the better part of a quarter hour primping at the sink, slathering her lips with a greasy tomato color and crimping her short hair into waves, spitting on her fingers and plastering curls to her cheeks. She did have a pleasant way with customers, particularly with the young ones, mostly her acquaintances from Barnard College where she would return once the summer was done.

The city had spent the last three days oiled in summer humidity, automobiles blatting blue smoke up and down the streets, clothing limp the minute it was put on. Ezekiel watched the girl through a mirrored window he had installed in his office some years ago, after George had finally moved to Paris.

George wrote often and had written that his new home was "just steps from Jacqueline Fournier's. You MUST visit. Pierre and I will show you the wonders." He had had the tact to never mention Soap, but Ezekiel knew from Sloan's yearly missive that she still lived with Jacqueline Fournier. He also knew, from the newspapers, that she was celebrated on the continent for her work. Her early work was compared with that of Berthe Morisot, in Europe, and to Mary Cassat in the States, but she had eventually moved beyond comparison and had carved a style of her own, one he had not seen.

He kept up with the goings-on of Bob Henri through the occasional stories of prizes he won, or some jury or board he sat on. He had traveled all over Europe, had married—twice, the first wife died not long after they wed, the second, whose name was Marjorie Organ, was an illustrator of some note and years younger than Bob.

Sloan finally left Philadelphia for New York with Dolly, the same tiny woman who once kept company with Soap, so long ago. Sloan met her through Davis, who had paid her to "do something about Sloan's virginity." Sloan fell in love with her, and they lived in sin for some years before he married her.

Ezekiel knew Dolly and Soap still had some connection, though he did not know what that was. Among the fellows who followed Bob Henri, Sloan was the only one who had never been to Europe. Some years ago, he had moved from New York to New Mexico. Sloan often wrote of his frustrations making a living on his art and continued to grouse on the plights of the common people, the underpaid laborers, the negroes, women. He quoted W. E. B.

Ezekiel endeavored to convince himself that Sloan's philosophizing was drivel, that his letters meant nothing. But they did, and each time he held one, or saw Bob's name written, it was as if the day he last saw Bob and Soap had just happened.

The telephone's watery bell startled him again. He did not answer. It was up to the people working the front of the store to answer the extension behind the sales counter. It rang again before *Candy* answered, "Harrington

Fine Arts." Her voice, Ezekiel had to admit, had a pleasant and tuneful tone. She stretched her neck in order to reach the mouthpiece. "Yes, sir," she said. "Who may I say is calling?" She listened, her red lips puckered. "Pardon?" she said. "I am sorry, I did not hear your name." There was a pause. "I'll tell him you're on the line, sir."

Ezekiel had no desire to talk on the phone, wished she would take a message. He picked up his newspaper, shook it straight in front of his face. He heard her lay the earpiece down on the shelf, the tap of her heels on the floor, her shoes going quiet as she made it across the Aubusson carpet. He had seven employees now, all preparing to go to their homes for the weekend. He had no particular affinity for any of them, save Hainsworth. Ezekiel was proprietor of three stores again: this one dealing in art, another on Broad Street stocking crystals, china, enameled boxes and trays from the East, and the third, a jewelry store on Rittenhouse Square. Hainsworth worked for him in the Rittenhouse shop, had been with him nearly twenty years now, happy to be in another's employ, content to be waiting on another's customers, whistling as he fabricated jewelry designs and selling them to enrich Ezekiel's coffers. His brother, JJ, years ago had gone off on his own, was now an owner of two jewelry stores in New York.

Ezekiel's business had grown in the ten years since the war. Much had changed in his life, but more had not. He had lived in the same house now for thirty-three years, had sat in the depths of this office over forty years. He had never married. Though, as his finances grew and his situation in the community increased, he had been introduced to several women, widows mostly. A decade ago he had been a sometimes, convenient companion to one attractive spinster who, like Julia Berwind, had her own means but apparently had no inclination to marry. His feelings for Soap had taken whatever zeal he had, and he never pursued another woman in earnest.

He was sixty-one years old now. It had been many years since he glimpsed anyone who resembled his father. For years, a seamy transient would catch his eye, or some meanderer who carried himself in a flash of fluid anger, or a man with debauched cheeks and gap-tooth mouth who might conjure that night long ago. His father would be eighty by now, and Ezekiel knew it was unlikely he had lived this long.

And now he was faced with this *Candy*. Candy knocked on his office door. He heard her chewing gum snap as she waited. He had reprimanded her some time ago for chewing, had insisted she spit it out when waiting on customers. But it was three minutes after closing, and he had no leverage in the issue now.

He stood to let her in and, as he did, a Stutz Speedster automobile pulled up and parked outside. Its top was collapsed back, and its three young people, their round faces fresh, pink and expectant, turned toward the store. The driver blew the horn twice. In the backseat sat a girl with a long scarf wrapped at her neck in a manner after the fellow in Fitzgerald's *The Great Gatsby*. Ezekiel had not deigned to read the book but had heard of it and knew young people these days fancied themselves part of a Gatsby throng.

He folded *The Inquirer,* laid it on his desk. The day's papers were splattered with the details of Philadelphia's heat and humidity, the deaths, faintings, and a few high-tempered fistfights were blamed for it. The news from markets in Europe had begun to take up much of the financial sections. The instability of the stock market in Germany was beginning to give his stomach a bit of trouble, though the Paris Bourse had closed a bit higher the day before.

A fan on his desk whirred but did little to cool the effete air. The three fans on the sales floor did some better but were so loud it was difficult dealing with sales so he insisted they be used sparingly.

Candy stood there looking back at him, eye to eye, a bony, sloop-shouldered indecency of bobbed hair, red lips, and skirts nearly up to her knees. There seemed to be no hint of modesty in these young women anymore. "Mr. Harrington," she said, "there is a Mr. Sloan on the telephone."

She began closing the door as if he had dismissed her. "Sloan?"

Over her shoulder she said, "Yes. He said he was calling long distance from Santa Fe, New Mexico." She pulled the door closed and tapped her way out to the Gatsby crew in the Stutz Speedster.

Ezekiel grabbed the neck of the telephone so hard the arthritis flared in his knuckles. He laid his other hand on the receiver, stroked its curve with his thumb and considered not taking the call. It could not be good news; over the years Sloan had written but had never made a telephone call. Ezekiel finally took the receiver in hand, put it to his ear. "Hello?"

"Harrington?" Sloan said. "That you?" Sloan's voice was not hard, as Ezekiel remembered it, but thick, like he needed to swallow.

"Yes."

"Sloan here."

"Sloan," Ezekiel said.

"Our friend Bobby." Sloan paused as if overcome. "It is not good."

Chapter 102

By the next morning, the obituaries in all the Philadelphia and New York papers carried long columns about Bob's death, detailing his inestimable career and his deep influence on the world of art.

Sloan said there would be a "gathering" in New York. Ezekiel had begun a note to him that he would not be able to attend but had not mailed it. The day Sloan called he had seemed so tender, so unlike himself that Ezekiel had, in the end, written he would come.

As the day approached, he regretted his decision. Bob's death brought up memories and angers Ezekiel had thought he was done with—and it intensified thoughts of Soap again. *Would he never be done with her?* Her old gear and painted canvases were still in his attic knotted up in the ugly clump she had wrapped them in. He had long ago instructed a housekeeper to store them out of his sight.

The years had seen a peeling away of people in his life, either in death or in some other miserable vacancy. Prune died of a lingering trouble of the lungs, much in the same manner his own mother had. He'd seen her just once, years ago after the disaster in Europe; at the time she had seemed tired. She died two weeks later. Totten died five years ago, twelve years after Prune. He had remarried after selling the bank to First National and retiring to a country estate in western Pennsylvania. Ezekiel's distribution from the sale of the bank had been generous, and he had recently put it into the stock market, along with the two and a half million in the equity he had built in his businesses. He had even borrowed on margin in order to buy more stocks. His portfolio had nearly doubled in value. Stocks were making him richer.

Sloan wrote that he had set up a foundation in Bob's name and was hoping to bring in two million dollars for it. Ezekiel knew he would likely be approached to donate when he arrived in New York—but he would not. He had written Bob Henri out of his life decades ago. He was attending the gathering solely on account of Sloan, nothing more.

Chapter 103

He began waking again in the nights, his body wet, his ears ringing. He reasoned the restlessness might be the return of his old unease about finances, as it once was. But nothing, no column or statement, gave him cause for anxiety. The thing, the one thing, he woke to was the memory of Sloan's gathering. He had never known Soap to lie, yet if she was telling him the truth, it put a lie to his last thirty years. The last moments in Paris had driven his entire life since then, every decision he had made; every cruel firing of an employee Ezekiel thought learned too slowly or did not abide precisely his every order; every conversation he met with silence; every person he turned away from, unless they could enrich his pockets. Paris had blotted out every bit of trust in him, had proven suspicion something to cling to. What was he to make of things now? Of Soap? Of Bob? There was no understanding anything.

When he had left Jacqueline Fournier's that day in Paris and made his way to Bob's studio. The streets were a blur of ice and rain and the afternoon so crackling dark that lamplighters were lighting the streetlamps early.

The door to Bob's studio had been pulled closed but not latched. Ezekiel pressed it open, hearing voices quietly mumbling back in the studio. He had not called out or announced himself. In the following years, he had come to understand why: The fates meant him to see what he saw.

In the studio, Bob had propped a new, stretched canvas on an easel and had made some preliminary swipes on it. The chaise had been pulled toward the windows as if he was preparing to use it in the image he planned.

Bob was straddling the divan, his long legs on each side. He was bent over it, fussing at someone lying naked on it. She giggled. Bob laughed, then he stood back as if to survey his arrangement. Soap was as nude as a grub, a blanket-rug draped behind her. Ezekiel watched as Bob knelt on the seat, then lifted a strand of her hair and arranged it over her breast. It must have tickled. She laughed again. Neither of them knew Ezekiel had come in until he blurted, "I see."

As he bolted out of the room, he heard Bob shout, "Easy!"

Ezekiel ran to the hotel, threw his things into his bag, thrust both their return tickets into his pocket. He strapped the bag, made way to leave, then drew out Soap's ticket, crumpled it in his fist, and threw the wad on the bed. He vowed leaving the ticket would be the last thing he ever did for her.

Neither of them had been in contact with him, over the years, neither had tried to explain. He knew two things: Soap would have been too stubborn to justify anything, and he would not have believed her if she did. It had been so easy to believe what he had believed, so easy to slice both of them from his life. But if things were not as he had believed, *what then were they*? He no longer knew. He was no longer certain of anything at all.

Chapter 104

The function was at a modest hotel in what Sloan had called the Lower East Side. In the lobby, vases of roses had been set around here and there, but the space was devoted, almost singularly, to Bob's art. Easel after easel had been set up with his paintings: a bull fighter posing in his suit of lights, a blind woman playing a guitar, portraits of Dutch children, gypsies, scenes from his early days in Pennsylvania. His brush had matured over the years, his subjects sliding from landscapes and Irish cottages to portraiture, which had no doubt earned him his keep. He had finally become, Ezekiel could see, a good artist, but one who did not break new ground or find some small peculiarity of his own.

At the far end of the room, beyond the circular seating, beyond the hotel's desk, hung a recent photograph of Bob. It faced the room like royalty. Ezekiel could not have guessed the effect seeing it would have on him. It was the image of the man he knew—older but the same one he had left in Paris, high-cheeked, slant-eyed, compelling. The image showed he had grown a bit heavier and his hair was no longer a raven's black. It was a piercing image, the eyes carrying secrets, puffed and exotic as an Indian's, just as they had always been.

In the ballroom, two hundred people milled about, patting one another on the back, some laughing, some slouching and standing aside. Ernest Lawson, Butts Glackens, and Everett Shinn were held together in an old mens' clutch. He looked for Sloan, saw tiny Dolly first, then Sloan near Dolly, wiping his eyes. Dolly was talking to an elderly woman a head taller than she.

Everyone had changed in forty years. The men Ezekiel knew from 806 were all grayer, balder, either fatter or thinner. Sloan had gone even sharper, his jaw edgier. Dolly was rounder; though she wore a decent, tailored suit, now, it still could not cover her frumpiness.

The older woman they spoke with was well dressed and braced herself against a cane. Ezekiel could see by Dolly's earnestness that she was likely proselytizing, holding forth on one of her causes, either Labor or unions, or, more likely today, the Henri Foundation.

Ezekiel greatly regretted coming. Now he was here, he had lost sight of why. He had never been able to be comfortable among people, had never truly figured out how it worked, what to say. He had always been one to hang away, to keep a remove.

He turned to leave, took a step, and something hit him in the shoulder with such a force it hurt. He swung around to face a woman whose face was purple with rage. "I tot I would see you here." She spat in his face. She raised her fist again. He grabbed her wrist.

God, why didn't I realize she might be here?

"You son a bitch," she said, and she yanked her arm away and socked him right in the jaw. He saw flashes. "Why you leave me der?"

His mind was a mess. He could grasp nothing at all. She was relentless, her fists pounding his chest. It made him want to laugh. It made him want to strike her back. Here they were, two aged people, he gone entirely white, she still dark, her black eyes set in a face rumpled with wrinkles, two old gimps fighting a forty-year-old battle. He grabbed her wrists, felt her try to pull away. "You," he said. "Bob."

"Don't even say his name," she said. "Why did you leave me der?"

"I left you a ticket to come home."

Again she spat in his face. "Puh, then what?"

"You didn't come back."

"Jacqueline took me. You didn't."

"You and Bob," he said. It was not in him to utter anything more. He had no words.

"Me and Bob *nothing*," she said. *She had been there naked, lying stretched out in Bob's studio.* "Bobby was going to paint my *PITCHER*." She swept his arms away, sliced at what she said. Behind her, Dolly was still carrying on with the older woman, who looked around, searching, her eyes finally coming to rest on Soap: Jacqueline Fournier. She poked her cane at the floor as if to come their way, then stopped.

Soap wiped spittle from her mouth with the back of her hand. It seemed to calm her. "You and Bobby," she said, "was the only men I thought I could ever want. And Bobby wouldn't have me like a man does. He knew I was yours. And you! You run away. Why did you run away?" She punched him again, softer this time. "Why you run away? Hah. I always wanted to know." There was nothing hidden in the way she looked at him, her anger was spent, and she was left with only the open, unprotected aspect of an older woman who has come to accept but not to wonder.

How had he been so wrong? "I don't know," he said, "now." He had nothing more to give.

"Well," she said, "I didn't never have it so bad with Jacqueline." She rubbed her wrists where he had held them. The bracelets she wore were gold now. Her eyes watered but the fight gone out of her. She began backing away. "Zo long, Easy," she said. "Take care of yourself."

Chapter 105

It had been two months since the gathering in New York. There was a sense of shifting in things; the financial market had grown changeable, the sun was casting longer shadows, a light frost had begun dusting the early mornings. The market changes were affecting the men at the Club, had sent them into a kind of manic show of optimism, making deals, buying stocks by the cartload at prices a third of what they had sold for only months ago.

For so long, Ezekiel had not bought, had believed in the sanctity of cash and gold. But then he had begun to feel the fool; men were making hundreds of thousands, *millions* in the market, and so he, too, began to buy, conservatively at first, then by the fistfuls. He became ravenous. He bought up good stocks: Bethlehem Steel, General Electric, and Montgomery Ward.

For a while, he felt a yank of apprehension at the speed with which he had spent nearly every ounce of his gold. Then, he began to borrow in order to buy on margin. He was a millionaire four times over and was convinced, along with everyone else, that the stocks would rise again, just as Totten's bank had risen after the crisis of 1893; history proved this out, and those without the foresight to get on board always lost.

Mornings, his housekeeper turned on the furnace the minute she let herself in. Ezekiel had yet not allowed himself to think of Bob's gathering or what Soap had told him. If a thought of her tiptoed into the drift just before sleeping, he woke and shoved it away. And, if in the morning, the undertow brought it back, he bolted from bed and held his head under a cold faucet.

In spite of the market, in spite of the rewards it promised, he found himself tired as never before, found it difficult to get up in the mornings, difficult to muster an appetite. He thought he might see a doctor about it, yet had nothing specific to tell one. He felt restless. Incentive, his constant ally, bled away. Who was there to prove anything to, anyway? Bob? Dead. Totten? Dead. And Ezekiel had long ago quit looking over his shoulder for the ghost of his father.

He locked up the store, made his way out into in the wind. Dust threw grit, his eyes teared, and he wiped them. Leaves skittered along like live creatures. He had worked a short day that day, getting in just before the store opened and leaving the moment he turned the sign. He took a streetcar home, let himself into the house. The housekeeper had already gone and had set out the damp leavings of dinner: a drying ham slice and peas, under a lid in the oven rack. A wet rag was draped over the edge of the sink, bread in the bin. He ate what he could of it, threw the rest in the can.

He took himself and the evening newspaper out to the high wing chair he had bought three decades ago because it once made him feel important. He read the paper, then threw it aside to use under kindling in case he wanted a fire. He made to set his eyeglasses on the table where he always put them; instead, he settled them again over his ears.

He huffed then thrust himself forward in the chair and grimaced an old man's grimace as he grabbed its dark arms. He pulled himself up.

He had not passed through the small door off the kitchen since shortly after he bought the house. The stairway seemed strange, now, as if it belonged to another place. The steps moaned as he shuffled up. They smelled dry of dust and old wood. His knees crackled and hurt, and he had to stop twice to catch his breath. The bare bulb at the top did little more than prick at the dark.

He finally reached the last step, stood under the bulb and breathed. His old trunk was pushed against one wall. The shapes of Soap's box and the roll of her old canvases lay under a cloth in the corner where the floor met the rafters. He bent under the roof's slope, gave out a yip as his knees cracked. Spider webs draped the joists, some had fallen away and hung limp under the weight of time and lint. He set his hand on the cloth, let it lie there a moment. He removed the cloth, tossed it under the eave. It sent up a storm of dust. He flapped his hand and spat grit.

He opened the box first. It had her brushes in it, her pallets, her painting knives, and her blank sketching pads, now riddled by silverfish. He set the things on the floor. They brought back the image of the girl she had been when they left for Europe, the smell of her scalp and her hair a bit past needing a wash, of the soiled and threadbare hems of her skirts. It was a soft memory and one that made him regret the modern Soap at Bob's memorial, whose slim dress revealed narrow ankles and whose graying hair had cut stylishly short.

He took hold of the roll of canvases. The twine that tied them was dry, the knots nearly untieable. He worked the knots with his nail and, as he did, his breath came easier. The last knot finally gave. The old canvases crackled and cracked, and the paint stuck where it had still been not quite dry, when she rolled them. There were four. He laid each out on the floor and weighted them with things he could reach: a broken lamp, a trunk, a vase. Each was painted with an image from long ago, a scene from the river, another of people in a park, a study for a portrait of Prune.

And the last, the painting of a hugely fat, nude, and grotesque man. The fellow stood on a dais, leaning against a walking stick. His face and nose were bloated, his breasts drooping like pudding over a gut that burbled over his thighs so only the round purple tip of his manhood showed beneath it: the drunkard at Bob's studio so long ago, Bull something, Luks' joke of a model.

At first, he could not understand why the painting was here. Then, it came, he *did* understand: *She* had painted it. *She* was the small boy with the beaten face, the boy with the too-large clothes, the boy who came to Bob's classes wearing a cap, even in the stifling heat; a cap that collected and hid all the tangle of her hair.

Soap.

Chapter 106

The crash came on a Tuesday. He heard it first hollered through a newsboy's megaphone: "Stock Market Crashes. Stocks Crash in New York." He had not gone to the Club, or he likely would have known there was some worry before the newsboys began their yelling. He would hold, he would not sell; things would soon swing back. But thousands swamped the markets; in hours trading was two and a half hours behind. By Friday, the market could not even open.

He began going to the Club again; he could not stay away. Talk of recovery was, so far, a salve even as the markets continued to fall. He was losing weight and could see others were as well. He drank down seltzer by the gallon. Some of the men bragged that they had sold early and now had the dilemma of what to do with so much cash. Ezekiel did not know how much of this was true, none of the braggarts looked particularly peaceful in their claims. Ezekiel mustered along with the charade that he was sound with stacks of gold locked away in his safes. But if he put his nose in the prospectuses he held, he was going broke; many of his stock rendered worthless.

By Christmas, he had shuttered all but the home store. He had barely cash enough to pay the mortgage he had taken on the house to leverage for even more stock. He had held out some hope for sales during the holidays, but by the time the store closed on Christmas Eve he had sold less, in the month, than he once did on a decent day.

In the snap of a finger, the world had changed. Philadelphia had gone from the noise of progress, of hammers, and saws, and pile drivers, of the voices of the young flappers and the honks of their roadsters to the stunned shouts of panic around the Philadelphia Exchange. Movement had come to a stop. Men stood for hours at the soup kitchens, waiting; children lined up at the doors of the churches for a watery soup to take back to families too embarrassed to ask for it themselves. All along the streets, lean men with nothing to do stood against walls, hands in their pockets, and left a line of smudge shoulders high.

Ezekiel was, if he allowed himself to think it, back in the same place he had been when he was nineteen years old. He still owned the building, but was in debt to the banks for margins that could be called any day. If the store was taken, he had nothing.

Chapter 107

The Ides had passed a week ago. March turned fickle, warm, and scented with spring one day, blown on frozen sleet that rattled the panes the next. Up and down every street, businesses were boarding over windows, clamping closed the doors with thick, impenetrable hasps. Banks were closing as well, their great columns rendered toothless.

After the first of the year, though the Market was still down nearly a third, it had crept up somewhat from its lows. Ezekiel had managed to rid himself of some of his stocks, but the losses he took were tremendous. If calls went out on what he held, he still did not have enough to cover them. He had fired all employees except one young fellow who agreed to work for nothing if, in exchange, Ezekiel let him set up a bed for himself in the storeroom in back. His name was Teddy Winslow. He had dropped out from his studies at Drexel when things became hard but, planned to return when things improved. He was a nervous sort whose mouth twisted and who chewed the insides of his cheeks. He stood back and his eyes took in every move Ezekiel made. Ezekiel could see some of his own ruthless youth in the young man and he did not trust him.

He had gone home early that day, after feeling a bit of nausea, a pinching in his gut that surfaced now most every day. He had the house to himself, now, had fired the housekeeper after the first of the year, and was managing on his own, catching a meal when he could, filling his pocket with bread for a morning meal the next day. He was considering giving up the house and taking one of the rooms over the store, but the thought of trudging up the stairs with his bad knees gave him pause.

That evening he sat in the chair, laid his hands on its oily arms and merely sat. He did not pick up a newspaper, did not sleep, did nothing but sit.

A knock came at the door. He was expecting no one; there was no one to knock any longer. He huffed, grabbed the arms to pull himself up. He must have been too slow, for the knock came again, louder this time. *Why don't they ring, for God's sake? I still have a damned bell.*

He shoved his feet into his slippers, tied the sash of his robe. He could hear feet stamping outside. By the time he got to the door, shoes were tapping down the steps, and he considered letting go whoever had been here.

The beveled window was dark. He peered through but could see nothing. He turned the knob, cracked open the door. A woman turned. He could see in the streetlamp only the pale coin of her face. "Easy," she said.

Chapter 108

Her movement was still smooth as a young woman's. She wore dark stockings under a coat trimmed with a fur collar. The coat was of striped wool and fitted, European made. The fur whorled in the wind. "I was hoping you was still in this place."

He asked her in.

She said, "No. I got to go. My daughter thinks I should be back to the hotel by now."

"Daughter?"

"Yah," she said. She seemed to grow shy, as if she did not know more to say. She pulled the coat tighter. "She's a good girl."

"I didn't know you had a daughter."

"She always lived back home."

"In France?"

"Ho no," she said, "in Poland." *Soap had a daughter before she came to America? Why didn't he know this? Why had they never told each other these things?* "I am great-grandma now."

He searched for something to say to hold her there. "Jacqueline? How is she?"

"Old," she said and laughed. She reached into a bag trimmed to match the coat, drew out an envelope. "George tinks things is maybe getting hard here." It was wonderful to hear her voice, to hear George's name. "Tings," she said, "is better back over there for me and Jackie." She pressed the package toward him. It was a large envelope, thick and rustling like it might contain journals or magazines.

"What is it?" he said.

"I go now. Open it. You gonna see. Something you gonna use. Jacqueline says she be mad if you don't." She raised her hand and turned. At the bottom step she shook her finger at him and said, "Use it."

The store was cold. He could see his breath. The rooms upstairs must have been cold as well, as he had not turned on the boiler for days. No one complained; no one would risk eviction. When things were good he would have heard about it. Now, no one complained, not the families, or the laid-off longshoremen, not the women who said they were seamstresses but who slept in the days and let themselves out at night. If he did toss them out, then what? He had lowered rents, had jettisoned the renters who missed paying, and had every room rented to only the ones who had met every month's rent for a long while.

He continued to bring himself to work as he had for nearly fifty years, but the skip and cock had gone out of his step. He was slow now, getting from the house to the store was a slow slog, something done in the same haze as one paid a bill or dusted a shelf one had dusted a thousand times again and again. He had once dealt in color, in the salve and thrill of pinks and yellows, blues, and delicate grays. His life now seemed brown, not the brown of earth but of a dog's turd.

Though he had worked with Teddy Winslow several months, Ezekiel was still wary and did not much like the young man. But every morning by the time Ezekiel made it in, Winslow was already up and working. He kept the displays clean, arranged and rearranged things as Ezekiel told him to. But Winslow had no eye of his own, would not have been able to tell art from a grade-school sketch. He kept himself clean, kept the one suit he owned brushed and pressed. It was a suit Ezekiel recognized as the sort to come from the church bins. How Winslow ate, Ezekiel did not know but suspected he lined up at the kitchens, along with the out-of-work men, as soon as the store closed. He could not have articulated what bothered him about the boy, but there was something in the way he came in while Ezekiel worked at the books and stood a bit too long, his eyes jittering over the ledgers.

When one day Ezekiel asked what Winslow had been studying at school, the boy simply said, "Business." Every evening, every midday, when Ezekiel left the store, he closed the safe, spun the dial, and double-checked that he had locked the office.

Since the night, a week ago, that Soap had appeared at the door, he'd found going home not the lonely walk it had been for so long, but something else, something that took away the stiffness in his joints, soothed the pain in his knees. Half a dozen times he had reached toward her envelope but had let it lie beside his chair, untouched, unopened. Had he been asked what made him do so, and had he been truthful, he would have said shame. Shame. He had once known none of that. In his certainty, in his superior intelligence, his *rightness*, he always *knew* and was proud and sure of himself. The package shouted that he knew nothing, never had. What could be in it? More truth? More shame? Seven days since she brought it. Seven nights he had sat with the sack-colored thing lying there under the light.

He set down the newspaper, took off his eyeglasses. There was nothing in the news but misery, unemployment, marches for women's rights, labor strikes, stories of children delivered to orphanages in order not to starve, rage and bile that President Hoover was not doing enough to bring the country around.

He set the eyeglasses on the table, laid his hand beside the envelope, it was a gnarled old-man's hand, a thin terrain of veins and spots. His breath came in waves; he could hear his pulse in his ears. He could not catch strength enough to lift the package.

He laid his fingers on the paper and his breath came easier. He ripped a sliver at one end, listened to the slow hiss as he slipped out what was in it: a sheet bearing a sketch of a cottage in a garden of flowers and a woman with a very broad sunhat. In a childish script was written the word "Me" and an arrow pointing at the woman's image. Soap's writing. She had not known how to write, now she did. Just below the sketch, she had written USE IT.

Under the sheet of paper was a folder.

Inside the folder was a one-way ticket.

To Paris.

It expired in twenty-three days.

At midnight.

Chapter 109

It was a short request, seemingly innocent, Teddy Winslow leaning on the office doorjamb, his legs crossed in a mimicry of casual. "Mr. Harrington," he said. He torqued his mouth to the side, took a good chew of his cheek. "I was thinking."

"Good," Ezekiel said. He did not ask what thinking Winslow had actually been doing.

Winslow shifted his mouth, took a grand nip at the other cheek. "I was thinking maybe I could sell better if I got paid for it."

"You know our agreement," Ezekiel said.

"I know what we talked about. But I'm not looking to be paid unless I sell."

"A commission," Ezekiel said.

"Yes."

"What *kind* of commission?" He knew his tone was harsh.

Winslow shrugged, shifted his feet. "Ten percent." It was what he had once happily paid George.

"You're already get free lodging."

"I know," he said and gave Ezekiel an expression meant to convey appreciation. "But, see, I have the offer of another place." He twisted his mouth, making real inroads at another good chomp. It was a lie, Ezekiel could see it. "So, I just might take them up on it."

It was not an unreasonable request. In fact, was it not the very thing he had once proposed to Mr. Reading when the old man was beginning to fail? Mr. Reading had been weak then, his business under duress, and Ezekiel had seized upon the vulnerability. Was weakness what Winslow saw in

Ezekiel now? So many years ago, at his own proposal, Ezekiel had seen a flick of humor and admiration on the old man's face. Did Winslow see something of the sort now in *him*? He found himself hoping so. The store was selling so little, ten percent of his sales would yield Winslow near nothing—but near nothing was better than he was getting now. "Five percent," Ezekiel said.

Winslow's face flared, his forehead pinched up. He looked down at his feet, gave a single shake of his head. He had rehearsed this, Ezekiel knew, trying to put doubt where there was none. "I don't know," he said. "I have another prospect."

"What?"

This caught him. He had not planned to be questioned. "Cookies," he blurted.

"Cookies?" Ezekiel said.

"Uh-hum."

"I see." Ezekiel picked up a pen, turned it, let Winslow squirm. He did not look up. "Then I guess you might as well take it."

"But see," Winslow said, "I like this business. I could make a go of it here, if I had a chance."

"You think you would earn more here than you would with, what is it again…cookies?"

"Yes." Winslow was chewing his lip, now; a ring of blood crusted the corner of his mouth. "But I don't see a future in cookies."

"Maybe you better think on it."

"I'll take it if I can have a room."

Ezekiel threw himself back in the chair and belched out a laugh, then another, and another. He was liking the kid more and more. Finally, he sat up, took off his eyeglasses, wiped his eyes with his handkerchief. "A room," he finally said.

Winslow's face glowed. "Upstairs," he said. He was not giving up.

"A room upstairs," Ezekiel said. He slipped his spectacles behind his ears, looked directly at Winslow. "You have a place to sleep down here."

"Doesn't have to be much of a room."

"Doesn't have to be anything," Ezekiel said.

Chapter 110

Ezekiel had never had a natural eye for art; he had spent his life in the imitation of understanding and had been good enough at the pretense that he had earned a reputation as someone who *knew,* someone who had a sense of style, and color, and beauty. In truth, his understanding was nothing more than an intellectual game of seeing what he needed to know in order to serve his purposes. He had to allow himself that he *had* learned, he *had* learned color, he *had* learned line, and light and composition, and he knew all of that had added up to beauty. But what he had not seen was beauty as Soap saw it from some intangible part of herself—nor had he seen what George saw or Bob. Most of all, he had not seen the beauty in all of them, in their certainty, their clarity, their love.

At the store, he behaved as if nothing had changed since Winslow approached him with his proposal. He observed the boy observing him. He watched him step into behaviors that were not natural to him but that he needed in order to get what he wanted. He did not seem to have an instinctive head for business—at least Ezekiel had once been good at that. But, like a fish hawk, Winslow hovered, observing what kept the doors open when other businesses were going under, watched how Ezekiel set things up to attract the few customers there were, and then glanced into Ezekiel's office whenever he got the chance.

Every day, Ezekiel saw his young self in Winslow, in his drive and vigor, an intensity that seemed to shoot sparks. He was fast and solid and never needed to be told twice. Ezekiel knew what drew him: ambition. Ambition had once wakened Ezekiel in the morning, driven him through the years and jettisoned him right where he ended up. He tried to resurrect some of his old vigor now, endeavored to conjure the old lift in his step. But whatever might have been in him then, some heart, or spirit, would no longer come.

He was tired.

Chapter 111

The ticket lay where he had put it the night he opened it. It expired in two days. He would not, he knew, touch it until after then, when it was good for nothing but the waste bin. But some essence of it had opened memories, and they came, unbidden. He could not push them away, but he found them not unpleasant; they were all he had from his past but the old trunk with his books, the trunk he had hauled from Cozad to Philadelphia and had lived with his entire life. Sam Schooley told him that, before she died, his ma insisted Ezekiel bring the trunk with him. He had opened it once or twice after he first came to Philadelphia. The things in it were shaken about, the books tumbled, the school papers his ma had saved were mussed, cockeyed. He could have tidied them like he tidied everything in his life but had not been able to for the emotion in it. He had closed the trunk and not opened it since.

The trunk was in the attic some housekeeper put there decades ago. He had not been up here again since he discovered Soap's paintings after Bob's memorial. Her paintings were framed, now, hanging on his walls, all but the one of the fat man and his rippling nakedness.

It seemed the stairs had grown steeper in the last few weeks, and he stopped often to soothe one knee, or the other, then had to will them up the next step.

The trunk lay under the fabric of cobwebs and dust. He sat on it to catch his breath. When his heart finally slowed, he knelt beside it, lifted the hasp. He did not bother to dust the seat of his pants. He eased the lid back. The books were there, just as he knew they would be. There were layers of them: Dickens, Kipling, Melville, Poe, as well as his childhood readers and his notebooks from school. Each had left its mark on him and his life.

The books and his papers tumbled one to another without order as if they had been put there at the last minute. His mother, of course, would have expected him to take them out immediately and arrange them, but he never had. He stacked the books around himself, making piles of his mother's hope for his future, until only a few and a crumpled paper were left in the trunk.

He pulled out the last of the books. Under them, on the floor was a torn envelope, yellowed with age. It must have been put there at the bottom for security against loss. He had never known it was there. It was not sealed. Silverfish had eaten a corner, but the writing on it was still clear. It was addressed to him in his mother's handwriting; the writing weak and shaky, bringing back the pain he felt in her last few days.

The envelope bore no address, only his name. He opened the flap, took out the letter inside, which consisted of two pages.

Dearest Ezekiel,

I have asked Sam to put this where you will find it after I am gone. The letter in it is a copy of what I have given your uncle with instructions for your future. Oh, how I hope I am there to see it.

Her pen was beginning to drag a trail of ink from one word to another, the writing becoming thin.

You are a good boy and you make me proud. I know you will

Here, the writing changed

(This is Sam writing now. Your mother has asked me to write while she tells me what she wants.)

I know you will do well, my dear, if you seek counsel from your uncle and love from your aunt. They are wonderful people and will see to it you grow into the fine man I have always known you would be. I wish I had.

But there was no more to the letter. Ezekiel unfolded the second page. It was dated two years before she died. Her writing was strong and fluid.

Dear Sister and Brother,

I am making a copy of this for my son, in hopes it softens some of the cold aspects of my will which I have finalized and am sending. Thank you for accepting the responsibility it throws your way. I realize its dry language leaves out much from what I want to say about my son. So, if anything happens before he is grown, I will say it now.

Should the worst come to pass, I wish him to come live with you and your wonderful boys. He is a clever, hard-working boy, but I am afraid he is growing quite stubborn. Totten, please give him your strong hand, he will need it. Prune, from you he only needs your love and kindness in order to develop into the fine young men you have made of Cornelius and Oliver, who I hope will welcome him as their friend and brother.

You can see in my will that I wish you to sell the house here in Cozad. It is paid for and has some value. I wish you to use the funds in my accounts, and the proceeds from the sale of the house, to afford Ezekiel the best education the money can get for my son. I insist neither you, nor he, waver from this, no matter what he might think of it. He has already begun to argue for staying here when he is grown. Cozad is a fine place, but has no more to educate him than secondary school. I am resolute, he will get a college education before anything else, whether I am here to see to it, or not. If he refuses, and I am not here to

marshal him, see he does not get any of my estate until he marries, or finishes his college, or turns twenty-five years old.
But most of all, my dearest family, love him, care for him as neither his father, nor I, were able to.
Your Loving Sister,
Mary

Ezekiel laid his chin on his chest. He was powerless to the weeping. He wailed for all he had misunderstood, for all in his life he had squandered, for all whom he had tossed away as if some kind of trash. Nothing ever was as he believed it to be; Totten had done his ma's bidding, even Sam had. Bob. Soap. The rafters swallowed his moans.

Chapter 112

The day had the makings of a good spring on the way. By eight o'clock, robins were singing and working the curbs for worms. A woman walked three spaniels on leashes, others ushered their children through the doors of the schools. It was the sort of day that slathered the city in hope and made even the out-of-business signs seem less worrisome.

Ezekiel did not have an appointment, but the legal secretary rang Fennet right away and showed him in immediately. The attorney's office was hushed, now, with carpet and a silence of thick drapes. The desk was fine-carpentered rosewood and, on a credenza behind it, stood photos of Fennet with presidents Coolidge and Hoover.

Fennet grunted when he made to stand, grabbed his back with one hand, reached to shake Ezekiel's with the other. "God, Harrington," he said, "we're old men." Gone was every red hair on Fennet's head; he was completely freckle-bald.

Ezekiel laughed. "Speak for yourself, Fennet."

"When was the last time I saw you?" They discussed this a moment. Neither could remember, though they had done business together many times over the years. They sat, not at Fennet's desk, but in two high, leather chairs to the side. The secretary brought them coffee. They talked a while about the state of the economy and people they both knew.

Ezekiel finally laid out what he wanted. Fennet wrote on a pad, then called in the clerk. They talked some more as it was being typed. When it was time to go, Fennet said, "Good luck, friend," and patted Ezekiel's shoulder.

He went to the house, sat at his office desk in the back, made three telephone calls. When they were finished, he pulled down the shades in every room. He filled a valise with what he needed. By the time he left the house, offices and stores had already spat out their people and locked up. He had been gone from the store the entire day. It was eight o'clock when he let himself in. "Winslow?" he shouted.

Some rustling came from the back, a whispered cough. "Sir?" There came the sounds of a scramble of movement. When the boy appeared in the doorway, he was without a shirt, his hair mussed. He stood in the storeroom doorway as if blocking Ezekiel's view of it. He was blinking, as one did when he could not think. He had someone in there with him.

Winslow's discomposure made Ezekiel smile. "You can relax," he said. "I will leave you alone soon. What I have to say will take only a minute. It involves a very large favor." He pulled Fennet's letter from his pocket.

"Have I done anything wrong?" Winslow asked.

"No," Ezekiel said. "I am leaving in a few moments."

"Leaving?"

"Yes."

"When will you be back?"

"I don't know. I want you to take care of things while I am gone." He handed Fennet's letter to Winslow. "I have asked someone to oversee. You will make a report every week to the person mentioned in that letter and take direction from him until I return."

"May I ask where you will be, sir?"

"It does not matter," Ezekiel said. "What matters is that you are in charge of running the store for a while. You will be compensated. You will see in the letter I plan to pay you the ten percent you wanted."

"Thank you, sir."

Ezekiel patted Winslow's bare shoulder. "I know the store will be in good hands, son."

"Thank you again, sir."

Ezekiel turned to go. When he reached the door, he looked back at Winslow to say good-bye. Composure had come back to the young man's face. Ezekiel tipped his hat. "So long, Winslow."

"Sir," Winslow blurted, "I want a room if I'm to do this. I won't do it without a room thrown in."

"Ha!" Ezekiel had been waiting for this. "You can have Number 8," the windowless closet he had lived in, himself, those years.

Epilogue

The night was still, the streets calm but for an occasional shout from one of the saloons or a passing automobile. An observer would feel nothing but the first hint of spring and would notice not much else but the soft night, unless he spotted the aging man standing in the spare illumination of the streetlight. The elderly fellow stood straight for his age, his bearing simple. He wore a hat, a suit of good wool, and he carried a valise and an envelope labeled RMS *Majestic*. Should the observer be a friendly sort, he might point out the envelope and say, "Why, it looks like you're going somewhere." And the gentleman might tip his head and say, "Ah." And he might nod his head then with a sort of finality and say, "So I am, young man. So I am."

Book Club Topics

What other books did "Come the Morning" remind you of?

Did the plight of women of the time ring true? Were Soap's life choices believable?

Did the plight of Henri and the rest of the artists ring true?

How credible/believable did you find Ezekiel to be?

Did you have a favorite quote or passage in the book? If so, what was it?

Which character did you relate to the most, and what was it about them that you connected with?

What might have made the setting unique or important?

Did the book change your opinion or perspective about anything? Do you feel different now than you did before you read it?

How do you picture Ezekiel and Soap's lives after the end of the story?

Was anything left unresolved or ambiguous?

How satisfying or disappointing was the ending of the story?

What insights from the reading experience may be applied to your current life/situation?

Do you think the art culture has changed today as far as accepting out-of-the-box artists? Would Henri and his artist friends have been readily welcomed into the art culture today?

If the book were being adapted into a movie, who would you want to see play what parts?

Acknowledgments

Everybody's heard the old saw that we work in the dark. Indeed. Writing is done in a very lightless place, at least for me; I never know what I'm doing.

Like most writers, my life is spent in the singular and dogged pursuit of "getting it all down". Except for the fortitude and company of a stable of characters, "getting it down" can feel interminable and alone.

But, in the end, there *is* light; a writer is never alone. In order to come up with work worth reading, writers needs a cadre of intelligent, generous helpful sorts along the way. And there's the light. I count myself lucky to have had a passel of them.

From my every fiber, thank you to these wonderful people—many in credible writers—who have lit my way and come to my aid:

Lisa Alber, Jerry Berberet, Dick Morgan, Rachelle Rodriguez, Carol Hirons, Anne Hawley, Marlene Geiger, Peter Osborne, Jan and Mike Laus, Rae Richen, Sue Parman.

Above all, my thanks to author Craig Lesley whose care and mentorship so long ago have been invaluable in so many writers' lives, like me. He is a treasure.

Bibliography

Perlman, Bennard B. (1988). *Painters of the Ashcan school: the immortal Eight.* Mineola, NY. Dover Publications, Inc.

Henri, Robert, and Ryerson, Margery. (1923). *The art spirit.* Philadelphia, PA: J.R. Lippincott

Perlman, Bennard B. (1991). *Robert Henri: his life and art.* Mineola, NY: Dover Publications, Inc.

Burt, Nathaniel. (1963). *The perennial Philadelphians: The anatomy of an American aristocracy.* Boston, MA: Little Brown and Company

Skaler, Robert Morris. (2005). *Society Hill and Old City: Images of America.* Charleston, SC, Chicago, IL, Portsmouth, NH, San Francisco, CA: Arcadia

Sandoz, Mari. (1960). *Son of a gamblin' man: The youth of an Artist.* New York, NY: Clarkson N. otter, Inc/Publisher

E. Digby Baltzell. (1979). *Philadelphia gentlemen: The making of a national upper class.* New Brunswick, NJ, London, UK: Transaction Publishers

Loughery, John. (1995). *John Sloan: Painter and rebel.* New York, NY: Henry Holt

Hepp, John Henry. IV. (2003). *The Middle-class city: Transforming space and time in Philadelphia, 1876-1926.* Philadelphia, PA: University of Pennsylvania Press

Moore, George. (1893). *Modern painting.* London. Walter Scott, Limited.

Moore, George. *Modern painting.* Gutenberg eBook. (2005). eBook.

Other literary fiction by Jeannie Burt

The Seasons of Doubt

A Library Favorite

In fall 1873, Mary Harrington's husband abandons her and their son in their sod house on the Nebraska prairie. Three months later she and their five-year-old son, Ezekiel, are freezing and starving. They head out into snow and a bitter wind for help.

The times are not kind to women. Mary begs for work, but finds she cannot be paid without her husband's permission. Every choice she makes will determine whether she can survive and raise her child.

When Patty Went Away

Critically Acclaimed

Summer of 1976, scrappy fifteen-year old Patty Pugh disappears. Her tumultuous behavior causes the community to bid her good riddance. Only quiet farmer Jack McIntyre and his beloved daughter seem to care she is gone. Although she was always trouble, Jack believes she is also a survivor.

Alone, Jack searches for the girl, a quest that leads him to a deep understanding of his own life.